Also by Mark Harris

The Shtetl and other Jewish stories
The Chorister and other Jewish stories
The Music Makers and other Jewish stories
Last Days in Berlin
A Virtual Reality

A

VIRTUAL

REALITY –

SECOND *EXODUS*?

Mark Harris

Matador
9 Priory Business Park,
Wistow Road, Kibworth Beauchamp,
Leicestershire. LE8 0RX
Tel: (+44) 116 279 2299
Email: books@troubador.co.uk
Web: www.troubador.co.uk/matador

ISBN 978 1838594 183

British Library Cataloguing in Publication Data.
A catalogue record for this book is available from the British Library.

Printed and bound in the UK by TJ International, Padstow, Cornwall
Typeset in 11pt Bembo by Troubador Publishing Ltd, Leicester, UK

Matador is an imprint of Troubador Publishing Ltd

"Given the millions of billions of Earth-like planets, life elsewhere in the universe, without doubt, exists. In the vastness of the universe, we are not alone."

Albert Einstein
(1879–1955)

One

I STILL couldn't get wholly to grips with the mind-skewing and non-virtual reality that I was a willing passenger, with my equally disposed wife Naomi and our seven-year-old twins Joshua Joseph Aaron Josce and Sarah Ruth Rebecca Miriam – and alongside numerous thousands of other Jewish people – on a huge and technologically incredible spacecraft… one of many similarly laden, and accompanying our vanguard mother-ship. And it was only then beginning to dawn on me that we were some seven weeks into an incredible, apparently two-month, 40-trillion-kilometre voyage across the Milky Way galaxy from Earth to our final destination, an exceedingly long-time inhabited exoplanet orbiting in, what our space scientists have termed, the Alpha Centauri star system. A world, my more than 'alien friend' Diva – who had actually changed her facial appearance in my presence – assured us, that would be wholesomely welcoming to millions of members of my ancient faith, Judaism, so needing to embark on an 'Exodus' – which we referred to as the second to that of our ancestors from biblical Egypt – because of a globally widespread, ever increasing and now scarily aggressive anti-Semitism. This was the centuries-old, oft-recurring but ironically post-modern version of Jew hatred that had been instilling horrifying notions of a potential second Holocaust, or *Shoah*, to rival Hitler's Third Reich murder of six million Jews.

Extremist political changes in supposedly civilised and refined countries had been prompting, if not inciting national parliaments to pass legislation with parallels to the Nazis' racially discriminatory 'Nuremburg Laws' of 1935, which had been devastating for purportedly cultured Germany's Jewish communities; though not nearly as cataclysmic compared to what was to come. There had been already certain statutory illustrations, including many countries' legislatures making and implementing laws banning *Shechita* – the Jewish ritual slaughter of animals for food – and *Brit Mila*, the circumcision of a Jewish male child at eight days old. And these moves had been recognised by Jewish communities, and not only in Europe, as more to do with nationalistic and populist anti-Semitism than the animal welfare and humanitarian motivations so claimed. I'd felt frequently that there was so much occurring in the world of the 2020s that could be taken as frighteningly reminiscent of what had transpired in central Europe during the 1920s and into the 1930s, about which I had read extensively. But in this the 21st century, it was all happening so extraordinarily quickly.

"I don't believe that you, David, and any of your brethren making the understandably overwhelming decision to flee Earth will live to regret the benign relocation to a new abode on our, as your astronomers allude to it, planet Proxima b," Diva had remarked to me, both earnestly and warmly empathetically, on her last visit to my historic and renowned, university hometown of Cambridge UK. Certainly, I could think of no grounds to doubt the sincerely expressed words of a woman who, some years earlier, had saved the lives of me and Naomi, my then wife-to-be. It was a quite startling coincidence to learn from Diva that around six million Jewish people – but excluding a vast majority of the so-called *Charedi* or ultra-Orthodox element of the faith, and maybe for their own understandable reasons – were determined to escape our threateningly evil world for the other side of the galaxy. Unsurprisingly, all but a relatively small proportion of the "prospective Jewish refugees" – as Diva had informed me, and described them – originated from Europe, North and South America and even the State of Israel. But other emigrant representatives of our belief, she'd told me, came variously from around the globe, including the Antipodes and South Africa. The overall intent, if I can put it this way, was worlds apart from Hitler's original thought of transporting all the Jews of Europe to the Indian Ocean island of Madagascar.

But the numbers heading for Proxima b still left a very extensive section of my fellow Jews, about eight million souls in total, resolving to remain on planet Earth. Aside from the likely theological motivation of a significant proportion of these 'stay-putters', a substantial segment seemingly holding firmly to the view that the amazing and unbelievably rapid spread and growth – or, debatably, revelation or exposure – of a vicious form of otherwise latent anti-Semitism athwart the world was merely a passing phase that could, and should, be weathered determinedly for its hopefully relatively short duration. Existentially, their almost complacent and maybe sublimating attitude had reminded me, and no doubt other readers of Holocaust history amongst my fellow space travellers, of the many thousands of German Jews who'd believed, fatally, that they could readily survive the Nazis' racial storm of the 1930s. They were Jews who'd refused categorically to leave the fascist nation, for whatever foreign country that would open its doors to them, after considering their families' loyal patriotism and contribution to the Fatherland over numerous preceding decades, if not centuries.

On the other hand, I'd pondered, it was necessary also to appreciate that the projected journey – albeit of probable salvation and deliverance – could amount to a terrifying prospect for many people. It would be a voyage into the literally dark unknown for millions of already horrified, even traumatised, members of the Jewish faith; and especially for those men and women with young children, elderly parents or other vulnerable close relatives; and despite being guaranteed – by Alpha Centauri's encouraging leaders via Diva, their principal Earth delegate – a "safe though lengthy trip through the cosmos, and a benevolent welcome to their new home". Though I could imagine many of those Jews intending to remain behind asking themselves, and others of their kith and kin, questions like: What benefit or advantage will the Alpha Centauri star system get out of the arrival of millions of Jewish immigrants on Proxima b? And, by the way, what do you think its current inhabitants look like in actuality? How and where would we live there? And how would the existing population of the planet be able immediately to cope with, let alone integrate, six million more people and of an entirely different history, learning and culture?

During our space transit – when, almost unbelievably, kosher food and drink and provision for religious services and other facilities, such as *mikvaot* or Jewish ritual baths, were afforded to all who required such amenities – certain prepared literature, in English and some other material Earth languages, was made available to every passenger. This incongruously 'printed' matter set out well the detailed preparations put in place for the incoming millions of Jewish people, and in all their diversity. Doubtless many of its very attentive readers may've continued to harbour fears that the positive, and reassuring, information provided was designed to lull suspicions; and that they were heading, possibly, into some kind of disastrous trap. Admittedly, there was no misgiving or distrust in *my* mind, having discussed matters with Diva, that the leaders as well as the indigenous population of the Alpha Centauri system by any standard outshone – in morality, integrity and decency, as well as technical achievements – their debatable 'equivalents' on Earth. As she'd advised me way back, her 'high-tech' fellow citizens and colleagues were not only millennia in advance of our scientists and technologists; but also in attaining the zenith of goodness, in the way so many would hope or pray for in a 'Golden Age'. A time when all people, and despite their potential differences in any respect, are able to live together in peace and harmony, replete with an acceptance of diversity and an absolute comprehension of 'the other' in their midst. In the final analysis, Diva had projected, all those who made the indisputably problematic and necessarily mind-blowing choice, to transfer from Earth to what they understood to be planet Proxima b, should be instilled with great hope. And a strong belief, that life in the 'New World' is lived – and would be lived by them – as life had been intended to be lived from the beginning of *Time* in the eternal cosmos.

Though I couldn't help wondering – as I lay on the comfortable 'bed' in my technologically efficient, if somewhat claustrophobic capsule accommodation and with a tad of maybe misplaced amusement – that an ostensibly "lengthy voyage" in the minds of Diva's extraordinarily advanced scientific community would, unbelievably, be no more than peanuts in space-time travel terms to us Earthlings in the awesome circumstances. Considering that – at the stage then attained in our former home world's journeying-across-space science – it would've taken, incredibly, hundreds of thousands of years to arrive at our now fast approaching, planetary destination. Also bringing the hint of a grin to my cheeks was the knowledge that a not inconsiderable number of my, so to speak, associate Jewish 'cosmonauts' would've already had the previous, and somewhat dubious experience of whiling away weeks largely incarcerated inside a relatively tiny cabin space aboard a mammoth, town-like cruise-liner. Generally, this would be for the wave-tossed period of an allegedly relaxing, if not lazybones' ocean voyage with intermittent landfalls to visit famous cities – by coach, and with a guide – for a few hours of superficial sightseeing.

Two

AS I lay on my capsule bed not knowing what Earth-day of the week it was, nor whether it was metaphorically 'day' or 'night' in the cosmic environment of our incredibly celeritous mother-ship – if that made any sense, and not that my lack of knowledge mattered to any extent – my thoughts time-travelled back to when I'd first met Diva, around eight years back. It was on the flag-stoned terrace of the The Anchor gastro-pub, overlooking the River Cam's waterfowl-sprinkled Mill Pond in my former hometown of Cambridge. In the unusually warm February afternoon sunshine, I was sitting alone at a smallish table whilst nursing a pint of my favoured Dutch lager and puffing away on one of my spasmodic, Spanish cigarillos. Suddenly, I perceived this lone, youngish-looking and apparently Oriental, maybe Chinese woman – with an unlit cigarette held between her slender fingers – approaching me, in a rather slinky manner, from the steps linking the terrace to the river-bridge beside Queens' College. She halted in front of me, adopted a kind of sensually posed stance and requested – politely in perfect Queen's English – a light from my still shiny, old Ronson lighter propped upright against my silver cigar case on the table.

Being a semi-retired, freelance investigative journalist – a slim and tallish, at that time divorced and single guy with a mop of genetically inherited, darkish hair and, as I've been told, looking reasonably good for his age – I was somewhat flattered when, after I'd illuminated her super-long fag, she began an everyday sort of conversation with me. Then she invited an exchange of first names, and remarked particularly on the unexpectedly fine weather. But, as it turned out, Diva had spoken too soon. No more than a few minutes or so later, the radiating solar orb vanished behind some billowing black clouds; so, just in case, we both made a smart beeline for the glass terrace door of the now trendy old, riverside inn. Little did I know, as we entered its virtually customer-free lower deck to ensconce ourselves at a niche corner table, what an extraordinary and life-changing experience was about to begin for me there.

It was during our subsequent time within the tavern's walls that astonishing winter's afternoon, now emblazoned on my memory, that the attractive woman I'd just encountered transformed her facial appearance from Oriental to Occidental features. And if that wasn't startling enough, Diva went on to perform other mind-blowing acts – like vanishing for a while, and before my incredulous eyes – ahead of revealing to me that she'd come fairly recently to Earth from the Alpha Centauri star system, trillions of kilometres away on the other side of our shared, Milky Way galaxy. I could barely credit that we agreed to meet again. But the prospect was compelling;

and I was so curious, as a writer, to know how and why this alien from another world was visiting our Solar System planet. It seemed, from what I could deduce implicitly out of her words, amazingly like she wanted to ask *me* something specific. Over the following few days, we got together at a variety of Cambridge's iconic sites; and at some historic 'watering holes' such as The Pickerel Inn opposite Magdalene College and close by my waterside, apartment development.

What was especially surprising to me was that I couldn't help but believe what Diva was telling me. Though during our intriguing chats, and to say the very least, she never actually explained fully the reason or reasons why she'd been despatched across the galaxy; and clearly, as she'd informed me, from a civilisation millennia in advance – scientifically, technologically and otherwise – of that on Earth. The suspense was excruciating to bear; but, eventually and after my expressions of deep frustration, Diva succumbed finally. Oddly, she began by asking whether I harboured any fantastic dreams, ambitions or aspirations. I could hardly absorb what I was hearing when this now Western-looking woman responded that she could deliver on my fantasy. This was, and perhaps strangely for a largely non-practising member of the faith, to travel back in time to the Jewish community that had existed in medieval Cambridge, then known as Cantabrigia. However, she advised earnestly that there would be a requisite pre-condition for enabling me to fulfil my otherwise 'castle-in-the-air'. Perhaps oddly then

– though not as matters transpired – I thought instantly of the walled, Norman citadel that had stood dominant on Castle Hill overlooking the river in Cantabrigia, and for some centuries after William's Conquest. Somehow, Diva knew for sure that I would do virtually anything to make her astounding offer a reality, and to accomplish such an unimaginable mission.

But then, on hearing what Diva required in return for transporting me back in time to the 13th century, I was utterly stunned and rendered almost speechless. Diva needed, she said matter-of-factly, to have sexual intercourse with me! Finally – after recovering a balanced composure, and naturally – I enquired about the motivation dictating this requisite price for my historic ticket to the distant past. All my potential paramour would say was that she'd been instructed to get herself pregnant – and that would be achieved definitely, Diva had added confidently – by an Earthling. So that when she returned to her home planet, which our astronomers have termed Proxima b, Alpha Centauri scientists could pursue researches into the development of an Earth-human embryo. Nevertheless, as she was at pains to reassure and convince me, the further exploration undertaken wouldn't be carried out for any nefarious purposes… far from it, she concluded.

Needless to state, but our exchanges did spur me to wonder why *I* personally had been selected – assuming that had been the actual case – to meet this requirement; or whether it happened, as seemed likely to me, to be a random selection. But I was really amused to learn, if

I'd understood Diva correctly, that picking me might've had something to do with my occasional past references – expressed to others entirely by virtue of a whimsical intent in apt situations – to yours truly having "come from Alpha Centauri". Whether for good or ill, I did sense in a convincing way that my new-found, alien friend and companion was being absolutely honest and sincere in her dealings with me. I couldn't help but be smitten by her personality and charm, both physically and intellectually. In the prevailing situation, how could I possibly resist such an attractive woman; at least in her presentational appearance to me, but bearing also in mind the goal of time travel, imagined but never before experienced by anyone on Earth.

Ultimately, my faith and trust in Diva's genuineness and candour proved to have a life-saving, if not survival affirmation. And so, one night, she and I did have sex in my spacious, two-bedroom flat overlooking the Cam; and on the other side of the river to the appealing architecture – some going back to the early 15th century – of Magdalene College. Although a singleton, I'd decided not to purchase a one-bedroom apartment after my divorce – my ex-wife had departed Cambridge to live with her new partner in Israel – because my son Michael, our only child, visited me from his home in New York about twice a year. Sadly, he'd experienced his own relationship problems in the past; though, eventually, he did find happiness and married the love of his life. After our sexual liaison, Diva kept to her promise – goodness only knows how, technically speaking — and sent me packing back to 13th century Cantabrigia. And to the precise year and season I'd requested, knowingly: that was spring 1275, a fateful year for the town's Jewish community harassed continually by anti-Semites. So no change there then, I considered pensively — but unsurprisingly, from a 21st century, post-modern perspective — as I lay on the bed in my capsule accommodation.

Three

I CONTINUED to lie on my not uncomfortable 'bed', albeit squeezed into a fairly compact but life-supporting capsule aboard one of the extraordinary fleet of huge mother-ships. These were transporting their millions of reluctantly willing though somewhat obviously overwhelmed, Jewish-Earthling passengers to planet 'Proxima b' in the Alpha Centauri star system, and on what we thought could be termed 'a second Exodus'; though the journey to that 'promised land' would take, happily, rather less than 40 years.

As my head rested, eyelids closed, on what passed adequately as a pillow, I thought about my wife Naomi and our boy and girl twins packed into a neighbouring, but only moderately larger, accommodation 'pod' – for want of a better word. Then my much-activated mind switched brusquely to another series of wildly varied contemplations, as had been happening an awful lot across these astounding, galaxy-transiting days since we departed Earth orbit some weeks back. First, this reflecting time around and in that last context, I recalled again my many years of extensive globetrotting as a freelance investigative journalist in mostly focused searches for – or following up frequently tenuous leads on – at least very interesting, maybe sometimes intriguing if not exciting but even exotic and sensational stories. And I did in fact discover and write some really significant ones, or so I've been told by a few of my most loyal, commissioning newspaper and magazine editors.

Nevertheless, the subjects of those features could never have matched – by way of exoticism, sensationalism or, indeed, any other 'ism' – the targeted and awesome voyage, science fiction become fact, I'd embarked upon now. I could still hardly credit its mind-blowing back-story, a potentially devastating scenario of worldwide anti-Semitism that was happening little more than 80 years after the Nazi Holocaust; and the annihilation of six million, innocent European and Russian Jews. Nor could my global travels compare, to any degree, with the astounding journey that I undertook in time travelling back from the contemporary 21st century, and my university-city of Cambridge, to its 13th century predecessor... Cantabrigia. I'll never forget landing alone below the battlements and palisades of its Norman fortress, rising on what later became known as 'Castle Hill', with its commanding position beside the river and the medieval town, sprinkled with church spires and towers and surrounded by farmland and countryside. A slight miscalculation of the intended drop-zone nearly cost me dearly. Diva had been aiming for my proposed arrival spot just on the edge of Cantabrigia's 'Jewry' area, where the majority of the municipality's Jewish community had resided; but somehow she fell short, literally, of my expectations. Nonetheless, I felt disinclined to ever complain to her; especially after a wonderful and – for an Earthling – almost inconceivable time-travel experience across some 700 years.

Whilst shifting my head awkwardly on the pillow, I remembered painfully what had transpired just outside the castle. A couple of uniformed but rough-featured and decidedly anti-Semitic soldiers, on a patrol of the fort's perimeter walls, had abused me with some time-honoured tropes, like 'Christ killer', and maltreated me physically with some vicious kicks. Apparently, they had espied the 'Jew-badge' – comparable to the Nazis' 'Yellow Star' Jew identifier – stitched onto my Diva-supplied, medieval apparel. Fortunately, they stopped short of a serious, if not fatal assault on my person with their long-bladed swords; and I managed to find my way down, gradually but safely, from the heights and over the river bridge leading into the town. Eventually, and virtually breathless but in one piece more or less, I arrived at the originally planned landing spot.

I was standing, but shivering with apprehension, in a narrow cobbled lane between the triangle-shaped, largely Jewish neighbourhood – but with Christian residents, too – and a church I knew to be All Saints in the Jewry, which would be demolished in the 19th century. However, my travails, as my virtually uncontrollable trembling indicated presciently, had not ended yet. I was set upon suddenly and shockingly by a brute-faced ruffian of a robber, doubtless another anti-Semite, brandishing a really terrifying knife or dagger and seeking to grab my stick-attached bundle. The bag was stuffed with extra garments, both outer and under, and other necessary or useful items supplied thoughtfully, if not vitally, by Diva; and for what I'd scheduled to be a relatively short, maybe about a week's mind-boggling sojourn in Cantabrigia. Luckily, my personally unprecedented screams were registered by two, neatly bearded men; though both of them looked to be rather younger than clean-shaven me. In the struggle with my viciously mean-looking and filthily garbed assailant, I'd fallen to the cobble-stoned ground. But the hurried and noisy approach of, as I was to learn momentarily, the two Jewish brothers caused me to glance up and note that they appeared to have emerged from a nearby and large, stone-built house. At once, and effectively, they succeeded in driving away my miscreant attacker, rescuing me – and my quite precious pack of supplementary attire – from his evil-minded clutches. Following that, they hoisted traumatised me from off the ground; and, together, assisted me in reaching and entering their miraculously protective sanctuary.

Thankfully, and maybe not unsurprisingly in the final analysis, Diva had left no stone unturned in providing me the vitally essential wherewithal to integrate with my new, medieval experience and environment. Apart from the relevant clothing of the period, of course, I'd been afforded also the astonishing ability to comprehend the language that would be spoken. It meant that I was hearing an instantaneous, post-modern idiomatic, English translation of what was being said to me. Perhaps even more implausibly, I enjoyed also the capacity to speak the prevalent vernacular of this time and place in the Middle-Ages. So there would be no difficulties of communication for me, at least in that connection. In addition, I'd prepared a hopefully believable, personal back-story that I was an unmarried tutor living in London; and that I was visiting Cantabrigia on a kind of break from work, with the idea of staying in the Jewish hostelry which I understood existed within the Jewry.

Thus, very shaken indeed, I was helped into the imposing residence by the kindly pair of gentlemen, Joseph and his younger brother Aaron. After the strong-looking, thick wooden and iron-barred front door was closed and secured, I was assisted up a winding stone staircase to the first floor. I was then seated, for my immediate rest and recovery, in a comfortably high-backed chair at a long table in the spacious and airy, dark-wood panelled chamber. I will always remember the bowl of hot, herb and honey soup – highly recommended, apparently, for my then shocked state – that Joseph had requested the very young, though impressively efficient, housemaid Miriam to ask her mother, the family's cook, Rebecca, to prepare hastily for me.

I was soon to gather that Joseph resided in the house with his widowed mother, Sarah, and a single, older sister, Naomi; and I would shortly meet these fine ladies. His wife and children, I learned, were staying currently with some close relatives in London. Aaron, who dwelt with his wife and their offspring in the nearby town of Huntingdon, assisted his brother in the family's banking business. This was run from the basement of the lovely abode where I was now being benevolently cared for and sheltered. The financial enterprise had been founded by their late father and patriarch, Joshua. But I was saddened to hear that he'd lost his life at the hands of some brutal, anti-Semitic louts almost a decade previously. I was well aware, from my reading of this era's history, of the often rampant Jew-hate; and had myself that very day personally, and terrifyingly, experienced it. Of course, I knew and before Cantabrigia's Jewish community did – in this my arrival year of 1275 – of its imminent expulsion, en masse, to Huntingdon by King Edward I; and of the ultimate removal of all Jews from England by that monarch's notorious Edict of 1290.

I was so grateful to accept his offer, when Joseph insisted characteristically that – instead of lodging in the evidently uncomfortable, dormitory accommodation at the Jewish hostel in the Jewry, as I'd intended – I stay with the family. This would be in my own private bedroom on the uppermost floor of the house; and for the duration of my proposed, comparatively brief sojourn in the town. In just a day or two ensconced within the welcoming household – eating alongside Joseph, Aaron, Sarah and Naomi and talking to them about life for the Jewish community and its accompanying problems in Cantabrigia – I felt almost like an actual member of the family. This warm, safe and comforting feeling was enhanced when, for example, Joseph felt able to tell me –

though I'd virtually guessed already – that his beautiful and well-educated sister was unmarried. Apparently as a child, he went on to give the reason for this "troubling state of affairs", Naomi had suffered from a quite serious medical problem. Fortunately, I was informed, the infirmity had been cured; though its outcome was the melancholy side effect that his sister was now unable to bear children.

Naturally, in conversing with family members, it was horribly problematic for me to lie about myself; albeit understandably, if not necessarily in my extraordinary circumstances. But I did happen to tell my kind and generous hosts, and early on in my temporary residence with them, that I wasn't married; and this was the complete truth since my divorce. I couldn't help but harbour a particular notion – based on barely concealed exchanges of expressions between the brothers, and also between them and their mother… and especially, protocol aside, on the placement of their sister in the chair next to mine at the dining table – that they might've been wishfully thinking a certain something. However, their hopeful optimism may've increased somewhat when, undoubtedly, they noted that Naomi – to whom, in fact, I was becoming rather attracted – and I had been meeting together to enjoy some interesting conversations; as well as to have some walks around the town and its near environs. I had to admit to myself, as I lay on my bed at night before drifting into a dream-filled slumber, that I was beginning to sense an even deeper connect with this appealing maiden. What was more, I sensed also a kind of reciprocation from my sweet and charming, though occasionally quite wan and sad looking, newfound female acquaintance.

There was one other person I was introduced to at the dinner table, one evening early in my stay, as a merchant and landlord and a very close, family friend. Josce, scion of a wealthy Jewish dynasty in England, lived with his wife and children in Cantabrigia, though I never met them. Again, I was truly dismayed to learn quietly from Joseph that Josce's late father Saulot, the one-time patriarch of his family, had been murdered by anti-Semites in the 1260s. It was Josce – luckily, at the material time, supervising the unloading of cargo from a flat-bottomed river-craft moored beside the town's Quayside – who'd played an important role in getting Naomi and me safely back to the house. This was after a horrific and near-fatal, anti-Semitic incident during a stroll we'd embarked on together, perhaps foolishly, along the Cam and well outside the town boundary. Stones and verbal abuse were hurled at us by a gang of brutish and scraggily-attired men, whilst we were consuming a midday picnic prepared by Rebecca earlier that morning. They were grouped initially on the opposite bank of the river to us; so, providentially, we had a little but crucial time to flee the danger.

However, as Naomi and I abandoned hastily our poorly-chosen lunch spot, running as fast as we could across the tufts of grassland, we glanced back. To our utter dismay and panic, we perceived that the hate-filled hooligans had swum across the narrow water channel and were now, albeit soaking wet, in pursuit of us. Miraculously but dreadfully, for without doubt we would've been slaughtered after Naomi had been raped, we managed reluctantly to force ourselves into hiding within the former protective – but then garbage-filled to the rim and rat-infested – King's Ditch, which encircled much of Cantabrigia. Burying ourselves, potentially for ever, beneath the muck and human and animal filth, but gratefully succeeding in gouging out some barely adequate breathing space, we managed to elude our murderous and foul-mouthed, Jew-hating pursuers. Finally, when I was confident that the coast was clear, we extracted ourselves – with some heavily cloying difficulty – from the elongated rubbish pit then staggered back, terribly bedraggled and traumatised, along the riverside path towards the town and home.

Thankfully, we were spotted and just about recognised by a horrified and incredulous Josce as we struggled – Naomi weeping constantly – across busy Quayside. After some essentially prompt medical attention by a nearby-based, doctor relative of the family, Naomi and I were pronounced physically alright, more or less; but we were in real need of some seriously recuperative rest over the next day or so. Our joint experience had proved to be beyond appalling; though one beneficial outcome, if it could be termed such, was that our suffering had brought Naomi and me closer together emotionally. So much so, that she felt able, after recovering from the shock of it all, to speak to me authentically about her intimate, barren condition; and the profoundly depressing feelings she'd needed to grapple with about never being physically capable of becoming a Jewish mother. Naomi told me that, nevertheless, she prayed to the Almighty every Sabbath in the synagogue, which – I was to discover on the Shabbat I accompanied the family to morning service there – was reached by a secret underground tunnel from the house's basement. This expansive cellar, where the banking business was based, was soon to become the scene of a horrendous and calamitous raid by the city Sheriff's armed officers.

That ultimately tragic invasion, no less, occurred near the projected end of my time in Cantabrigia when, candidly, I was totally perplexed about the developing relationship between Naomi and me; but knowing that my deepening affection for her was matched by her own feelings for me. Just like she'd found the capacity to confide in me, I held no qualms about confiding in an astonished – to say the least – but, beneficially, intrigued woman that I was a time traveller from the 21st century, and could prove it. Witness, I held out to her, my mobile phone! It so happened that Naomi and I were helping Joseph with some sorting out in the underground chamber when heavily armed constabulary burst their way in. The officer in charge declared that Joseph and the rest of us were under arrest for coin-clipping offences; and that the entire house would now be thoroughly searched, from top to bottom, for evidence before trial. We knew that false allegations of this sort were aimed continually at the Jewish target, with several of those wrongly accused being found guilty at trial, sentenced to death and hanged on the gallows in a public place. Inevitably, our protestations of innocence had no affect whatsoever on the ears of our malicious accusers.

Then we were chained securely and marched off to the gaol at the castle on the hill. Passing Quayside with our armed escort, we were espied by Josce as soon as we saw him. Naturally, the family's close friend couldn't believe his own eyes; and his jaw dropped in stunned amazement and incredulity. When we prisoners reached the fortress, the three of us were thrown into ground floor, open-barred cells, Naomi's adjoining the one into which Joseph and I were pushed so roughly. Though, very shortly afterwards, my caring host – as the alleged principal culprit – was told that, on the morrow, he would be transported to the Tower of London, where he would be held in solitary confinement until his appearance in court and likely execution in due course. Joseph was dragged down to a subterranean holding cell and we never saw him again.

I was pulled from my cell and, with a sobbing Naomi doubtless observing my terrified expression, escorted upstairs for interrogation. To my complete horror, I was subjected to an invasive body search; and, of course, my mobile phone was found. Without me providing a full and satisfactory explanation of that object, and its presence on my person, the item was confiscated and stored away in a then locked wooden chest. Before being led back to my cell, I was advised by a now glaring officer that I would soon be joining my criminal friend Joseph on his journey to the capital the next day. With the awful loss of my smart-phone, especially adjusted by Diva for the purposes of my seeking a safe return to 21st century Cambridge, I couldn't take on board the impossibility of doing that now. I could hardly absorb and comprehend the dire situation in which I and, of course, Naomi found ourselves; and, painfully for me, I could hear her continuous sobbing in the adjacent cell.

In my enclosed, mini–cell–like, mother–ship capsule, I was becoming somewhat restive with these still scarifying recollections. Then my memory reminded me that nothing less than a miracle happened next. All of a sudden, as our guard snored loudly and persistently whilst slumped at the desk, Diva appeared; and articulated her concern that she hadn't heard from me to arrange my time travel journey back to the future. After Naomi and I expressed our now deep love for each other – but, on her part, not without an achingly heavy heart for the family she felt were being abandoned by her – my darling soul-mate agreed to accompany me to 21st century Cambridge. Sadly, Joseph couldn't be taken with us.

On our safe and sound arrival in my famed university hometown, there was much to regularise for my beloved Naomi; and rather more for her to learn, and with which to get a post-modern grip. We got married in a synagogue; and my son – who, at that time, I didn't tell about Naomi's provenance – flew over from New York to attend the ceremony, and the small reception that followed it.

Not that long afterwards, and to our total gob-smacking astonishment, Diva arrived unannounced at our apartment beside the river and presented us with the twins of whom, as Naomi understood, I was the natural father; and, in a sense, by virtue of whom she'd come to be my wife. We named the boy, Joshua Joseph Aaron Josce; and the girl, Sarah Ruth Rebecca Miriam... in treasured memory of those held dear to us.

Four

I WOULD see Naomi and the kids, if they weren't asleep or being supervised in the children's extensive play-zone, fairly regularly at our appointed mealtimes in a hugely spacious hall within our gigantic mother-ship. It appeared, I imagined, more like the enlarged interior of a modern cruise liner's engine room, with lots of exposed metal pipe-work of various descriptions and other, indubitably vital engineering festooning the walls and ceiling. But these inexorable, environmental and technological necessities didn't overly concern us Jewish passengers... well, most of us. We didn't even want to know about any drills with 'lifeboats', whatever form they might've taken on such a spacecraft. It was just marvellously relaxing to be able to stretch our limbs; and, if we wished, suitably animate our bodies after being cocooned in the dormitory pods.

It was also good for our enormous number of passengers to get the opportunity to mix, talk and generally socialise with other close family members, more distant relatives and possibly friends, old and new, in their vicinity on the same dining shift. The children had the chance to make some new pals, too; and they could play happily together in the special areas set aside for this purpose. The meals were excellent, cooked from frozen but tasty and filling; and kosher food was readily available for those who required and requested such rabbi-supervised fare. All passengers – whether male, female, children and even babies – were obliged to dress in an identical kind of uniform. On embarkation, when the fleet of mother-ships was stationed stealthily somewhere in Earth orbit, we had been supplied with a sort of bluish-hued, lightweight tunic top to be worn over what appeared to emulate, and felt akin to, pantaloons; and, in addition, similarly tinted caps and footwear in a style that could pass for trainers. The rationale behind our compulsorily unified apparel wasn't really clear; nor was it explained to us. Some brethren opined, doubtless inaccurately, that it was because the colour blue was sometimes associated with Jewish people, maybe due to the basic shade of the Israeli flag. When all of a particular shift's innumerable passengers were making their gradual way from the entrance and through the vast hall, to take their allotted places at the beyond lengthy tables, the overall scenario – if viewed from above – must've appeared like the waves of a sea-tide rolling into the shoreline.

In any event, the apparent need for our especial headgear was useful and conducive also to the strict tenets of the Orthodox men amongst our brethren. Though the bearded *Charedi*, or ultra-Orthodox male element, probably would've preferred to don the traditionally wide-brimmed, black hat over their *kippah* or skull-cap. The Orthodox women, whether married or otherwise, were really appreciative to be offered thoughtfully a type of long skirt as a substitute for the trousers-like, lower garment unconcernedly worn by other – but not so, or at all, religious – passengers of their gender. This was because they held strictly to their religious tenet that women shouldn't wear the kind of clothes worn by men. Some of the wedded, Orthodox womenfolk actually looked quite cute with the issued blue caps pushed down onto their community's requisitely worn – supposedly modest but, sometimes, maybe unduly attractive – *sheitls* or hair-pieces.

When Naomi and I, and other passengers allotted the particular shift, assembled together and were first allocated seating arrangements at one of the unbelievably long, metal tables in the incredibly huge dining and social area by members of the definitely humanoid crew, we found ourselves seated directly opposite a married French couple likely, we estimated, to be somewhere in their forties with the husband balding and the wife manifestly pregnant. Our twins were present, of course, at this earliest time in the hall; they were tucked together, and perched quietly between Naomi and me. My wife could speak and understand the modern French language almost perfectly, based understandably on her Norman-French of the medieval period. My own moderate comprehension of the lingo was rather less fluent, and at the GCSE O-level grade from way back. However, and fortunately for me, Maurice and Mirelle – both of whom had worked professionally in Paris' financial sphere – spoke and understood English extremely well.

The first words spoken to the couple by us, or rather by my spouse – as she lowered her eyes to Mirelle's well pronounced 'baby bump' – were:

"Mazeltov on your forthcoming, happy event!"

Maurice smiled graciously at our good wishes. But Mirelle – and to our acute surprise – instantly drew in her lips, closed her eyelids tight shut, screwed up her otherwise pleasing features then, seemingly, couldn't stop herself bursting into tears. Promptly, the husband placed an arm around his wife's shaking body and drew her close to him, so that her head – with its long and dark, shiny hair – rested, as she wept, on his shoulder. Naomi and I gazed at each other discreetly but somewhat quizzically and crestfallen, noticing too that our little son and daughter appeared to be frightened a little by the woman's strange reaction to the expression of our congratulations. We noted also that other passengers in our immediate neighbourhood, distracted by the sobbing sounds, were taking notice of their source. But they didn't display any overly surprised reaction, which may not have been that odd. Though this could've been due to their and others' sad experiences, to say the least, in the context of our wholesale Jewish emigration from Earth to the Alpha Centauri star system light years distant.

"I'm so sorry," Maurice said softly, his voice filled with an aching sincerity and his baleful eyes revealing their own suddenly acquired dampness, undoubtedly exposing his own profound emotions also. "Please give me a moment or two, then I'll explain… and thank you so much for your kind good wishes."

Naomi and I seemed to be sharing a little, but maybe acceptable difficulty in launching a smile in this oddly ambivalent situation. So, fairly simultaneously, both of us merely nodded slowly once or twice. I was thinking of telling Maurice that he didn't need to explain anything to us; but then the food was served by an almost indescribable but, technically, so efficient a method. No further words were exchanged between us and the French couple sitting opposite until after we'd consumed our meals. By which time Mirelle had, we thought, recovered her composure and – after a meaningful gesture from her husband – appeared to be on the point of addressing my wife and me.

"I-I'm so v-very sorry for my b-behaviour just a while ago," she said, lifting her gaze to Naomi then me; and albeit with an initially quivering moment or two in her Gallic-accented voice.

But immediately following her brief sentence, she placed a hand to her mouth, looked downwards again then delicately touched Maurice's nearest hand resting on the table. He took the hint at once, and turned his attention to us.

"I believe my wife wishes *me* to explain her recent conduct to you," he said, making me – and, I think, Naomi also – feel a trifle sensitive, uncomfortable and apprehensive about what he was now going to tell us. So, finally, I felt that I had to say:

"Maurice, you don't have to explain anything to us, really you don't… we don't want to see you and Mirelle upset in any way."

But Maurice just shook his head, and said:

"We want you to know."

We nodded with resignation, and without more.

"Well, David and Naomi… thank you, of course, for your *Mazeltov* and good wishes on our approaching happy event, and which is much appreciated," Maurice began, though his delivery seemed somehow to lack the inherent joyfulness we might've expected. But he appeared instantly to pick up on the implicit nature of our facial expressions.

"I know we should be displaying our gladness at this wonderful time," he said, "but, as you've sadly witnessed just before, Mirelle and I have dreadful memories about what happened to our late beloved children, Alain and Madeleine, at the hands of terrorist anti-Semites a couple of years ago …"

As low-level sobbing sounds issued from his wife, the facial expressions of both Naomi and me would've shown, and abundantly clearly, the shock and horror at what we were hearing now. Not that what we were being told was exceptional in these devastating days for the Jewish people on Earth. I couldn't but help recall the shooting dead, by a terrorist, of a rabbi and pupils at a Jewish school in Toulouse several years back; and even some time before the opening of the deadly, 21st century floodgates of murderous Jew-hatred. We'd heard, read in the newspapers, seen on TV news programmes and even witnessed firsthand so many terrible, and frequently deadly, incidents over recent years. We could never become immune to the fearsome and alarming outcomes of such tidal waves of increasingly violent anti-Semitism sweeping the globe.

For certain, and without question, this was the crystal clear motivation for the presence of Maurice and Mirelle, Naomi and me and the millions of other Jewish passengers onboard this astonishing fleet of Alpha Centauri mother-ships; and for this voyage across the Milky Way galaxy to our, and their, new planetary home. And being informed about a personally shattering experience of losing dearly beloved ones, especially young children, struck us to the core of our Jewish beings and souls. With my wife's hinted concurrence, I stretched out my right arm across the table, the palm of my hand open upwards indicatively. This action, together with the almost pleading look on my face, held the reiterated message that Maurice really wasn't constrained to go on with his report of a dreadful parental loss. I'm sure he received my sympathetic intimation; but his split second reaction to my action convinced me that he was determined to continue his doubtless agonising account; and for his own, perhaps explicable, reasons.

"It was a weekday morning, though I can no longer remember which day of the week," Maurice started again. "As usual, Mirelle and I were escorting the kids, Alain was eight and Madeleine ten, in my car to their Jewish primary school, before riding the Metro from leafy suburbia to our respective bank offices in central Paris, not that far from L'Opera. We'd been living in the suburbs since marrying a dozen years earlier, and it was just a short drive from our house to the school. When I pulled up near its entrance gates, the children jumped out from the backseat shouting 'Au revoir, Maman et Papa!' then eagerly joined a stream of other arriving pupils. As was my custom, I wound down the driver's side window and… w-waved to… P-Pierre, the s-school's external security guard …"

He bit his lower lip and stopped speaking for a few moments. I sort of gathered from his palpably emotional pause that probably something awful had happened subsequently to Pierre. I could detect that Maurice's breathing had quickened, whilst his wife sat silently and quite rigidly now, her eyelids closed more than firmly. Then her husband went on, after sighing deeply.

"I received the sorrowful telephone call from the police later that morning. Apparently, two heavy-set and hooded anti-Semites, armed with submachine guns and revolvers with attached silencers, shot dead Pierre at the main gate without making a sound. The security man hadn't stood a chance. Similarly, the school's other sentinel, on duty just inside the entrance portal to the main building, was killed with a single and noiseless bullet to the head. It seems he may've opened the door after looking through the spy-hole, and not seen his colleague standing where he should've been. Having gained entry, the two murderous invaders systematically and quickly toured the building, from the ground to the third… that is, the top floor. They burst into the classrooms and staff offices, spraying the terrified and screaming children, teachers and non-educational personnel with a cruelly lethal gunfire. Some of the adults and pupils, though not that many and quite enigmatically, managed to survive by escaping rapidly to conceal themselves in toilets or cupboards. Or by fleeing through the ground-floor kitchen and windows into the school's garden-playground area to the rear... and even over its boundary fences and hedges ..."

Maurice halted his horrendous narrative once more; and his poor spouse moved restively, now tearful again. I recalled reading, or seeing news items on TV or my smartphone, about this cowardly and heinous attack on a Jewish school in Paris. But, sad to contemplate, it wasn't a unique disaster for our victimised communities – whether in Europe, the USA and Canada or elsewhere in the world, including South America and the Antipodes – during these ever more insecure and sickening times for them. However, less than a century after the Holocaust and the wholesale annihilation of six million Jews by the Nazis, it was hard to believe that there had been so numerous and frequent such fatal anti-Semitic assaults occurring, and so extensively, around the world. Though, in fact, many brethren did consider that this particular, targeted, senseless and inhuman hatred was eternal; and, therefore though sadly, should be expected to recur from time to time and to varying degrees of fatality.

Then the Frenchman went on with his account:

"With other, atrociously anti-Semitic attacks beginning to occur so widely at the time, what I was hearing from police officers would've come as almost predictable, generally speaking. But in this instance, needless to say, the matter was unbearably personal and overwhelming. My head almost felt as if it was exploding after I heard the terrible news. I now needed to contact Mirelle and somehow find the strength, let alone the words, to inform her of the disastrously violent, wicked and fatal attack on our innocent children's school by terrorist gunmen. The police required us to go there at once, to confirm or otherwise whether our kids had been killed or wounded; or whether they were missing and, thus, had possibly survived the bestial shooting massacre. My wife and I could only hope, and pray to the Almighty ..."

Maurice paused yet again, gazing directly into the deeply saddened eyes of Naomi and me. Then he shifted somewhat on his seat, and held tightly onto his now quietly weeping wife. We were rendered totally speechless, even presuming Naomi and I could've found anywhere near the most appropriately sensitive words to expound and convey what we were feeling at that moment.

"When finally we arrived, in our indescribable mental states, at the school, which was surrounded by armed police and soldiers, we learned that both attackers had been shot dead by speedily alerted police marksmen as they tried to flee the gruesome crime scene," Maurice continued. "There were also several ambulances in attendance. I'll not describe in detail the appalling sights that confronted us, and other stunned and assembled or arriving parents, inside the school building. But there were no less than actual streams of blood flowing out of the classrooms and offices, into and along the narrow corridors and down the stairways. It was incredibly ghastly but direct evidence of murder and mayhem. The bodies of the dead had been carried to the assembly and activity hall on the ground-floor, and covered over individually with blankets or other material to hand. Emotionally devastated fathers and mothers, many of them hysterical, were seeking, as best they could in the horrific circumstances, to identify their dead children, if that turned out to be the awful case. Understandably, and with an extreme reluctance, the parents were lifting very tentatively the temporary body coverings to reveal the often blood-drenched cadavers. Elsewhere in the building, they could discover the attendant and surviving pupils, whether seriously, moderately or slightly wounded or even, maybe and luckily, uninjured... though all of them displayed obvious and variable signs of trauma. The kids were being treated urgently on the spot by paramedics before being taken to local hospitals, now on full alert to receive them. Armed patrols had been despatched around the neighbourhood to search for missing adults and pupils, hopefully safe and alive in some secure hiding place ..."

Maurice halted his account yet again, and took a deep breath.

"Mirelle and I didn't need to visit the room where the injured and shocked children were being cared for, and given necessary medical attention. We found our beloved son and daughter in the main hall ..."

In a way, it was fortunate for us that the signal was then given for the end of this meal shift. The passengers got up from their places – our twins had to be awakened from their slumbers, leaning against each other and their mum on the seating – and commenced moving in lines towards the exit. We could see our French acquaintances rising, harrowingly heartbroken, from the metal bench to head back gradually to their respective dormitory capsules, both of them to an undoubtedly agitated, sleepless and mournfully tearful night. It went without any words passing between my wife and I that, in our own metal cocoons, we would likely have a pensive, next several Earth-hours; and not only by reason of any thoughts we might ponder of a time some 700 years ago …

Five

THAT NIGHT, my slender wife slunk fairly comfortably into my, even though quite compact, capsule. This did mean that we needed to hold each other very closely; but, as you would expect, that wasn't a real problem. En route back to our respective dormitory pods with the kids, Naomi told me she couldn't face being alone in her pod all night; and I assumed, of course, that took on board implicitly the presence of Joshua and Sarah. My wife spoke with a voice brimful of emotion; but, anyway, I could guess that, like me, she was continuing to feel deeply upset about what the French couple had been distressingly telling us earlier that evening in our mother-ship's immense dining hall. How could we not be so affected about the extremist and anti-Semitic slaughter of their two young children during the carnage, a couple of years back, at a Jewish primary school in a Paris suburb?

Naomi added that she wouldn't be able to get to sleep for mulling over the bloodbath butchery. Not that we hadn't been aware, from media reports, of that and many other lethal attacks on Jewish communities in the ever-growing milieu of Jew hate and persecution around the world. Our family had been fortunate to have escaped involvement in anything so inhumanly destructive physically; though the vilest forms of verbal abuse were not at all uncommon. Clearly, it was hearing firsthand from sorrowfully still mourning parents – who'd sustained such a dreadful personal loss, and necessarily thinking about our own much loved children – that had truly hit us hard. And that was especially the case when Maurice and Mirelle gazed equivocally across the table at our young twins during the husband's ghastly narrative.

Subsequent to returning from our evening meal shift, Naomi had put the kids to bed in the capsule they shared with her. Perhaps unsurprisingly, I learned, they'd both fallen asleep in little more than a few moments. Their mum had doubtless felt very envious at our offspring's virtually instant launch into the Land of Nod. In fact, she mentioned this to me soon after tapping on my capsule casing and gaining entrance to the pod. It was good to hear also that my wife was hopeful that *her* much desired slumber would arrive swiftly in my all-embracing arms. Regrettably for her, however, that wasn't to be so; though, of course, I'd been glad to hear that Joshua and Sarah were now, with any luck, in a happy and tranquil Dreamland for them.

"Are you asleep yet, darling?" I enquired whisperingly, and only a short while following my cradling of Naomi's willowy body in my upper limbs.

Maybe I wasn't so amazed when I got a reply to my optimistic question.

"No, David my love… I'm not!"

I knew from our personal history together that, sometimes, the sound of music would help her become absent from the real world; and, particularly, when something was playing on her mind.

"Shall I sing you a lullaby, Naomi?" I offered *sotto voce*.

She shifted awkwardly against me.

"Please don't, David," she murmured at once, and with emphasis.

I drew her even closer, if that was possible, and understood her reasoning.

"Don't suppose I need ask what the problem is …"

"You're right," she responded, kind of wistfully. "But why have these terrible atrocities been happening again to the Jewish people? Can you answer me that, David?"

I couldn't see her face, and she wasn't able to see mine, in the dimness of our cocoon. There was just a faint, rather dull glow hovering from somewhere outside the capsule. But whatever was the facial expression representing our respective and innermost feelings, both of us knew that we didn't have the explanation for her poser. Save maybe for the regularly automatic reference to human beings having been accorded freedom of thought and deed, as a result of which there has been both good and evil in the world. And which both of us had learned – though centuries apart, and very early in our lives – from the stories in the Old Testament. Naomi and I had covered this debate on more than a few occasions in the past as well as more recent times. But on this night, and bearing well in mind the lateness of the hour, I remained silent; and, thankfully, my wife did, too.

Eventually, I did fall asleep. Had I known beforehand the unbearable intensity of the tormenting nightmare that was to continue haunting me even on my awakening, I would've strived to remain awake all night; and probably would've ensured Naomi did, too… just in case. Unfortunately, she didn't fall into the soothing arms of Morpheus; and so, unhappily, she thought continuously about the horrors of which Maurice had spoken. My terrifying, bad-dream images were not so much concerned with his emotional report of a tragic personal loss; but rather constituted a profoundly disturbing compendium of analogous, anti-Semitic incidents that we'd become fearfully aware of from our newspaper reading, radio listening and TV viewing. And that was coupled with the sort of Maurice-type, individual accounts that Naomi and I were yet to hear from fellow passengers we were still to meet during our journey across the galaxy to the Alpha Centauri star system, and our new home on exoplanet Proxima b.

The numerous, horrendously shocking and heartbreaking instances of death and destruction that we heard about, from our fellow 'Jewish astronauts', included one concerning aged grandparents being shaken awake – eyes bulging with terror – in bed, in the middle of the night, to have their throats slit by inhuman, anti-Semitic invaders of their home. Other stories covered synagogues being explosively demolished or set ablaze, frequently with trapped community members burned to death. And not unlike the innumerable similar conflagrations ignited by fanatical Nazi mobs during *Kristallnacht* – the 'Night of

Broken Glass' – across Germany on 9th to 10th November 1938. Joyful weddings, *bar-* and *bat-mitzvahs* – coming of age ceremonies for boys and girls – and other *simchahs* or celebratory occasions in synagogues, hotels and other venues had been attacked with homicidal intent by obsessive, Jew-hating fanatics firing sub-machine guns.

And as if the lack of morality and humanity could end there, large numbers of Jewish people attending – at various cemeteries – *levoyahs* or burials of dearly beloved relatives or close and life-long friends were suddenly mown down, without mercy, by gunfire from semi-automatic weapons wielded by wild-eyed anti-Semites. At one Jewish old-age home, all the residents and care staff – and any relatives or friends who happened to be visiting during that appalling and sickening afternoon – were hauled, pummelled or otherwise hounded upstairs to the roof garden and hurled shrieking over its safety barrier to their bloody deaths on the street below. In those recent, continuing and seriously anguished times for Jewish communities worldwide, there had been so many other gory examples of annihilation. They vied virtually with the wholesale slaughter of Jewish men, women, children and babes-in-arms in the gas chambers and death camps of Hitler's *Third Reich*. And such deadly incidents could be compared also with the mass executions by shooting at the blood-soaked hands of the evil Führer's *Einsatzgruppen*, or paramilitary death squads, and their national associates in the forests and ravines of Nazi-occupied, East European countries.

I awoke fuzzy-headed and with a start, hitting my head on the upper part of my capsule. The shock of the sudden metallic contact certainly had the effect of rousing me from my cerebral wooziness; but, at once, I acquired a bit of a headache. Nonetheless, I'd noticed – on first struggling to raise my eyelids – that Naomi was no longer ensconced with me in the pod, doubtless having decided to return to her own; and, ostensibly, to check that the kids were alright. My head was now really hurting, so I followed the given routine for seeking any necessary medical advice and assistance in this, to all passengers, very strange and unique situation. I pressed an appropriate 'button' – which illuminated instantly – on the capsule's internal side panel, explained my problem into a small 'speaker' then awaited the promised pill, which – and very soon afterwards – I found had arrived. This was after lifting a lid in the upward curving end of an adjacent, thin metal pipe. As advised in excellent English, I swallowed the quite tiny, white tablet immediately. After a mere few moments, my cranium had ceased aching and I felt – at least physically – absolutely fine; due, I was sure, to the wonders of an extremely advanced medical science.

But as I lay my head back on the 'pillow' to seek some much needed R and R, the psychological hurt of my gruesome nightmare content, blocked only temporarily by my headache, returned to haunt me... and with a vengeance. Passengers on our gigantic spaceship enjoyed the thoughtful facility – built into their capsules – to call, or receive calls from, other voyagers. I really wanted, albeit rather selfishly in the circumstances, to contact Naomi and speak with her. But, then again, I didn't wish to disturb her if, hopefully, she was managing to gain some shuteye; or even if she might've been ministering to one or both of the twins in some requisite way. However, I took comfort in knowing that I would see my wife and children very soon; and, incredibly, I felt my eyelids closing gradually before losing consciousness and drifting into what turned out to be a fortunately peaceful, dreamless, calm and soothing slumber.

Six

THE FLEET of colossal, Alpha Centauri mother-ships had escaped rapidly the Earth's gravity – in more senses than one, I considered, for their millions of erstwhile persecuted Jewish people on board – and begun the voyage to a new planetary home, over four 'light years' away, at a phenomenal speed. This was a velocity vastly in excess of the current scientific and cosmological capabilities of NASA; or any other rocket-launching bodies on our former world. I was aware that many thousands of onboard Jewish professors and academics active in various fields, scientists and technologists, including a few Nobel prize-winners, and rabbis from all shades of Judaism, as well as countless others – including Jewish atheists – would be onboard passengers. I just knew they would be debating, both within their own specialist or belief groupings and with others, profound and possibly further divisive scientific, theological and philosophical questions – singularly or in combination – concerning the so-called second 'Exodus' of the Jewish people after their first, biblical flight from Pharaoh's Egypt thousands of years ago.

But as I'd mentioned to Naomi – during one of our own private and personal, though perhaps not so intellectual but nevertheless interesting discussions – there could be no doubting that many thousands of our fellow space travellers wouldn't necessarily be Jewish, either by birth or conversion into whatever degree or compartment of our faith. Possibly, these passengers would've married, or at least become a self-styled 'partner' to, a Jewish man or woman; and we were aware, from USA statistics, that the 'marrying-out' rate there was exceeding fifty percent now. Or maybe such galactic voyagers had been born to a non-Jewish mother in whatever relationship with a Jewish man. But, undoubtedly, the basic questions being turned over and over by the mother-ships' capsule contents – that is, the human passengers... and definitely not members of the fairly inconspicuous and, we believed, essentially automaton, android or robotic crews – could be encapsulated, my wife and I felt, in one word... *Why*?

These widely held discussions – some heated, others taking a more sociable and perhaps whimsical style of discourse, all often engaging a screen-monitor Skype-format integrated into our accommodation pods – were, we supposed, a good enough way of passing the time onboard. But, we thought also, they could distract passengers from worrying continuously about what precisely lay ahead for us on Proxima b. We all knew, or had to admit and accept – save, perhaps, for those with rigidly extreme, religious views – that mere mortals couldn't know or attain the absolute answer to the monosyllabically-expressed, but momentous *Why* interrogatory. A question which could be expanded into: *Why was all this happening to us, the Jewish people, both in relation to its cause and its effect?*

Of course, it was conceivable that only a relatively small proportion of the arguing and maybe hubristic Earthlings would've been mindfully occupied – then and in the past – by their grain-of-sand significance, and individual place in the mysteriously infinite and eternal cosmos. But, amongst the space-journeying millions of Jews, I'd been the first to be told by Diva – way back at our first meetings in Cambridge, and at one or other of its cosy riverside inns – that not only was Alpha Centauri's science and technology millennia in advance of such as exists on Earth. But also that the entire citizenry of the exceedingly far distant, star system had long-learned how to live together harmoniously, peacefully and securely, benignly and tolerantly, cooperatively and generously, as well as kindly and lovingly… so that the total population of Proxima b was living in a kind of 'Golden Age'. And my friend, from that far away flank of the Milky Way, didn't appear to be running out of superlative adjectives to describe her home planet's co-inhabitants. Only a pause to swallow some of her apparently non-alcoholic, orange beverage had served to call a halt to the seemingly endless flow of glowingly descriptive words.

In stark contrast, Diva went on to talk about her research-based understanding of the history of Mankind in our Solar System, Earth's constant wars and enduring hatreds from the very beginning to the current, post-modern era of terrorism and extremism, the comparatively celeritous recurrence of corrupt and evil governments, the continuing prejudice and now repeatedly terrible persecutions against the world's, barely 15 million Jewish people. She'd added, quite unnecessarily, that huge numbers of human beings, and despite being so-called civilised and cultured, appear to have learned no lessons from the past; and would likely never change their thinking, attitudes and bigotry; and likely because they really didn't want, or see the need, to do so. Clearly, Diva had read up about the rise of Nazism in 1920s and 1930s Germany; and miscreant National Socialism's compulsive anti-Semitism leading to the Holocaust and the merciless obliteration of six million Jews. She'd pointed to the so-called *Kultur* of the German *Volk* and, yet, its fervent belief in Aryan superiority and supremacy; but also to the fact that the people supported and voted for Hitler's malevolent regime largely – she felt, too – because it represented what *they* actually desired.

The alarming increase in anti-Semitism in the United Kingdom, continental Europe, North America and elsewhere in the world was confirmed emphatically to Diva on one of her later, once-a-year visits to Naomi and me in our Cambridge riverside apartment; and, naturally, to delight in seeing again the growing twins. I'm sure she could perceive, on chatting to them, that they'd inherited some of her own astounding capabilities, including the ability to read other people's instant thoughts. My wife and I were somewhat doubtful whether the kids were entirely aware, to date, of that powerful and potentially useful, even if invasive and maybe uncomfortable, aptitude or talent.

On that visit to our flat, she learned further and unhappily of the fear-provoking and deeply stressful situation of Earth's widespread Jewish communities or *Diaspora* – a distress felt also in Israel, and not only by those of its Jewish citizens with family still living outside the middle-east State. But Diva, too, became involved firsthand in a personally shocking incident. When she left us, after as enjoyable an evening as possible in all the melancholy circumstances of the times we were living through, a heavy-set man apparently noticed her leaving our apartment. On the external, side-jamb of its front door is displayed a *mezuzah* – the smallish, elongated symbolic emblem and container holding a manuscript prayer and marking a Jewish household. She returned to our flat, just a short while after departing it, to tell us what had transpired subsequently. It was quite scary for Naomi and me to have our doorbell rung unexpectedly at that time of night; and, needless to state, I peered though the portal's spy-hole to identify the late caller. It was a relief, albeit an ambivalent one, to see that it was Diva.

She reported that the man had followed her down the stairs – she hadn't taken the lift, Diva told us, for his rather than her sake – to the building's exit and onto the then night-darkened and deserted, riverside boardwalk area. Our extra-terrestrial friend said that she swivelled round quickly, on starting to walk in the direction of Quayside, on hearing what had to be the same man's heavy footsteps on the wood-planked pathway very close behind her. With a wicked smirk creasing his bestial face, she said, he was now brandishing a long knife that glinted in the muted light from a nearby, old lamp-standard. Little did he know what was coming to him... Our dear Diva apparently had raised and outstretched her right arm and hand to a horizontal position, then pointed an index finger directly at her imminent assailant's evil heart. At the same time, she placed her left index finger against her left temple. Instantly, we heard from her, the lengthy dagger had fallen from her doubtless anti-Semitic attacker's grasp, bounced off the ground and into the water with a dull splash. Her assailant's face had crumpled in terror and agony, and his body went rigid for a few moments. After that momentary paralysis, he'd grabbed at his chest and uttered the deepest of sighs before his entire body speedily and completely disintegrated.

In one sense, Naomi and I – although surprised initially to have Diva return to the flat only minutes after she'd left it, and before hearing her explanation – weren't so amazed to learn of the likely intended-to-be-fatal attack on her person. It was clearly a case, at least in acceptable theory, of her life or the murderous brute's... with no additional comment required, we felt strongly. But being a terrible incident very close to home, and for sure, it had made us fearfully uneasy about us and the twins leaving our apartment in the following couple of days; though we and they did, but always together. Clearly neither Naomi and I nor – probably, I suspected – the kids would've possessed Diva's powerfully responsive and effective capabilities.

The very personal and grisly episode she'd experienced, our dear friend told us before this time finally and safely leaving the flat that miserably memorable night, had prompted her to reflect further on the seriously worrying, anti-Semitic developments across the globe, as we'd spoken about earlier. My wife and I definitely pricked up our ears when Diva conveyed her thought that Alpha Centauri's leaders needed to determine how the increasingly persecuted Jewish people on Earth – at some point maybe confronting the cataclysmic possibility of another Holocaust – could be helped to survive extermination and extinction.

"After all," she'd added, "in Genesis, the first chapter of your Old Testament, it's stated very plainly that the Almighty 'created the heaven and the earth'."

And she'd concluded:

"In consequence, therefore, I believe that the Jewish people shouldn't feel troubled about taking some benefit from the entire *Creation*!"

Her parting words, spoken with such unpredictable intensity and emotional sincerity, left Naomi and me with a vital hope, of a kind that had served to sustain our people in years past and that had been sadly evading us. We trusted that it would inspire us to believe in a contented, benevolent and positive future for our children's generation and all Jewish generations to come …

Seven

I COULDN'T help but reflect on Diva's reference to the Jewish people's escape from slavery in ancient Egypt to the freedom of the Promised Land. It did seem to me now that we millions of Jewish passengers on board the Alpha Centauri mother-ships were embarked, indeed, on a second *Exodus*; but one of maybe far greater than biblical proportions in the numbers involved. Not this time around was it an emancipation from the slavery of being forced by their taskmasters to construct pyramids and treasure cities for the Pharaohs... But it was the deliverance from a slavery of fear for their safety, if not survival from a new wave or even deluge of 21st century, anti-Semitic discrimination, persecution and, ultimately, a prospective total destruction.

Diva had researched so much about the history, heritage and culture of Judaism; and aside from the faith itself. I ruminated also on her allusion to the Almighty's *Creation* of "the heaven" as well as "the earth", and as so stated in the very first verse of Genesis, the opening book of the Old Testament. In effect, this was designed to allay any apprehensions, qualms or uncertainties held by angst-ridden Jewish communities on Earth, the amazingly prospective voyagers across the Milky Way galaxy to another star system. I smiled at my recollection of Diva's delivery to us in Cambridge of the twin boy and girl, as conceived between us – and later explained to a wholly accepting Naomi – for the purposes of furthering Alpha Centauri's scientific, genetic, physiological and other studies of the human embryo until birth. This was the pre-condition, presented to divorcee and single me by the attractive and – I was convinced, and essentially so for loyalty reasons – totally honest and dependable Diva, for my being accorded the exceptionally stupefying opportunity to travel back in time to 13th century Cantabrigia.

Her earlier acquired and growing knowledge of all things Jewish became marvellously apparent when, subsequent to her departing our flat after leaving the adorable babies with us on that truly mind-blowing but wonderful evening, we discovered that our son Joshua had been circumcised, doubtless eight days after his birth and in accordance with Judaism's ritual practice. But I hadn't informed Diva, as yet – though she probably knew anyway – about the developing kids' increasingly perceptible inheritance of her power to read another person's immediate thoughts; and whether or not they were then orally expressed. I recalled their 'natural' mother remarking that it wasn't possible for her to read another individual's mind like a book. Above all, I remembered what she'd proposed just before leaving us on the night when, atrociously, a blade-wielding anti-Semite had tried to kill her on the riverside boardwalk alongside our apartment building. In effect, Diva had told me that she planned to discuss with Proxima b leaders whether help of some valuable kind could be provided – assuming they would welcome an offer of such assistance – to the virtually besieged and downtrodden, physically and abusively maltreated as well as intimidated and increasingly frightened, if not terrified Jewish population on our Solar System's only inhabited planet. Earth was a world that afforded a home to a mere 15 million members of their long-standing but continually assailed religion, out of a global total of around eight billion, self-styled *homo sapiens.*

It was on her next visit to our flat, to see my wife and me as well as the children, that she'd invited me alone – Naomi was then, unfortunately, bed-bound and suffering from a bad dose of the influenza virus, with the twins staying over at a friend's house in the town – to accompany her for a chit-chat amble along the Cam's riverside pathway. It so happened that, on the day in question, I had a *yahrzeit* – in this instance, the anniversary remembrance of my late father's passing away a couple of decades earlier. And for which I would say aloud in the presence of at least a requisite *minyan* or quorum of 10 men, ostensibly students during term-time, the relevant memorial prayer during that weekday's *Shacharit* or morning service in my local synagogue which, otherwise, I would attend rarely each year. So I'd told Diva to meet me opposite the early 15th century College of St Mary Magdalene and on nearby Quayside – with its hectic punting operations for tourists, and offering some eclectic restaurants and bars – after the service had ended. I gave her the approximate time of its conclusion which, I was informed by the rabbi, would probably be about 08:00.

However, on leaving the synagogue building at about that time – and perhaps because I was hurrying along with my mind focused on meeting Diva – I'd forgotten to remove the black *kippah* clipped to my mop of darkish hair. When I met up with my dear friend from Proxima b, she didn't tell me that I was still wearing my skullcap, a necessity for a Jewish man to don when reciting Hebrew prayers; and whether or not inside a synagogue. But before we started off on our Cam-side stroll, Diva thoughtfully had given me a pill for my wife to swallow at once; and advised that Naomi would be as fit as a fiddle on my return home after our walk. At her manifestly implicit urging, I went back briefly to the flat that early morning to administer the proffered remedy to my suddenly awakened and quite woozy other half. And, indeed, Diva's 'violin' prognosis was the healthy outcome of the, I supposed as you would've thought, 'magic potion' from Alpha Centauri. In view of the instant cure and my wife's rapid recovery to wellness, on my later return home I felt it, albeit reluctantly, apposite – though it was really difficult, and not only due to my having a *yahrzeit* that day – to tell Naomi about the exceedingly unpleasant incident that had occurred on my trek with Diva. Sadly, it would bring back to my Cantabrigia-born wife's mind, as it had to mine, dreadful and painful memories of another, even more horrible occurrence that had befallen us outside the town back in the 13th century.

Diva and I had begun our moderately paced hike along the stone-flagged pathway – between the duck and swan sprinkled water and the tree-fringed areas of greensward and parkland – under a cheerily blue and sun-splashed sky, dotted with a few sheep-like clouds. My, as always, attractive companion – and I didn't believe that I was being disloyal to Naomi for thinking such – was garbed in hugging denims, trainers, a colourful top and an open, lightweight anorak with a hood... just in case, she'd said glancing upwards. Diva had turned to somewhat less casually dressed me, apparelled in a dark suit with a white shirt, striped black and red tie, shiny black brogues and a still out-of-sight, out-of-mind *kippah* clipped clingingly atop my head. Then she'd started to reveal the – to me, startling even incredible – outcome of the detailed proposition, about helping the more and more victimised Jewish people on Earth, that she'd presented to the compassionate and altruistic leaders of her own planet.

"It's becoming a really lovely spring day," Diva commented initially whilst gazing at a pair of stately swans, that I'd noticed too, gliding across the tranquil waters of the sun-dappled River Cam.

Swivelling smartly to face me directly, she added:

"But, on quick reflection, I'm sorry to have said that... you may be feeling sad on the anniversary today of your father's demise."

"No, not at all," I responded at once. "Fortunately, my Dad enjoyed a long, good, productive and happy life, especially with his wife Abigail, my lovely Mum, who outlived him for just a handful of years… and I possess many pleasant memories of him, and my mother of course."

After a short while, we'd reached that stretch of the slow-moving river beyond the antique and handsome architecture of Cambridge's historic colleges that extend alongside its banks; and which soon that morning would be plied by myriad punts, filled to the brim with tourists from around the globe. A goodly proportion of these enthusiastic and fascinated sightseers, reclining comfortably on the famed, flat-bottomed and wooden pleasure-craft, were from the Far East; and especially the escalating visitor droves from the People's Republic of China.

As we'd progressed, side-by-side, along the now quite deserted path – passing the weir with its tumbling waters, the lock gates and soon to be busy lido, colourful residential narrow-boats, the university's boathouses and some recent, upmarket apartment developments – Diva reported:

"Well, David, when I got back home to Proxima b, after my last visit to Cambridge and a brief period of time to organise matters, the principal global and regional leaders met together at what you would consider to be a kind of conference, in order to discuss my ideas with respect to helping your people here on Earth …"

As ever, it was an authentic awareness and thoughtfulness on Diva's part to talk to me in such terms, utilising a sort of descriptive language that would be usefully meaningful for me. I was almost certain – but only so far as I could be, as an Earthling – that the system of government, authority, control or whatever on her home world, and its advanced technology of inter-active communication, would've been rather more complex; and not to say, linguistically too.

"What was decided, if I may ask?" I enquired, my face possibly brightening hopefully.

"After much debate and consideration," she continued, "it was resolved to put forward a complete, positive and constructive plan of assistance, the approval of which would be conditional on the affirmative result of a planet-wide referendum. But naturally and assuming a confirmatory outcome in the voting, which was virtually beyond doubt, it would also be subject to a willingness on the part of your brethren here on Earth to take up our offer."

Diva's procedural references prompted me to think – though, thankfully, speedily – about the United Kingdom's fraught, initial referendum on the question of leaving the European Union… thus, whether to *Brexit* or not!

"W-What was the plan put forward?" I asked, highly intrigued by the topic but slightly distracted by a gaggle of glossy Mallards – at least the males – and a variety of other waterfowl splashing about noisily in the middle of the river. "And how did it make out in the global ballot?"

Diva whimsically shushed the ducks then replied to my eager queries.

"The project that I'd placed on the table," she said, "and which was discussed and finally agreed by our leaders, though conditionally as I've mentioned, was to invite Jewish Earthlings to escape their dreadfully widespread and developing problems at the hands of anti-Semites of one grouping or another by, so to speak, another *Exodus*… by leaving their long-time planetary domicile, or place of origin, and journeying across what you refer to as the Milky Way galaxy – within a time span of about eight weeks – to a promised, welcoming, safe and secure new home on Proxima b in the Alpha Centauri star system."

She paused, and my jaw must've dropped in awe at what she'd just informed me.

"W–Were there any dissenting voices at this special gathering, Diva?" I asked when finally I found my voice, and soon after absorbing afresh the glowing and definitely warming spring sunshine.

"Not as such …" she replied earnestly.

Logically, I needed some clarification of these words.

"What do you mean by that?" I kind of interrupted.

"Please do give me a chance, David!" she urged quite emphatically, staring at me and maybe a bit like a schoolmistress at a pupil who'd committed a classroom misdemeanour. "I was just about to explain to you."

I sort of hung my head, but only in a teasing pretence of shame and embarrassment.

"Sorry, Diva," I uttered in repentance.

She came up with a predictably winsome little grin then went on.

"Well, David, some of the leaders wanted to know from me whether there were any other oppressed minorities on Earth at this time, that's aside from adherents to Judaism. I gave a confirmatory reply, of course, as you would undoubtedly expect. But I added that, nowadays and yet again, Jewish communities were the primary target of world-wide hatred and persecution... and, therefore, most immediately and vitally in need of help and protection."

Diva paused, and I pondered for a moment or two.

"Did anyone mention the State of Israel as the likely proper and potential saviour of world Jewry?" I enquired with a close interest, my ex-wife having made *Aliyah*; that is, had settled in the 1948-established State with her new partner after our divorce some years back.

"Before answering that question, David, I should say that no queries or points were raised at the conference by our leaders in any way other than with a good intent or motivation ..."

"From what you've told me in the past, concerning your truly civilised and cultured fellow citizens on Proxima b, Diva, I accept completely what you've just remarked," I said, and because I really wanted to say it to the person who'd saved my life, and that of my darling Naomi.

"Yes, Israel was mentioned," she continued. "The leaders wished me to confirm, or otherwise, whether the comparatively tiny yet marvellously enterprising, national homeland of the Jewish people could be the rescuer of Jewish communities living outside its borders in the so-called *Diaspora*. I explained to them about the *Law of Return* and the making of *Aliyah* by Jews, who thereby returned to their *Promised Land*. But I noted, too, that Israel was itself encircled, if not besieged and continually attacked. Though adding that the nation was well able to defend itself against one form of terrorism or another, by various armed movements, groups, cults and countries that sought the State's utter destruction. And one or two of which, I said, could develop or acquire, if they hadn't already, and potentially deploy an atomic bomb or other nuclear weapon or device. No doubt, I continued, and just like numerous citizens of Israel, many Jews dispersed widely outside its borders would possibly consider they might feel insecure residing within them. In any event, I commented to the leaders, it would hardly be feasible for the compact Jewish State to arrange and organise, let alone make provision for, the *Return* of many millions of Jews over an inevitably limited time scale …"

There was much food for thought for me in my dear friend's reportage.

"So, Diva, what did the Proxima b leaders think of your, if I may say so, fine discourse on the subject?"

"Thanks, David," she said smilingly, "… and, well, they took on board every word I'd spoken, and very wholeheartedly and sympathetically. As I've mentioned, they concurred one hundred percent in my proposed plan… and I can say that, as definitively expected, it was approved also in the subsequent and planet-wide referendum."

"Was anything else of interest or concern raised by the leaders during… the conference?" I enquired further.

"Yes, there was one matter mentioned by a few of the leaders," she responded, her otherwise endearing blue eyes now replete with what may've appeared as an ambivalence about telling me of it. "They were well aware of the serious environmental problems and challenges that Earth faces and appears incapable of solving, such as climate change and global warming, bio-diversity collapse and air and ocean pollution of so many appalling varieties. As a result of the ecological crisis that seems to be looming on the planet, they felt the need to express the opinion that, in any event, there would be a real and pressing risk of human extinction in the not too distant future… But they accepted, of course, that the immediate matter to hand was even more real and pressing."

"Very interesting," I said, with typical English irony and understatement. "But returning to Proxima b's referendum, what was the actual statistical result of the voting?" I asked with some nervy anticipation.

Diva smiled at me, and I kind of knew – even without her extraordinary capacity to mind-read – what my dear friend was now on the brink of relating to me.

"Unanimously in favour of the strategy!" she said. "Though, I have to tell you again, we were not expecting anything less than that."

I nodded slowly and pensively, with my lips bunched somewhat emotionally; and, in fact, my head moved similarly several times. But before I could enquire additionally about the then ensuing, and crucially important, thought to be given to the all-important, practical arrangements for the proposed further *Exodus*, the ghastly incident – of which I would report, though hesitantly, to Naomi on my return home – befell Diva and me.

Eight

IN THESE seriously troubled times for the Jewish communities on Earth, I should've known better than forget to remove the black *kippah* attached to my mop of hair on leaving the synagogue that morning, and before embarking with Diva on our riverside walk. Perhaps my several nodding responses to her noting for me the completely affirmative, referendum vote on Proxima b to help such communities should've been more vigorous than gentle. Then my skullcap might've been shaken off my unthinking head; and, thereby, we could've avoided the vicious episode that, unfortunately, was to happen shortly. And maybe I should've taken even more notice of the concentrated stares or, rather, glares at me from a few of the scant passers-by on the Cam-side pathway. With the dubious benefit of hindsight, at least in this instance, I should've understood or recognised that they were probably anti-Semites who had espied my conspicuous headwear and were, in consequence, revealing by facial expressions their noticeably negative attitudes towards Judaism and Jewish people.

Now we were approaching the broad, Elizabeth Way concrete road-bridge across the river – with an external stone stairway connected to each of its flanks, and leading from the pathway to the highway above it. I was just about to ask Diva about the assistance plan agreed by, and popularly approved for, the leaders on her home planet. But quite unexpectedly, bearing in mind the weather so far that morning, it had started to rain; and quite heavily, too. As we neared the spanning archway, beneath which ran the riverside way, the former radiantly sunny sky had suddenly transformed and filled with threateningly bleak clouds. Happily, as Diva and I both probably thought at that instant, we were just a short sprint from the deserted and now darkening shelter of the bridge.

We'd halted, at least for me to catch my breath, around the middle of the overhanging and curved span. Smiling approvingly at each other, we'd shaken the many runny raindrops from our clothing. I could tell from Diva's revealing but amusing smirk that she felt one-up on me for having the foresight – if not the certain knowledge – to don a waterproof outer-garment. Standing together silent and still, we'd listened and watched as the downpour hitting the river resoundingly sent up fountains of spraying water. Despite the belting noise of the slamming rainfall, only slightly diminished from reality at our interior position, we could hear also the echoes of perched pigeons cooing from somewhere above us, though I couldn't espy where they were located. Then we'd heard other sounds reaching us from the open-air path we hadn't attained as yet.

We'd turned simultaneously to see three youngish and roughly bearded males, all wearing typically dark and intimidating hoods, darting into the tunnel-like shelter and ahead of us. It would seem they'd just descended hurriedly from the road-crossing, via the exterior stone steps adjoining the bridge, to evade the heavy squall. The men, possibly in their late 20s or early 30s and dressed in jeans and leather jackets, then spotted Diva and me sharing the useful cover. They began to swagger in our direction. This was a little worrying, especially when they stopped just a metre away from us. I glanced at Diva with a concerned look, but she didn't appear to be overly troubled. Then I recalled the endgame of her confrontation with an assailant on the riverside boardwalk alongside my apartment building. One of the coarsely hirsute, and menacing, male trio – his cowl encompassing a facial expression seemingly midway between a grin and a glare – then opened his mouth to speak.

"Excuse me, sir and madam, but have you got a few quid for us poverty-stricken guys?" he grunted hoarsely, and sounding more like a demand than a polite enquiry. "We're jobless and need to eat."

Of course, Cambridge wasn't the only city in the country where there were many rough sleepers and beggars. In most situations, of course, they could be ignored or avoided by pedestrians if that was the intention. But I knew we were now in an altogether different kettle of let's say, trapped fish; though I did feel really secure with the extremely capable and reliable Diva by my side. She and I remained rigid and quiet. However, my mind actively wandered back to 13th century Cantabrigia and my horrific riverside experience with Naomi that easily could've ended fatally for both of us at the hands of murderous anti-Semites. In an area not too distant from where Diva and I now stood, we'd been so fortunate to escape their terrifyingly imminent clutches by concealing ourselves comprehensively within the former defensive but then rank, foul and decomposing rubbish- and detritus-filled King's Ditch that had almost encircled the medieval town.

"Could you let us have some money for foodstuff?" the awful guy repeated, leaning forward with apparent malice-aforethought in his voice and posture.

We said nothing, and I doubted whether any cash given to the threatening threesome would be expended on food… more likely, alcohol of whatever brew or distillation they favoured to get themselves sopping drunk; or even narcotics of one kind or another. Not having received, as yet, the response they required, each of the three hooligan highwaymen of sorts stepped back together, though only a tad. They reached inside their jackets and pulled out sharp, six-inch blades. Brandishing the knives at us, they screamed alarmingly and in unison:

"Give us the cash you have on you, and right now… or else!"

Next, the gang member who'd first demanded money with menaces suddenly looked at my head then threw me a horribly smirking frown.

"They're Jew bastards!" the villain shrieked, his countenance a gruesome mask of malevolence, and added instantly: "They must have pots of money on them… Hand it over, you bloody sneaky Hebrews, and now!"

Automatically, I copied Diva's action in stepping back slightly. But this was followed at once by one of our assailants moving adroitly around and behind us, waving his steely weapon and blocking off any possible attempt at retreat. I peered quickly in both directions – forward and back – but there were no other walkers, or even cyclists, in sight. Not that I was surprised, with the heavens still gushing barrel-loads of rainwater. Then I felt Diva's hand on my arm.

"Be ready, David," she said *sotto voce*.

I wasn't at all sure what she meant, though I clung to a reasonable notion.

"What did you just say, you Jewish whore cow?" the apparent gang leader shrieked at the non-Jewish Diva, whilst lifting his dagger-gripping hand with malicious intent.

Without more, the object of this brutal and venomous loudmouth's pointedly racist invective raised her right arm with a deliberate motion, directed her index finger first at her verbal abuser then at his wicked-eyed sidekick and, finally – after swivelling around – at the third, contemptible gang-member. Within moments, all three of our dreadful and, to me, really scary attackers screwed up their agonised faces, dropped their knives and collapsed to the ground; only to be lifted, one by one, and thrown into the Cam by my powerful and heroic Diva.

"Let's go now," she said. "Unlike the fate of my earlier aggressor outside your block of flats, these louts will float along the river for a while then recover consciousness. Doubtless, they'll be astounded by the situation in which they find themselves. But they'll have no recollection or memory of anything that has happened to them... they'll clamber out of the water, and race away."

I nodded, smiling with admiration. But I couldn't prevent myself from thinking that she was a truly merciful individual, in all the contemporary circumstances. As she began to speak again, I noticed that the rain had stopped and the sun was emerging from behind the dispersing grey clouds.

"Do you know of a good pub in this vicinity?" she enquired evenly.

"Y-Yes I do, as it happens, Diva," I replied, struggling inwardly to recover my normal composure now I was safe from harm. "The riverside Fort St George... it's a cosy and relaxing inn with some excellent craft ales, and just a fairly brief amble back towards town ..."

Diva nodded with a smile.

"And you're right," I went on, "we, I mean *I*, do need a drink after that, to say the least, disturbing incident, for *me*, just before."

"And in a way, for me too, David," she responded, as I took my dear companion's arm and led her along the route we'd taken earlier. "It was just another confirmation, if I wanted any more, of the necessity for such a plan to aid your people as I'd placed before our Proxima b leaders. And when we've settled into your recommended hostelry, I'll at last be able to answer your brutishly interrupted questions about the clearly significant, practical issues that have to be addressed and solved in order for the scheme to be implemented, as it will be... so lead on, David."

Nine

EN ROUTE to the Fort St George riverside pub with Diva, we'd remained silent. She was taking in the peaceful scenery on both banks of the Cam; and I, with my *kippah* now tucked out of sight in a trouser pocket, couldn't stop myself reflecting on the really nasty episode we'd recently experienced under the Elizabeth Way road bridge. That now not uncommon, physical and trope-splattered confrontation was, I knew, ugly and terrifying enough. But, of course, it couldn't compare with other vile, aggressive and, indeed, fatal anti-Semitic attacks against individuals; let alone the wholesale massacres of innocent Jewish men, women and children that had occurred in various other countries.

But I'd thought also of the widespread intolerance, transparently disguised or actually defended vigorously, now surfacing again; and often amongst politicians, the so-called intelligentsia, the professional classes and other purportedly well-educated and supposedly cultured sections of the Establishment in nations across the globe. Not so shocking when you knew, from reading and otherwise, that many leading officers of Hitler's *Einsatzgruppen* – which had followed Nazi Germany's advancing armies and mass-killed entire Jewish communities in Eastern Europe and the Soviet Union – were led by professors and other academics, medical doctors, lawyers and other professionals. Yet so many of those with robust anti-Semitic leanings had never met, and certainly not spoken with, an adherent to Judaism; nor had they an inkling about any aspect of true Judaism. In a sense, nothing of this situation was new, as evidenced by the history of the last two millennia – from the Roman Empire, though medieval Christian Europe and Catholic Iberia to Tsarist Russia and the Third Reich of Nazi Germany. It was the eternal hatred of the Jewish being that was feeding on itself, growing apace, propagating lies and perpetuating an exclusively focused demonising of anyone and anything connected to the faith. And, since 1948, the detestation was aimed also at the State of Israel, its people's ancient and national homeland, with anti-Zionism employed often as a cover for anti-Semitism… a baseless and resentful hostility against the Jewish religion and a severe, existential threat to its members.

In fairly short order, Diva and I had reached the charming and traditional tavern – a cottage-like and part 16th century, Grade II listed building with rustic-looking roof tiles, Inglenook fireplaces and wood-beamed ceilings. To avoid falling into a depressive state for the remainder of my current time with her, I'd forced myself to track my thinking towards the mind-blowing, Alpha Centauri project for safeguarding the continued survival of my Jewish brethren. Certainly it had helped to part the black clouds scudding across my, literally and metaphorically, grey matter. This had given me some cause for optimism and a hope for our children, grandchildren and future Jewish generations. My good-hearted and generous friend – who'd doubtlessly deduced my sadly flagging emotions from both my facial expressions and some of my thoughts – settled me into a comfortable, wall-backed seating arrangement in the snug then made her way to the bar counter. With the historic hostelry almost empty of customers at that time, she was served instantly by a friendly young barmaid.

Returning with what she'd assumed, and correctly, would be a much desired double malt whisky of renown for me – though carrying a non-alcoholic cocktail for herself – Diva sat herself down beside me and placed the drinks on the polished, dark wood table in front of us. At once, she reached out to grasp her colourful concoction and took down more than a sip, prompting me to pick up the old-fashioned glass of golden liquid from the Scottish Highlands.

"How did this old pub get its name, David… Fort Saint George?" Diva enquired after imbibing.

"I believe it was so titled," I replied, wiping my lips with a tissue and happily able to oblige her, "because, apparently, it resembled, at least partially, the old East India Company's fortress at Madras in India …"

"Ok," my companion responded, pursing her lips.

"However," I added, "if you take a glance at the pub sign, displaying an illustration of the Company's extensive, high-walled, towered and turreted fort, and swinging over the pretty, seating area outside and opposite Midsummer Common, you may well think otherwise."

"Ok," she repeated, downing another swallow of her drink.

Then Diva suggested that, at least for a short while, we should merely recline quietly and calmly in our seats, relax and savour our respective drinks. Afterwards, she said, I would be given an outline of the basic aspects of her, as she put it, "survival plan for the Jewish people on Earth".

Nevertheless, and initially, after she leaned back her head and closed her eyelids I took the opportunity to send a text to Naomi. Thankfully, I received an instant response that she was "feeling fine" after taking Diva's proffered pill. My wife asked me to pass on her sincere gratitude to my fellow walker, which I did subsequently. I would need now to await my return home to see for myself how well she was actually doing; though I doubted not that my dear friend's curative assistance had done the complete trick. For the present, I decided to adopt her sensible advice that we should just rest "quietly and calmly" for the time being. I did try really hard to make my mind go blank which, regrettably, proved to be utterly impossible. And for what seemed a fairly obvious reason: my cerebral facilities couldn't help but bring back to my contemplation the researches I'd carried out – on first meeting Diva some time back – into the Alpha Centauri star system and her orbiting home planet, Proxima b.

There were lots of websites about Alpha Centauri which, I learned, was first recorded during the second century by Ptolemy in his star catalogue. I understood that it was a triple star system, comprising Alpha Centauri A and Alpha Centauri B – which, together, are said to form the binary star Alpha Centauri AB – and Alpha Centauri C. The latter is otherwise known as Proxima Centauri; and, as its name implies, it's the nearest of the trio of stars to our Solar System at 4.24 light years distant. The binary A and B are relatively close together so that, with the unaided eye gazing from Earth, they appear to form one star and one point of light. But it doesn't require outstanding astronomical technology, like the Hubble Space Telescope, to separate them; that can be accomplished with a tolerable pair of binoculars.

Alpha Centauri A is the largest and brightest in this multiple star system on the far side of our Milky Way galaxy. And together with its very close solar companion, they form into the most brilliant 'star' in the southern constellation of Centaurus; and the third most radiant in the night sky, after Sirius and Canopus. Proxima Centauri is a smaller and faint, red dwarf star that can't be observed with the naked eye. My researches had indicated that it orbits AB at a general distance of 13,000 astronomical units.

Alpha Centauri A is clearly the primary star in the system; its radius is some 20 percent more than that of our sun, making it approximately 10 percent heavier. But, above all, I'd been especially over the moon to take on board a variety of comparatively recent analyses. In 2012 and 2013, two possible planets were thought by our astronomers to exist in the AB zone. Although no firm evidence of Earth-like planets exists, I'd read grinningly, it was estimated at an 85 percent probability that such proof will be discovered. I'd noted also that the Alpha Centauri star system had been listed, by NASA's Space Interferometry Mission, as a "Tier 1" target with the aim of detecting the sought-after proof. Apparently, in 2015, the Hubble Telescope had observed an Alpha Centauri transit event. This could've meant the existence of a planetary body; but it may've been too near to its sun to be capable of sustaining extraterrestrial life of any kind.

A slightly larger than Earth, rocky exoplanet termed Cb – but which I rather knew as 'Proxima b' – is said to have been found in the "habitable" or "Goldilocks" zone of Proxima Centauri in 2016. Scientists on Earth had pointed out the several challenges to its being a habitable planet; and even considered that its habitability prospects could lie beneath the surface. Notably, the astrophysicists, or whoever, hadn't discounted the chance that Proxima b possessed an atmosphere and surface water, even oceans in its warmest areas; so that, in consequence, above-ground habitation was also a distinct possibility. They would *really* be interested in a long chat with Diva, I'd pondered with an undoubtedly broad smile at the time of my reading about these various factors.

I'd been even more intrigued to discover that crossing the phenomenally huge distance between our Solar System and the Alpha Centauri star system would take, with Earth's present spacecraft technologies, several millennia! But I'd read also that nuclear-pulse propulsion, or laser-light sail science, could potentially reduce the galactic travel time to mere decades. So, inescapably, I'd wondered about how long a period it had taken Diva, and any accompanying colleagues, to transit the 40 trillion − 40,000,000,000,000 − kilometres; and about the supremely celeritous means by which they had done so… a unique and fantastical method of propulsion or the navigation of 'Worm Holes' were my speculations. I'd gathered that consideration, by the Breakthrough Starshot Initiative, would be given to sending a fleet of ultra-fast and light-driven 'nanocraft' to explore the Alpha Centauri star system. In 2016, the European Southern Observatory had announced that Proxima Cb might well be a target for such an exploratory effort. Finally, I'd found out that, in January 2017, there came into existence between 'Breakthrough' and ESO a collaboration "to enable and implement a search for habitable planets in the Alpha Centauri system."

After digesting all that compelling information, I did wonder − justifiably, I'd perceived − about whether any powers, with a potentially very advanced intelligence and that might well exist in the Alpha Centauri star system, could've become rather intrigued by the attention being focused on it by astrophysicists and astronomers here on Earth. And as a consequence, I'd considered with fascination whether this might've readily explained Diva's arrival on the only habitable and, indeed, inhabited planet in our Solar System.

It was no surprise that these recollections of my earlier researches had sent me to sleep eventually but impolitely;

and which fact I gathered from Diva, when she nudged me awake and said that now was the time for me to learn a bit more about the proposed project and Proxima b's invitation for my world's Jewry ...

Ten

AFTER DIVA had stirred me from my not entirely surprising though brief and wayward slumber – but prior to her actually beginning to explain her Alpha Centauri approved proposition of inviting the oppressed Jewish communities on Earth to emigrate to a new and welcoming home on planet Proxima b – she concentrated again on her non-alcoholic cocktail. This pause had afforded me a reasonable chance to reflect, albeit fleetingly, on the first *Exodus* of the Israelites from ancient Egypt, and as described in the eponymous Book of the Old Testament.

The Almighty had appointed Moses, assisted by his brother Aaron, to seek from Pharaoh the freedom, from hundreds of years of slavery, of the Children of Israel. "Let my people go!" were the ringing words representing the key demand. But Pharaoh's continual recalcitrance – agreement then denial and agreement then denial, and so on – had led, as a direct consequence, to the imposition by the Almighty of the 'Ten Plagues' which, ultimately, compelled the dictatorial ruler of Egypt to let them flee from his land. This inexorably hurried departure has been marked, every year since, by Judaism's festival of *Pesach* or Passover. This eight-day observance – when the 'unleavened bread of affliction' is eaten, commemoratively – nominally recalls the 10th plague when, at night, the Almighty 'passed over' the dwellings of the enslaved Israelites to forever close the eyes of the Egyptian firstborn.

But once again regretting his consent to the mass departure of usefully hardworking slaves from the Land of Egypt, Pharaoh despatched his chariot-borne army in pursuit of them. But only for his military forces to be deluged and drowned in the Red Sea, after the Moses-led Children of Israel had succeeded in crossing through it – between miraculously, but temporarily, parted and towering walls of water – to attain sanctuary on the opposite shore. Reflecting further on my last thought, one thing was abundantly and satisfyingly clear to me. If ever Diva's proposed plan actually did get off the ground, almost literally speaking, and those Jewish people – who desired above everything to escape persecution on Earth – actually began to escape the planet, it would be completely impossible for them to be pursued!

Then, all of a sudden, I was jerked out of my contemplative musings or reverie by Diva, who'd now given up nursing her glass and returned it to the table.

"Well, David," she opened, a tad forthrightly, "it would be possible for us on Proxima b to launch a fleet of our gigantic mother-ships to transverse the galaxy and hover, after a voyage of approximately eight Earth-weeks, somewhere appropriate in your Solar System. The precise quantity of these giant space vehicles needed would be dependent, of course, on the numbers of your Jewish brethren prepared for an inter-planetary transit, though many of them might prefer to hear the word *cruise*, across the Milky Way."

"O-Ok, Diva ..." I uttered gob-smacked, if not nonplussed. "But, forgive me for enquiring, how would your planet, about which I know only the indubitably inaccurate speculations of our Earth-based astrophysicists, be able to absorb, integrate or cope with a sudden influx of perhaps millions of people?"

She looked straight into the eyes of an undeniably flummoxed face.

"I don't think I need go into all that at this moment in time, David... except to say that your people could rest assured that they'll not be at all disappointed with the extensive provision that would be set up for them. And in a peacefully conducive environment and atmosphere, which will enable the Jewish immigrants to make the kind of valuable contribution to society they've always made, and wherever they've settled, in the past."

"Many thanks for saying those kind and considerate words, Diva... they're much appreciated," I responded. "And, naturally, I understand fully that it's early days yet... though I, and for sure my fellow Jewish human beings, of necessity will be extremely eager, if not anxious to learn in due course the finer details of such *provision* of which you speak. And, of course, before they can make any constructive decisions that will undoubtedly transform their lives, likely and appreciably for the good, but in an extraordinarily fundamental way."

"You're right, David," my longstanding, extraterrestrial friend remarked with a whimsical nuance of a smile. "And your comments lead on aptly to the more immediate matter to hand …"

"And what's that?" I intervened, somewhat precipitately, followed swiftly by: "Sorry, Diva."

"That's ok, David… and I do understand your apprehensions and compulsions in the, to you, exceptional and utterly incredible circumstances of our project …"

I merely nodded this time.

"But, as I was on the point of mentioning," she continued and, I was glad to note, without the would-be school-ma'am stare, "the more urgent objective for us is to resolve the most satisfactory method of communicating our proposition via the leaders of the Jewish communities on Earth… and you, yourself, may have a key role to play in that context. Initially, it could be quite difficult, to say the very least, to convince your people of our authenticity and wholesomely sincere intentions. They would have every right to be exceedingly cautious. But in their presently distressing and dangerous situation, I believe they would be accepting on the basis of what we could reveal to them. And I'm confident they would be prepared to give the Proxima b plan a proper hearing. It could well be that the display of our genuine and redeeming hope for the continuity of Judaism and its joyfully observant future, would be like music to their ears …"

Diva paused and I nodded again, while the challenging thought of what the thousands of rabbis, representing a variety of Judaic elements, might think about all this instantly crammed my mind with an ambiguous anguish.

"So, David, my colleagues and I are working on the best process for all that," she went on. "I'll be in close touch with you, and quite shortly, about this vital part of the plan and how you may be able to assist us."

I moved my head up and down yet again; but this time I said something, too.

"But what if those governments, rulers, heads of state, political movements and others in key control positions outside of world Jewry and its leaders, both secular and religious, get to hear of these secret communications?" I queried with, I felt, some justified cause. "And there could always be whistleblowers, for whatever their motivations, too!"

During another brief pause before receiving Diva's answer, I'd recalled my knowledge of Nazi Germany – after Hitler came to power and during the 1930s – urging, or rather implicitly demanding with threats that all of its Jews, now without German citizenship, emigrate from the Aryan-only Fatherland, albeit having to leave behind their accrued assets. Large numbers had felt presciently bound to leave; though many thousands couldn't bring themselves to reach such a decision. They had hoped and prayed that the Third Reich – with its rampant, bullying and statute-backed anti-Semitism – would be just a passing political phase in affecting their loyal and prospering contribution to what was thought to be a cultured nation. A large number of German-Jewish soldiers, serving in the muddy trenches of the Western Front during the Great War, had been awarded the Iron Cross, several of them First Class, for their heroic bravery in action. And we knew, with hindsight, the tragic consequences for those Jews who'd passed up the ever-diminishing opportunities to flee the Führer's Third Reich for a fresh beginning in another country. After the disaster of *Kristallnacht*, in the autumn of 1938, the writing was undeniably on the wall for them. The vast majority of remaining Jews perished at the Nazi death camps established by the German occupiers in Poland during the Holocaust in the Second World War.

There was no doubt in my mind that Diva had now read my immediate thoughts. And it was she who started nodding on this occasion.

"If the plan is exposed or disclosed, by whatever means," she continued, "then maybe its idea would be generally, and sincerely, welcomed by those individual heads, groups and others that you mentioned just before. But then again, they might well be fearful of any potentially disastrous, if not earth-shattering retribution from Alpha Centauri if they would seek to intervene, say militarily, in the rescue mission …"

"Please excuse me for interrupting, Diva," I apologised, "but should or must one consider also what might catastrophically befall those members of the Jewish communities on Earth who, for one reason or another, didn't or couldn't take up your benevolent invitation of a new and hopefully contented freedom and life on Proxima b?"

"I imagine you've been thinking about the Nazi Holocaust, David?"

I was right… my friend probably had been reading my thoughts.

"Yes, Diva, I have," I said, maybe rather superfluously.

"Assuming that the plan could become known as you've surmised, though we do have especially applicable methods for seeking to prevent such happening," she said, with what I took for a subtle wink, "I believe all those concerned would take serious note of the patently superior powers we have at our disposal… and against which they would have no defence whatsoever."

"But, Diva, wouldn't this mean that those born of the Jewish faith and remaining on Earth for whatever reason, and their enemies would know this, could easily be caught up fatally in any hugely destructive assault by your people? And, therefore, wouldn't the anti-Semitic foes of these Jews feel safe and secure in their belief that you wouldn't want their Jewish human shields, so to speak, to be harmed in any way?"

It seemed to me that Diva was fidgeting somewhat.

"We would and could deal with these kinds of situations, if they were to occur," she commented, her expression now quite serious. "I realise totally that the mind of a human being can, logically or illogically, argue in circles before becoming enlightened, if that does happen in due course …"

I nodded humbly, as a signal of my understanding of Diva's understanding.

"But, for the time being, let's concentrate on the *priorities*," she emphasised, picking up then draining her glass.

I could detect the whimsy or irony in her equivocal statements, but left it at that.

"As I mentioned just before, I'll contact you again and in the not too distant future," my long-time pal said finally, rising from her seat and adding with the little wave of a hand: "Bye, David!"

Diva then departed Fort St George, which was starting to host rather more thirsty customers than when we'd first entered the old, timber-framed inn.

I'd got up, almost at once, and followed her out of the pub. There was now a brilliantly blue sky again; it was pleasingly sunny and reasonably warm. But I could see no sign of my Alpha Centauri friend, and in whichever direction my eyes searched. No doubt, she'd performed one of her truly amazing, disappearing 'tricks'... I took the riverside pathway back towards town, maybe as deeply pensive and contemplative as I'd ever been in my entire adult life so far, and headed gradually homewards.

Eleven

ON MY return to the flat, I'd been delighted to find my beloved wife looking fantastically well recovered from her horrid flu virus. Thanks to my administering of Diva's thoughtfully prescribed pill earlier that day. Though I'd harboured no doubts whatsoever that such would be the predictable, inevitable and virtually immediate effect. Naomi was in the kitchen, apparently preparing a late, but delicious luncheon snack of bagels stuffed with smoked salmon. She asked me if I would like to join her in the tasty bite. I accepted the kind offer gladly, informing her that I hadn't eaten anything since breakfast.

On entering our apartment, I'd noticed that the curtains – unusually for that time of the day, and if someone was at home – were still drawn in the living-room. So I moved along the hallway to open the lined drapes on that now beautifully sun-sprayed day. But it hadn't been an entirely happy one for me, or Diva, after that abhorrent, anti-Semitic incident alongside the Cam. When I entered our spacious lounge/diner, however, I was quite surprised to see the twins seated on the settee and reading their current books in the light of table-lamps sited at each end of the sofa. They looked up quickly, a trifle startled at my sudden entry.

"Hi, Dad!" they called out, and in unison.

"What are you two doing at home?" I enquired with a quizzical look, and maybe understandably confused – by earlier and yet ongoing, troubling events – into thinking they should've been at their nearby primary school.

"It's half-term, Dad... Remember?" Joshua replied, with a cherubic little beam.

"Ah, yes," I said. "Just forgot that for a moment."

My son and daughter re-focused attention on their books; though not before Sarah nudged her brother with an elbow, then explained smartly:

"As you know, Dad, we've been staying at a friend's house while Mum got over the flu... Mum came to collect us this morning now she's feeling much better, and we're soon going to have some lunch together."

I nodded, resigned to accepting that the girl – whether understood specifically by her, or not – had been reading my about-to-be-expressed queries.

I parted the curtains, flooding and illuminating the comfortably large room with a radiantly bright light, turned off the reading lamps, left the kids happily absorbing their – I'd perceived – Harry Potter paperbacks and returned to the kitchen. Naomi had just finished putting together the traditional Jewish food item; but I suggested that, before we all sat down at the table to eat and drink, the pair of us should perch ourselves on the bar stools whilst I outlined my morning or so with Diva. My wife assented, though maybe a tad reluctantly. After I finished telling her of the bad experience we'd been subjected to, as well as the perhaps more beneficial news – and with a respective pessimism and optimism – I could see clearly, and comprehend fully, the flabbergasted expression on Naomi's face. This no doubt stemmed from – whether partially or entirely – her still incredible, 13th century origins in Cantabrigia.

My wife sat stiffly on the high, short-backed stool and stared at me. But, oddly, just as if I were invisible – though I couldn't really match Diva's stunning skills in that regard – and she was gazing *through a glass darkly*. I was beginning to grow a little concerned at her reaction; so I addressed her by name a few times, and gently drummed my fingertips on the backs of her knee-resting hands. Then she appeared to return to a kind of pseudo-normality, with a sort of jerky recoil; but, fortunately, I managed to prevent her from slipping off her fairly lofty seat.

"I-I'm r-really s-sorry, D-David," she stuttered initially, on trying to recover her *sang-froid* and a normal posture. "What you've just been relating rather took me by surprise, and in more ways than one… I'm sure you can follow what I'm struggling to say."

"Of course I can, my darling," I said softly and empathetically, helping my wife down off the stool and embracing her snugly in my arms.

We parted after a long minute or so, and I planted a hopefully reassuring kiss on her slightly quivering lips.

"Please don't despair, Naomi," I urged. "I'm as confident as Diva that everything will turn out fine for us and the kids… and our brothers and sisters of the faith."

I was pleased to witness her nodding at my expectantly comforting language.

"Let's have lunch with Joshua and Sarah now," I said, picking up a couple of the bagel-topped plates from the shiny, black granite work-surface.

My other half moved her head up and down again, looked directly into my eyes and stated:

"I'm pretty sure we would agree that our votes will be for us and the children to join our so wonderful and faithful Diva, and her people, on Proxima b… isn't that so, David?"

I nodded my smiling assent then leaned across the crockery I was carrying to peck Naomi on the cheek. She rubbed her forehead, presented me with a tender beam, hastily washed her hands and collected some of the other enticingly appetising food platters.

"Where's our lunch, Mum?" was a cry we could hear emanating from the sitting-room. "We're starving here!"

"It's coming right now …" I called out, "and as if you didn't know, you cheeky little devils!"

Their mother followed me along the hallway into the lounge-diner space and put the plates on the table. The kids abandoned their hallowed reading material, and dashed to sit down; whilst we repeated our transport tasks a few further times, then settled ourselves alongside them.

From time to time during an otherwise silent meal, when I – and, assuredly, Naomi too – couldn't stop thinking as much as we were munching, either Joshua or Sarah would ask a question, such as:

"What's a *conference?*" or "What's a *mother-ship?*" or "Where's *Auntie Diva?*" or "What's *Proxima b?*"

We sort of knew what the kids were playing at, even if the saucy imps might not have known for the most part; but they were becoming quite good at the game. Quite possibly they did appreciate their ostensible, mind-reading talents. Diva might well have cause to be proud of them; though – not having mentioned to her the offspring's genetically developing, cerebral powers – I couldn't be unreservedly definite on that score. Naomi and I hadn't spoken to Joshua and Sarah on the general topic; and not only because we didn't credit the twins' comprehension at their present age. But we could've been wrong on that issue, too. They were seven years old now, and we could hardly believe how rapidly time seemed to have flown by us. Though we knew well of Albert Einstein's aphorism that, *the distinction between the past, present and future is only a stubbornly persistent illusion.* And, of course, there had been and were many a child genius not much older, if not younger than our kids. Mozart, one of my favoured classical music composers, was a prime example.

Nonetheless, in response to the children's intelligent interrogatories – and whether rightly or wrongly on my part – I replied variously and irrelevantly, notably egged on by my wife: "Eat your delicious salmon bagels... you said you were starving!" or "Eat up... we'll answer you sometime soon!" or "Too many questions whilst you're eating... stop now, or you'll get indigestion!" or "Hurry up and have your lunch… before it gets *cold*!" And that last, teasing retort to yet another poser – on this occasion, from Joshua – reaped a mischievous, grin-accompanying rejoinder from my, not that immature son: "*Cool*, Dad!"

Twelve

I CAN'T recollect when exactly Diva had next visited us in Cambridge. There was so much happening, almost entirely bad, for Earth's Jewry at the time. Disastrously, several horrific terror bombings and shootings had occurred around the world, with numerous Jews – men, women, children and babies – killed and much larger numbers wounded or maimed for life. So many in-shock families were now heartbroken, holding *levoyas* – burying, then sitting *shiva* and mourning – for their lost, beloved ones and reciting the *kaddish*, or memorial prayer, for the close relatives murdered by extremists and militant anti-Semites. Naturally, security had been increased and intensified palpably; though, in innumerable instances, only by the *Diaspora* communities' own defence and protection organisations. The State of Israel had in place, of course, the safeguarding mechanisms long needed against those who sought to destroy its Jewish citizens, and to eliminate their national home.

I suppose it must've been a few months after she'd explained to me Alpha Centauri's most extraordinary and approved proposal to rescue the increasingly persecuted, and now precariously situated, members of the Jewish faith that Diva had called on me in Cambridge again. And at a time when there were millions, potentially, who would be prepared and deeply thankful to be launched on a cross-galaxy *Exodus* from Earth to the red dwarf star Proxima Centauri's orbiting exoplanet, and Diva's home, Proxima b.

On that glowingly sunny morning's stopover by our extraterrestrial friend, she'd suggested – and at once – that we not embark on a hike along the river path. But rather that we should imbibe a fairly judicious and safe Americano – and what she'd observed, quite earnestly, would be a longish chat and maybe Q&A session – in one of the university town's several popular coffee shops. I'm not sure why precisely, but I'd thought it might be more conducive if we strolled along to one of the college's student bar-cafés. Diva had agreed without more; and I suggested the cosy, and generally tranquil Red Brick Café overlooking the landscaped gardens of Robinson College, founded in 1977 by the entrepreneur and philanthropist Sir David Robinson. It was only a short walk from the city centre, and not that far beyond the opposite bank of the Cam. I'd said we would take the slightly less direct, but definitely more picturesque route along 'The Backs' or greenswards of the ancient riverside colleges... St John's, Trinity and King's; and by way of the loftily severe landmark of the near Soviet-style, 1934-opened structure of the UL or Cambridge University Library.

Diva didn't object to my proposed itinerary; although her expression more than hinted that she had some rather important information to impart to me, and wished to do so as soon as may be. So off we went. Before we departed the Cam-side apartment, I'd scribbled and left conspicuously in the kitchen a succinctly written note for Naomi, who was then out shopping in the Grand Arcade mall and elsewhere in town. The warmish and sun-splashed, early summer weekday was duly reflected in our respective choice of casual and lightweight apparel. Diva had favoured limb-hugging, faded blue jeans, a white- and azure-striped top with a pair of neat and athletic shoes to match. A yellowish, leather-look shoulder-bag swung by her side as we'd walked together along the tree-lined path between the river fringing 'The Backs' and vehicle-busy Queen's Road. I'd sported straight-leg denims, a short-sleeved and light-blue shirt with a navy-blue baseball cap and colour-matching trainers.

After we'd arrived at Robinson, passing the Porters Lodge entrance under the archway at the top of the entry slope, I offered to take my companion on a speedy tour around the college's expansive landscaped grounds, with its fountain-centred lake and splashing waterfowl. She declined my idea instantly, but tactfully and not at all brusquely, saying that she would prefer we had the hot drinks and started to talk right away. I could understand where she was coming from… so I led her to the then virtually deserted café, and got our black Americano coffees brewed behind the serving counter by one of the amiable staff. Then we settled into a pair of comfy armchairs at a small low table alongside the café's panoramic window that boasted a commanding view of the lovely gardens.

"Thanks for bringing me here, David," my dear friend said with a subdued smile then taking the quickest and tiniest sip of her steaming black Americano. "You know, the Red Brick Café does have a really good feel about it... so I can see why you choose this more outlying place as one of your conducive thinking and scribbling spots away from the hustle and bustle of town."

I nodded my assent, but refrained from drinking any of my piping coffee, as yet; though recalling, strangely, a newspaper article I'd read about some medical research concluding that imbibing beverages when very hot wasn't at all good for the heart. I could see my fellow coffee-drinker smiling at my thought.

"That nicely sums it up, Diva," I commented with a sort of grin, "and they usually have a selection of scrumptious cakes here, too... Would you like to go and pick out one to enjoy with your coffee?"

"No... I'm fine thanks, David," she said. "But you go if ..."

"I'm good for the time being," I reacted, though maybe too promptly and unthinkingly. But I did have uppermost in my mind now her implied yet robust desire to get started on the crucial matter at hand.

"So, Diva," I urged but evenly, "please tell me how far you've got with the new *Exodus* proposition."

"After much thought and especially due to the foreseeable and extreme complexities... though not on our part, you'll understand," she began, "we have worked out a plan of approach to this tragic matter at hand ..."

Diva paused momentarily. I said nothing, and took merely a tentative sip of my coffee.

"First of all was the major question of communication," she continued. "How to inform the world's Jewish communities of Alpha Centauri's, doubtless to them, extraordinarily implausible and literally out-of-this-world notion that could become a rescue mission... and to enlighten them in a way that they would believe, wholeheartedly, was one filled with our good intentions ..."

Again a pause; and, furthermore, I didn't react in any way.

"Possibly," she went on, "whoever we informed initially of our notion could well, and unsurprisingly, consider it to be a terrible trap of some kind. And who could, in theory, argue against that fearful apprehensiveness and distrust? But, as you'll doubtless remember from our own first meeting at The Anchor inn, beside the river here in Cambridge... it wasn't long before you were able to accept the albeit astounding veracity of who I am, where I come from and what we on Proxima b are capable of doing ..."

This time I nodded once, but did no more than that. Then I took a little more of my Americano, as Diva did from her cup.

"So our thoughts revolved around the world-wide Jewish leadership... political, religious, administrative, scientific etcetera, and with which we should make contact in the first instance. And as I've mentioned, David, you may be in a good position to play a significant role in that procedural framework ..."

I sort of nodded again, though I was indicatively speechless now.

"Your eyes speak for you, David," Diva commented pointedly. "Once we have convinced your people's leaders, as we shall do, of our benevolent and beneficial motivation, and have satisfied them also of the reasoning for that sincere intent, no doubt we'll together create a meaningful and workable strategy on how best to pass the hopeful offer of a peaceful, safe and secure haven in the light of a distant star …"

At this point, I found my voice.

"I've scant reservation that you will persuade and reassure maybe all our leaders, as you specify, of your authenticity, Diva …" I said. "And in precisely the same way that you relatively swiftly and scrupulously overcame my original and utter disbelief some time back now. So perhaps I *can* play an, albeit minor confirmatory part in the process …"

"Thanks, David."

"But I'm staggering in endeavouring to imagine how millions of my brethren, spread so extensively around the world and even with some substantial centres of gathering, will be informed systematically, comprehensively, credibly and convincingly of the outcome of your proposed *conference*, if I can call it that, with the principal leaders of Earth's Jewish population …"

I seemed to ramble on, but then seized a quick deep breath.

"And in such a meticulous manner as will allow families, individuals and so on the detailed opportunity to give a 'Yes' or 'No' and even maybe a 'Don't know' response to the amazing but incredibly challenging offer of liberation, as presented."

Diva appeared to be taking on board what I felt to be a logical and rational series of material thoughts.

"You shouldn't tax your creative brainpower too much in those, though not unimportant respects, David," she responded, after downing a mouthful of her beverage and passing on to me a real sense of optimism. "Please don't forget... though I don't want persistently to appear as boasting about our million-year advance on Earth's science and technology, amongst other matters... that so many things are possible of achievement for us in the Alpha Centauri star system. And which couldn't even be conceived of in the minds of your planet's greatest scientific and other thinkers ..."

I nodded slowly, and probably with an expression of due contrition for my lapse. Momentarily, I glanced into the abundant greenery of the college garden through the café's wide picture window.

"Please don't look like that, David," Diva remarked, her appealing blue eyes replete with sympathy. "It's only natural that you would have such harassing, or rather rightly anxious thoughts. But there's one factor that I contemplated you might've mentioned, too ..."

"And what's that?" I enquired, and so prematurely again.

"I was about to say," my dear friend remarked, with that whimsical school-ma'am look she sometimes conjured up for my edification, "that, sadly perhaps, there could be stark differences of opinion within families and other groupings about whether or not to accept our offer of salvation or deliverance from evil, if I can so phrase the concept. Needless to say, that could result in a huge and dreadful amount of distress within families, as well as communities. Just as an illustration, there would be many thousands of instances where serious disabilities, fatal illnesses and other analogous medical problems are certain to affect decision-making. This is, naturally, expected to be inevitable in the circumstances. I'm sure, beyond question, that anything and everything possible and practicable would be done to allay the qualms, uncertainties and suspicions, if not terrifying fears. But particular situations that so many people are confronted with on a daily basis will mean, in any event, that they wouldn't be in a position to accompany us to a safe new home on Proxima b."

On this occasion, I waited until I knew she'd finished speaking on her additional and so piquant thought that, worryingly, hadn't entered my head... at least, at the time I'd been raising points a little earlier.

"You're so right, Diva... and I say that with the greatest of respect," I remarked somewhat solemnly. "And what you've just noted brings to mind something I may've referred to at another time. As I'm sure you know now, the situation you describe was faced undoubtedly by many Jewish individuals, families and communities in Nazi Germany of the 1930s. The anti-Semitic writing was on the wall, literally as well as metaphorically, from the moment Hitler was elected, democratically, into power… becoming Chancellor in 1933 and the nation's virtually worshipped Führer. Before the Second World War began in 1939, Jews in their many thousands had decided to emigrate from the Fatherland, to which they had contributed so much loyalty and industry over a lengthy period. But those who remained in the country, and for whatever reason, faced increasingly relentless, severe and cruel persecution and harassment; and most of them were annihilated eventually in the Nazi death camps during the Holocaust …"

"Yes, David," she intoned, with a benign and compassionate tone to her voice, "we can only hope for the very best outcome to our plan… and the rescue of as many of your people as practicable in all the prevailing circumstances."

We both nodded then finished off the remainder of our excellent Americano coffees.

"Your leaders, no doubt," Diva added suddenly, "will wish to know in detail the process we might have in mind, and by which those millions of your fellow Jews, who do decide to come to a new home and future on Proxima b, will be assembled… and where, on Earth, they will commence their epic galactic voyage …"

I took up nodding again.

"As you may expect of us, David," she continued, "we do have a meticulously detailed, scheduled plan to accomplish the gathering together of the Jewish emigrants; and a necessarily parallel proposal to ensure secrecy, as well as the requisite prevention of whistle-blowing. This operation will commence before they're embarked on the sizeable space shuttles, of a stealthy format, that will serve to convey them to our gigantic mother-ships. These will be hovering surreptitiously, if not clandestinely, away from any prying Earth-astronomers' eyes and somewhere suitably apt in the Solar System."

With one, even if restrained smile at the wonder of it all, I slow-nodded my ultra-amazed, if not stupefied head. Diva nodded at my, to her, highly predictable reaction.

"Your leaders," she continued, "will definitely desire, and require, in-depth knowledge of not only the time it will take to reach the target destination from Earth, but also of the natural environment in which their people will live on Proxima b... And also an awareness of the sort of accommodation and facilities they should expect to be prepared for, and available to, the Jewish migrants. Inevitably, there will be countless other questions arising for your brethren, including those relating to climate, livelihood, the ability to observe their faith and to practise all the religious rituals and other requisite aspects of Judaism... But in addition, undeniably and with overwhelming curiosity, some data about their new home planet's indigenous population."

"You're absolutely right on the button with all that, Diva," I said, with yet more nods. "And I'm sure that, in due course, you'll be in a position to answer these posers to the questioners' overall satisfaction. I think you've told me how long, or rather how unbelievably short, the inter-planetary journey is likely to take… around eight weeks, am I correct?"

Diva nodded.

"But with your evident power to morph your outer shell, so to speak, I still don't know for certain, Diva, what you and your fellow Proxima b-ites actually look like," I went on, "as compared, that is, to us human beings so-termed …"

"Sorry about that, David," she said wistfully. "But I can absolutely assure you, as well as our potential new arrivals, that there's not a significant difference between your and our apparent physical bodies and facial appearances. Though, with the advantage of being a million years ahead of you Earthlings, and there I go again, I can state with confidence, if maybe immodestly, that we're generally rather more attractive! So put that in your pipe and smoke it …"

I had a bit of a giggly fit and rather loudly, because someone who'd just entered the Red Brick Café – to join a few other customers, aside from Diva and me, present there now – gazed across at us and beamed outlandishly.

All at once, my companion looked worryingly pensive.

"I've got to leave you," she said earnestly, starting to rise from her armchair but indicating, with a hand movement, that I should remain ensconced in my own for however long.

"Ok," I acknowledged. "And yes… I might stay here, and maybe have another coffee then a thoughtful stroll around the handsome gardens… But when will I see you again, Diva?"

"Please don't concern yourself about anything, David," she said, "during your *thoughtful stroll* in the Robinson College grounds… Everything is going to turn out fine. I and my colleagues will arrange the next steps, according to the outline I've now given to you. I'll contact you again, and probably in the near future, if you are needed for the kind of reason I've suggested. Is that ok by you?"

"Yes, that will be ok by me… and I look forward to hearing from you as soon as may be," I replied with a renewed sense of hope for the future. "Both of us know that life isn't likely to improve, rather the extreme contrary, in the foreseeable or any future now for Jewish people on Earth. And as you've observed, the Almighty did *create the heaven* as well as the Earth."

Diva nodded whilst placing the thin leather-look, bag strap over her right shoulder.

For just a moment, I glanced through the window at the college's gardens. But when I looked back into the café again, Diva had vanished.

Thirteen

I PONDERED the remarkable conversation with Diva that morning, at The Red Brick Café in Robinson College, as I squeezed up with a slumbering Naomi in my compact capsule on one of the extensive fleet of mighty mother-ships heading for Proxima b in the Alpha Centauri star system, and light years from Earth. I couldn't prevent myself from continually repeating those incredible words, *mother-ship*, at least in my head. The term *mother* seemed more than apposite to describe this and other similar spacecraft in which I and millions of my fellow Jewish passengers were being so well cared for... like by a loving parent. I could hardly believe it was just a few months back that Diva had outlined the rescue plan to me; and it was equally unbelievable that we were now a mere Earth-week away from our planetary destination and new home.

As Diva had promised, I was contacted not that long after her last visit to Cambridge; and to my unjustified amazement – despite what she'd told me – I was invited to attend and speak at a, let's say *conference* of political, rabbinical, administrative and certain other Jewish leaders from across the globe. It had been organised – really speedily and extraordinarily in this particular faith context,

I thought somewhat whimsically – by our extraterrestrial friend and her Proxima b colleagues. I was more than intrigued to note that the critical gathering would take place in Israel; and I learned, with even greater interest, that the decisive meeting was to be held at Yad Vashem – The World Holocaust Remembrance Centre – in Jerusalem. I agreed to go to the Jewish national home, of course, and flew British Airways out of London Heathrow to Ben Gurion Airport two days before the 'secret' *conference* began at an inescapably symbolic venue for our people.

I arrived in the Holy Land earlier than necessary but intentionally, so as to have an opportunity to visit my ex-wife Sonia and her partner in Netanya, the popular seaside resort a short distance north of cosmopolitan Tel Aviv. By a wonderful and unexpected coincidence, my atheist son Michael, similarly thinking daughter-in-law Dinah and their young son Gill were visiting from New York. Apparently, Michael had been given some family news quite recently, but which hadn't been transmitted to me. What Michael and his other half knew, and I didn't, was the motivation for their then presence in Netanya with the grandson.

Soon after unpacking in my room at a fine Jerusalem hotel, I phoned Sonia to tell her – of necessity, with a white lie – that I was currently in Israel on a writing commission from a London-based magazine. After expressing her somewhat subdued surprise and gladness, she advised me somewhat emotionally that her partner had deserted her for another, and younger, woman. And that she'd been proposing to give me the sickening news when I next called her from, she would've thought, the UK. Our son had just happened to be first to contact his mother, and from the States, following the sudden separation; hence his prior knowledge and admirably immediate and sympathetic, long-haul flight to Israel in order to comfort her. Subsequently, when the five of us were assembled in her near-beachside apartment, I discovered that the abandoned woman was now planning to sell up and leave the country to reside close to Michael and Dinah's home in New York. At the same time, I was delighted to meet again our son's lovely wife, who was a copywriter at the same advertising agency where her husband was a senior accounts executive, and the growing grandson.

A while later, I discovered happily from Diva – who'd conveniently made the appropriate enquiries for me – that my ex-wife, our son, his wife and their child were amongst the passengers listed to be onboard one of the mother-ships, but not mine, en route to Proxima b. Marvellously, however, I was able to converse with Sonia then Michael via the incredible technology made available, for specific purposes, in my neat pod. I suspected that I understood why my son and daughter-in-law were heading adventurously for a new future with their son. Probably, Sonia – who, very much alien to me, had become quite religious in the years before our divorce – had taken the view that there was nothing for her to lose by doing so. She'd expressed, from time to time in the past, her developing and melancholy apprehensions about living in an Israel virtually surrounded by relentless enemies and subjected to increasingly murderous, terrorist atrocities. Jewish life in Earth's post-modern, so-called 'society' was becoming horrendously complex for so many.

My personal, Diva-organised experiences – including the unique, time-travel trip back to medieval England – and other authentic support at the Jerusalem *conference* were helpful, I thought, but in a relatively minor way. The principal thrust – empathetic, humane and for their ultimate benefit – to convince participants was primarily down to the exceedingly and astoundingly advanced, scientific and technological 'signs and wonders' presented by Diva and her team to an increasingly starstruck audience. It almost goes without noting that there were a couple of leading, Jewish astrophysicists present at Yad Vashem. Naturally, they imputed certain serious problems of which they were professionally aware from specific researches; and their perception or interpretation of them as such. They covered these scientists' beliefs that, although Diva's home planet orbited within the so-called 'habitable zone' of Proxima Centauri, its closeness to this red dwarf star seemed to mean that its emitted UV radiation would inhibit, or even prevent, any life from forming and existing on Proxima b. After a detailed explanation of the actual evolution then continuation of life on that world and its raison d'être – expressed by the Alpha Centauri team at their listeners' own accepted and relatively primitive level of scientific understanding of the universe and its components – the Earthling physicists couldn't help but, metaphorically, bow their heads with a profound respect and wonder.

There was mention also, by the Proxima b working delegates, of the availability of a certain, multi-purpose area of land on their rocky – and, in that sense, Earth-like – planet. The terrain in focus stretched alongside a sea and was slightly larger in size than the State of Israel. The climate in the region concerned would be conducive to human life; and relevant, recognisable and hopefully acceptable accommodation would be provided for all who settled within its ambit. It was stated confidently that a 'society' with great prospects could soon develop; and one that would be for the good of all. The presentation was virtually miraculous; but I, and doubtless most other invitees in the large hall beneath the *Shoah* museum, didn't have the whiff of a clue about what was transpiring when advanced scientific and technological aspects were covered in the main discourse. But in the final analysis, however, all we really wanted or needed to know was of a positive – and thus encouraging and fear-allaying – scientific reaction and conclusion.

The *conference*, so to speak, had ended with almost unanimous agreement to the Alpha Centauri proposal. Participants from around the world had harkened beneficently to its humanitarian motivation, in view of the foreseeable and potentially cataclysmic situation developing apace for the many millions of souls within the Jewish communities on Earth. Inevitably and sadly – and this needed to be faced, too – not everyone could be saved, viably or practicably, by their seeking to make *Aliyah* to the Jewish homeland. Nor would it be possible – bearing in mind the titanic and spread-out numbers involved, and this wasn't an *Entebbe Raid* situation – to rescue or safeguard them with any action initiated by Israel. And it was on the symptomatic cards that many hundreds of thousands of Israeli citizens themselves would resolve to leave for Proxima b.

A significant proportion of the millions of people concerned with the result of the Jerusalem *conference* weren't Jewish, either by birth or conversion. Jewish men and women with non-Jewish spouses or partners had reached large and ever-increasing numbers in recent decades; and especially in the US of A. But there was no difficulty about including them, and their Jewish or non-Jewish children, in the new *Exodus*. Although, it was accepted, that – as within totally Jewish families – there could be divisive and stressful, if not painful differences of opinion in the context. Nobody had claimed that the mind-boggling question would be an easy one to answer, and for all to resolve without consequences. In that connection, and bearing in mind that the *conference*'s determination could never have been absolutely unanimous in any case, it was witnessed overwhelmingly that many invited heads of ultra-Orthodox Jewish sects or groupings would have nothing whatsoever to do with its outcome. *So be it* was the three-word and equivocal reaction heard to be expressed by other participants in this instance.

But there was only one word considered, generally, as apt to describe the arrangements to be put in place for assembling furtively on, and launching from, Earth – then transferring across the Milky Way via mother-ships gathered clandestinely in the Solar System – all those Jewish families and individuals who would decide to embark for a whole new life on Proxima b... *Fabulous!*

Fourteen

DESPITE CRADLING the still slumbering Naomi warmly within my encompassing arms inside the capsule, I couldn't help but contemplate my navel despite efforts to obtain some shut-eye myself. Continuing reflections on the amazing *conference* in Jerusalem had deprived me already of a goodly stretch of sleep-time; and they would be ongoing that day.

I shifted gently a tad – I couldn't have moved much in excess of that, even assuming I'd wanted to – in order to achieve slightly more comfort in the, so to speak, *pressing* circumstances of the pod. I didn't wish to awaken my wife suddenly and, perhaps, frighteningly for her. After largely taking care of the twins for the preceding seven Earth-weeks, in a situation miles – if not light years – apart from our normal daily lives in Cambridge, Naomi certainly deserved the cosy rest she was obviously enjoying from the beam glossing her reposing face. Whilst kind of envying her, I wasn't able to match, as yet, her speedy into the *arms of Morpheus* accomplishment.

And so my present, though occasionally punctured, thoughts of the *conference* held furtively at Yad Vashem awkwardly persisted. Now – and quite randomly again – I recalled meeting, and talking to, one of the other members of Diva's team from Alpha Centauri. It was during a drinks break in the intensive *seminar*, of sorts. A youngish-looking and attractive woman of about my height approached me, and introduced herself as "Ziva". Initially, and maybe startlingly, I could've sworn she announced that her name was "Diva". In actuality, she bore a remarkable resemblance to her colleague and my first personal contact from Ziva's home planet.

Like my longstanding friend from Proxima b, Ziva appeared in her tunic as a slim, blue-eyed and blonde Occidental. I couldn't help but recall my original sighting of Diva – on the riverside terrace of The Anchor gastro-pub in Cambridge – when she'd assumed, in a facial transformation, the appearance of an Oriental female. Name-wise, I speculated momentarily on whether the identical *IVA* ending of Ziva's name was common amongst her world's population, at least on an English transliteration. I was pretty certain, of course, that the latter combination wasn't anything to do with a planetary insolvency. Ziva sat down beside me as we both imbibed our delightfully cool and refreshing glasses of water.

"My name is Ziva… Z-I-V-A," she spelled out, just like her colleague had done when we'd first met. "Diva has told me all about you, David… and your exploits together a while ago," she said with a cute kind of smile.

I hoped, probably uselessly, that she wasn't including the one-off, sexual intercourse aspect of such *exploits*. Diva had required that particular *exploit* as a 'research project' condition precedent to my time travel journey back to 13th century Cambridge. A sexual episode, happening when I was a singleton after my divorce, which had resulted – as Naomi and I were stunned but overjoyed to discover later – in our delightful twins, Joshua and Sarah.

"O-Oh… that's good," I responded, sounding somewhat equivocal.

"Yes, well I'm a close friend of Diva, as well as being an assistant team-member," Ziva explained. "So she tells me everything, at least everything I can't gather for myself but need to know. I think you may understand what I mean."

Just as I'd thought, I thought.

"How are you likely to be involved with the new *Exodus* plan, Ziva?" I enquired with a searching curiosity.

Both of us drank some more water. The hall was kind of air-conditioned, of course and for want of a better terminology. But it was really warm outside of it. Not that I minded much, being fairly adaptable to climate change from my many years as an investigate journalist travelling the world for stories. But I was unsure about the temperatures generally sustainable by Ziva and her extraterrestrial compatriots. I suspected there wasn't a real problem for them, my expectations based on their origins at the other side of the galaxy to us. And also on the welcome footing of a clear assurance, from Diva, that the weather patterns prevalent in our proposed living zone on Proxima b wouldn't be at all incompatible with the physical tolerance capacity of us Earthlings.

"I would be involved, as you put it and alongside many others, with organising the journey from your Solar System to our star system," she answered evenly.

"Ah, the transport of us Jews from Earth to Proxima b, Ziva ..." I said.

"With respect, David," she went on, with something of an edge to her voice, "we should avoid using the term *transport*... we know that it may well have very sensitive connotations for Jewish people."

"What *connotations*?" I asked quizzically, but without thinking the point through.

"Are not the Jews of Nazi Germany and Nazi-occupied territories in the Second World War, and during the *Holocaust*," she replied, "referred to as having been *transported* or pushed into rail *transports* or cattle-trucks for their final journey, of unsuspected annihilation, to the gas chambers of the death camps that the Nazis set up in Poland, and elsewhere?"

"Y-You're right, of course, Ziva," I responded, figuratively hanging my head with the words. "And it's a very delicate and sympathetic way of thinking by you and your Proxima b colleagues. Having in the past met some survivors, who had themselves lost many beloved family members in the *Shoah*, I myself should've been aware of a more appropriate expression to use in the present context."

"No problem, David... but, naturally, there would be the understandably arising question of apprehension and trust in this, to you and your brethren, mind-shattering project," she continued, raising her head noticeably and adding: "Looks like we're soon to start the next session on the agenda."

I nodded. Quickly, we drained the now tepid water from our glasses then stood up to go to our respectively allocated *conference* positions. Just before we did all of that, Ziva had time to say:

"We're so sorry it has come to this for your people here on Earth. I, too, have learned about anti-Semitism's age-old and abominable tropes, many of which have persisted or mutated across the millennia. I don't need to tell *you*, of course, but I've noted how such hatred seems to have been based successively on religion then race. And, from nineteen forty-eight after the United Nations' decision on Statehood, on the existence of the now and, with double standards, so often exclusively and unjustifiably demonised Israel... and that, in spite of the consistent presence of your people in that land across the generations. It's as if only your people are to be denied the right to self-determination, and a life.

"Those who decide to take the unique and, literally, out-of-this-world voyage with us, on what probably will be the one and only chance for them in such mission of rescue from a rapidly developing and murderous evil, can rest assured. They will be safe and secure in making a new home for themselves for tomorrow and all the tomorrows to come in the eternal cosmos. They will be able to form a society or societies of their choice with, if they wish, the varied ingredients of Jewish communities and generally as on Earth today. And they can construct the societal environment and infrastructure within which they will carry on their day-to-day lives and livelihoods.

"But believe me, David, I can well comprehend the dilemma of an absolutely terrifying and virtually impossible choice, between a rock and a hard place they could think, that will now confront your people on Earth. And despite being offered the ability to escape the extremely perilous situation closing in on them here …"

Walking to my allotted seat, I found myself heartily agreeing with Ziva's closing thoughts as she left me, with a sort of reflexive smile, to return to her own fixed place in the hall. But I knew the authenticated contingency planning, now being unfolded and revealed that day in Jerusalem, would convince a very large proportion of those millions of Jews to be informed of it subsequently. The detailed proposals put forward by the Proxima b team of experts were pragmatic and empirical; and appeared to have covered all known aspects of the venture definitively. Accepting, philosophically, the exceptionally advanced and deliberative processes within the Alpha Centauri system, the fundamental proposition shouldn't have been perceived as incredible; even though it was definitely such for me.

Not that there wouldn't be agonising decisions to be made by the wide-eyed, jaw-dropping recipients of this extraordinary offer of salvation. And – as later I wasn't entirely surprised to hear on our spacecraft's extensive and informative grapevine – a not insignificant ratio of its passengers was questioning their earlier determination. Many of them were feeling a sad spectrum of regrets about their departure, which had been relatively hurried, from their homes on Earth. In a way not unlike, I supposed, the complaining thousands of Israelites fleeing slavery in ancient Egypt under Moses' leadership. Though, generally, the transferring Earthlings would be leaving far more behind in our modern era.

Religiously Orthodox passengers – who gladly possessed the option of gathering together for prayer services led by their ministers and using *Sifrei Torah*, the sacred Hebrew scrolls of the Five Books of Moses, brought with them from their erstwhile communities – were unhappy about travelling on the Jewish Sabbath. Such would be *prima facie* in contravention of *Halachah* or Jewish Law. But the vast majority of them were consoled, in a sense, by their rabbis' ruling that there's no breach if, as in this case, the context concerned a matter of life and death. Members of Liberal, Reform and Progressive religious groupings on board weren't necessarily worried by such questions.

But it was quite apparent that everything was being done to make the inter-stellar trip as comfortable and on-the-ball as possible in the prevailing conditions and state of affairs. In view of the millions of Jewish people en route to Proxima b, the accommodation provided – and especially the capsule make-up of it – couldn't be quite the same, practicably, for, say, a family as a reasonably sized, three-bedroom, semi-detached, suburban house. Nonetheless, the facilities and amenities afforded were, by any stretch of the human imagination, extraordinary; as, I reckoned, it needed to be in such a mind-stunning situation.

Almost inevitably, though sadly, during the eight Earth-weeks' journey across the Milky Way – and bearing in mind the numbers, as well as age ranges, of those on the fleet of mother-ships – there would be many deaths from natural or, indeed, other causes. Bodies needed to be stored without burial for a period longer than that required traditionally by Jewish law. Nevertheless, interment – according to *Halachic* rites and rituals – would take place as soon as possible after landing at our destination. But also, and not unexpectedly, there were happy events, too, including weddings, abundant births and *bar-* or *bat-mitzvahs* to celebrate. The maternity provision, in addition to the broad-spectrum and considerably 'futuristic' medical services, supplied couldn't be faulted in any way regarding positive and beneficial results. And even on the assumption that we could've understood all the ramifications of these remedial applications. So, in the final analysis, passengers would be experiencing – arguably in a whimsical, though basically serious, manner of speaking – the best of all possible worlds!

Then I must've actually fallen asleep, still clutching Naomi in my capsule, because – and I wasn't aware then of how long afterwards – I was woken by my wife, and at least in the first instance, whispering in my ear.

"David, wake up… David, wake up… please wake up, David …" came Naomi's words into a consciousness gradually expanding in line with her increasing volume. "We've got to collect our little ones now, David darling… and then queue up for the dining hall …"

Fifteen

AS NAOMI, the kids and I stood in the smoothly moving procession for our next meal, Joshua tugged at my sleeve.

"Daddy… can I ask you a question?" he said – in his maturely cute though, naturally, child-like style of speaking – looking up at my enquiring little smile.

"Yes, my boy… you certainly can," I replied. "Fire away, son."

"Are we there yet, Dad?" he asked, then returning my grin.

Two could play at that game, I thought at once.

"Are we where yet, Joshua?" I responded, hopefully transforming my benign expression for my boy's benefit. But, indeed, also for that of his adjacent sister, who was staring up at me with a glowing anticipation whilst holding her mother's hand.

"You must learn to be precise in your use of language, Joshua," I went on; and maybe in more than just a continuing manner. "So do you mean the end of this queue for our meals or the landing on Proxima b, our new home planet and about which you and Sarah have been told?"

"I mean the planet, of course," he retorted; and arguably, had it not been for his very young age, with a somewhat adult and even sardonic ring to his pseudo *lad* - like delivery. "But there's no need for you to answer me now, Dad... I know, and *exactly*, what you're going to tell me."

As our lengthy column moved on apace, then halted for a few moments, I detected my closely listening daughter joining her brother in an impish grin. Impulsively but fleetingly, I ruffled my hand through the wayward mop of fairish hair on Joshua's head as he tried, though unsuccessfully, to duck away from my swift action; and to the amusement of closely following passengers.

In a short while, we reached our allocated seats at an ultra-long table, one of innumerable in the vast 'hall'. As usual, Naomi and I sat ourselves on either side the twins, with Joshua sitting next to me. Again directly opposite us, of course, was the young French couple. Sadly, they appeared so tense, even thoroughly depressed, as they sat really close together. His left arm encompassed his wife and her head – with its red-rimmed, despondent eyes – resting forlornly on his broad shoulder. Naomi and I, having exchanged rapid glances with each other, implicitly considered it best merely to nod in their direction when they came to notice us. Just to acknowledge their presence. Then we would continue to focus our attention and – with the amazing, though now familiar technology efficiently to hand for the purpose – implement our decisions on what we and the children wanted to eat and drink at that scheduled meal session.

We and the other diners on this shift would normally need to wait only a very brief period for the incredible, automated facility to deliver the high quality repasts. Such would be in strict accordance with individual requirements or preferences for whatever reasons, including medical and religious. In the meantime, and as on a number of other occasions during the previous seven Earth-weeks or so, Naomi began chatting with the friendly, middle-aged couple seated beside her. She'd told me that they originated from Manchester; and that their name was Rubenstein. But I'd not spoken to them myself, as yet. At the same time, I engaged in conversation with the octogenarian gentleman, a widower from London and a long-retired Solicitor, ensconced on my left flank. Until the food arrived, Joshua and Sarah were keenly plugging in to quietly play games, or whatever, on their hand-held, electronic gadgets. I hadn't spoken to the ex-lawyer for several of the recent meal times, as he seemed to be in close dialogue with a youngish couple, apparently from Manchester, seated on the other side of him to me.

"How are you, Alex?" I enquired, turning to face my elderly and pensive neighbour, who looked reasonably well-preserved for someone in their late eighties.

"M-mustn't g-grumble at all, David," he replied, quickly coming out of his meditative reverie, smiling at me and remembering my name. "As I think I've mentioned to you, I did have some troubling medical problems which, as required of all passengers, I needed to report on boarding our, if I may put it this way, very welcoming cruise-liner ..."

I nodded, recalling my family's thankfully negative, health-check registration.

"But with the advantage of some incredible remedial help, from our marvellous Alpha Centauri saviours, during the last month or so," my relatively new acquaintance continued, "I'm feeling considerably healthier today than I did before leaving my home in Hendon... a truly marvellous outcome, David!"

"I'm so glad to hear this, Alex," I remarked wholeheartedly.

I was hoping to match the appealing smile emanating from across his entire and fairly elongated face, from a not completely bald pate, over a lightly-creased forehead to mildly lined cheeks then cutely doubled chin and slightly wrinkled neck. Unfortunately, and embarrassingly, he could've caught me taking in – maybe even re-assessing – his above-shoulder features.

"Of course, David," Alex went on, "I've received the medical benefits of the treatment, for which I'm so grateful... on the inside, not appearance-wise. Maybe, and with their advanced technology in all fields, they could've made me as fine-looking as you, with your doubtless genetic legacy of abundant hair foliage. But I don't believe I would've accepted the chance to look younger, even if it had been a possibility and I was offered it."

If Alex had been a lawyer for the prosecution in the context, he would've won his case hands down. Actually, my mortification was making me feel like pleading *Guilty* immediately, then taking the inevitable Judgement and its punishing consequences. But I only nodded slowly then gave my meal neighbour the sweetest and most endearingly caring smile I could muster at that awkward moment... for me rather than him.

"So I take it you've got no regrets about coming on this voyage... of discovery, so to speak?" I asked; but, necessarily, without supplementing it with my next following thought... *and even at your age, Alex.*

"None whatsoever, David," he said fervently. "I've been quite lonely since my beloved Freda passed away, nearly ten years ago now... how time flies, eh?"

I nodded, spotting a smidgeon of moisture glinting in his hooded eyes.

"Sadly," he added, "and as I think I've mentioned to you during one of our previous chats, Freda couldn't have any children... and she didn't want to adopt any."

"Yes, you did... and I'm sorry for your loss, and that you've been feeling lonesome."

"Thanks... but that's alright, David," Alex said, tapping with a partially liver-spotted hand on my arm that was resting on the table. "During more than fifty years of marriage, I had plenty of time to accept and adjust to our childless situation ..."

Alas, he hadn't perceived that my expression of being sorry for him was meant, by its specifics, to avoid reference to his late wife's apparently sole and determined resolution not to have an adoptive son or daughter. Evidently, however, Alex had loved Freda so much that her maybe unchallenged decision hadn't in any way affected their profoundly loving relationship across half a century or more. So I merely nodded again.

"I do have nieces and nephews, etcetera," he continued, "but I haven't seen them that often... they live all over the place. Some of them, I suppose, could be on board one of these huge mother-ships, if not this one... I don't know, David. Freda herself was a child survivor of the Nazi genocide of six million Jews. She was born and brought up in Lithuania but lost her parents, siblings and most other relatives in the Holocaust. My darling wife-to-be was rescued by the Soviet army from a camp to which she'd been deported and, eventually, managed to get to England after the end of the war ..."

As he paused, his dark brown eyes watering a little, all I could do was bunch my lips and nod compassionately yet again. Then I was pleased to perceive a tiny sparkle of solace and reassurance in Alex's moist eyes.

"I've been so very thankful to be able to attend one of the many so thoughtfully improvised synagogues on this enormous space vehicle... for the Shabbat services, conducted by the onboard rabbis," he commented. "At one of them, I could recite the *kaddish* memorial prayer when I had *yahrzeit* a couple of weeks ago, on the anniversary of my beloved Freda's sad passing. But I've not seen you and your family at the synagogue I've attended. Perhaps you go with them to one of the other Shabbat services held to cater for those of us requiring such. And, almost unbelievably, there are always the traditional *kiddush* refreshments afterwards, I'm delighted to say."

I puckered my cheeks, whilst noting that our meals seemed to be taking a little longer than usual to arrive for that dining session… though I could've been *out* on that one, too, with time playing some tricks on me.

"We're not very religious, Alex," I explained, "However …"

And then the food and drink turned up on the scene, as if by magic, bringing a sudden close to my sprinkled-with-sadness conversation with Alex. I was just about to tell him that, despite being little more than 'a once-a-year Jew', I was delighted that he – and no doubt countless others on the fleet of massive spaceships headed for the Alpha Centauri star system – were enabled to continue their adherence to the religious tenets and traditions of our ancient faith.

Sixteen

AFTER OUR tasty meal dishes, I took the kids to their lessons then returned to my capsule where, as we'd moved off in disciplined line from our table, Naomi said she would be waiting for me. We could've gone together to the huge socialising hall which, initially, I'd thought was the transformed dining hall; though it couldn't have been, because of the numerous meal shifts. Usually, there was some space remaining, even for latecomers, to chat amiably with new people. It was virtually impossible to find previous days' acquaintances amongst the immense number of passengers present. But it was usefully informative for us to converse with our English-speaking compatriots from around the world we'd all fled relatively recently. The array of languages, and the range of dialects and accents in which our own mother-tongue was being spoken, was quite amazing; and the Tower of Babel gamut of sounds – although somewhat ear-shattering initially – self-consciously, and rather sensibly, calmed down eventually. However, it was good just to be alone with my darling wife whenever possible; and that loving togetherness, in a way, also gave us some sense of proportion, if not to say 'normality'.

I was scheduled to meet with Diva in an hour or so; but, before that, Naomi and I cuddled up for a cosy little chat.

"So how is the Rubenstein couple, Naomi?" I enquired, as we got as relaxingly snug as possible and I planted a quick peck on a proximate cheek.

She reciprocated with an attempted kiss on my forehead, largely though understandably misplaced on my nose. I'm fairly sure she had her eyelids shut during this display of affection, because she quickly opened them when the tangible flesh composition on her lips couldn't have felt quite right. After we exchanged post-contact and whimsical looks, she replied to my question.

"They're ok, I suppose," she said. "But, undoubtedly like many thousands of our fellow travellers, they're so melancholy and upset about their close family members who'd decided to remain on Earth …"

"Yes, Naomi… but, naturally, we've heard this far in excess of once, and even within the comparatively minute circle of passengers open to us to meet," I commented earnestly. "Who in fact might the Rubenstein pair have especially in mind here?"

"I was just about to say, David …"

"Sorry."

"Gerry, and he said I could call him that, and Leah have four children, two sons and two daughters," she explained. "They're all married, have kids of their own and, except for one son based in London, were living in the Manchester area and reasonably near to their parents. The couple were pleased to tell me that two of their four children, the daughters, together with the grandchildren from them, were onboard another of the mother-ships en route to Proxima b. Gerry and Leah speak to them, and as often as possible, via the technology available to us. But so very sadly for them in a way, the parents told me, their other two children, the sons, and their families had managed to make *Aliyah* and to settle in Israel a fairly short while back. Their boys, they said, harboured the deep hope and some confidence that they would all have a safe, secure and meaningful future in the Jewish homeland. Although, as Gerry mentioned, his sons did appreciate somewhat the potential downside, and maybe disastrous possibilities. But, their father added, they were determined to defend the country, if necessary, and were very willing to do any requisite service in the Israel Defence Forces… and they were loyally supported by their wives in that connection."

"I see," I said, fully comprehending the grandparents' profound emotions. "So many here have expressed the opinion that we've all faced an almost impossible predicament, to whatever degree, of having to resolve a terrifying kind of Catch-22 conundrum… whether or not to embark on this nigh on stupefying *rescue mission* from trillions of miles away across the Milky Way."

Naomi sort of nodded horizontally from her supine position then fell into slumber mode immediately, softly and rhythmically murmuring in her sleep.

I needed to stay awake for my arranged meeting shortly with Diva who, no doubt due to our close connect, considered she should keep her Cambridge contact in touch with proceedings and our progress through the heavens. When the time came for me to depart my pod, and unfortunately, I couldn't avoid – but inadvertently – rousing my dear wife from her calm and quiet slumbers. It just wouldn't have been possible for me to slide out furtively and without disturbing her. She didn't seem to mind in the circumstances.

As I made my circuitous way to Diva's quarters – employing an intriguing type of 'SatNav' or direction-finder gadget she'd supplied to me – I knew there were some important questions I was really desirous of asking her. As it turned out, Ziva collected me at the entrance to her team zone – for various reasons – and led me to Diva, whilst staying in the background during our session.

When en route to Diva, I'd pondered the interrogatories nagging at my mind. I and my fellow passengers had been informed earlier, of course, that an extensive, appropriate and conducive area of habitable land was to be made available for us on Proxima b; that necessary and relevant accommodation would be provided, and which could be extended and/or enhanced by us, the particular region's first inhabitants; and that our own Jewish 'society' would undoubtedly develop at a rate of knots. But we hadn't been advised of how, and with what content, a requisite government would be constituted; not an easy matter, one might've thought from the historical experience on Earth. Neither had we been told whether the land to be provided – apparently spreading along, and into the hinterland from, an extensive sea – would become an established, democratic and independent nation for us. Nor had it been explained whether we would, in any scenario, be subject to the without doubt benevolent leadership or whatever that existed presently, and in whatever constituent form, on the Proxima Centauri world.

I couldn't recall Diva having told me anything about these significant elements of our future life on her home planet. Naturally, the discussion in my head was totally influenced by certain political systems, arguably primitive in many respects, which existed on Earth. It was highly likely that nobody from our neck of the universe would be able to grasp the likely sophisticated political, supervisory, administrative or whatever arrangements in place within the Alpha Centauri star system. Not that you could always – if ever, many Earthlings might say – get your head around the workings of systems, democratic or otherwise, on *our* now far-distant globe.

After putting what I considered to be some imperative queries to Diva, she smiled at me from her seat across the desk, if that was its function; but in a way that I couldn't honestly interpret.

"Why are you smiling at me, Diva?" I asked, indubitably appearing nonplussed.

She blinked a few times; and I couldn't help but admire her poise, as well as her lovely blue eyes.

"I'm not smiling, David ..." she countered, "just exercising my facial muscles."

"Very funny, Diva ..." I counter-countered, "but I'm trying to be serious."

Her facial muscles and eyelids took a rest, and my friend appeared to breath deeply.

"I know …" she said evenly, "though I thought you, of all people, would appreciate some fanciful banter to lighten what seemed to be a heavy weight resting on your shoulders."

"My apologies, Diva," I said, trying hard not to look downcast.

"No problem," she offered, turning towards Ziva and requesting her to bring us some cold drinks. "Even though you may not know or believe it, the questions you just posed were all sorted out at Yad Vashem. They needed to be, of course. You weren't validated to be included in the then confidential discussion sessions in Jerusalem. It was a complicated, if not highly complex area of debate… at least for those in attendance as the leaders of Jewish communities on Earth. And perhaps even more so in the national political environment in which the conference was being held. But at the end of the day, literally, there was a comprehensive acceptance of the vital subject's necessary resolution. I don't want to boast, David… that's not our style, as you know. It's merely a matter of fact, as I know you've long understood …"

Ziva returned with our drinks and placed them on the desk then moved back to her seat in the wings.

"Thanks, Ziva," we both said in unison.

"As I was saying," Diva went on, "our civilisation is so far in advance of that which exists variously on Earth… and as you're well aware, David, I'm not speaking only in relation to scientific and technological knowledge."

All I felt able to do was nod resignedly a few times. After that acceding exhibition of mine, we each took a swig of our cold drinks; they looked like still water, but tasted pleasantly fruity to me.

"We're now not far off from our destination, David," Diva continued, "and, in an Earth-day or two, all passengers across the fleet will be given fully comprehensive and comprehensible data to enhance the current knowledge they possess about their forthcoming new home... and which, we're certain, will answer every question they might have ..."

I nodded again.

"And before you ask, as I know you would, David," she added quickly, "there will be a one hundred percent consensus with all aspects of the, so to speak, blueprint for the future of your people on Proxima b. So don't worry, my friend... about anything."

I knew she was reading my imminently expressible thoughts; and, on this occasion, I was glad Diva was able to do that without my having to say the words... largely because I was rendered speechless.

Seventeen

FOR OUR next meal in the 'Great Hall', Naomi and I decided to swap places beside the children at the table. Primarily, this was because I wanted to have a chat myself with the Rubenstein husband and wife, with whom I'd not yet engaged in conversation. I was sure that my food neighbour Alex would appreciate a pleasant gossip with Naomi. Probably, the children wouldn't notice any alteration in the seating plan; even now, they were extracting the gaming gadgets from their tunic pockets.

On sitting down, however, I noted that there was a gap opposite us where the youngish French couple had been sitting for the past seven Earth-weeks or so. After exchanging puzzled glances with Naomi about their sudden absence, I hoped that either wasn't or both of them weren't unwell. I knew, and clearly understood why, they were continuously feeling depressed; the murderous loss of their children was so wretchedly sorrowful. But, apparently, no medical aid had been sought for the condition they were, and maybe more particularly the wife was, sadly experiencing. I just hoped that the bereaved pair's justifiably ongoing mournfulness hadn't made them ill physically.

Then I felt a gentle tap on my right arm. It was the Rubenstein man.

"Hello ..." he said with a somewhat surprising flatness, the dark brown eyes in his almost round face – with its slightly greying head of hair and matching moustache – looking at me with an oddly ambivalent mix of positive acknowledgement and negative dejection. As he began to speak again, and after I'd nodded in response to his equivocal greeting, I noticed that his wife was staring at me across her spouse's shoulder with an expression not dissimilar to her husband's melancholy look.

"I'm really sorry to have to tell you ..." he continued, balefully, "and the terribly sad news is now being passed down the line, that the French couple, who'd sat directly opposite you and your family, have passed away ..."

Naomi must've heard what he'd just articulated, because my quick glimpse back confirmed her gazing at me unbelievingly over the twins' heads.

I could sense that the mask spreading across my facial features was beginning to match the Rubensteins' appearance... though it could well have been hardening into shock.

"H-How... W-What was ...?" I began, but couldn't quite get the words out of my vocal cords and across to my informant.

"That's ok... David," he said with an empathetic tone. "I know that you and your wife have had a number of conversations with the late young couple. We had a few with them, too, and I can readily appreciate how you're feeling..."

"B-But… but how could they both…?" I started to break in, quizzically not being the word to describe my unfinished and incredulous enquiry. Naomi had told me the Rubenstein guy's first name. But, personally, I just couldn't bring it to mind in the present dreadful circumstances. And I would've felt a bit discomfited to ask him, especially as he was using mine.

"It's reported that they've committed suicide," he responded. "It seems the alert came, via the unbelievably advanced technology with which we're surrounded, when there were no signs of breathing in the husband's occupied capsule… it's said that, at the time, the pod was holding him and his wife in close embrace."

"But how did they manage to kill themselves?" I asked, with mystification. "When the millions of us boarded our allocated shuttles for the Alpha Centauri mother-ships, the screening was impeccable even if, happily, non-invasive. It was so far ahead of the kind of, let's say, airport security operational on Earth. And the safeguards on board the fleet are designed to ensure that all of us, of whatever age group, don't hurt or harm ourselves in any way."

"I really don't know *how* they managed to carry out this dreadful act…" he replied. "That wasn't mentioned in the information coming down the line just before. But, sadly, not that it matters now."

It was a short while later that I learned from Diva that the French couple had cut their wrists… and that the gruesome outcome was a horrifying deluge of blood when the capsule was opened.

"Alas, that's so," I agreed. "And as we so dismally know, of course, this is by no means the first time during our space voyage that such an abysmally sorrowful episode has occurred."

My new acquaintance nodded forlornly.

"Unfortunately, you're right, David," he said, sighing intensely. "The ghastly statistics for fellow passengers committing suicide, and across the entire fleet, may well go into many thousands now... it's beyond putting into words."

I nodded, also taking a very deep breath then expelling the air towards the empty places on the other side of the table.

We requested our respective meals; and they arrived in good time, as per usual. Not a word was spoken by anyone in the vicinity during our consuming of the wholesome and delicious fare; and everyone could follow the rationale for this contemplative silence. During that period of doubtless profound reflection, my mind wandered back to the initial boarding of the shuttles to the mother-ships hovering stealthily somewhere in our Solar System. It had become known, and understandable, that the luggage passengers could bring with them would be limited. Much in the way of assets would be left behind for, if possible, others remaining on Earth, necessarily so; and, needless to state, that would include real estate. Financial considerations in that context would be virtually meaningless. And that would be in stark contrast, it then crossed my mind, to the situation when the Israelites made their *Exodus* – via the rocky desert wilderness to the Promised Land, and not by means of inter-planetary, galactic spacecraft – from Pharaoh's Egypt in the biblical epoch. But it was a question of life or death. As we knew, a whole new society would be formed on Proxima b; and, self-evidently, that society would need to reflect all those vital ingredients, at least, of our former lives on Earth, which would be far too numerous to list.

Suddenly, as we neared the conclusion of our meal shift, a low buzz of conversation struck up again in our sector of the vast hall. After glancing around, I turned to Gerry, whose name had just come back into my head.

"Seems like we and fellow passengers in this immediate location have now come to the end of our and their reflective meditations, Gerry," I remarked.

"Yes… seems like it, David," he reacted, though pensively whilst nodding his head slowly.

"My wife tells me you're a chartered accountant, Gerry…"

He nodded again.

"And Naomi informs me that you were an investigative journalist," he said.

"That's right," I said, "and, presumably, you're hoping if not planning to continue in the accountancy profession after we settle on Proxima b?"

"You're correct, David," he replied. "I was, and in effect still am, a partner in a long-standing firm of chartered accountants. I'm extremely glad to say that all my fellow partners, together with their families, embarked on one or other of this fleet of huge spaceships heading for our new planetary home. And all partners have been in fairly constant touch during this amazing journey."

"So do you accept, as hopefully all passengers do, my friend," I put it, "that we millions of emigrants from Earth can establish a blessed, happy, functional and productive society for our own successful future and that of generations to come?"

"I've no doubts whatsoever about that, my friend," he replied.

I was pleased to note his parallel usage of my amiable appellation.

"In one important sense, David," Gerry added, "we're not starting from scratch ..."

I gazed at him enquiringly.

"Well," he continued, "it's not like we don't know about the overall format as existed formerly. Consequently, we're certainly well aware of what needs to be accomplished, and constructed... and as soon as practicably possible. So that our lives can go on as they did on Earth, though potentially enhanced and without the threat of anti-Semitic annihilation hanging over our heads."

I nodded then opined:

"You put it very well, my friend... if I may say so."

Gerry nodded in turn, and with a wry little smile.

Soon afterwards, the signal was given for our meal stint to file out of the expansive chamber. On departing, and with much sadness in view of the terrible news about the French couple, we were advised that the fleet would be landing on Proxima b in precisely two Earth-days, or 48 Earth-hours, time.

Eighteen

MUCH LATER that day – bedtime, in fact – and after we'd spent quite a lot of time with the kids, I wrapped myself around Naomi… on this occasion, in *her* pod; the twins were currently occupying mine. Well, I supposed and as it's said, a 'change is as good as a rest'; though, personally, a 'rest' of the sleep variety would've been really good if attainable. Before my wife fell into other arms – namely, that of Morpheus – and which she fairly quickly did, I spoke to her about my chat with Mr Rubenstein. Indeed, I myself was so in need of some slumber that I didn't even think to ask her to remind me of his first name, which I'd duly forgotten again. Naomi, like me, thought he'd been commendably confident in his categorically positive attitude regarding the future of the soon-to-be-landed, Jewish immigrants on Proxima b.

We were becoming aware, of course, of the combination of neo-excitement and natural trepidation seething through other passengers, as well as ourselves. The substantial majority had taken well on board the heart-warmingly welcome concept of *'goodness'* now primary and prevalent – but only after a lengthy evolution of the truly civilised society – in the habitable zone of

Proxima Centauri. I knew how Diva would express her planet's essential philosophy, which she'd founded on her now extensive studies of Judaism and Hebrew. The words I'd heard her use came from 'Psalms'… *olam chesed yibaneh* – the world will be based on kindness. Most of us would fully understand, and be thankful for, what she meant; and the requisite adjustments to be desired. Also, we knew well enough – from socialising, so far as practicable, in a massive chamber – that a goodly number of passengers, particularly but not exclusively youngish 'Diaspora' couples with families, harboured a similarly especial notion…

But now that the fleet of mother-ships was almost on the point of arrival at our ultimate destination, numerous passengers were beginning to wonder whether they had surrendered their Jewish lives on Earth too readily and prematurely. Largely of the parental variety, they seemed to be sharing a common feeling of guilt… a sense that they had abandoned, if not deserted those of their kith and kin remaining across the world; and who'd resolved to maintain their faith there, and to resist the unrelenting anti-Semitism now evilly, and potentially fatally, enveloping them. Those amongst the passengers who were rather more religious than others kept repeating that the Almighty had *Created* the Earth; and that they should've continued living on His *Creation* – and also within the albeit globally demonised and 'besieged' Jewish homeland… the Almighty's *Promised Land*. Whilst others – of varying degrees of secularity – would, nonetheless, seek to comfort the more piously faithful fellow passengers, and maybe also themselves, by asserting that in the opening verse of the Old Testament's first Book, Genesis, it's stated that the Almighty "created the heaven and the earth". The 'Diaspora' secularists – a not insignificant proportion of whom might well have sought to make *Aliyah* to the Jewish nation state – would add, of course, that it wouldn't be possible for Israel to absorb within its borders the several millions of Jews residing outside of them. And that serious thought had needed to be given to the safe and secure future of their children.

Naomi and I dwelt for a short time on the few assets, mainly some valuables, that we were allowed to bring with us on embarking the shuttles for the mother-ships. Of course, we knew that the value of possessions carried onboard could vary enormously from individual to individual, and from family to family. But one factor was certain. A pre-condition for acceptance as passengers – and it was a qualification imposed not only by Proxima b leaders, but also jointly by the all-accepted representatives of world Jewry – was that any real estate owned by millions of them couldn't be placed for sale on the general property market; and for quite obvious reasons. Only particular private property sale transactions, donations or other gifts of real estate – buildings, houses and land – would be permitted in order to acquire currency. That would be for exclusive use on Earth, for example to purchase moveable assets for future use; though, if manageable, for restrictive storage onboard the spacecraft.

These property transactions or gifts needed to be processed confidentially to family members or to other fellow Jews who would be remaining behind on Earth, for whatever motivation. Or even to those planning to leave the planet and who, not being very well off, could be gifted the real estate for *them* to sell; though only on the requisite confidential basis, that is to non-departing Jews. Since my reasonably comfortable ex-wife, and our professionally successful son with his wife, would be joining the galactic fleet, I made a stealthily private sale of our leasehold apartment in Cambridge. It was to one of our longstanding, somewhat irreligious Jewish friends and a modest landlord in the city, who was staying put for reasons of his own.

Naomi and I were aware also that a large proportion of those departing the Solar System had made donations of property, some quite considerable, to Jewish charities running residential homes for the elderly and/or disabled. Those couples or individuals concerned, and for the most-part, wouldn't see or be fit to undertake the inter-planetary voyage. And we were so proud and admiring of the selfless staff and volunteers who'd stayed behind on Earth to keep the many homes functioning properly, and regardless. My wife and I were incredibly impressed also that, of all the millions of prospective Jewish voyagers to Proxima b – and whether or not they owned real estate, for sale or gift – there wouldn't and, indeed by virtue of Alpha Centauri's mightily advanced powers, couldn't be any leaks by would-be whistleblowers and their ilk.

It was hardly any wonder that, after our most boring of supine conversations, I felt Naomi go slack in my embrace and start the few moments of murmuring in her early drifting off. I reached out to grab a tissue, and gently wiped away some dribble about to drip from her lips onto her tunic. This action gave me pause for a reflection on something really extraordinary in context. It was always going to be the case that the amount of everyday clothes we could bring with us on this 'luxury accommodation cruise – not' would be severely limited. Once aboard the mother-ships, as I was informed by Diva beforehand, all passengers – and of whatever age-group – would be supplied with two sets of comfortable-to-wear, lightweight textured and silver-hued under-garments plus overlaying tunics.

It was ensured – thoughtfully, and as many would come to know gratefully – that the Orthodox religious elements amongst the space travellers wouldn't be overly offended by the nature and constituents of this uniform apparel. Women members of such groupings could opt to wear a one-piece outfit of the tunic from neck to ankle. The alternative, selected by the men-folk and a large majority of female passengers, was a two-piece get-up with top and trousers. But these easily stored, not totally unattractive – though maybe arguably 'Chinese Cultural Revolution' look-alike – items of gear possessed a remarkably practical attribute; and especially so, bearing in mind that they were to be worn throughout our eight-week, galactic journey.

In effect, the underwear and the one- or two-piece tunics were miraculously self-cleaning; and almost instantaneously so, once they'd been removed from the body. 'Fantastic' was the only superlatively descriptive term applicable! And when I learned of this incredible method of laundering, I thought: 'Hey, washing machines... eat your hearts out!'

A strangely imposing, but dreary sensation of washing tumbling around and around inside such apparently – to Diva and her mates – antediluvian white goods invaded my over-taxed consciousness. In just a handful of moments, I felt myself losing contact with this surreal and existential world then drifting into a firmly beckoning slumber. Before finally crashing out, a hazy thought or two came to me. One was that, very soon now, we would need to attune our burdened and weary minds to entering the new 'New World'; and, in a philosophical manner of speaking, to the novel design of apparel we might possibly need to don. But just prior to losing consciousness, my mind screened a prescient image of me wearing jeans, a sweater and a baseball cap on Proxima b.

Nineteen

THE FOLLOWING 'Earth-time' afternoon, on the day before we were scheduled to land on our new home planet, Proxima b, Naomi and I accompanied by the twins – and a very substantial number of our fellow passengers – were congregated in the massive socialising hall. But there were, of course, huge numbers of the Jewish space voyagers also elsewhere on our mother-ship, including those thousands reading, relaxing or whatever inside their capsules. And doubtless there were similar onboard distributions throughout the extensive fleet at that time. All of us, however, had been informed in the morning – and by one means or another – that there would be a 'broadcast' to all passengers, wherever they were situated, at a particular Earth-hour. We were told also that it would be in the form of a lecture, or talk, about Proxima b; and that it would be given by… Diva. Of course, information of various kinds had filtered through to all those on this astounding venture, both before and after it had been launched – literally; and subsequent to the incredibly amazing *conference* held at *Shoah* museum in Jerusalem.

But on this occasion, apparently, there would be an outlined overview which, it was hoped, would be helpful for passengers in preparing their minds, as well as bodies, for imminent arrival within the habitable zone of red dwarf star Proxima Centauri. Though, necessarily but as expected, the discourse would seek to eschew use of the complex language specific to Proxima b's extremely advanced scientific and hi-hi-hi-tech powers. And even though there were thousands of senior Jewish scientists of every description – including astrophysicists – onboard the fleet's spaceships. These Earthling experts could, and probably would, have sought to perform their level bests in efforts to comprehend the millennia-ahead research, developments and discoveries of Proxima b's scientific aces. But, naturally, it would be borne well in mind that the vast majority of the several million passengers should be given the environmental and other material data in as easily understandable terms as possible. As I waited alongside Naomi with the kids, and whilst we chatted spasmodically with some other passengers with whom we hadn't spoken previously, I speculated on the likelihood that our Earth boffins might well have been in maybe potentially useful touch, for the relevant purpose and by whatever applicable method available onboard, with their 'technological equivalents – not'.

Suddenly, there was a sort of beeping signal heralding the start of the talk, and I recognised Diva's voice instantly…

"Good afternoon, everyone… we do hope that you are all keeping well. As you know, we will be landing tomorrow on Proxima b, in the Alpha Centauri star system. After your eight-week journey across the Milky Way galaxy, which we trust has been made as easy and comfortable, and even as enjoyable, as possible for you, we hope everyone is looking forward to a happy, peaceful and successful future, for yourselves and succeeding generations, on your new home planet. All the indigenous residents of this world are fully aware of what you have been going through on yours, and what you may well have had to dreadfully experience if you had not departed it. But, even so, we comprehend also that it could not have been an easy decision for you to make... far from it, we believe. As you have known for some little while now, you are assured of a sincere welcome on our planet, in all senses, if I can borrow the term, a utopian and not, as sadly on Earth, a dystopian world.

"Our planet Proxima b is, as doubtless now known by all of you, a staggering forty trillion kilometres, or twenty-five trillion miles, distant from Earth. But we must bear in mind that our shared universe contains billions of galaxies, which each hold billions of stars. And the total number of planets orbiting all those stars is virtually countless. But this speaks not of the eternal cosmos, into which our universe has been expanding since the so-called 'Big Bang' some thirteen billion Earth-years ago. Even our scientifically advanced civilisation knows not of what universes may exist in the cosmos outside our own universe.

"But enough already of such overwhelming statistics... let us concentrate on your new home planet. And I will continue to use your terminology. Proxima b, which is about a third larger in mass than Earth, orbits within the habitable zone of its sun, Proxima Centauri, that is also referred to by your astrophysicists as a 'red dwarf star'. As many of you know, there are two other, much larger and very close together suns in the Alpha Centauri star system, in the constellation Centaurus. They are Alpha Centauri A and Alpha Centauri B. The habitability of our globe has been much questioned by your scientists, in large measure but not exclusively, perhaps, because of the close orbit to its star. Proxima b is orbiting just seven and a half million kilometres from Proxima Centauri. Earth is about one hundred and fifty million kilometres, or some ninety-three million miles, from its Sun... and which is rather more massive than our own star. All this means that our planet takes around eleven-point-two Earth-days to orbit its star. So there is nothing like an Earth-day on our planet.

"Of course, your questioning scientists have, with the greatest of respect, only an extremely rudimentary knowledge and understanding of our star system and the long-inhabited, overwhelmingly scientifically and technologically advanced Proxima b. We know that your space-research specialists have speculated that there would be quite a number of perilous and pertinent conditions prevalent in our Proxima Centauri system, not least with regard to our host sun, that would make any form of life on Proxima b virtually impossible. Standing here on my world, having landed via a shuttle from your lead mother-ship a short while ago, I can advise you with great confidence, though I am more than certain I do not need to do such, that your scientists are so wrong about the existence and long-time continuation or survival of life on this planet. However, insofar as they speak of particular and potentially dangerous effects within our red dwarf star system, they do have a point. But, again with respect, your boffins do not know, as an undeniable fact, which of these physical activities or effects exist... and, if they do, to what precise extent and affect on Proxima b. Moreover, they could not know in their wildest imaginings, and thus be able fully to appreciate, what can be done by an unimaginably developed society, in goodness as well as science, to deal with and thus overcome completely and effectively any such physical threats, perils or various system-arising disadvantages, if they might be so perceived, that otherwise could or would be faced by our civilisation.

"It is true that there are certain natural and material hazards in our Proxima Centauri zone. These are caused generally by the juxtaposition of our star and orbiting planet, and we cannot prevent them from happening... even despite our advanced scientific knowledge. However, over thousands of years, our indigenous people have developed the means by which we have been able to thwart what, otherwise, would be the downside outcome of seeking to live easily and comfortably within our star system and on the surface of Proxima b. Indeed, had we not fashioned and evolved such protective provisions, it could be highly unlikely that I would be safely speaking to you here and now.

"It would take me a very long time to explain thoroughly all meticulous details of the, so to speak, involved technology... and to endeavour to make an effort to do so in your own current Earth language of science which, at its contemporary level, is also complex. I do not wish to sound, in any way, haughty or self-aggrandising about all this. Believe me, that is not our scene. Given the same duration of time for R and D that we have experienced on Proxima b, your scientists, technologists and astrophysicists, including those amongst you now, would have attained undoubtedly at least a not dissimilar level of research, knowledge, comprehension and practical application. But in the short period we have available at present, I would just wish to outline some of the applicable and physical considerations to which I have been alluding.

"As you are aware at this juncture, Proxima b orbits very close to its sun, Proxima Centauri. Incidentally, I would merely repeat here, though we are sure you must know now, that we are using your own astronomers' and astrophysicists' nomenclature and established terminology for, amongst other things, our own heavenly bodies ..."

I've got to admit that I gulped somewhat when I heard Diva express her last few words.

"... The proximate orbit would mean, of course, strong and so-called *tidal forces* emanating from our sun. These are so powerful as to virtually *lock* our world to its red dwarf star. The consequence is that one hemisphere of our planet always faces Proxima Centauri, whilst the other is forever facing away from it. As a result of this unavoidable configuration, our globe experiences three quite different climate regions. Naturally, the Earth from whence you have come has varied climate zones, too. Such as the freezing temperature areas around its Arctic and Antarctic poles and the very hot equatorial and desert expanses, with comparatively more temperate stretches of land and water between these extremes.

"But you need to bear in mind that, on Proxima b, the equivalent of an Earth-year is just over eleven Earth-days. And because of its exactly circular orbit, we have nothing corresponding to Earth's seasons as such. The hemisphere constantly opposite our nearby, albeit fairly smallish star is nevertheless always brightly sunny and quite hot, of course… about ninety degrees Fahrenheit. The other flank of our planet is, by and large, perpetually very cold and dark. The broad sector, circling the planet between the consistently, so to speak, day and night areas, experiences a natural and ceaseless dawn or dusk light, with climatic conditions comparable with Earth's more clement and bearable regions. The major part of the one billion or so inhabitants of our world, though not all of them by any means, live and work in this quite extensive *Twilight Zone*, as you might possibly allude to it.

"It is in this most conducive, habitable region that you will be settled together, at least for an initial period of however long a necessary duration. Because there would be nothing to prevent any of you from transferring to another part of our world depending, of course, on your own wishes, requirements and circumstances. Unlike the melancholy if not dire situation of so-called humanity on Earth, on Proxima b we comprise one society, one big and contented family, however differently we, as individuals, might think on occasions… being *all for one and one for all.* Happily, we have learned to live harmoniously together.

"So… back to our star which, being rather smaller than yours and closer to our world than your Sun is to Earth, will appear some ten times larger than your sun would have looked to you on your former home planet. And even though Proxima Centauri is only twelve percent of the solar system Sun's mass, and just fourteen percent of its radius. But do not worry… you will soon get used to this situation. At least you will not need sunscreen, as ultraviolet light is hardly radiated by and from our star. Despite that absence of UV rays, we do have an abundant plant life, and of a whole variety of species… primarily in areas of the more amenable, climatic zones. But this is the case even in some other, and maybe less commendable, areas… for some elements of warm air can transfer, via winds wafting gradually across the equatorial belt, from the hottest to the coldest parts of Proxima b. And straddling ocean currents can convey spectrums of heat over the intervening divide.

"But like in relation to certain other specific physical matters, our developed science and technology has equipped us to ensure these, if you like, environmental add-ons or enhancements. And I might interject here that any dystopian, so-termed *Greenhouse Effect* has been consciously avoided, and from time immemorial to us. Similarly so, I should say, in connection with the important question of solar flares. These extremely energetic, solar storm emissions are not infrequent from our active red dwarf star, and could prove fatal for any planetary life forms. Naturally, your Sun also emits such flares from time to time. But nevertheless, and unlike Proxima b, the Earth rotates significantly... and, consequently, it possesses a natural magnetic field which shields its life forms from the inherent and potentially catastrophic dangers ...

"And so, in the distant past, we needed to create such a magnetic field, which has been operational now for a very long period of time in efficiently safeguarding life on the surface of our planet... including the preservation of our ozone layer and Earth-like atmosphere. And, thereby, we have established also a sturdy rampart against X-ray radiation and destructive stellar winds. Plentiful liquid water exists in the more habitable areas of Proxima b. Indeed, the warmth from Proxima Centauri has given rise to lovely seas, oceans and lakes, some straddling the equatorial band from the bright hot side to the dark cold side. But the hemisphere confronting our star, despite its proximity, is not so hot that evaporation and water loss would occur to a deleterious effect.

"You will no doubt be very glad now, after your eight-week voyage across the galaxy, to be settling, and soon, into the especially more comfortable context of our primary habitable zone. Part of the terrain concerned flanks a sea, one end of which is in the consistently *day* side of our world, whilst the other end just laps into the ever *night* hemisphere. In due course, this geographical arrangement could afford you a potential range of active or, if I may say so a tad whimsically, *inactive* leisure possibilities... from sunbathing, through sailing to skiing. Arguably, this could be akin, in order, to being in Eilat, on the Sea of Galilee or up Mount Herman... if you know Israel, as a large number of you will do undoubtedly. So enjoy.

"As I have mentioned, almost the entirety of Proxima b is inhabited... though, as you might expect, from large through medium to sparse degrees. I do not need to tell you, however, that there are rather more people residing in New York than Antarctica. So I conclude now by saying you should please rest assured that we have your wellbeing, happiness, success and prosperity on Proxima b well in mind. Please do not have any apprehensions or misapprehensions. Every aid and assistance you may require, within your novel environment, in establishing and developing a society integrated with ours, as you may or will wish, is to be forthcoming. And you will benefit from all the opportunities of doing your own thing, so to speak.

"Together, we can carry onward the adventure of life in our extraordinary universe, making and sharing fresh discoveries in the wonderful, infinite and eternal cosmos. If we, as you, might express it... *The sky is the limit!*"

Naomi and I almost felt like crying... for *joy!*

Twenty

"ARE WE there yet, Daddy?" Joshua and Sarah enquired of me, as often they did, in unison and with saucy smiles; and after I'd noted them winking at each other. I was seated opposite, with Naomi next to, them on one of the inevitably numerous and crowded shuttles that were ferrying passengers from the fleet of 'orbit-anchored' mother-ships to, apparently, very near our allocated abodes for the foreseeable future.

"As you *well know*, my little sweeties, we'll very shortly be landing close by our new home," their mother answered in my stead; and quickly too, having noted me shaking my head at the twins but with a wry grin doubtless skimming my cheeks. "So no being *clever clogs* with your father... else he might forget to collect our luggage, such as it is, before we disembark."

This time round, I nodded my head; though with a sluggish and pensive deliberation, pondering just how long our compact-bundle pick-up might take to complete. Next to no time, I concluded and pretty smartly. Being totally aware of the incredible efficiency – bearing in mind the several millions of *Jewish* passengers involved – experienced from the Alpha Centauri crews and teams throughout our staggering, trans-galactic voyage from Earth. The remarkably adept, if not perfectionist approach of our representative hosts spoke worlds – and maybe even more so than the almost unbelievable transit – about the ultra-far-advanced situation of their incredible civilisation. I couldn't help but continually think in superlatives about it.

"If you youngsters are implying you're feeling hungry," their mother added with a cautionary look creasing her features, "it's your own fault… I did tell you to eat more for breakfast!"

"No… we're *not* hungry for food, Mum," Joshua responded, manifestly for both himself and his sister. "It's just that Sarah and I want to be where we're going… we're becoming impatient to see our new home *already*."

Naomi and I exchanged smiley glances at his final word, with its customary Jewish take; and I guessed she would reply aptly to the boy, which she did in fact.

"Yes, we do know what *already* means… and don't we all wish to be at our destination *already*, you little scallywags!"

It was more than obvious to us, from the kids' immediately preceding and well-understood facial expressions, that they knew what their mother was about to call them before she uttered the amusingly derisory label. Naturally, thoughts of Diva and her mind-reading capabilities came to me again. But my thoughts arrived too soon… fortunately, about her telekinetic talents and nothing else.

"Joshua and I are wondering whether Auntie Diva will be meeting and greeting us when we finally get off this... this... oh, this... this *thingammywhatsit!*" my daughter enquired, though somewhat earnestly.

"Wouldn't think so, Sarah," I replied, for a change. "She's bound to be up to her eyeballs in helping to sort things out... far too busy to welcome us personally when we arrive. Unless she's got the ability, and perhaps she has, to say *Hello!* to *all* of the millions of Proxima b newcomers... and wherever they're likely to be setting foot in an extensive region of the planet so kindly afforded to us."

That mouthful seemed to have done the trick, because – until we did disembark from the shuttle vehicle – we didn't hear a further peep from the twins. Unsurprisingly, they had been sort of right in their speculation. When, at last, we did again step foot onto *terra firma*, Diva – and also her junior colleague, Ziva – were present to receive and heartily welcome our not inconsiderable group in a kind of endearing media format. Other Jewish immigrants from the large, inter-planetary fleet probably were being greeted similarly, but elsewhere in our allocated area of the habitable temperate zone, by other members of the organising teams.

I hadn't forgotten to collect from storage our meagre belongings, practical items largely – plus some valuables and heirlooms – that would serve the family, but only temporarily. Though the marvellously self-cleaning clothes, with which we'd been supplied, would be really useful to the family. But above everything, in this mixture of subdued excitement and natural apprehension, all passengers had been continually reassured – and, indeed, were now almost entirely confident – that a mutually conducive 'society' would be in place relatively quickly to cater for all everyday and other needs and requirements of the incoming Jewish settlers. During their transit across the Milky Way, and as Naomi and I understood it, countless meetings – and by various extraordinary, organisational means and methods of compilation – had been held between innumerable former service providers, professional and otherwise, on Earth and certain appropriate and broadly equivalent participants in Proxima b *society*.

So, undoubtedly, numerous and relevant discussions had occurred, involving a long list of such suppliers including bankers, lawyers, accountants, administrators, property developers, builders, architects, surveyors, estate agents, manufacturers, retailers, transport specialists, academics, teachers, surgeons, doctors, dentists, opticians, nurses, age and disability practitioners, faith leaders, scientists, technologists, technicians, designers and artists, horticulturalists, sports people, media operatives, entertainers, hoteliers, food and drink specialists, leisure experts – not necessarily in any particular ranking – together with many other requisite elements of a flourishing 'society'. And one enabled to work in determined harmony – as that of Proxima b had learned to do – for its future happiness and prosperity. I hoped we people from a sadly divided and conflicted Earth could achieve that Utopian state of affairs, too.

In the meantime, the family were to be found amidst lengthy lines of, now happily ex-spacecraft, passengers moving directly from our shuttle on a neat kind of near-horizontal escalator. We progressed through a light, airy though attention-grabbing, opalescent-opaque tunnel; and then into a huge, brightly illuminated and − happily not literally − breathtaking sort of reception hall. Its ceiling towered above us, and there were numerous exposed floors riding high.

Being fairly proximate to the front of the seething queue of Jewish humanity, and having just ridden a type of elevator-stairway gradually upwards, we found ourselves assembling on the first of the many but well-separated floor-levels. All of them were shielded by opal-lit, protective barriers from the ever-increasing plunge the higher you were located in this colossal structure. No windows of any category appeared to be present in this enormous edifice. That seemed to reflect the fact there hadn't been any 'port-holes' or whatever − at least for the passengers, so far as we were aware − either on the mother-ships or in the subsequent space shuttles to our new home planet. The appearance of a big and lofty dome high above the, I supposed, atrium − and of the interior's slightly curved walls − were ubiquitously reminiscent of the translucent, but not transparent material of the lead-in tunnel's glowing constitution.

After a reasonably brief wait − during which exceedingly welcome and very tasty liquid and solid refreshments were supplied to the so sizeable gathering by a unique and virtually indescribable technique – we exited our storey through a now revealed passageway. Then we stepped directly into an apparently further form of transport, the exterior design of which we couldn't know. Naomi and I gazed with resignation at the kids, half expecting another cheeky *Are we there yet, already*? It never came... but the twins did look, and quite understandably, really sleepy-eyed; we didn't feel so wide-awake ourselves. Once our travel batch was duly installed, we were off again. But I couldn't tell what type of vehicle – land, air or even water – we were now row-seated silently within. What we did know, because we were duly informed gleefully, was that this would be the final stage of our transfer from Earth to our ultimate goal... the neighbourhood where we would now be residing alongside other brethren from around the world we all once inhabited.

After moving off, it seemed to take mere moments – all on board the somewhat anonymous transport delighted in discovering – to attain our new home within the donated settlement territory. As we stood, on disembarkation and for the first time in several weeks, in the open air on firm ground and in a comparably breathable, Earth-like atmosphere, I'm absolutely certain that not a single one of us Jewish men, women and children could believe our boggling eyes ...

Twenty One

THAT NIGHT, I was lying beside Naomi in a double bed... yes, a bed! Both of us were stretched flat on our backs, heads resting on firm pillows and eyes staring up at the whitish ceiling. The bedroom... yes, the bedroom was illuminated softly, and almost romantically, by dimmable bedside lamps. No doubt akin to the millions of our fellow Jewish newcomers to Proxima b, we were somewhat traumatised – though not in any adverse way – by flashbacks to the environment we found ourselves standing within when walking off the concluding conveyances to our new dwelling place. And this after leaving the astoundingly huge, inter-planetary mother-ships that had transported us to the Alpha Centauri star network from the Solar System's Earth.

Neither my wife nor I – and both of us had made our own extraordinary, but time-travel voyages some years earlier – could get to sleep for the astonishing images criss-crossing our very conscious, insomnia-wracked minds. We were totally silent, aside from some heavily reactive breathing at times; and we hadn't spoken to each other since before slumping onto the crisp, brilliant white sheets a while back, and with the hope of some ultimately reviving shut-eye. Certainly, it wasn't the sexily low-key lighting that was keeping us from our well-deserved slumbers. And for sure, I – and doubtless my loving spouse also – harboured no lascivious desires in our current states of mind. There would've been no cerebral space for them, in any event.

Rather monopolising my own senses was the scene that had confronted my disbelieving eyes – which had perused many a phenomenally futuristic, sci-fi novel – on disembarkation at our prior-allocated, residential locale. But all of a startling sudden, I nearly jumped out of my skin and erupted from the comfortable bed! Naomi had actually started speaking. Not something that, normally, would've provoked such a dramatic reaction on my part; though, at least, moderately explicable in the then non-plus circumstances. As my ticker began to re-acquire its former beat mechanism, and I calmed down a little, my wife's words found a devoted hearing. Apparently, she'd noted that, in my temporarily befuddled condition, I'd missed her first utterance.

"Again… do you know what, David?" she re-started.

"W-What …?" I kind of mumbled.

"Utterly surprisingly, even stunningly," she went on, nudging me so that I turned my head to see her glowing eyes, "I was more gob-smacked by my surroundings when we landed here earlier, than when I arrived in twenty-first century Cambridge from medieval Cantabrigia! Despite some of the things we've been told, I was expecting to be totally overwhelmed by the sheer futurism of our new dwelling place."

"I can well comprehend that, Naomi," I responded in, I was sort of glad to note, a fairly even verbal keel. "That had been my expectation, too."

"The spacious and Earth-like, green lawns we set down on were lovely and welcoming, and the personal feeling seemed so normal," she remarked as I attempted, rather awkwardly, to nod from my reclining position.

"And that sense of utter familiarity," my wife added, "was so amazingly reinforced by the variously lofty, superbly designed and, again, Earth-like apartment developments circling the park and extending well beyond."

"I couldn't agree more," I said, again peering directly upwards but with a grin. "So here we are, on the top floor of this excellent, state-of-the-art, modern building with our darlings Joshua and Sarah sleeping soundly in their own separate bedrooms… absolutely unbelievable!"

"Pleasingly, the twins have been really good… and, seemingly, equally fascinated by what they've seen here," Naomi commented. "They deserve their rest… not that we don't, of course!"

"What about the fantastic vistas we enjoy from up here, and near the heavens?" I enquired, smilingly.

The views from the windows of our attractively furnished, lounge-dining room were excellent. For some reason, they reminded me of Tel Aviv; but I couldn't quite put my finger on the reasoning or impulse. Gazing from our flat's height across what appeared to be an Earth-style, post-modern metropolis, we could perceive not only very lofty buildings but also, beyond gaps between them, numerous rows of houses and what gave the appearance of shopping precincts. All interspersed with what looked like tree-fringed parks and gardens; and inter-crossed with what appeared to be streets and roads, though we couldn't spot any motorised vehicles of whatever kind. Early days as yet, we supposed.

Above all, and probably, my comparative reminiscence of Israel's trendy coastal city was prompted by the expansive, water-side location of our new Proxima b conurbation. I guess this could've reminded me of Tel Aviv's location beside the Mediterranean. And even though, as we understood it, our habitable area – within the planet's equatorial temperate zone – had, as did this sea straddling it, extensive very hot and very cold regions flanking it. I imagined that those of the incoming Jewish population desirous of a more Med-type – as opposed, of course, to an Arctic or Equatorial – climate, might prefer to holiday in, or perhaps move permanently to, the rather warmer end of the expansive and lake-like water-feature, if practicable at any point… in time or place.

"The views are wonderful," Naomi readily confirmed. "As is the weather we enjoyed outside for a while… and the sky, too, for that matter."

We'd spoken about the *sky* as we walked, utterly bowled over, around our delightful and highly liveable-in, three-bedroom flat. The Earth contemporary-style apartment boasted a master with en-suite, a family bathroom, a kitchen and a spacious through lounge-diner. Naomi and I had gazed, thoroughly smitten, through its picture windows and upwards to the heavens. Naturally, we'd first registered the sky and the calibre of illumination embracing our environs when leaving our transport in the neighbouring park. It had been explained – and to all the mother-ship fleet's passengers early in their galactic voyage – that a technologically advanced, improvised scheme of diurnal light and relative darkness would mirror the Earth's day and night modes for the millions of new residents in Proxima b's habitable zone; and, at least, for the foreseeable future.

We could hardly credit the commendably empathetic lengths of superb preparation the Alpha Centauri leaders had put in motion for us Jewish escapees from Earth. And having also the ultra-benevolent aim that we, as the *aliens*, shouldn't be completely flummoxed – to our psychological disadvantage, and to say the very least – on our arrival. Even so, we were thrilled to witness, at a time between the artificially-lit skies above us, the awe-inspiring sight of a natural and beautiful, twilight phenomenon.

"You've said it all, Naomi," I opined, reaching for her arm and gently manoeuvring so that we were in a more frontal embrace. "But we should really be utterly lost for words… just like we were when sliding into this bed, so pensively, a while ago."

My wife lifted a hand to stroke my exposed cheek.

"Well, let's get lost for words again …" she murmured, kissing me tenderly on the lips, "by trying to get some sleep now."

I nodded wistfully.

"After all," she continued, "when we awaken from our hopeful slumbers, it will be the extraordinary yet ostensibly normal beginning of our new lives on Proxima b."

I delighted in Naomi's then warm and loving mouth contact.

"Goodnight, my darling," I whispered, freeing her body from my clutches and allowing my beloved wife to rest back on her pillow.

Then I allowed my eyelids to drop; as, undoubtedly, she did hers. But not before she repeated my closing words.

Twenty Two

NAOMI AND I awoke with a terrifying start. We sat up straight and sudden, the duvet sliding instantly to the polished wood floor. There was a huge amount of banging, the target of which seemed to be the front door of our apartment; and which we could hear deafeningly through the closed portal of our bedroom. Our stricken ears were also picking up much shouting accompanying the front door walloping; though, at our location in the flat, we couldn't make out what was being hollered.

My wife and I were staring at each other with expressions of horrified non-comprehension when we almost leapt from our skins. All of a sudden, the bedroom door burst open. But, thankfully, it was only the twins – in their colourful jimjams and bawling their heads off, understandably – that flew into our room. They hurled themselves onto the bed to hug us tightly, Joshua with his mother and Sarah with me.

"W-What's h-happening?" my daughter screamed, then buried her tear-moist face into my striped pyjama top.

"W-We're r-really s-scared!" the boy cried out, virtually in tune with his sister's shrieked query, whilst lifting his head slightly from his mum's dark nightwear.

"We don't know what's going on, kids," I responded, forcing myself to maintain a level and parentally responsible stance – if that's what it amounted to – in the furore. "But let's get organised and try to find out, eh?"

Naomi and I slipped hastily from the bed, gently pulling one or other of the twins with us. My instant thought was that she and I should get dressed quickly, and before approaching – if we did, hesitantly – the apparently strong and secure front door, which was still being hammered severely. For certain, we needed to seek some understanding of the assault on both our woodwork and our eardrums. It was clear that Naomi and I were just as frightened and nonplussed as the offspring. What could be happening... and why? Whatever the totally out of the blue and intimidating rumpus was all about – and, frighteningly, so soon after the peaceful and friendly welcome to this new world – it could've been involving only us in the building... or maybe not.

I was aware of the artificially light sky filtering through our bedroom curtains, but didn't feel we had the luxury of time to open them and gaze through the window high above ground-level. Not that, necessarily and for that reason of height, we would've espied anything significant related to the persisting noise of combined thumping and raised voices. The kids were still panicking close around our legs; and we definitely had to get 'with-it' as soon as possible. But before we had the chance to do that, a real thrust of terror erupted from our senses! The four of us had just emerged into the hallway of the flat when, in a mind-shattering split second, the front door kind of exploded inwards.

The family froze with an absolute horror that riveted us to the spot. Though we should've better ducked down to avoid the shrapnel of sharp wood splinters and fragments flying towards us. Then, as one unit almost, we began screaming when into the hall rushed what appeared to be two terrifyingly grimacing, black-uniformed and helmeted storm-troopers carrying what looked to me like – and doubtless were, of course – futuristic sub-machine guns! Even the twins' compact eyes were bulging manically, with their little jaws agape and vocal cords at once squeezed into utter silence at the grotesque, unbelievable and cerebrally numbing sight confronting us now. We cowed quickly against the wall.

What is happening? I just managed to mutely ask myself, but with some emphasis. My silent question led instantly to another, incredibly personal interrogatory. Had we and all our fellow Jewish, galactic voyagers to Proxima b been led into a disastrous *trap*? I couldn't... I couldn't grasp intelligently and credulously anything that was entering my mindset. Surely my good and long-time friend Diva couldn't have been part and parcel of such an horrendous trick, deception, ruse, scam... call it what you will! No, it really couldn't be... *could it*? I pondered frantically, whilst beginning to tremble uncontrollably.

But then, as the beyond menacing invaders of our new home started to prod us brutishly – and even the ultra-terrified children – with their vicious 'sci-fi' weaponry,

171

they also commenced shrieking words that I knew of, that caused me almost to vomit and that deeply assailed my emotions, as well as my religion, in a way that left me unable to create meaningful utterances.

"Juden raus!… *Juden raus!*" the storm-troopers yelled at the tops of their harsh and guttural voices.

I could make out similar threatening sounds reverberating around the relatively spacious, internal communal area beyond the now open and smashed doorway of our flat. Very strangely, the German language was being used, translating to English as 'Jews out!' But why was it being used, for heaven's sake? Was the 'Master Race' on Proxima b endeavouring to be devilishly evil and nastily mordant at the same time? Joshua and Sarah, so sadly petrified, couldn't possibly have understood the infamous connect; or so I believed. But I was undoubtedly wrong about that – as I ought to have realised earlier – on hearing my son whispering nervously to his sister: "Why are they shouting, 'Jews out'… and to us, now?"

As we were brutishly shoved and prodded into the communal space, for sure Naomi – whose cheeks glistened with tumbling tear globules – and I did believe we knew the answer to Joshua's question. From documentary films, movies and history newsreels shown on television and other media screens, both of us were recalling – without doubt, but with manifest horror – jackbooted Nazi troops and black-uniformed SS driving Jews from their East European ghettos. Onwards they were marched, with many being shot to death cold-bloodedly en route to the railheads. There they would be packed into foul cattle-trucks for transportation to the Nazi death camps, such as the notorious Auschwitz-Birkenau, where they would be the howling victims – thousands at a time – of Zyklon-B asphyxiation in its gas chambers.

As we were forced down the broad stairway of our towering residential development, joining up with other terror-struck Jewish residents – families and otherwise – from each succeeding lower floor level, I couldn't fully absorb or make acceptable sense of what was taking place. But as I carried Joshua – and Naomi, Sarah – down the increasingly and unimaginably overcrowded stairway, a dreadful notion entered my already crammed head. Just as Hitler's Nazis had, and to keep them calm, deliberately misinformed the Jews, who were about to be deported, that they were being transported for 'resettlement' outside the war zones, so – and I couldn't credit that I was thinking this – it could well be that we'd been spun a yarn, too.

Broadly likewise, we Jews would – by being brought across the galaxy to the Alpha Centauri star system – be made to feel safe and secure from an anti-Semitic and potentially cataclysmic and fatal denouement for the Jewish people on Earth. But the truth, seemingly, was turning out to be something different entirely. Never could I have believed that Diva and her people were anti-Semites; and nor could I have understood what the motivation might've been for such Jew hatred on Proxima b. Not the least because she'd saved Naomi and me from certain death at the hands of violent anti-Semites in medieval Cantabrigia.

As we all stumbled our way downwards on the now heaving staircase, I began to speculate about the veritable rationale for my needing to have sex with Diva as a pre-condition for a time-travel adventure back to Cambridge of the 13th century. Perhaps the projected and focused studies of the human embryo, and the early stages of development after the birth of our lovely twins – which Diva had mentioned as relevant – were designed to do no more than ascertain the most suitable method of killing rapidly all those millions of Jews who would likely decide to emigrate, or rather flee from a world tragically falling apart for them.

Everyone more or less directly in front and behind us on the hundreds of steps – we could hear, and with emotion – were sobbing their hearts out… the old, the young and all age groups between them. Someone, somewhere ahead of us in the human deluge, cried out suddenly.

"We were duped… the bastards!" came the words, then the sentiment: "And we fell for it again, fools that we were and are!"

Immediately after that, we heard loud screams echoing around the claustrophobic walls, followed by flashes of piercing light. And an invisible someone, from the same direction down the seemingly never-ending well of a stairway, shrieked in an utterly horrified tone of voice:

"They're hurling out of the windows the old Jews they've just killed!"

What could we do? How could we react? How might we save ourselves? But these were totally useless questions.

It was impossible... there was no way of escaping our destiny, whatever that would be. Now we realised this happening to be an inescapable state of affairs. All that the flood of people, moving inexorably and hellishly downwards, could do was increase the volume of their pitiful howls at what fate appeared to have in store for them. Naomi, myself and the kids were doing nothing more, nor less, than be part of the helter-skelter of Jewish residents being compelled viciously to hasten down through the lofty building by the look-alike and sound-alike Nazi storm-trooper guards.

How, again for heaven's sake, could all that was befalling us have come about? And what were we, in fact, heading towards? My internalised queries were almost strangling my brain of air, especially as I couldn't help but feel a certain degree of guilt in this matter. If only Diva were here and even just momentarily, I thought wildly and gaspingly, I would definitely have some pointed questions for her... and no mistake!

Finally, we vertical column of descending Jews reached ground level; and then were herded, en masse, to the familiar area where we'd been landed from our shuttles not that long ago. When we'd stepped off the transports, how could any of us have possibly imagined that, not much further ahead in time, we would be facing potential disaster and tragedy? As we were assembled brusquely on the tree-fringed swathes of lawn, surrounded by our heavily-armed sentries, I noted that many thousands of earlier arrivals on the expansive green site were being embarked on another fleet of huge craft, which were taking off skywards in swift succession. *Where are they headed*? I wondered, with a deeply heart-rending sense of unvanquished terror for my beloved family; and, indeed, for all my co-religionists in the same dreadful and terrifying situation as us.

Whilst still clasping a sorrowfully weeping Joshua tightly to my chest, I did my best to wrap an arm around Naomi's quaking shoulders. As she held onto our other sobbing child, her watery eyes and dreadfully pallid face told me everything my wife was emotionally experiencing, too. Soon we were being pushed aboard our allocated vehicle, which was already so full of my fellow Jews that we could barely breathe; and we all stood tightly packed together like alien sardines. Before we'd stepped aboard, I took what – I pondered scarily – might well be my last glimpse of the heavens. Through the lightness of the improvised *day* illumination, I could perceive the now pale hues of what would be the permanent and mesmerising twilight of Proxima b's equatorial region.

The flight took no time at all for the craft, within which Naomi, the twins and I were being crushed alongside the countless other passengers. Far from what I would've wished, I couldn't help thinking about the hell-like and lengthy journeys for deported ghetto and other Jews in their cattle-truck, train transports to the concentration and death camps, with so many of them collapsing and dying en route. So I expected that all of us shuttle inmates were, at most, glad – if such could ever be an apt word in the circumstances – we hadn't been subjected to that horror.

On our mass disembarkation, only Earth-minutes after rising into the sky, we found ourselves in an unbelievably extended, broad but closely bunched queue on what appeared to be a virtually endless platform-ramp of sorts. And, yet again, the awful Auschwitz-Birkenau image of train arrivals, through that distinctively evil-looking archway entrance at the most notorious of Nazi death camps, screened itself in my mind's eye.

Until Naomi, Joshua and Sarah – together with other women, babies and young children ahead of and alongside us – were separated from the men-folk and driven by the heartless, brutal and inhuman guards to join another queue that ran parallel to ours along the platform or ramp. To where or to what, I couldn't make out. It was too far to the front of us to discern precisely what was transpiring at the head of the columns of now wretched and psychologically broken Jews. I may've harboured a miserable but convincing idea of what was going on, based firmly on the irrefutable facts of history. Nonetheless, I just couldn't bring myself to accept the rigidly enforced and ominous segregation from my adored wife and children, whose facial expressions on being dragged screaming from my side were heart-crushing. To my possibly catastrophic peril – and likely without any thought on my potential fate for doing so – I made my difficult way through the throng of adult Jewish men, of all age groups, blocking the path to my darling family. Then and hurriedly, I sought to transit the few awkward metres that divided the column of adult males from that of the women, children, aged and disabled.

I was heading directly for Naomi and the kids, moving quickly forward to the nearest flank of their line to me. She and others became frighteningly aware of my approach, my wife with added horror and alarm. Why was I doing this? What difference could I make to the situation? Wouldn't I be making things so much worse for us? The searing questions raged through my head with nothing less than the hot speed of light. Not unexpectedly, and before attaining my objective – whatever that might've been exactly – one of the numerous, miscreant guards ran up and dug me in the ribs with the somewhat sharper end of his weapon. I cannot describe my last quick glimpse of Naomi as I fell and hit the ground, an aching body turning involuntarily to lie outstretched on its back. I peered upwards in terror, and just as I was expecting the bestial thug of an anti-Semite to finish me off with a hail of bullets… I awakened shuddering from my nightmare, to find Naomi standing at my side of our bed and prodding me in the ribs.

"You've been snoring horribly and it's time to get up now, David!" she declared. "Diva's joining us for breakfast… Remember?"

Twenty Three

NAOMI WAS taking the twins – and somewhat earlier that particular morning than would be, subsequently, the normal time for departure – for the first day at their allocated local primary school, when Diva arrived at our flat. So my wife wasn't able to join us for breakfast after all. Of course, when the doorbell rang at the arranged hour, I knew it was Diva; it was she who'd requested the get-together, for whatever reason. We were happy to oblige... Naomi and I owed her so much that we would've been prepared to do virtually anything for her, or so I thought.

I opened the door to our apartment, an action which – happily, only for a fleeting moment or two – brought my horrendous nightmare to a now fully conscious mind. And I saw at once that Diva was accompanied, and somewhat unexpectedly, by her younger and equally attractive colleague Ziva. Whenever I would hear the names Diva and Ziva, I couldn't help but recall the lovely, mountain-embraced town of Riva at the northern shore of Italy's beautiful Lake Garda, which my ex-wife and I had visited on a couple of occasions during our long marriage. It made me wonder, a trifle whimsically, whether it was very likely that the name Riva was taken by at least one of Diva's other team members. Although, quite often, I felt like enquiring about that possibility, I never did. In any event, Ziva was very welcome to visit our flat; and it wasn't that we didn't possess – and quite amazingly so – enough coffee and other breakfast refreshments in our kitchen for the additional guest.

The three of us exchanged smiles, though Ziva's appeared a little edgy, as I greeted the familiar faces on my doorstep. Promptly, I led the pair along the hallway towards the lounge-dining room with a welcoming "Make yourselves at home, please"; but not before closing the, thankfully, solidly pristine and secure portal of a front door. On joining the indigenous women in the sitting-room area, I could see they were now comfortably ensconced on the settee. As I pondered momentarily on the question of why Diva had brought Ziva with her that morning, the much longer known-to-me citizen of Proxima b was the first to speak.

"Don't worry about making us any breakfast, David," she said. "We're not hungry... though a black coffee would go down very well, eh Ziva?"

Her sofa neighbour nodded, somewhat self-consciously I thought; and just giving me the impression she was entertaining something special on her mind.

"No problem, Diva," I replied, directly to her; though I glanced quickly at a quiet Ziva before heading for the kitchen. "I'll be back quite shortly."

It took little more than my vague time estimate to prepare the caffeine shots and return to my guests with a smallish tray of steaming cups. Such a simple brew-up would become an inevitably 'without thought' routine eventually. But during that early period after our arrival within the Alpha Centauri star system, it seemed – with a full awareness – thoroughly far-fetched to be making such a hot beverage; and just as if I was back in our Cambridge flat. Naturally, that wasn't the only kind of act which made our new planetary home, trillions of kilometres from Earth, so unbelievably and ambivalently peculiar in those early days after setting foot on it. In the alien context, having the utility of hot and cold water pouring from a tap – and whether for drinking, washing, bathing, showering or cleaning of any sort – was almost beyond human acceptance of its feasibility and plausibility. But we shouldn't have laboured under any sense of denial that the long-time inhabitants of our 'New World' knew all about water. I placed our piping hot 'Americano' coffees on the low table between us, put the tray on its under-shelf then sat down on a comfy armchair facing my two guests.

"I've no doubt, David, you're wondering why I asked for this meeting with you this morning," Diva said. "And why I've brought Ziva with me …"

I nodded in a kind of acquiescent way, and she continued.

"And even though you know we know what you're about to say at any immediate time, please do say it… ok, David?"

"Ok, Diva," I responded, possibly with the hint of a qualified smirk.

"At this point, I also need to say that we knew, of course, that Naomi would be occupied taking Joshua and Sarah to their new school... and for the duration of our visit."

I must've frowned with some perplexity; and silent Ziva's blank expression was quite mystifying, too. The two youngish females, eye-catching even aside from their figure-hugging tunics, must've known I was about to ask what it was they wished to discuss that wasn't for my wife's ears also. And I did put the question to them, but not anticipating that Ziva would break her quietude and answer me.

"Maybe we could come to that point a little later ..." she remarked evenly and, intriguingly, as if she had some especial involvement in its explanation.

"I agree with that, of course," Diva said, after taking a quick sip of her coffee. "But first let me just ask, David, how you, Naomi and the children have been getting along after your recent arrival here?"

I accepted a need for patience regarding any material reply to the significance of my spouse's absence from this coffee break; and, doubtless, it would've been pointless to press the matter.

"It's been really astonishing, Diva," I said. "It may be impossible for me to find the words, let alone express them, to describe how we feel about this our new abode on Proxima b. But I think I have to try... the climate, the environment, the huge amount of construction work that's been put in place for our benefit, the convenient availability of nearly everything we've been used to having and enjoying, the almost instant establishment of every good, necessary and useful aspect of society, from professional to artisan, from industrial to commercial, from primary to advanced education, from health services to provision for those with special needs... I feel now that I could go on and on, but I do believe you understand fully what I'm seeking to say. Everything is so incredibly amazing, not least the matter of full employment, with almost everyone working at what they were doing on Earth... really mind-boggling and so much appreciated, especially regarding the Jewish religion aspects... I hope we can show our gratefulness to all on Proxima b, and in a meaningful way, at some future point... And I'm certain that all my fellow immigrants feel the same way about things... But, for now, I do think I should stop babbling on..."

"It's really good to hear what you've been telling us, David," Diva said with a smile. "We want all our new fellow inhabitants on this planet to be productive and more than content here... and that has been, and continues to be, our first priority."

"T-That comes over so clearly, Diva," I commented with, seemingly, a touch of poignancy in my tone of voice. "If only all the people on Earth were as thoughtfully responsible, and as dedicated, in showing goodness and kindness to others as the benevolent population of your, and now thankfully, our world... Sadly and unfortunately, many millions of those now living on our former planet have learned nothing from the dire lessons of its, to say the least, long but extremely disturbed history …"

Diva picked up her cup again and, before imbibing, she said:

"Thank you so much for the very welcome sentiments you've expressed to us, David… they're much appreciated, and we're so glad we've been able to help. Having stated that, it wasn't only our Proxima b team that had arranged, or brought about, all the necessarily contributing elements of your new home. On the voyage here, and as I'm sure you well knew, innumerable productive meetings and discussions were held apropos what was needed to be in place for a fully-functioning society including, of course, a wide-ranging and non-politically inclined committee. This body would be designed impeccably for the role of overseeing and administering, with any requisite assistance from us, the extensive territory you've been accorded… but without prejudice, of course, to future mobility on the planet."

"And I do know that you and your team, and all others concerned with our well-being and welfare and who hold such concern in their hearts, have our eternal gratitude," I said, noting that Ziva was draining her cup of coffee.

Diva had nearly finished hers; but mine was untouched and, anyway, probably stone cold now. Then I further noticed Diva giving a short, curt nod to her colleague, who reciprocated likewise.

"I think we can now come to the point you raised before," Diva said and, I thought, in a fairly serious tone. "Aside from wanting to hear the views on your early experience on Proxima b, here's the principal reason for arranging this meeting with you in Naomi's absence."

"Right, Diva," I said. "Fire away."

"It's quite a sensitive and personal matter, David," she went on, "and it will be for you to decide whether or not you mention to your wife what we'll be asking you to consider by way of helping us in a particular manner."

As Diva spoke, I espied some fidgety hand movements on Ziva's part. Diva's reference to "helping us" not only reminded me of my own words, slightly earlier, about some day showing our appreciation for the aid so benignly and wholeheartedly given to my people. Also, it caused me some apprehension about the kind of "sensitive and personal" help being sought.

Diva went on:

"I trust you can remember our sexual liaison, David …" she said.

When she spoke those two unexpected words – "sexual liaison" – I'm fairly certain that I gulped significantly and began to blink rapidly. Apart from this activity, I felt riveted to the spot as my one-time, functional paramour continued speaking.

"…back in Cambridge and a while ago. And also, I hope you would undoubtedly recollect the motivation behind my approach to you on that intimate relationship which led, of course, to the births of your darling twins, Joshua and Sarah."

At that moment, my mental capacity permitted me to remember but not to speak. Then, though gradually, I found my tongue. Diva was obviously waiting patiently for me to actually express my thoughts.

"W-Why are you reminding me of all this now?" I managed to enquire, maybe cheek-reddening a tad; and especially so, as a third party was present.

I could detect that Diva was harbouring guiltily a bit of a saucy grin, so probably I *was* blushing slightly.

"It's because we would like you to do it again ..." she replied, "But not with me this time."

As my one-time and one night, intimate partner uttered the last words, she glanced at Ziva for a moment then everything instantly fell into place for me. For a few moments, I was struck dumb again. But to avoid slipping into numbed disbelief, I needed actually to say something quickly and determinedly.

"I-Is this the reason for your colleague's presence here today?" I queried unnecessarily, but bearing in mind again Diva's clear request that I state what I'm instantly thinking.

"Only in one sense," she said, and with another noticeable little leer at me.

"And in what sense is that?" I responded, but without due thought.

It should've been quite clear to me that Diva didn't mean Ziva and I should have, and imminently, sexual intercourse in my apartment. I shook my head, an act aimed primarily at my foolish self. Coincidentally, Diva reacted likewise and,I suspected, with a similar target.

"As you would expect, David," she said, supplementing her action, "Ziva would need to know, personally and directly, your answer to our request."

Ziva and I exchanged – perhaps understandably – non-expressive looks, as I endeavoured to formulate some material phrases to deal with this suddenly mind-crunching, if not explosive situation presented to me... and very early on in my 'New World' context.

"But Diva, I was a *singleton* when you put your well-rationalised, intimacy proposition to me in Cambridge and back a while," I began. "I was a divorcee at the time... but now the equation includes Naomi, whom I love very much."

Diva replied at once.

"I don't need to tell you, David, that this exercise doesn't feature or affect the concept of *love*," she met my point emphatically. "It's just a natural continuation of the project we started some years ago, and which is felt will provide us with additional information and research data, the study of which could further assist us in helping your people, now really here on Proxima b, to live safe, long, full, productive and enjoyable lives."

I couldn't attack, or even fault, the logic that, without a shred of doubt, had assisted our rescuers, nay saviours, in making such phenomenally amazing and comprehensive preparations for our arrival and survival on our new planetary home in the Alpha Centauri star system.

"And what do *you* have to say about this matter?" I said, directing my question at Ziva.

She sat up straight from her reclining, though perhaps not entirely relaxed position on the sofa then re-placed her cup on the coffee table.

"It's not really for me to comment now," the admittedly appealing example of womanhood replied. "I was asked whether I would wish to volunteer for the project, and I readily did… my reasoning for doing so having been described precisely in the words used by Diva just before."

I nodded without more. But in the then prevailing quiet of the room, another pertinent interrogatory entered my brain cells. I turned to address it to Diva who, of course, was totally aware of its specific nature.

"But why select me again?" I enquired succinctly.

Diva smiled warmly at me.

"What do they say… 'Better the *little devil* you know'… eh, David?" she countered wryly.

Yet again, how could I challenge her common sense? Though I noted the given axiom's extra, *small*-like word supplied; as well as the stressed syllables to indicate, I felt sure, her intent to aver that I wasn't actually a *demon*.

Once more, I merely nodded.

"So what do you think about this proposal, David?" she added finally.

I reflected edgily for a moment or two.

"I trust you'll understand, Diva, that I can't give you an answer right away," I said evenly. "However, and in all the circumstances, I don't feel that I can give you an outright negative decision… But you may see why that makes me feel somewhat embarrassed, if not guilty. With hindsight, I can appreciate the reason for you not wanting Naomi present this morning. Though, I can tell you, she's a post-medieval and more relevantly post-modern, open-minded individual very prepared, and willing, to consider objectively all sides of a question. Nonetheless, though not without a noteworthy tinge of hesitancy, unease and trepidation, I'll need to discuss all aspects of your proposition with my wife... and I'll definitely do that tonight."

"Thanks, David, and we can't ask any more of you," Diva said empathetically, rising from the settee and taking Ziva with her. "We do note fully your justified thoughts and feelings in this matter... it's only that we want sincerely to aid your fellow new citizens of our planet to the best of our capabilities, and in all relevant respects."

I nodded, for the last time during that memorable 'breakfast' meeting then escorted the two ladies to the front door.

"We're sorry for putting you through all this, David," Diva added finally, "but we're certain you'll appreciate our motives for doing so. If anyone might be able to assist us further in our mission, we knew it would be you... and that you would accept the fact we aren't casting any aspersions by thinking such."

After Diva and Ziva had departed the flat, I slumped onto the sofa and buried my head in my hands.

Twenty Four

PREDICTABLY, WHEN in bed that night with Naomi – yes, Naomi – she asked me what Diva had wanted to talk about when she'd come visiting that day. My wife was interested to hear that Ziva had accompanied her to our flat. I wondered fleetingly why she hadn't enquired about the so-called 'breakfast' meeting earlier. But I kind of knew that she'd been rather preoccupied with thinking about how the twins were acclimatising to their new school, to which she'd accompanied them that morning; and that had meant her necessary absence from what turned out to be a very different sort of 'coffee break' get-together to that expected.

Admittedly, I harboured some reluctance, if not a conscientious doubt about informing Naomi about Diva's intimate proposal concerning Ziva and me. But, of course, I did tell her there and then… as I'd promised my Proxima b friend that I would do; and I always kept my vows. I possessed no real certainty as to how my second wife of several years would respond to the startling repeat request, even though – as I'd mentioned to Diva – I have clear knowledge and experience of Naomi's liberal attitudes. So I wasn't entirely surprised when she rolled over towards me in the bed then posed a rather particular question.

"I think that I understand, darling, but why didn't you offer to make a small donation... you know what I mean?" she asked evenly.

I may not have been taken completely by surprise regarding her poser. But I could've readily kicked myself, as a dutiful spouse, for not having thought to do what my undoubtedly broad-minded, free-thinking and, indeed, sensible wife was now suggesting. Perhaps I was so shaken by Diva's sudden and unanticipated request that I'd felt, in the instant, my brain – and for some undisclosed reason – to be incapable of a rational compromise offer for her consideration. I suspected that I was seeking, at least in my head and momentarily, to defend the lack of a loving husband's likely reply – taking into account my wish to be of grateful assistance to Diva and her colleagues, if possible – to what would constitute adultery.

My response to Naomi, as I swivelled to look into her probing eyes, was on the weak side.

"I believe that I understand too, darling... but why I didn't think of, and put forward, what you just mentioned escapes me."

The loving face, only a few centimetres from my own, smiled whimsically; and I felt, gratefully, a bit like I'd been let off the hook. I puckered my lips, and my wife followed suit with hers. Then I put my arms around her, held her to me in a close embrace then we kissed fairly passionately and lingeringly.

When we paused eventually, I said:

"Are you sure, Naomi?"

"I am," she replied at once, and without further comment.

After that succinct exchange, we made love.

*

The next day, I made media-contact with Diva and put the counter-proposal before her, mentioning that it was Naomi's idea and one that I should've had in mind when I was presented, early the previous morning, with a request to have sexual intercourse with Ziva. Noting my present marital status, I asked for the rationale supporting a decision not to put the proposition to me in the same way. A way of which I was more than confident that Diva knew would've been somewhat easier for me to take onboard and discuss with Naomi. Naturally, my friend had a ready and convincing answer to my tentative but, I considered, none the less justifiable enquiry.

"David," she began, "I was entirely aware of the situation, alternatives and possibilities. But I am sorry for maybe not being more sensitive to the circumstances… though there was a reasonable notion behind that. And perhaps I should not actually have brought Ziva with me, so that you and I could have spoken alone initially."

I was becoming curious.

"What was the *notion* of which you speak, Diva?" I wanted to know.

She paused for thought, but for just a moment or two.

"I am positive that Ziva will not mind if I explain to you that, after I had described to her my research-inspired love-making with an Earthman in Cambridge a number of years before, she had desired very much to have the same experience… it was nothing more than that, David."

I couldn't deny it was "nothing more than that". But, arguably a trifle belatedly, it did inspire me to wonder about the history of, and the current, reproductive procedures in the Alpha Centauri star system. I believe that a grin may've creased my features at that point. But all that I could bring myself to remark was:

"Thanks for that, Diva… but I am feeling a bit flattered to hear your explanation."

"So be it, David," she said. "I will contact you shortly in this specific connection, and I must emphasise that your important services would, as always, be much appreciated. And not only by the Proxima b team, but also by your brethren if they could know how our additional studies will help us to further assist them in so many technological and other aspects of their *New World*."

I nodded at the mouthpiece, and Diva added finally:

"But I do know, and can tell you David, that Ziva will be somewhat disappointed not to have had, looking back in due course, the benefit of a full experience opportunity in this matter …"

*

That night, after we slipped between the cool clinging sheets, Naomi and I began a conversation sparked by the reproduction process we'd agreed I could participate in at Diva's revised proposal; and following the submission at my wife's behest. Being fully aware of my sexual liaison with Diva, which had given us eventually our wonderful twins, Naomi had noted that our copulating session in Cambridge a while back – and despite the coupling being with an extraterrestrial – had been quite normal by Earth standards. At the time, and for the short period prior to the sex actually occurring, I'd speculated seriously about that topic. But knowing also that Diva – and, potentially, at least a proportion of her fellow inhabitants on Proxima b – could morph her facial features, I'd speculated about what else of a bodily nature could be transformed temporarily.

When I'd first encountered the 'alien', she'd taken on the convincing appearance of a Chinese woman; and then had become an Occidental. So I'd wondered, maybe understandably, what might be her true physical identity. And this subject was rather worrying to me, having in mind some Hollywood movies of the sci-fi genre which had featured other, and somewhat horrifying, galactic species. Nonetheless, my thinking had evolved and developed favourably in the direction of accepting that Diva and her kith and kin are, and fantastically, hominid in biological form and constitution. But this didn't mean necessarily that sex – whether, importantly, for the production of offspring or, if it featured at all in the equation, purely for personal enjoyment and satisfaction – on Proxima

Centauri's habitable-zone planet would be the same, in all respects, as for Earth humans.

Being a million years ahead of Earthlings in the science and technology stakes, in all significant fields and amongst other virtues and advantages, it seemed highly probable that Proxima b's biological and other sciences had, over millennia, come up with a radically different mode of sexual reproduction; and for reasons plausibly related to efficiency, viability, preventability and determinability... or whatever. And in such a way, and over an incredibly lengthy and generations-spanning age, which could've existed during the planet's earliest populated epoch as sexual intercourse – in the style that Earth males and females would manifestly comprehend – but which had fallen into desuetude, for whatever reason.

These several ruminations had figured in our intriguing and overwhelmingly speculative, bed-time discussion encouraged by Naomi raising an especial question with me.

"David," she started, "why do you think Ziva would be disappointed, as was suggested, not to have had a full sexual experience with you... one assumes of the Earth variety, as described to her by Diva, and in order to give birth in due course?"

Before I could reply at that initial stage of our subsequent exchanges, my wife added:

"And do tell Diva that any child or children resulting, as inexorably will be the outcome from this imminent reproduction exercise, should be given out for adoption by a couple who are unable sadly to have their own offspring. Though in the light of virtually miraculous, medical advances on this world, of which I'm pretty certain, such a pair might not have a problem in conceiving now."

"Yes, Naomi," I said, while nodding in agreement, "we do have our hands rather full and tied at the minute with Joshua and Sarah, bless them …"

My spouse nodded keenly, too.

"And, incidentally," I continued, "we know presently only of their extraordinarily inherited ability, but not from me, to read people's minds regarding what they're on the point of uttering. Of what other extraordinary capabilities or inherent skills they may potentially possess, we have no knowledge of at the present time …"

Naomi nodded again, perhaps more deliberately than enthusiastically.

"You know, Naomi," I went on, "way back in Cambridge and after the *intimate event*, I carried out some brief and limited research on the internet about what we've been talking about, generally speaking, and which included conjecture, supposition or guesswork by academics, scientists and others concerning the question whether possibly existing aliens engage, or not, in sexual activity of the kind pursued by human beings on Earth. But I was very attentive even when reading about the almost endless variety of ways by which creatures on our former home planet reproduce sexually. Some, indeed, are hermaphroditic… and, presumably in consequence, they can perform both sides of the reproductive process. Some of Earth's species are asexual, and don't need to indulge in sexual activity in order to create progeny ..."

It looked like Naomi was about to ask me a question.

"Please don't ask me anything, darling," I pre-empted her. "I'm not an expert in these delicate matters, but only a passable ignoramus."

My wife's slow nod was accompanied by a coy little smile.

"Of course," I carried on, "sexual intercourse and the admixture of genetic variations or DNA input can be extremely useful, maybe vital, in the evolutionary development of a species... especially as environmental challenges – whether climatic or otherwise – and surrounding circumstances can, and certainly do, alter or evolve across time. Change needs to be confronted and dealt with, often for the purposes of survival of the species. Whether or not the indigenous resident population on Proxima b have appetites for sexual intercourse, or none, I don't believe that anything here can be any stranger than what takes place amongst the varied species on Earth. Perhaps I should have a word or two with Diva on the subject... and justifiably, I feel, in view of my invited involvement in a reproductive process here. B–But n–needless... n–needless to s–say... only w–with your p–p–permission... m–my... m–my l–love ..."

"You have it, my darling... but no personal demonstrations from either side, ok?" Naomi responded instantly; though, at the same time, she was eyeing me oddly and with a wry grin. And her voice sounded to be quite far away.

"Naturally," she added, "I've noted Diva's altruistic motivation in all this… the researched outcomes and objectives of it being for the benefit of us tomorrow, and for our future generations. I take it that your trust goes along with …"

Apparently, she stopped speaking at that point; though I wasn't aware of this at the time, as I'd fallen fast asleep.

Twenty Five

NEXT MORNING the family enjoyed breakfast together in the flat. I hadn't previously gotten a chance to speak with the kids themselves about their new school, and how they were getting on there.

I was just about to do that, as we all sat round the table eating and drinking, when Joshua and Sarah said in unison:

"The school's great, Dad... so spacious, and with a lovely sports field attached... and our teachers are wonderful, too... so kind and inspiring."

"Well, that's very pleasing to hear," I responded, exchanging the usual resigned glances with Naomi.

"But we haven't exactly started our curricular lessons as yet, Dad ..." the boy added.

"Why's that?" I enquired looking at my wife, whose current expression implied that she wanted to tell me something.

"We suppose it's because the tutors are taking time to introduce us to our new surroundings, Dad," our daughter explained. "Groups of us are being led around the building, which has everything we need and more... And we've had some assemblies in the really large downstairs hall, where the headmistress has been trying to tell us about the wider environment, too. It's all so amazing, and taking time to sink in."

"Ok," I said, feeling quite proud, "but now tell us something we don't know."

The twins giggled, as I turned to Naomi. She was looking a tad preoccupied.

"Did *you* want to say something, darling?" I asked, with a touch of tetchy curiosity in my voice.

"Sorry, David," she said, "but it's just some personal news that, somehow, slipped my mind to tell you."

"What *news*?"

"Well, when I took the children to school yesterday," she went on, "it was confirmed to me by its office that I've been accepted as a part-time, classroom assistant. I'm so glad, and so are the kids. Aren't you, my little darlings?"

"We are... we are, Mummy!" they sang aloud in chorus mode.

"And I'm very happy for you, too, Naomi," I said with a smile, recalling that she'd applied for one of these posts when we were journeying across the galaxy in one of the fleet of mother-ships. "How often will you be working at the job, and when do you start?"

"I'll be in class every other school day," she replied, "and I'm starting today, in fact... so let's get a move on, kids. Your mother doesn't want to be late on her first day, does she?"

"No, Mum... you don't!" brother and sister declared, to wide grins from their parents.

When my family departed for their school day, of one kind or another, and while washing up the breakfast crockery and cutlery in the kitchen, I reflected on the kind of not so regular work that I would be doing. Contingency planning on the mother-ships, for our people's future on Proxima b, involved lengthy and detailed meetings, seminars and discussions within every imaginable category of profession, vocation and trade, etcetera. And all with the valuable, if not vital contribution and essential assistance of the Alpha Centauri teams, comprised of requisitely expert members in their various fields of operation.

Although I'd retired basically from the, literally, *world* of journalism, I really wanted to be able to continue being a writer for publication, as I had been in Cambridge and if possible; though on a rather reduced scale. So I participated in many relevant, potential media aspects en route to our new planetary home. I was delighted when it was resolved to found and publish a weekly Jewish newspaper for circulation throughout the territory we'd been allocated. An editor had been appointed, requisite staff had been engaged; and even before we arrived in the star system. I was really grateful to Mike, the much experienced editor, for recognising the numerous years of investigative journalism that had been my career path on Earth. He had no doubt, and I certainly agreed with him, that there would be so much of wide interest to write about as we settled into our extraordinary new world. And he considered there was unlikely to be a problem as regards commissioning me from time to time. Naomi, who'd been warmly encouraging in my hopeful efforts, was equally elated with the outcome for me. So I was awaiting patiently Mike's call about my first literary assignment for the pristine newspaper, which was to be given the banner title of *Jewish Centaurian*.

I'd only just finished putting away the cleaned and dried breakfast paraphernalia, when there was a ringing of the doorbell. Who might that be? I wondered. I wasn't expecting anyone to visit that morning. Wouldn't it be so coincidental and great, I thought, if it was a despatch from editor Mike with an early commission to pen a feature on some fascinating topic of compelling consequence to the paper's potentially huge readership?

Unfortunately, it wasn't such an, albeit kind of incongruous delivery at the apartment's front door. I accepted that confidently on opening the portal. On the threshold stood not a helmeted messenger but Ziva, who appeared to be unaccompanied. The charming young woman wasn't clad in black leather gear, but was attired engagingly in a neatly fitted, light blue, tunic-style dress hemming a few inches above her knees; and she sported a darker blue, leather-look shoulder-bag. She smiled wanly at me, and I reacted sort of in kind; though, I thought instantly and a little apprehensively: *What does* she *want now*?

"Good morning, Ziva," I greeted her in a sort of formal tone, but with an evident slice of inquisitiveness in my voice. "What can I do for you?"

"Can I come in please, David?" she responded. "I do *need* to have some time with you."

She needs to have some time with me, I speculated inwardly on her somewhat emphasised words. And I recollected immediately, if hesitantly, Diva's allusion to her colleague's *disappointment* at being denied an opportunity to have sexual relations with me. Was this the reason for her sudden and unexpected presence on my doorstep that morning? Without a shred of doubt in my mind, I knew she would be aware of Naomi's absence from the flat for much of the day. Was Ziva about to plead for me to have sex with her? But before any more sexily pertinent – or, maybe, impertinent – questions assailed my grey matter, however, she repeated her question.

"Can I come in please, David? Actually, I have something to give you... and there's an urgent necessity."

Somehow, I didn't feel staunch enough to deny the woman entry to our apartment, so I was presently inviting her inside. On beckoning her in then closing the door, and with a pulverising disinclination, I said achingly to myself: *Oh, my goodness! What am I letting myself in for?*

Ziva knew for where to head from her very recent one and only, previous visit alongside Diva. So that, when I entered the sitting-room soon after my visitor, she was ensconced comfortably on the settee already. She'd crossed her legs, resulting in the dress riding up to reveal a firmly curving and smooth thigh.

"Would you like a coffee?" I asked, gulping unavoidably at her alluringly and – I wondered – possibly invitingly revealed, upper leg.

She shook her head a couple of times.

"No, David," she added, vocalising her actions. "I don't have *that* desire at this moment."

Oh, my goodness! I thought. *And what* desire *does she have at this moment?*

"Please sit down beside me, David," she continued, with what I felt to be a sultry edge to her vocal cords. "I have something intimate to give to you."

Oh, my…

Before I could complete the reiterated and unspoken notion, Ziva grabbed my hand and drew me down beside her. I sort of slumped onto the sofa, released my digits from her firm grasp and sidled away from her body. She seemed to sigh deeply at my shifting manoeuvre.

Oh, my …

Then my eyes focused diligently on Ziva's shoulder-bag, which now sat on her lap. She straightened up, opened it and withdrew a beer-bottle-shaped packet.

"This is what I have to hand you, David," she said in, I considered, a gratuitously subdued voice. Then she gave me the package.

"What is it?" I enquired, rather foolishly with later hindsight.

"It's for your donation, David… Don't you remember?"

After a few shameful moments of pregnant pause, if I can put it that way, I nodded with absolutely everything – and I mean, everything – then falling into its rightful or wrongful place for me, and in the order of things.

"Please will you do the necessary now, David," Ziva virtually insisted, but with a not insignificant beam. "I need to get this container, with your much appreciated contribution, back to Diva... and as soon as possible."

I nodded again, disappeared into the bathroom and, about ten minutes later, returned holding the recomposed parcel and returned it to the delivery girl. She placed it carefully inside her bag then made to rise.

"Before you go, Ziva," I said, with a palm gesture suggesting she should resume her former seated position, "could I just ask you a few questions that have occurred to me since our last meeting?"

Thankfully, she sat down again.

"Please be quick, David."

"Will do, Ziva," I began. "Sorry if my queries are rather on the sensitive and delicate side but, first, can you tell me whether, on Proxima b, reproduction of your species is by sexual or other means? In asking, and I'm sure you know what I'm saying, I bear in mind what Diva discussed with you in this context."

"Other means," Ziva replied succinctly. "What's your next question?"

"Was reproduction ever sexual in the very long history of this planet's indigenous population?"

"Yes, David... but that was an extremely long time ago. Akin to your Neanderthals, and undoubtedly, it was likely to have been *nasty, brutish and short*, to re-coin a proverbial phrase I'm sure you know."

I nodded, followed by:

"So no romance involved, then?"

"No, just like other animals… instinctive is probably the most apt term. Next question, please, David."

"I'm guessing it fell into a sort of desuetude then, with your species' particular evolutionary process."

"You're right… without any orgasmic element, as Diva explained the process to me, there was a need for physical exertion or effort, but little point… Especially in light of advances in our physiological sciences across the countless millennia on this planet. Next one, please, David."

"So I'm taking it also there's no such thing as *love*, that is romantic love, on this planet?"

"That's correct… and whatever that Earth expression or essence actually and objectively means or involves."

"In a way," I went on, "I can see where you're coming from, literally and philosophically. As one of our ancient Greek philosophers once opined, *Love is neither equal nor durable*… so arguably, I suppose, what *is* the point?"

Ziva began to get up again.

"I need to be off right away, David," she urged. "But I would just leave you with this question. *Why do males have nipples?*"

What a weird enquiry, I thought. Maybe she was saying, maybe whimsically, that here was a point that was pointless; but was seeking to communicate some profound message about what we'd been talking about. Anyway, I left her query floating in the air, as she began to move towards the hall. Before she reached the front door, and just ahead of me, she turned.

"But, you know David," she added further and voluntarily, "even without sexual reproduction, we are very happy, respectful and with good motivation, and whatever the terminology is said to involve, in our lives and relationships. And we've been able to, and can still, transmit those virtues to our generations present and future."

In the moment, I decided to say something more.

"So we might say that *love*, in whatever sense it's used subjectively, objectively or otherwise by us former Earthlings, hasn't, doesn't and won't make your world go round ..."

Ziva nodded, with a minimal smile.

"Maybe that's been of some benefit... in a potentially indefinable way, and even for us," she commented.

"Thanks, Ziva... I'll let you go now," I said finally.

I reached around her to unlock the door, and she left the flat after very gently placing the dark blue bag over her shoulder.

Twenty Six

MUCH LATER that day, after our cheeky little ESP scallywags had retired to their beds, Naomi and I were sitting on the armchairs in our living room and drinking coffee. The lounge area did possess what would've passed on Earth for a flat-screen television, but it was actually imbedded into a wall. It had been so mounted when we'd moved into the apartment a short while back; but were told that we would be informed when the TV and radio services had been established, and that broadcasts were expected to be made very soon.

In truth, Naomi and I weren't at all put out by the absence of a glowing goggle-box to watch. Though, admittedly, it could've been useful to have had a news channel to keep us up-to-date with any developments and happenings in our Jewish settlement territory. Mike had mentioned to me that he hoped to publish a first issue of the *Jewish Centaurian* a comparatively brief time after our arrival on Proxima b, and which we looked forward to reading. In the current and believed brief absence of any media input to our lives, like on that night, Naomi and I could talk to each other; and which, we both agreed, would be a very good way for a husband and wife to pass their available free time.

She described for me her first day as a classroom assistant at the twins' school. It seemed like she'd relished the period of hours spent there; and, happily, the job was just as she'd expected it to be. Naomi definitely went along with our children's view that the teachers were marvellous and – since the curriculum teaching had commenced that day – had verified that opinion. But not only regarding the education staff members' speciality, educational subjects. Naomi also expressed her approval of the kosher meals served to everyone, including herself, in the lunch break.

My own input to our night-time chinwag wasn't, unfortunately, as straightforward as the wife's contribution. Of course, I spoke about Ziva's significant visit to the flat earlier that day; and I didn't feel too reticent about admitting honestly my untoward thoughts after she'd turned up, suddenly and unannounced, on the doorstep. During my narration of the early stages of that morning's exchanges with Diva's colleague, I seemed – according to Naomi – to be becoming a bit fraught and fragile. But she encouraged me, in her characteristically kindly and non-judgemental manner, to take it easy... the notions that had occurred had occurred, no problem; and what had transpired had transpired, again no problem. I thanked Naomi for her comforting and empathetic attitude.

We leaned towards each other, almost instinctively, and shared a brief kiss on the lips. This brought to mind my questions to Ziva concerning her species' reproduction process, to put no finer point on it, prevailing on Proxima b; as well as the rather mystifying elements arising in our one-to-one, Q and A session. I mentioned all this to an intrigued listener imbibing her black Americano. She did appear somewhat saddened to learn of the evolutionary details; but more particularly, or so it seemed, to hear of the absence of *Hollywood-style romantic love*. Possibly that was the dilemma, I countered... perhaps it's a too subjective concept, stirred or motivated by dubious life rudiments. Naomi seemed a trifle reluctant to accept that contention or analysis, whatever it amounted to. Though, like me, she was non-committal about the likely indigenous, Proxima b species' questionably 'cold' procedure of rationally and logically ticking boxes, or not, in forming permanent relationships or otherwise. Although, being a million years ahead of us former Earthlings, maybe they had learned something profound that we hadn't during our rather shorter evolutionary period. Whatever, Naomi and I decided to go to bed... and even though we weren't feeling that fatigued.

*

The next day, a non-working one for my wife, we resolved to register for membership at the local, orthodox and Ashkenazi synagogue and community that we'd heard had been established now; though we knew also that a formal dedication service was yet to be held. A Chief Rabbi for this grouping of Jewish houses of worship had been appointed, commendably and efficiently, as we'd voyaged across the galaxy on our mother-ships. Such had been accomplished similarly for the Sephardi, as well as the Reform, Liberal and Progressive movements now set up in our allocated, temperate region of the planet.

Naomi and I weren't very religious, generally attending the orthodox synagogue in Cambridge only on the High Holydays of Rosh Hashanah and Yom Kippur; but, occasionally, at other times of the year. On visiting our proposed house of worship that morning – and it was just a short stroll from our apartment development – we were able conveniently to meet with its salaried secretary. We signed the requisite documentation, and were officially welcomed by her as members of the new community. We'd set up a joint account at a local branch of the bank now established in the territory, so we could sign the equivalent of a monthly direct debit to meet our subscriptions. It was still so amazing to be able to do such mundane, Earthly things; and to have such commonplace, Earthly organisations in our so extraordinary new world. In fact, a new area currency had also been introduced, with the so-called *proxima* being a relative parallel to the US dollar, the British pound sterling and the EU euro.

Of course, we would also have burial rights included via our subscriptions; and we were advised that the community's cemetery had been created now, as a vitally necessary priority, in a level area just inside a fringe of our territory. The middle-aged secretary informed us that – inevitably but sadly, of course – there had been a number of interments already; and she added that all the burials had been as a result of the deaths, by natural causes, of men and women well over the age of eighty, with one deceased lady being in excess of 100 years old. On hearing this, I did speculate on whether, as an outcome of probably benefiting in due course from Proxima b's highly advanced scientific and medical provision, our human or possibly evolving bodies would enjoy an even greater longevity.

After Naomi and I had signed up, the busy full-time secretary nevertheless kindly escorted us on a quickie tour around – what, I suppose, we former Earthlings would call – a 'modern' building. The beautifully designed, traditional synagogue itself, having a seating capacity for several hundred congregants, boasted also lofty, arched windows, a ladies' gallery, a simple but attractively fashioned *Aron HaKodesh* or Ark – within which were housed the *Sifrei Torah* or mantled and silver accoutred, sacred scrolls of the Law or Five Books of Moses – and a raised dais of a *bimah* with its reading desk. Upstairs, we were shown some rooms to be used for the *cheder* or Hebrew and religion classes for children up to *bar-* and *bat-mitzvah* – or coming of – age being, respectively, 13 and 12 for boys and girls. The spacious main hall – for weekly *kiddushim* or blessed refreshments after the *Shabbat* or Sabbath morning service and for other purposes, such as family *simchahs* or celebrations of one kind or another – was in the basement.

Naomi and I thanked the secretary for her time and the tour; then told her how impressed we were with the newly dedicated structure, and with how rapidly it had been provided for the community by all those concerned. Our guide noted that she couldn't have agreed more with us, adding – and before saying farewell at the building's imposing front portal – that she looked forward to seeing us at services. On leaving the forecourt, I doubted that such would be too often. But as we walked back home, reflecting gladly on our experience that morning, we decided on attending – with Joshua and Sarah, of course – the next Shabbat morning service in the synagogue in a couple of Earth-days hence. And we were so pleased that we did.

On the day itself, Naomi and the kids occupied seats in the gallery, as I took up a place in the spacious downstairs, men's section. We arrived reasonably early because, as expected, the synagogue became filled eventually almost to capacity. But we didn't expect this to be the case on every future Shabbat, and by a long chalk. The youngish and trimly bearded *chazan* or cantor, originating from a notable New York community, led the service with his wonderful tenor voice and customary Shabbat liturgical music, composed by renowned Jewish composers of Central Europe in the 19th and early 20th centuries. He was supported by a large group of excellently conducted, male choristers that sang from the special choir stall constructed thoughtfully above the Ark. Crowning the service, I – and no doubt many other of my fellow worshippers – felt, was the marvellously inspirational *drosha* or sermon delivered by a well-known and learned, English rabbi; and now the principal minister of this new and particularly welcoming, friendly and co-operative *kehillah* or community. I just had the passing, maybe bizarre and perhaps controversial thought that we'd learned so much, and in such a relatively short length of time, from the philosophy of our fellow but indigenous citizens of Proxima b.

The rabbi, wearing a black *kippah* or skullcap and an all-embracing *tallit* or prayer shawl, rose from his special seat to the right of the Ark – the *chazan* seated in his own appointed chair on its left flank – and took his position behind the waist-high pulpit. He was tall, slim, looked in his forties and facially though tidily hirsute; but with a kind-hearted smile readily finding its pathway through the neat bush of dark hair. The congregation sat attentively in complete silence, with its many hundred pairs of eyes concentrating on the minister. He began by uttering certain words that he'd doubtless considered would instantly bring all of us together as one, as *the* community; and no matter the likely varying degrees of our personal faith and practical observance. After his succinct and manifestly heart-felt introduction – and from the glowing looks on the numerous faces I could perceive, whatever the age group to which they belonged – it was abundantly apparent that he'd succeeded in his worthwhile aim.

He explained that, for millennia, the Earth was held to be the centre of the universe. Humans believed, he said, and for so many years that when they looked up at the night sky they were seeing all the stars in the heavens – the billions beyond the Sun and our Solar System of planets – revolving around the Earth. This was the *geocentric* view, he continued, as expressed by Greek philosophers like Aristotle, and in the centuries before the commencement of the Christian era. The ancient Israelite and Jewish view wouldn't have been otherwise, or contradictory, as it kind of confirmed the Old Testament story. The Sun, its moon, the planets and the countless stars had been created by the Almighty in the beneficial context of the Earth. But the firmament of the heavens, and its limitless content, existed necessarily and possessed an endowment.

The rabbi intoned the first verse of the Book of Genesis, which declares: "In the beginning God created the heaven and the earth." In the mid-16th century, the minister noted, Copernicus' astronomical researches concluded that the Earth – just like its companion planets in the Solar System – orbited the Sun. The Polish scientist was supported, in the following century, principally by the works of German astronomer-mathematician Kepler and Italian physicist-astronomer Galileo.

In the 17th century, the rabbi related further, Sir Isaac Newton's studies on the subject of *heliocentricity* – the central position of the Sun – seemed to confirm a view of the lowly position of Earth in the physical scheme of things. Whilst some strong opposition from the established religions continued, despite the evidential discoveries and findings, gradually there came an inevitable and unavoidable acceptance by the vast majority of believers. In the 19th century, for example, Rabbi Hirsch began penning words to the effect that the Torah doesn't suggest otherwise.

The rabbi, at his pulpit, then said something of additional significance. Our presence now on Proxima b, he noted, as refugees from an overwhelming anti-Semitism on Earth – thankfully with the amazingly sympathetic help of this planet's citizens, for which we will be eternally grateful, to continue in freedom our religious beliefs – confirms, once again and beyond any shadow of a doubt, that the universe doesn't revolve around the Earth.

Following the service, we enjoyed a delicious *kiddush* prepared by the synagogue's Ladies' Guild in the large underground hall. Naomi and I – with the twins close on our tails – mingled with then talked to a number of our fellow community members and, seemingly, some potential friends. After that, we strolled silently back to the apartment deeply immersed in our thoughts from the morning's rabbinical address, as well as from the social contact chats over the tasty refreshments.

Twenty Seven

IN BED that night, Naomi and I reflected further, and aloud, on the rabbi's inspiring oration after the *leyning* or reading of the Earth-week's *sedra*, or portion of the *Torah* or Law, that Shabbat morning at the new and nearby synagogue we'd now joined; and despite our general lack of observance. The state of our religious affairs didn't mean, of course, that we had little or no belief in the Creator... in the Almighty. Far from that position; and we hadn't become members of this particular, newly-formed community merely for social purposes... our forecast irregular attendance at Shabbat and many other services wouldn't make for easy and consistent inter-connections, in any event.

My wife's and my own common thought as we rested supine, heads on pillows and gazing up at the ceiling, was that we had no problem – indeed, akin to our fellow congregants earlier that day – and much to be grateful for, on hearing the community minister's expression of his profoundly held tenet that the Almighty's presence is throughout our universe and outside of it. The Pentateuch, he'd said, might tell the long and human story only of the Lord's relationship and involvement with our distant ancestors on Earth. But, from the beginning of historical time, it's made crystal clear that our former home planet is just a small element, albeit a not unimportant one for us, in the heavenly scheme of *Creation*; and even in the broader conceptual scheme of things constituting the infinite and eternal cosmos beyond our universe.

As we stretched out close together on the cool white sheets, exchanging thoughts and notions on this mind-blowing subject, our voices reduced in volume and in line with our diminishing wakefulness. Very shortly afterwards, we both fell headlong into the waiting and appreciatively soothing arms of Morpheus. Though not before Naomi mentioned, virtually in a half-asleep whisper, that we should invite around to the flat, for drinks one evening, our new synagogue acquaintances. Ex-Londoners Brian and Elise, a married couple – in their mid-forties, we estimated – with one child, Martha, had been a GP and a Solicitor, respectively, back on Earth.

We'd conversed cheerfully with the friendly pair at the synagogue's quite imaginative *kiddush* earlier that day. Brian was slightly taller than me, a tad larger physically and balding but with a pleasant elliptical visage sporting a moustache and a goatee beard. Like me and most of the other gentlemen present, he was wearing a dark suit, white shirt and sober tie. His wife Elise was of medium height, quite slender, attractively featured and with curly auburn hair. In tune with Naomi and the majority of ladies alongside her, she was clad in a modestly below the knees and longed-sleeved dress. Their pretty daughter Martha was around a couple of years older than our seven-year-old twins; but she was running about the building, outside the synagogue itself, with them and other children during our devotions. This not completely noise-free activity made the morning in our astonishing context, if we'd thought about that – which, definitely, we did – nonetheless pleasingly familiar from our, albeit infrequent visits to a synagogue back on Earth.

Coincidentally, the family resided in an apartment at the same development, and even on the same top floor, as us. However, they were rather more into *Yiddishkeit* or Jewish tradition and adherence to Judaism than we were; though not in any extreme way. Had that been otherwise, Naomi and I might've continued circulating around the lengthy *kiddush* table and the milling, diverse Jewish crowd moving about its environs. Brian told me – whilst our spouses kept a watchful eye on the kids, and what they were taking from the plentiful food and drink buffet – that, aside from kosher eateries, they would eat out only at restaurants serving meals comprising vegetarian fare and permissible fish, that's with fins and scales. He said they enjoyed travelling the world, when they could; but wouldn't have been able to visit many of the places they had done if strictly kosher food had been required by them. I was on the identical thought level as the amiable doctor, and didn't hesitate to tell him so. But, naturally, I did explain our own observance – or, rather, general lack of observance – position. Nevertheless and liberally, he nodded his comprehension and acceptance of that fact.

Though the really pleasant guy went on to inform me that only kosher products would be consumed at their home, and that such would be required when eating in any other Jewish context.

We got on really well together, as did Naomi with Elise – and certainly Joshua and Sarah with Martha – so we gelled as families very quickly; and hardly spoke, at least for any length of time, to other members of the newly established community. Now Naomi and I were on the rim of slumber, and some likely snoring on my part if I didn't roll onto one side. In consequence of Brian's non-medical 'advice' that his family would eat only kosher food in another Jewish household, my wife and I knew full well, from past experience too, that we couldn't invite them to our flat, whether for lunch – say, after a rare Shabbat morning, synagogue attendance by us – or for dinner at any time. So an invite to our new-found friends would need to be for drinks exclusively. And, possibly, these beverages – alcoholic or otherwise – would have to be in paper cups if the couple only otherwise drank, in a Jewish context, from glasses or crockery that had been *toivel*… that is, religiously purified at a special kind of *keilim mikvah* or ritual cleaning facility for certain dishes, pans, vessels and other utensils. Somehow, we suspected Brian and Elise weren't ultra-Orthodox and more modern-Orthodox adherents to the Jewish faith.

*

So we invited the couple and their daughter to come to us for after-dinner drinks one evening during the following week. They expressed their delight at the invitation, turning up right on time the night in question and bearing the not entirely unexpected gift of a bottle of kosher red wine. Naomi and I accepted it gracefully and with thanks; but without enquiring about its source. We were aware that kosher food and drink, largely of whatever kind consumed previously on Earth, would be readily available for those who desired or required such. Our twins led Martha into Joshua's room to play some games – ones we'd approved, of course – on screen; whilst we four adults settled down relaxingly in the sitting room. Brian and Elise occupied the settee, to which I'd beckoned them, with Naomi and myself destined for the armchairs. Maybe a bit reluctantly, and before our invitees arrived, I'd placed four wine glasses on the occasional table. Nevertheless, I'd agreed with Naomi to arrange, in reserve on the kitchen drainer, several white paper cups... just in case. But, as predicted, there was no objection to our preferred holders for imbibing wine, the donated bottle of which I now opened with a corkscrew and then began pouring.

We could hardly hear a peep from the children, save for sporadic peels of laughter or victory exclamations. But any noise, such as it was, stayed low in background because I now closed the living room door. It was Brian who voiced aloud "*L'Chaim*!"... The rest of us then raised our glasses, together declaring the Hebrew word then drinking to the traditional Jewish toast to "Life".

"Quite an astonishing one for us now, to say the least," I affirmed, holding onto my drinking vessel as I started the actual conversation that evening. "Who could've imagined, even a short while ago and in their wildest and most fantastical moments of philosophical contemplation, that we would be spending the rest of our lives on a planet trillions of miles from Earth?"

"The mind boggles!" Elise reacted immediately.

Brian turned to his wife and nodded, as Naomi and I looked directly at her and performed likewise.

"We also have some very good malt whisky, if you would like that as well," my wife offered.

"We're ok for the moment, Naomi… though both of us are keen aficionados of the aptly Gaelic-named *Uisge Beatha*, the 'Water of Life'," Brian responded. "And, as I'm sure you must know, conveniently substantial stocks of the Scottish distillation together with, as I understand it, vodka, slivovitz, rum and the now increasingly trendy gin were transported, across the perhaps contextually inapt Milky Way, on the cargo-carrying mother-ships to Proxima b."

I nodded with a wide grin, and said:

"But I also believe that procedures are in hand, in our allocated territory, for the future establishment of appropriate distilleries or other meaningful facilities, and the production of the essential ingredients, for us to continue to enjoy these age-old spirits, of one kind or another and depending on your fancy…"

"At least we've got our conversation priorities right," Brian interjected, and quite amusingly.

We all guffawed heartily; and, oddly, coincidental to some now softened but doubtless boisterous laughter emanating from Joshua's bedroom beyond two closed doors.

As we supped the very drinkable, kosher Merlot – and chin-wagged congenially together – it was fairly inevitable that we would chat, initially and in the main, about our remarkably unique situation; and on what had been left behind, generally and personally speaking, on Earth. We just happened to note the very recent news that a road and rail, public transport network had now been instituted across our territory. This had been accomplished with a significant involvement by engineers who were former Israeli citizens. The speed and meticulousness, amongst other factors, with which the system's outcome had been achieved was, of course, down principally to the Proxima b teams. We all were sort of aware that much had been contributed beneficially by many of those people who'd joined us from the Jewish nation on our trans-galactic voyage. And this was quite understandable, as they'd been running all aspects of their own self-determinate society since its establishment in 1948.

Once we'd got through this inexorably still-amazing subject-matter, our conversation became more as it might've been had Brian and Elise joined us for drinks in our Cambridge apartment beside the River Cam a while back. At the last Shabbat's, synagogue *kiddush*, we'd discovered briefly each other's recent backgrounds. Though, needless to say, we said nothing to the couple about time travel, Naomi's medieval origins and our relationship with Diva, a name that, unsurprisingly, did ring a distinct bell with them.

"I take it that you've both taken up professional positions here now," I enquired of our guests, "and, no doubt, they were arranged during our space journey on the mother-ships."

Brian held out a pointedly waving hand for his spouse to reply initially.

"You're absolutely correct in your assumption, David," Elise began. "I'm a partner with a firm of Solicitors... and which we set up during our, only in one sense, longish voyage here. Of course, a judiciary and a system of tribunals, both civil and criminal with first instance and appeal courts, have been established now with agreed and relevant codes of law, practice and procedure. And miraculously, but necessarily, with the vital assistance of those professionals who'd occupied materially equivalent positions on Earth... albeit in an internationally varied, legal environment. My own speciality is real estate and the like. But in my former office I was needed to assist sometimes, though unenthusiastically from an emotional viewpoint, with certain criminal matters including rape ..."

"Do you think there'll be much criminal activity within our territory?" Naomi asked of the lawyer.

But before a reply came to my wife's question, I said:

"Sorry to put in my four-penny-worth, Elise, but we've been told time and again on behalf of the Alpha

Centauri inhabitants that, after millennia of evolution, they've become good and benevolent, if not perfect people always doing what is right and proper in, what we might call, a Utopian society. Our presence on this planet, our rescue from potential extinction as a people on Earth and for an entirely altruistic motivation is, maybe, the clearest illustration of what they are, and I am, saying. Optimistically, one day we'll all have learned and benefited from our now fellow, but long-standing, citizens of Proxima b... and may even have evolved into a species that doesn't commit criminal offences of any kind."

"No apologies required... and I note what you're saying, of course," Elise responded thoughtfully, despite my babbling on. "It goes without saying that some Jewish people commit such offences. Many of them have been sent to prison on Earth for their criminality and, hopefully, they would be rehabilitated and learn from their mistakes in life. Like you, David, and doubtless the vast majority of our brethren who are making this planet their new home, we trust and pray that no further criminal acts will be committed now we're here... And that the apparently excellent example of its indigenous citizens will be followed today and in the future. Hoping, wishing and praying are wonderfully benign activities but, unfortunately, we cannot take anything for granted. That's the rationale, as you may well be aware, behind the setting up currently of a relatively modest police force and prison service, which have come about also with the help of relevant professionals from the State of Israel."

"Very interesting, Elise," I said warmly, "and let's trust that the future will be trouble-free, peaceful and law-abiding for everyone… but we hadn't yet heard about the launch of a police force or a jail structure, had we Naomi?"

My wife shook her head, rather too busy with her glass of fine wine to utter any comment.

"Well, these aspects have only just got started, David," Elise responded. "You'll soon be noticing a few coppers in uniform patrolling our streets."

Naomi and I nodded then, turning to Brian, I asked him whether he'd set up a new GP practise.

"No, I haven't established such a surgery as I ran in north-west London, David," the doctor stated. "On our voyage to the Alpha Centauri star system, numerous conventions, if you like, were held with attendee medical people from around our previous world. There were doctors, surgeons, consultants, dentists, opticians, psychiatrists, psychologists, paediatricians and a variety of other medical professionals, of every known speciality, participating in these many and, fortunately, highly productive and forward-looking meetings and discussion groups. Again, as we know and have said in other instances, there was an extremely advantageous, not to say exceedingly useful if sometimes almost stupefying input by the Proxima b aces. They are so, so far ahead of us in the diagnostic and curative fields, and to such an incredible extent that we Earthling medics will need some considerable time even to get to grips with understanding the basics of their research, knowledge and practice, let alone implement such …"

I nodded in his short pause then Brian continued his discourse.

"Just as an illustration, David, on Earth there has been a certain amount of research work, and experimentation, done in the field of robotic surgery. That would be primarily in the context of pinhole surgery and the like... not too invasive but which would involve opening up of the body, so to speak. On Proxima b, so far as we are able to comprehend the situation, they've reached the evolutionary or revolutionary stage at which the body itself is capable of diagnosing any of the, for them, now rare and serious medical problems. The contemporary and indigenous, individual body itself is kind of programmed naturally to deal with such. And whether by way of some sort of miraculous self-surgery, on which subject and at this juncture in our own Earth knowledge and history of medical science and procedures, we haven't yet got to grips intellectually... or otherwise. There's an enormous amount for us to learn... not to speak of the medical equipment, amenities and wherewithal that, in due course, we'll need to absorb and put into practice. But, in the meantime, and with such help as our learned teachers and practitioners can provide for us, we'll be able to do so much more for our patients... and especially, we believe, for those suffering sadly from a currently incurable cancer. I haven't set up a GP surgery or neighbourhood clinic here... other doctors will be providing local and first-level, medical services in the territory. And, of course, there are hospitals now in operation across our allocated sector of the habitable zone. I'm going to be working at a kind of medical research centre that's been set up now, and hope to be able to contribute fully to the future, complete and comprehensive health and wellbeing of our people here."

"Absolutely and incredibly amazing!" were the words I uttered then, but wishing that I could've come up with even more superior superlatives. "We look forward to the day, Brian… and you, and your colleagues, have our full gratitude for all you're doing now and will be doing in the future."

"Thanks, David," the doctor said. "And with the astounding assistance of the Proxima b medical teams, we'll strive to achieve the healthy longevity that their people enjoy. But tell us, have you received any commissions yet from… hmm, oh yes, Mike… the newspaper editor you mentioned to me last Shabbat?"

"Not to date," I replied. "But both your and Elise's work suggests that you might have a fascinating and very newsworthy story for me at some time, presuming you would be able to talk about it and have it published widely… and assuming I can convince Mike to release any such article. What do you think, Brian?"

We were now coming to the end of the wine, the remnants solely in our glasses.

"But before you answer my question, would you like some more alcohol… maybe a wee dram of malt?"

"No thanks, David," Brian responded while glancing at his wife, who also was shaking her head. "We're fine."

"And we should be going soon," Elise added. "Martha kind of favours her full eight hours of kip!"

"As for a possible feature or news item," Brian remarked, "we'll see what happens... you never know, David."

Regrettably, you never do know... about anything. Indeed, the time was to come when I would be preparing to write up an entirely different story to the one I'd imagined penning about Brian and his colleagues' work. But at the end of that pleasant evening, after exchanging cheery goodnights on the doorstep with our new and very good friends Brian, Elise and sleepy but smiley little Martha, we all went off to bed happily.

Twenty Eight

NAOMI AND I didn't know, but maybe should've done, that Martha attended the same school as our kids; though, being some two years older, she was placed in an upper class to them. The detail just hadn't arisen during the recent and enjoyable drinks evening with her mother and father at our flat. Neither Joshua nor Sarah had spotted the girl in school, as yet; at least they hadn't mentioned doing so. It was a few of her alternate working days after our social get-together that my wife, posted temporarily as a teaching assistant in Martha's classroom, recognised our new friends' daughter. Naomi thought the little lass had acknowledged her at exactly the same moment; and recalled being smilingly on the receiving end of what appeared to be a nervously stealthy and rather self-conscious little wave from the pretty youngster.

A day later, Martha's mother rang our doorbell, at the start of a non-working day for Naomi, to invite us to lunch after the next Shabbat service. My spouse requested a second or two; then she contacted me 'telephonically' to check whether it was alright to accept the kind invitation. For an instant, the thought occurred to me – perhaps automatically now – that I didn't want to make it a habit for us to attend synagogue on a regular weekly basis. It really hadn't been our inclination or scene, for that matter; but I couldn't deny that the metaphorical '*kiddush* grapevine' could be handy to me, journalistically speaking. Doubtless, my Naomi had held a similar notion or two in her head; and, probably, that's why she'd called me for confirmation. On quick reflection, I knew that we could accept the thoughtful invite and still not attend the service beforehand. But a slight hint detectable in my wife's voice suggested that, on this occasion at any rate, we should attend as well as accept... so that's what I told her. Naturally, this didn't mean that we were compelled to go to the house of worship every Shabbat regularly. As Naomi brought our very brief conversation to a speedy close, and before she switched off, I just caught her saying to our near neighbour: "Thanks so much, Elise... and we're delighted to accept. We look forward to seeing you all at synagogue next Shabbat morning."

So, going forward, I supposed we could anticipate a genial engagement in a few days. Prior to that – in fact, on the day following Elise's pop-in – I'd received another invitation. I was asked to attend, which I would do enthusiastically, an editorial gathering arranged by Mike at the *Jewish Centaurian*'s offices. The attractively designed and six-storey, 'post-modern' building – of which the newspaper's editorial team occupied one spacious floor – was about a 20-minute, steady amble from our apartment. As I walked, in good time, along various thoroughfares to the mid-morning meeting, I could feel a kind of vitality exuding from the roads and streets as my fellow Jewish pedestrians headed towards the usual variety of societal destinations. Aside from the brightly illuminating and lemony sky, which we were getting fairly used to by now, everything seemed so awesomely normal; and not at all as extraordinary as it was inherently. Especially when witnessing the new and stylish, single- and double-decker, public transport buses plying the highways in all directions with their – and I could espy them through the clear and clean window glass – winsomely smiling or happily chatting passengers.

There were a dozen permanent members of the *Jewish Centaurian*'s staff, largely youngish men and women on around a 50-50 basis, seated on either side of the elongated table – plus a few likely or potential contributors, including me – with Mike at its head. The group make-up was intriguingly eclectic, including internationally speaking; though the common language was English. There were Jewish newspaper journalists and former editors originally from North America – the USA and Canada – and the UK, plus a couple of countries in continental Europe, as well as from Israel and the Antipodes. From networking briefly over our coffees or soft drinks before the meeting got underway, they seemed to constitute a really professional, experienced and friendly bunch of guys and gals. After colleagues had drained and disposed of their paper cups, and enjoyed some short but interesting exchanges, Mike called us to order and requested we take our name-marked places at the table. I was one of two attendees seated furthest from him; but, as our editor remarked immediately, the seating positions were randomly indicated to avoid a free-for-all of not knowing where to perch ourselves. Ok and if you say so, Mike, I thought.

When we'd settled down and at the outset, he called for each of us to introduce ourselves – and maybe a bit more formally, he added, than possibly over our earlier drinks – but reasonably succinctly. There was still much work to be done, he noted, before the newspaper's first issue would be published; but hopefully, he added, that would come to fruition in a couple of Earth-weeks' time.

"Why don't you start the ball rolling, Dan," the encouraging, affable and youngish editor invited, waving a hand towards the middle-right section of the table from himself. "What's up on the chief political editor's front, then?"

Dan, from Washington DC, was a lofty and skinny guy in his late forties with a swathe of prematurely greying hair on his now nodding head.

"Not a feverishly exciting amount at this present time, Mike, believe it or not," he began from his seated position. "I'll be reporting on this settling-in period, of course, for the administration appointed en route to Proxima b… There will be elections in the not too distant future, but no Party politics. I do believe we've learned significant lessons both on Earth and, already, from our good friends in the Alpha Centauri star system of which we're now a part. The voting will be to elect from those who will put themselves forward as candidates for a type of national government… you know, the kind of united rule that existed under Churchill during the Second World War. It's not, of course and happily, that we've got the same emergency, war-time sort of situation that existed at that time… But it's far from being a conventional set of circumstances, even though it may appear to be such for us on an everyday basis and in general terms. We'll be covering the preparations, and presentations, in due course."

"Thanks for that, Dan," Mike said now pointing, but in a polite manner, to Paula – originally from Sydney 'Down Under' – an attractive, short-haired brunette with lovely azure eyes and probably around her mid-thirties. "So let's move on to business, commerce and the like… Paula, the floor is yours."

She seemed to take the editor literally, and actually stood up. She was just a couple of seats away from me.

"Thanks, Mike," she started. "Well, this area of life in our allocated territory has been proceeding remarkably well, in a relatively short period of time and almost precisely as meticulously and contingency planned on the mother-ships bringing us here. All appropriate fields, including manufacturing, commercial and financial services from banking onwards are up and running efficiently as projected. I'll be writing about the entire operating network in detail but, for the present, I'm bearing in mind your request for brevity here and now, Mike."

"Fine, Paula," he responded, seemingly finding it a tad problematic shifting his gaze from the former Australian

'Business' journalist. "Let's have a little break from the heavy stuff, then… So what's happening in the sports field, Robert, if I can put it that way?"

Our editor pronounced the writer's name with a fair French accent; and maybe aptly so, because the paper's 'Sports' editor hailed from Paris. He looked to be in his early thirties and a really sporty type, clad – as he was – in what appeared to be a blue and white striped track suit. Actually, Frenchman Robert spoke English virtually without a Gallic tinge; and he felt somehow obligated to explain that almost absent accent by informing us that his sadly late father had been a Londoner.

"I can tell you, Mike and colleagues," he reported, "that, across our quite extensive territory, several professional football, golf and tennis teams and associations have been established… together with a few clubs for amateur participants in these sporting activities. There are also, as yet, a handful of swimming, athletics and gymnastics centres being set up. Like editorial colleagues, my own reporting staff will be describing the evolving and developing situation here. And they'll be writing up a number of interviews with the personalities closely involved, many well known from our former planetary home."

"That's excellent, Robert!" Mike intoned, unnecessarily. "I'm really looking forward to attending some soccer matches in the fantastic sports stadium that has been constructed… and not trillions of miles from these offices!"

Next, in order, Mike called upon Gavin, Ruth and Morris, who spoke about their respective editorial portfolios. Gavin – a lean and fair-haired guy, I estimated in his early forties and hailing from Toronto – gave us a rundown on his upcoming 'Entertainment' pages. These would have coverage of future drama and operatic productions, with musical performances of every description from classical through jazz to rock and pop, in the few but apparently superbly designed theatres that existed currently for us. As well as reviews of newly authored books – both fact and fiction, academic and leisure – produced by the now in-place publishing houses; and that would deliver traditional-style volumes in addition to e-books and their Earthly, post-modern ilk… until the publishers – and readers, of course – learned about, and took onboard, more futuristic options.

Not only Gavin, but also 'Education' expert Ruth – unfortunately, a physically stern-looking but nonetheless amicable, somewhat overweight and middle-aged woman from Tel Aviv; though originally from Manchester, England – mentioned, in passing, the newly set up libraries, archives and other research facilities of diverse kinds. These were stocked with many thousands of books brought across the galaxy from Earth; though doubtless they would be digitised, or whatever in futuristic terms, in due course. Ruth spoke also of the system of education up and running in the territory; and on an unbelievably compact time-scale. She alluded to kindergartens, primary and secondary schools and higher education institutions in the sense of university and technical colleges. The former teacher, a very experienced journalist in the education field, noted that there would be a huge amount to report and write about. Ruth added that she was in the busy process of organising interviews with school heads, college directors, university deans and professors in that connect.

Morris, a hefty and completely bald man likely in his mid-fifties – who'd divided his working-time on Earth, and for some decades, between California, Berlin and Jerusalem – would be responsible for editing the 'Community' and 'Religion' sections of the newspaper. He advised us that many synagogues had been built, and both Ashkenazi and Sephardic communities formed of varying heritages, for the modern- and ultra-Orthodox with, for the latter sector, adjacent or nearby *mikvaot* or ritual baths, *yeshivot* and seminaries or religion academies for young men and women. There were also, he added, many varying houses of worship for the Reform, Liberal and Progressive elements amongst the territory's assorted Jewish inhabitants. He mentioned that a very substantial proportion of the several millions of Jewish people now on Proxima b had become quickly affiliated to their respective communities.

Morris referred also to the assigned cemetery area, which had been divided and allocated now to each religious grouping; and where a number of burials, in accordance with the different traditions of the varied Jewish faith elements, had taken place. The *Jewish Centaurian*'s religion and community man said that he'd been compiling a list of communal leaders, rabbinical and otherwise, whom he would be contacting. In addition, he remarked, there would be another inventory of his that carried the names of managers or directors of a number of charitable and other benevolent organisations and bodies that, when and where needed, would likely be playing an important welfare role across the territory.

I and, I was sure, others seated around the long, meeting table had noticed Mike glancing at his wristwatch. When Morris had finished speaking, our editor commented:

"I'm sorry, everyone… but available time, and certain imperative and pressing matters, right now will not allow leeway for all present here this morning to have their say. We'll convene again soon and that, of course, goes without saying… even to non-editorial team members. Thank you, one and all, for your participation today… and that goes to those permanent staff from whom we've heard, and to our new and hopefully successful journal's prospective correspondents and freelancers. We shall be in touch with such potential contributors, like David over there or others unable to be here today, either to assign interesting stories or to invite and commission compelling suggestions for significant one-off features, regular columns and series, or whatever might be likely to appeal to our readership. So thanks again, to everyone here… and absent friends, too."

Mike got up from his chair and departed immediately. Several of the rest of us loitered for doubtless varying periods in the meeting room. Personally, I just shook some hands or waved my fingers in farewell then disappeared through the open, glass double-door. By no means was I the last to leave the gathering space, at least not that time round.

Twenty Nine

ON THE Shabbat we were invited to lunch with our new friends, we met up with them at the morning service in the synagogue. Brian and I had arranged that my family should call for his at their flat, so that we could chat en route to the 'modern' designed house of worship together, adults and accompanying children. After I knocked on the front door of their apartment – rather than ringing its powered bell, which might've offended our rather more Orthodox neighbours – it was opened by Brian. We exchanged an immediate *Shabbat shalom*, a customary 'peaceful Sabbath' greeting. However, he informed us that Martha had been a little sick earlier, though nothing too problematic thankfully; that we should proceed to the *shul*, or synagogue, without them; and that, in all probability, they would be arriving there very soon after us.

Fortuitously, that proved to be the case… Martha's father was a qualified doctor, after all. From my seat, I could perceive smiles on all faces as Elise and her daughter took their fairly prominent seats in that part of the ladies' gallery directly opposite me. That coincided with Brian sliding into his pew allocation – after donning his *tallit* or prayer shawl – at the main aisle end of my row, and with a winsome nod to me and Joshua by my side. There were a goodly number of both men and women attendees that morning; and at a surprisingly early stage of the proceedings, it seemed to me. Not being a regular synagogue-goer myself, I wouldn't have known – at least accurately enough – the average quantity to be expected for a standard Shabbat morning service. Both Naomi and I weren't intending to come along with the twins to *daven* or pray that frequently, so as to definitely confirm member attendance statistics.

Nevertheless, it did occur to me – as I leaned over my *Siddur* or Daily Prayer Book – that the attendance figures could well be greater than might've been the case for an Earth Shabbat; and for potentially comprehensible reasons. The primary factor, I speculated, being related to the prayers that congregants would likely wish to offer the Almighty regarding family and friends who'd decided to remain on our former home planet in the Solar System. I also bore in mind our most inspirational and caring minister who, like many others of his learning and community experience, had journeyed alongside us to Alpha Centauri and our new abodes on Proxima b.

His *drosha* or sermon that morning, after the reading of the Torah portion, again confirmed my thoughts about his so appealing ability to choose the most nuanced and appropriate words in the prevailing circumstances. The rabbi mentioned – and really empathetically – some of his own relevant feelings concerning those Jewish people who, for whatever important reasons, couldn't bring themselves to depart Earth for a promised and welcoming new home on the other side of our Milky Way galaxy. Even despite the dreadful and tragic catastrophe that might well befall them, and likely sooner rather than later. Nonetheless, the minister needed to construct his delivered sentences very carefully and sensitively, bearing strongly in mind a need also to avoid upsetting unnecessarily the delicate position of those, possibly many, congregants who may've felt a continuing sense of deep guilt about 'abandoning' loved ones who'd stayed behind on Earth.

It was almost impossible, I considered, for the minister to achieve his complete objective in that regard. During his address, and for a while after he'd finished speaking, several men and women could be heard making low, possibly self-conscious sounds of weeping, their tears of patent distress representing hearts broken inescapably by the absence of beloved relatives, and an ignorance of their fate. Yet again, in an extraordinary way and despite the muted sobbing, everything was likely to have appeared amazingly typical for the congregants in this authentic synagogue that could've existed on Earth. Well, perhaps not that conventional for me. The apparent normality experienced by the majority of my fellow congregants that morning would've continued; and whether or not they had been invited, which they hadn't, to the traditional Shabbat lunch fare prepared by Elise... a *cholent*, no less! A unique, 18- to 24-hour, overnight-simmered stew created initially to comply with Jewish law, which prohibits any cooking on a Shabbat.

We didn't linger – as would've been habitual for many – at the after-service *kiddush* refreshments, with Elise the talented chef and her hubby anxious to return to their apartment and get us all seated comfortably around the dining room table. But the first thing Naomi and I asked about when meeting up with our friends in the synagogue's subterranean hall was Martha's condition, hopefully now fine. Thankfully, that was indeed the case. Her mother explained that, occasionally, their little girl felt a bit sick when awakening in the morning. Brian told us such a queasy feeling wasn't that rare an occurrence in young children; and that there were a number of possible diagnoses, which he wouldn't go into then. The medic added that he'd succeeded – by various curative applications – in reducing the number of recurring instances; and that he was fairly confident the problem would end fairly soon. Naomi and I said that we wished Martha well.

Brian made the *bracha* or blessing over wine, and juice for the kids; then, as mandatory, we all washed our hands at the kitchen sink before sitting down, where directed, at the table. Here we each received a slice of the traditional *challah* bread cut, after his intoning another *bracha*, by Brian from one of the two loaves then sprinkled with salt by him. Our host sat at the head of the extended, white cloth covered table, with Elise to his left and me on his right. Naomi perched beside me and opposite Martha; Joshua and Sarah sat side-by-side at the end facing Brian. The age-old, Jewish potato, meat and bean stew from *der Heim*, the one-time sort of collective home of Jewish people in

Eastern Europe and Russia – and with all the concoction's other well-established ingredients – was dished up, piping hot, by our hostess to all present. Whilst the adults focused close attention, for the present, on their piled high platters of steaming *cholent*, we could none-the-less hear the three kids jabbering in the background over their somewhat smaller plates of customary Sabbath food.

"How come you two know what I'm going to say... and before I even say it?"

It was Martha directing her question at Joshua and Sarah.

My son glanced quickly and meaningfully at me, then at his sister and finally back at the munching interrogator.

"It just seemed fairly obvious you were about to ask Sarah and me whether we'd ever before eaten this kind of meal... *cholent*, I think it's called," Joshua replied evenly and, seemingly, with innocence.

"But why did you think the question I was about to ask you both, and which you answered in the negative, was *fairly obvious*?" equally bright Martha responded at once.

The busily and seriously masticating adults around the table managed to absorb smilingly, and additionally, the kids' endearing conversational exchanges. Then our daughter spoke.

"We spotted you staring at us with curiosity as we stared at our meals, Martha," Sarah said, with a really cute smirk. "That's why my brother told you, and before you asked us, that we'd never eaten *cholent* previously."

Our hosts' daughter was silent for a moment, as she finished chewing.

"Ok …" she said, before scooping up another fork-load from her dish, "but this kind of mind-reading stuff has happened between us more than once in the recent past, though I didn't mention it then… and I don't think my questions were so *fairly obvious* on those occasions, either."

"Well, Martha," Joshua said, "that might be a matter of opinion."

Martha shook her head with resignation and sort of sighed, then opened wide to get her mouth around a fork-full of meat and potato.

"Our young children are *so* adult," Elise remarked with a gentle chuckle.

Immediately, the three other adults in the room nodded their firm agreement; and with full and smiley cheeks.

While dear Martha was on the receiving end of some undeserved, sardonic verbiage from the twins, I asked Brian and Elise how their daughter was getting along at the new school, mentioning that our Joseph and Sarah had told us how very happy they were there.

"She thinks it's wonderful, too," the mother remarked with a glowing smile, after swallowing some of her tasty *cholent*. But having been listening to the kids' lively chatter, she added somewhat pointedly: "But why don't you ask her yourself… the distraction may well rescue her from your lovely kids."

I knew what she meant, of course, and I did. After exchanging wry grins with Elise, I sought to attract her young daughter's currently well-focused attention with a rather ostentatious hand-wave.

"Martha …" I voiced as well, but not very vociferously.

Her attention duly diverted, she reacted to me at once.

"Yes… er, Uncle David? Sorry… but should I be calling you that?"

"You can, if you like," I replied, glancing at her beaming parents for some supportive gesture.

They nodded smilingly to both their child and her new 'uncle'.

"Thanks, Uncle David."

I detected a fidgety movement at the end of the table to my right.

"And can we call you Uncle Brian and Auntie Elise?" our forward offspring intervened in unison, addressing the question to our beneficent hosts.

"You can, if you wish," Brian responded, all other adults present replicating his jovial countenance.

"How are you getting on at school, Martha?" I asked her at last, glad the children's 'ESP' chit-chat had concluded finally. "And what are your favourite subjects and pursuits there?"

"I really enjoy being at this school, Uncle David," she said cheerily. "I've made lots of friends already… and even some in other years, like Joshua and Sarah. Our teachers are brilliant, so clever and knowledgeable but also so proficient at explaining things to us in a clear and understandable way. There's the oddly and perpetually yellowish sky we see, looking up through the building's large windows and from its surrounding play and sports grounds during so-called *daytime*. But we've got used to that… don't think about it too much now. And our time at school seems so remarkably normal. It's just like we're still learning on planet Earth …"

"Lovely!" I interrupted. "Sorry for that, but don't many of the children have language problems, Martha?"

"Not really," the girl stated. "Most have English as their first language, and others generally had been learning it at their school on Earth. So, to carry on with your first questions… Our marvellous teachers are also telling us as much as they know about our amazing, new planetary home. It's all so unbelievable and astonishing… that's being at the other end of the Milky Way galaxy from Earth. But it's also a little scary, that's for us kids… not to say it isn't exciting, in a way. And our school meals are really delicious, too!"

Whilst she gave that succinct food review, I could sense some confirmatory nodding of our twins' heads.

"And we adore being taken on supervised walks around town," Martha went on, "as well as on bus trips to the waterside, and to the outer edge of the city area.

From there we could see some slightly higher ground or hill-like features in the not too far distance."

"That's great!" I jumped in again, "and it's more than Auntie Naomi and I have managed to get around to doing, as yet."

The intelligent little narrator nodded; and, after the hint of a one-upmanship grin, she uttered rather cutely:

"Don't worry… you will, Uncle David and Auntie Naomi."

Little did I – or, indeed, anyone around the table – know how soon such an exploratory venture, of the kind she'd mentioned, would come about… and as the outcome of an apparently ominous occurrence.

"And your favourite subjects in class, Martha?"

It was Naomi who sort of moved in to repeat my earlier poser; as I was rendered a tad speechless, though only momentarily, after the girl's last, cutely sweet remark to my wife and myself.

"Well, Auntie Naomi," the girl replied smartly, "the subjects I love learning about mainly include geography and history… also English and English Literature. So I suppose you could say that I go for the arts, rather than the science curricula …"

Admittedly, I was truly knocked for six that such descriptive language was emanating from a child under the age of 10. It sounded very much like a sixth-former speaking; though, I reflected, her proud parents did comprise a lawyer and a doctor. I hoped that Brian and Elise would hold similar admiring opinions of our Joshua's and Sarah's adult-like language usage.

"I really want to learn so much more," Martha added enthusiastically, "and as much as I can, about what we call Proxima b… our new home planet in the Alpha Centauri star system. Especially, I would like to study its geography and climate, as well as its very, very long history of intellectual life and habitation. And even though I'm not

247

that inclined towards the sciences, such as physics, biology and chemistry, I would definitely be keen to learn about the incredibly advanced stage of our rescuers' technologies… Technologies that, fantastically, could bring us trillions of kilometres across our galaxy, and in next to no time, so that we can enjoy my Mum's *cholent* on Proxima b."

The smiles-accompanied applause that followed from around the table was so well deserved. But all I could bring myself to utter, though somewhat needlessly *sotto voce*, was "Wow!" What I should've belted out was: "Bravo!" The notion then occurred to me: *What, in heavens name, did I learn in school then?*

For a short while, a pin-dropping silence reigned as we sorted through our crowding thoughts. But we didn't stop eating and, ultimately, completely demolished Elise's scrumptious Shabbat meal from the old country. Most of us – though probably excluding the kids, of course – had little tummy room remaining for the *parve* ice-cream and stewed fruit dessert, which thereby could be consumed after a meaty repast. The sweet was naturally light and refreshing, tempting enough to be given a digestive slot… and, needless to say, by everyone.

Afterwards, all parents enjoyed black Americano coffees, with water from the hot water urn, seated relaxingly in the sitting room whilst the kids disappeared into Martha's bedroom, ostensibly to read quietly. Before leaving the flat later that Shabbat afternoon, Naomi and I – after having a rapid word together when Brian and Elise vanished into the kitchen with the used crockery – agreed we should ask them to visit us again for post-dinner drinks one weekday evening.

This I did as soon as they returned, with all three children alongside, to the flat's living space. They accepted graciously, and we set a date and time in the near future. Having settled that contentedly, then expressed our grateful thanks to the hosts for a delightful and time-honoured Sabbath lunch, our family quartet – utterly replete and more than ready for a nap – left their apartment for our own not far away dwelling place.

Thirty

NOT THAT long after our welcoming, absorbing and delicious, Sabbath lunch with our very near and good neighbours, and on a weekday evening as arranged, Brian and Elise came to our home for after-dinner drinks. When I opened the front door to them, I noticed immediately that a family member was absent.

"Where's Martha?" I enquired, and recalling, maybe a trifle strangely, that she'd felt a little sick before recovering and coming to the synagogue recently. "Hope she's ok."

As I beckoned her parents into our apartment, her father said:

"She's fine, David, but thanks for asking."

And her mother added to her husband's words, as they entered the sitting room ahead of me to be greeted by Naomi.

"Martha was feeling rather tired after a full day of sports activity at school, so she desired to go to bed somewhat earlier than usual tonight."

"Snap!" Naomi declared with a smile, having undoubtedly heard the earlier part of the exchange about Martha. "Our kids are right now tucked up in bed, and in the Land of Nod... and for the same reason."

With grins continuing all round for a little longer, Brian and his spouse settled themselves comfortably on the settee. Naomi slumped somewhat ungainly into an armchair; though perhaps understandably after a tough working day at the school, followed by cooking the kids and me a tasty meal. Leaving my wife and our guests chatting lightly, I crossed the room to retrieve a bottle of a renowned and excellent malt whisky, an alcoholic beverage I knew all present would favour, and four old-fashioned glasses from the drinks cabinet. For a fleeting moment, peculiarly and almost uncomprehendingly, an image of the city of Cambridge against a starry universe backcloth entered my mind. I shook my head, somewhat bewildered, but managed to get down on my haunches to open the low cupboard's double doors and extract the requisite receptacles. After a single transit of the room, I set them up on the occasional table between the occupied seating then poured away.

"I see this one's a rather special Laphroaig edition," Brian remarked, inclining his head to read the distinctive label on the bottle tilted in my hand. "Just happens to be one of our all-time favourites, David."

I handed him and Elise a generously filled whisky tumbler.

"Coincidentally, ours too," I reacted, pouring two more tots-plus for Naomi and myself then taking my armchair seat.

"Like so much else we've been experiencing," Brian remarked contemplatively, after savouring and slowly imbibing some of the characteristically, Islay-flavoured, smoky-peaty *Uisge Beatha* or 'Water of Life', "it's so incredibly amazing that we're all sitting here, trillions of miles from the Western Isles of bonny Scotland, and enjoying one of the golden products from their famed distilleries... it just about, but fortunately not quite, whips my breath away."

"That could depend on how much of the malt we'll be downing this evening," I responded, only half-jokingly; and my comment did actually invoke some albeit hesitant and gentle chuckling.

"That's quite amusing, David," Elise said, half-encouragingly. "And just last week, I was conversing over morning coffee with one of my colleagues who'd resided and worked in Glasgow. Richard told me, in passing, that he'd been involved with arranging for a very substantial quantity of malt and blended whisky to be purchased and loaded aboard one of our accompanying, cargo-carrying mother-ships headed for Proxima b ..."

"Bravo!... To him and all the others concerned in that process and importation," I interjected, but a smidgen too histrionically perhaps; though my words brought some active nods, and a show of keen expressions, from my kind and chortling listeners.

"Let's make an apt toast," Naomi suggested at once. "Brian? Elise? David?"

"Your idea, Naomi," I said, a little provocatively maybe, whilst holding out an indicative palm in my wife's direction. "So you have the honour, darling."

Brian and Elise nodded their definitive approval.

"O-Ok… thanks," she said tentatively and appearing to mull over a thought or two. "You know that, back on our former home planet, people would often say, *There's nothing perfect in this world of ours.* And I do believe that all of us know what we and our fellow Earthlings meant by that sort of philosophical observation. Here, on Proxima b that is, and from our experiences over a relatively short period of time, I get the distinct and confident impression that we'll certainly learn, as Diva has continually promised us, how to create a perfect world for our children and future generations. So let's drink to that… *A perfect world for everyone!*"

Naomi rose to her feet at once; and those of us still sitting joined her, all raising their whisky tumblers then voicing in unison – but not so loudly as to possibly awaken Joshua and Sarah – the toast to "*A perfect world!*" Without exception, we gulped some of our malt then sat back down to recline contentedly on our respective seats.

"Our twins appear to be having a really great time at school, and have acclimatised to their new surroundings there so remarkably quickly," I said, resuming a subject from our earlier, Shabbat lunch gathering. "And they seem to be learning so much more productively than when they were attending their primary school on Earth …"

Naomi was nodding in agreement as I spoke, and took up the baton where I left off.

"It's absolutely incredible," she contributed. "I've been witnessing this excellent improvement firsthand, and not only where our kids are concerned, when I'm assisting in class, etcetera… I take it this applies to your Martha as well?"

My wife addressed her question to the girl's mother; although we'd heard previously from Martha herself about her really positive take in answer to a similar enquiry.

"You're quite correct, of course," was the instant reply. "And just like your own children, she's getting on remarkably well in her own school year, taking in a lot of knowledge from the truly inspirational teaching staff. She's also participating eagerly, and to her enormous satisfaction, in the physical games and other athletic and gymnastic activities with the marvellous facilities provided in and about the magnificent school building."

As my wife and I uttered the word "Snap!" again, Elise's doctor husband injected, so to speak:

"Healthy bodies mean healthy minds… and both are so very important for our children on Proxima b. Well, for everyone here."

All others present nodded then took some more whisky. I offered to top up our guests' glasses, but both shook their heads advisedly.

"Your pouring was very munificent, thanks David," Brian noted with a kind of schoolboy grin, glancing askance at his slowly nodding spouse. "We don't want to overdo it… and I'm not necessarily speaking as a medic, you understand."

I nodded, too.

"So tell us, Brian, since you've alluded to the medical profession, how's the work side of life getting along for you here and now?" I asked more seriously. "You and Elise know how much Naomi's revelling in her part-time, class assistant role at our children's school... and that I'm awaiting to hear from Mike, the editor of the *Jewish Centaurian* as you're aware, with a writing commission. Hopefully, that will turn up in early course. But, in the meantime, I'm penning a feature about our voyage from Earth and across the galaxy to Proxima Centauri and its habitable zone. Sorry about babbling on, Brian... we'll be interested to learn about your rather more vital work here."

"We'll look forward to reading your piece on our extraordinary, interplanetary journey, David," Elise said benevolently.

"If it's published," I indicated.

"Of course it *will* be," my wife said, with emphasis and to heartening nods from our guests.

"So Brian... let's hear how it's going for you."

"Well, David," our doctor friend was able to respond at last, "thankfully, the now established hospitals and clinics aren't too overloaded with patients having severe medical problems. But, naturally, they're prepared for any eventuality. As I'm sure you're aware, the vast majority of those potential migrants to Proxima b who were seriously or terminally ill resolved to remain behind on Earth. As I believe I've mentioned to you, I'm involved primarily in research at present and alongside a large number of professional colleagues and well-known experts... At least, they're well-known to me from their various fields of medicine, extending across the entire universe of the subject and not forgetting diagnostics, surgery, psychiatry, dentistry, optometry etcetera, etcetera …"

"And not necessarily in that order or exhaustively, I assume," I said superfluously, but adding: "I'm really impressed."

Brian nodded, and with a smiled thanks.

"Yes, well," he continued, "we've all, that's the entire and general medical profession represented here, have been finding ourselves in a kind of revolutionary situation. And I mean that in a good sense. With the welcome advice and assistance of the far advanced, indigenous medics on Proxima b, we hope to learn so much from them to help our people… and especially in the difficult area for us of preventing or curing all cancers. Inevitably, this is bound to take a considerable amount of dedicated time. But there's certainly a brilliant light at the end of the diagnostic and curative tunnel, and we'll do our utmost to seek implementation of full and complete remedies as soon as we possibly can."

"We wish you and your colleagues every success in all your endeavours, and ultimate victory very soon," I offered, to further nods from the wives. "Your incredible efforts will be so much appreciated by all our immigrant brethren… and, in due course, by future and possibly evolving generations here. And your work in this connection will certainly contribute tremendously in heralding the arrival of the *perfect world*, of which we spoke and drank to earlier."

Together, we raised our glasses again then supped a little more of the distinctive and distinguished, Islay malt. And I added, maybe a bit cheekily:

"Apparently, even the lovely red buses in our territory are running precisely and consistently on time, already so soon... that's public transport perfection, indeed, for us Earthlings!"

There were undeniably mobile grins all round, and I supposed one couldn't have expected less.

"And how's the legal profession proceeding, Elise?" I enquired.

"All's going exceedingly well, David," she replied. "I don't want to bore everyone but, since you've asked, I'm definitely enjoying very much the work our team is doing... and that's mostly related to land, property, company and financial matters at the present time. Speaking generally and as I may've mentioned before in brief, pun unintended, firms of solicitors, chambers for barristers, courts and tribunals, civil and criminal, have been set up with the necessarily associated, appropriate professional and regulatory bodies. So the infrastructure, with its universally agreed, endorsed and constituted *Code of Law and Practice* is now well in place. As I'm sure we've mentioned previously, too, there's now a police force operational throughout the territory... and also an established prison service ..."

"Does the jail system have any customers, as yet?" I asked, possibly a bit too whimsically inapt; and maybe pathetically though, in fact, quite seriously.

"Auspiciously, not that many," Elise answered, straight-faced. "Most of the inmates are serving sentences we discovered they would've served in their respective countries on Earth. It may take a little while for the system to deal with a number of relatively minor offences committed on the mother-ships bringing us here… such as assaults, of one kind or another. But happily, from what I've heard on the legal grapevine, a perhaps incredible total of nil crimes have been reported or detected since we all arrived on Proxima b, albeit not that very long ago."

"That's really something, Elise!"

It was Naomi who spoke.

"Let's hope it stays that way," my wife added.

"Excuse me for butting in again," I apologised. "But could be this is yet another beneficent illustration of how all our brethren are seeking wholeheartedly, and for good reason, to be *perfect* citizens in their new and enlightening home."

"Let's drink to that, too!" my cheery spouse invited.

And all of us did.

"Cheers!" I declared, to be echoed accordingly.

Then we were distracted by a slight noise emerging from the hallway. It was the bathroom door closing. One of the twins must've crept inside fairly stealthily. Very shortly afterwards, we heard the toilet flush then the door opening. A little head peeped into the sitting room. It was a sleepy-eyed Sarah.

"H-Hello e-everyone… and n-night n-night, Auntie Elise and Uncle Brian," our little girl managed to utter, then yawned gapingly and slunk back into her bedroom, its door shutting slowly behind her.

"Sarah looks really delightful in her lovely pink jimjams... ah, bless," Elise remarked with a glowing smile.

We chatted on for a while longer, conversing interestingly on a variety of current affairs and topics, ranging from food and drink production, supply and availability to what was likely to be produced in the way of entertainment for the territory's residents at the now established theatres and other venues. Finally, we all finished our originally not so wee drams... my justifiably said-to-be *generous*, single pouring of malt whisky from the Western Isles.

"Think we should love and leave you now," Brian said, having received a noticeably meaningful nod from his wife. "Elise and I thank you so much for your kind hospitality... We'll meet up again very shortly, I'm sure."

"Sorry we aren't able to make our offering more substantial, you know what I mean," I said. "But no problem, we understand completely."

"Thanks... and please don't concern yourselves," Elise said reassuringly. "We really enjoyed this whisky evening very much."

Brian nodded fulsomely then shook my hand. Elise gave Naomi a peck on the cheek. Then our good friends left the flat. As I closed and secured the front door with my wife waving beside me, little did we know how uncannily and sadly prescient Brian had been when stating a few moments earlier: *We'll meet up again very shortly, I'm sure.*

Thirty One

NAOMI AND I had been gradually and respectively washing up and drying the whisky glasses in the kitchen after a pleasant, chatty evening with our close neighbours and now very good friends. I was about to put away the tumblers in our drinks cabinet, when I nearly dropped a couple of them then almost jumped out of my skin. There was a sudden and scarily noisy banging on the front door of our apartment, accompanied by loud voices screaming something I couldn't make out in the din. Hurriedly, if not in a panic, I left the glasses on top of the low cupboard, dashed into the hallway and actually did bump into my wife, who was just emerging from the kitchen with a horrified look on her face. On colliding, we both nearly fell over; but I managed to maintain my, and Naomi's, reasonably vertical stance by grabbing her arm and waist in an effort to support the pair of us in that position. I knew, for sure, that I wasn't dreaming; though the continuous hammering and shouting – if not shrieking, at least from one pair of vocal cords – was of nightmare proportions.

"W-What's h-happening, David?" Naomi uttered wildly, with a riveting fear in her voice as she seized hold of me.

Sounds behind us caused my wife and me to quiver heavily, but no more than momentarily. Looking around swiftly, we saw with relief that it was Joshua and Sarah exiting their bedrooms. Pyjama-clad, they entered the hallway staggering with sleepiness then wrapped themselves around their mum and dad with a panicky and pitiful foreboding marring their innocent, young features.

"I-I really don't know, my love," I got round to replying to Naomi's troubled question at last; at the same time, sliding a hopefully comforting arm around my now whimpering daughter.

Almost phenomenally, through the pounding and hollering I just made out my name, and Naomi's, being called. My wife gazed at me with incredulous alarm. We continued to stare at each other, in silence but with utter bewilderment if not grim apprehension. But I needed to make a decision, I knew that. Gently, I steered the terrified twins into their mother's warm and secure embrace then made for the front door. Still with severe reluctance – and a kind of overriding fear for my family now cowering in the hall, eyes glued to me and the thankfully sturdy front door – I unlocked and opened it, little by little and warily. Then I was shocked to the very core of my being. Brian and Elise virtually collapsed with an anxious momentum into the entrance-way and right up against me. Once again that evening, and with a necessarily instant application of physical effort, I was able to remain standing, if somewhat stunned; and, therefore, in a steady enough position to prevent the couple from falling to the polished wood floor.

"W-What's the m-matter?" I uttered, stuttering with a stressful disquiet for their wellbeing. Simultaneously, Naomi rushed up – doubtless leaving our confused and horrified children to huddle together – in order to comfort a sobbing and patently distressed Elise. Not that Brian looked and sounded much different to his severely fraught spouse.

"Tell me, Brian… What's happened? What's wrong?" I pressed with, I felt and desired, much sincere and sympathetic concern – perhaps it was trepidation – in my, albeit emotional voice.

"W-We can't find Martha!" he blurted sorrowfully.

"What do you mean, you *can't find Martha*?" I enquired with perplexity.

Elise erupted into even more harrowing sobs as her husband, tears welling in his own burdened eyes, said with a deep ache in his delivery:

"She's not in our flat… we can't find her anywhere… we really can't stay here long… just checking… we've called the police, and they'll be along soon… and I've told them they can find us here, if we're not at home… I hope you don't mind, David."

I shook my befuddled head, shut the front door, grasped a so distraught Brian by the arm and – with Naomi bringing tenderly along his painful to see, hugely overcome wife – led him and them into the sitting room. The kids followed quietly and parked themselves, cross-legged, on the carpet close by the three-piece-suite. On its sofa, Naomi and I – each of us profoundly concerned by the evident circumstances – gently seated our dear friends then sat ourselves in the armchairs with a rigid focus on the palpably devastated couple. Brian placed an arm around a now softly weeping Elise; and she lowered her head onto his shoulder.

"What's happened to Martha?" I heard myself asking, evenly though a tad diffidently in view of what Brian had told us so far.

Her doctor father appeared to sigh nervously.

"When we got back to the apartment after our drinking session with you, just a short while ago," he began, gazing worriedly into the hall towards the front door and fidgeting edgily in his seat, doubtless with a compulsion to move on pronto, "we naturally went first to our daughter's room to make sure she was contentedly asleep …"

There was a short pause, clearly for the speaker to compose himself.

"… But Elise and I could see at once, with the duvet folded back, that Martha wasn't tucked up and slumbering peacefully in her bed. Nothing otherwise appeared awry and we just wondered whether, having heard us returning and maybe being already awake, she decided cheekily to hide from us somewhere in the flat… Not appreciating as a child, of course, that the absence from her bedroom would cause her parents to agonise unnecessarily. Unfortunately, to say the least, our exhaustive search of the apartment didn't reveal her naughtily concealed presence. Elise burst into tears, quite naturally, but we needed to remain as calm as possible. Although Martha had never been a somnambulist, we thought innocently that there's always a first time for sleep-walking. So Elise and I dashed from the flat to search for her elsewhere in the building …"

There came another pained pause.

"… from top to bottom, its common parts, up and down the stairway and into the basement storage area and the external bin store… and, of course, the lifts. We also hurried around the outside, so far as the perimeter of our communal garden and grounds… but Martha was nowhere to be seen. Now we were really starting to seriously panic, and our thoughts became less hopeful than previously. Then we were seized by the idea that she might've somehow by-passed us, and by means unknown, when we were returning home from your apartment. Our daughter could've awoken with a start for some reason and, forgetting about our trip to you for drinks this evening, she could've fretted about her parents' absence on calling for us from her bedroom. So she could've decided, in her bemused state of mind, to leave the flat to look for us. Then we felt, with perhaps some positive sighs of relief, she could've remembered her mum and dad were with Uncle David and Auntie Naomi. So that's the reason why we're here right now …"

Another pause …

"… but clearly and sadly, our baby isn't …"

Naomi and I were stunned, struck dumb with horror and choked with compassion for our friends, as Brian finished relating his and Elise's dreadfully unsuccessful attempts to find their missing child. He stood up hastily from the settee whilst helping his emotionally crumbling and tormented wife to raise herself, too.

"We've got to go home now to await the arrival of the police... they should be here imminently," Brian stated, adding: "We hope and pray Martha has just wandered off haphazardly, and will soon return home or be located... maybe fast asleep in a nearby shop doorway."

Naomi and I offered several fulsomely empathetic and sanguine nods, noting also that Joshua and Sarah each possessed a pair of tear-pearled cheeks. I was certain my wife also was hoping that nothing sinister, even tragically fatal had befallen the sweet, intelligent and pretty young girl; but never would we have expressed these pessimistic notions.

"I'm sure Naomi won't mind," I said, after a brief thought occurred as we all moved into the hallway, "if I accompany you to your apartment at this traumatic time, and perhaps stay around for a supportive while... but only if both of you would want that, of course."

I swivelled round on my heels to witness my wife, and even the twins, nodding.

"That will be fine with me, David," Naomi remarked at once.

Then I turned back to see both of our friends nodding.

"That would be very good of you, David," Brian said, shaking my hand. "But I think we'd better go... and quickly now, Elise."

With that, I planted a kiss on a cheek belonging to each member of my family then left the flat accompanying

Martha's, understandably, extremely anguished parents back to theirs. But as I'd pecked the side of Naomi's face a moment or so earlier, I whispered in her ear that she could contact our long-time, Alpha Centauri friend Diva… just to put her in the picture for the time being.

Thirty Two

BARELY A moment or two after I entered our angst-ridden friends' flat alongside them, and we moved to the living area, there was a ring of the doorbell. Brian rushed back to open the front door. I could tell that still constantly sobbing Elise could hear, as I did, that it heralded the arrival of the police. Her husband led the officers towards us. As they all entered the living area, I could see that there were three of them, including two youngish and tallish, dark-blue uniformed constables with colour-matching, beret-style headgear; one of the pair was female.

The clearly in charge third officer, a sturdy gentleman in a dark grey suit – almost matching, in hue, his full head of wavy hair – with a white shirt and plain navy-blue tie, and maybe in his early fifties, introduced himself as Detective Inspector Solomon. The policewoman – some blonde locks peeping from under her 'cap' – had a quiet, no doubt compassionate word or two with the still standing and tearful mother, then gently clasped her arm and sat down with her on the settee. The men remained on their feet, and Brian introduced me as a family friend and a close neighbour in the apartment building.

After the male constable, holding a bulky briefcase, asked Brian which bedroom was Martha's then vanished into it, DI Solomon began speaking.

"We've now organised for some officers to call at every flat in this development in order to search them," he addressed Martha's father first and foremost. "And they should've already started that requisite, eliminatory process. "They each hold copies of the issued Warrant to do that, and will show it to all residents if called upon to do so. We're not assuming any wrongdoing by any of your fellow residents, of course... but, needless to state, it's essential to leave no stone unturned in our search for your missing daughter ..."

The detective paused for a moment or so as Brian and I nodded; then he continued:

"Thus, by way of illustration, Martha could be fast asleep right now in the hallway of a flat where the deeply slumbering, and perhaps elderly, residents had left their front door ajar inadvertently before retiring to bed. Amazingly or not, such things can and do happen, you know. Also, we have other colleagues presently combing the development's internal common parts, as well as its gardens and grounds immediately surrounding the building. And we've now arranged with the relevant, indigenous Alpha Centauri team to, so to speak, artificially override, and rather earlier than its agreed, so-called *daytime* start, the dramatic albeit perpetual, natural and sunset-style sky that we know as *night*. This will give us the ability to launch far-seeing, and camera-bearing, drones in the active search for your daughter. Ground-based personnel will also be looking across other, near areas within our settlement territory …"

Another very brief pause, then:

"… I'm so sorry this has happened," Solomon went on, "but I can assure you that we'll do our utmost to locate your young daughter, and as soon as possible."

I was truly impressed with the efficiently planned, initial and hopefully successful operation by the police, as outlined by the officer apparently in charge.

"Thank you very much for that," Brian said, clearly as bowled over as I was at that juncture. "We're so very worried about Martha's safety and wellbeing."

"Of course, I can readily comprehend how terribly concerned you and your wife must be, at this exceedingly worrying time, about your beloved daughter's sudden and mystifying disappearance," DI Solomon responded. "And, as I've said, we're doing everything we possibly can at present to find her …"

A further short hiatus ensued, and then the detective continued.

"… In my occasional, though not dissimilar experiences as a police officer on Earth… actually in Sydney, Australia… there's been a happy ending virtually always in such cases. Adventure-minded kids, even quite young ones, shouldn't necessarily surprise us by their… well, adventures I suppose."

As I pondered Solomon's fairly mild Aussie accent, Brian was nodding balefully and looked to be on the point of saying something. But then he appeared to change his mind. My instinct – and not by virtue of any mind-reading powers, as possessed seemingly by Joshua and Sarah – told me that Martha's father was about to ask the very experienced, and assuredly long-serving, DI about those evidently few searches for lost children that hadn't ended so happily. A horrible word entered my head suddenly… *abduction*; and then a question: *Were we really living in a* perfect *world now?* However, I felt confident Brian was thankfully aware that his overwhelmingly distressed spouse – and even in her pitifully horrifying condition – was listening to the informative conversation he was having with Solomon. Indeed, I noticed her husband glancing fleetingly at Elise when he seemed to alter his thought pattern an instant or two back.

"Please excuse me, I need to leave you now …" the senior policemen said, gazing from Brian to Elise then again at her spouse, "but in the very capable hands of my two constables …"

The male officer had just returned to the lounge from Martha's bedroom and accompanied by the heavy-looking briefcase, which he handed now to his superior officer.

"… And, naturally," the DI went on, "I, or one of my colleagues of similar rank, will be keeping in touch with both of you… hopefully, and very soon, with some good news about your daughter."

I was hoping that the guy wasn't being over-optimistic, as Brian nodded appreciatively at his comforting words. Solomon turned towards the hallway to be met by another ring of the doorbell. I detected a really terrified expression creasing Martha's parents' already haggard faces. The male police constable opened the front door; and there, on the doorstep, stood Rabbi Stellman from our synagogue. His bearded visage, crowned with a wide-brimmed black hat, bore a seriously concerned expression. Brian beckoned him to enter the flat. The Detective Inspector nodded at the middle-aged minister – who, I'm sure, the officer recognised – as he moved around him and exited the apartment. The constable, who remained behind in the flat, then closed the door. The rabbi followed Brian into the living room, nodded after noting my presence and stared, clearly and painfully shocked, at Elise – still seated beside the policewoman – as, doubtless, he absorbed also the dire atmosphere.

"I'm so sorry," the rabbi offered, his intonation replete with both anxiety and sympathy. "I came as soon as I could after hearing that Martha was missing from home. I was just saying some prayers for her good health and safe return to you, Brian and Elise… may the Almighty hear my voice and plea. I feel so profoundly for both of you."

"How did you get to hear that our daughter had gone *awol*, rabbi?" Brian enquired whilst gesturing that the minister should seat himself in an armchair; and which he did.

I had little doubt that my friend had employed the *awol* military term – albeit perhaps mistakenly, and in more senses than one – because he knew that, during a relatively early stage of his rabbinic career on Earth, Rabbi Stellman had served as an army chaplain for Jewish soldiers.

"One of our congregants contacted me a little while ago," the now community minister replied. "He lives on the ground floor of this building... and he'd got to know about your sadly missing daughter when the police arrived at his flat, during their search of all apartments here, apparently for elimination purposes."

Brian and I nodded. Elise was still too deeply confined in her own horribly bleak world to make any sort of acknowledgement at all. Rabbi Stellman's armchair was positioned proximate to the end of the sofa where Elise was sitting with the consoling female constable, well trained for such situations, on the other side of Martha's mother and clasping one of her hands. Elise was staring downwards, her body quaking visibly as she continued crying, when the kindly minister leaned forward and placed his forearm gently on the dark-coloured settee's near armrest.

"Easy for me to say, I know Elise," the rabbi addressed her directly, "but you must try to be strong. Every effort is being made to find your daughter, and there's no reason for you to fear that anything amiss has happened to her. Please be full of hope and trust that Martha will be found well very soon... as I, and doubtless you and Brian, have prayed to the Almighty that she will be."

All of a sudden, Elise looked up and straight into Rabbi Stellman's totally sympathetic eyes, her own now quite reddened by her relentless weeping. It seemed apparent to me and, I thought, to the others present that she wanted to say something which was playing on her mind, and in response to her rabbi's benevolent words of solace. After a few strained moments – when obviously struggling to put herself into a less emotional state, and followed by a couple of mournfully intense sighs – Elise started to speak; and, somewhat surprisingly in this dreadful state of affairs, with a reasonably audible voice.

"R-Rabbi S-Stellman," she began, "p-please do forgive me for ignoring you when you came into the flat earlier, and ..."

"There's no need for me to forgive you of anything, Elise," the minister clearly felt an overpowering necessity to interrupt and express. "I can understand fully what you and Brian must be going through right now... and at this extremely worrying time for both of you."

The woman appeared to shake her head slightly.

"B-But I do think Brian and I need to seek forgiveness for what we've done, rabbi," she went on, maybe with some returning, and emotionally fathomless, thoughts causing her to whimper softly.

"What do you mean, Elise?" the attentive and caring minister enquired, with a querying glance at each of Martha's parents.

"W-Well, Rabbi Stellman," the mother said with a sob, "we shouldn't have left our young daughter alone in the flat and gone off to our friends, David and Naomi and albeit very near neighbours in the building, for drinks and a chat earlier this evening... And despite the fact that Martha had told us she was very tired from school activities today, and wanted to go to bed early. We feel so guilty and ..."

"But neither Brian nor you should feel guilty... to any extent," the rabbi advanced. "It wasn't your fault that she has gone missing. She might well have left the apartment, for her own reasons if she had any and surreptitiously, even if you had stayed at home, Elise... and were having a cheerful conversation with Brian in this very room."

Elise again seemed to shake her head a tad.

"I-I do hear what you're saying, rabbi," she said, fairly evenly, "but, with the greatest of respect, we'd never before left our baby home alone... And we could easily have postponed the social arrangement with our friends, or Brian could've gone to them on his own and apologised for my absence to stay with our fatigued Martha... Regretfully, we do feel responsible for what has happened."

After her kind of confessional statement, with its underlying and personal guilt complex so apparent, Elise burst into tears yet again; and the policewoman sought to comfort her by sliding an arm around miserably rising and falling shoulders. I felt really sorry for the rabbi, who was doing his own level best verbally to calm, console and bolster Martha's mother; but who was having a rather bad time of it. Even through her renewed bout of terrible sobbing, the guilt-ridden mother found some more words to utter, and with much palpable hurt.

"What if Martha hadn't stealthily left the flat to go on some jaunt or exploit of her own design... and, for sure, she's never gone sleep-walking either," Elise remarked and somewhat volubly, to the manifest embarrassment of at least her husband. "What if she's been *abducted*?"

Brian, who seemed to be on a delicately emotive parapet during the fraught conversation we were now witnessing, clearly felt the need to intervene at this juncture.

"My apologies, Rabbi Stellman," he said ruefully. "My dear wife just isn't herself at the moment, and I'm sure she didn't mean to …"

"No worries, Brian," the minister interjected, not wishing the husband to say any more about Elise's outburst. "As I've said, I understand the situation completely… but please place your trust and faith in the Almighty. There's no reason for you to feel guilty, or accountable in any way, for Martha going absent. Nor is there any cause for you to be unduly pessimistic about your daughter's present safety and wellbeing. Much is being done to find her, safe and sound."

Shortly after that sensitive series of exchanges, Brian suggested quietly that I should return to Naomi and the kids; and he thanked me sincerely for my wanting to be with them. Before I left, my friend said that he would keep in touch with any, hopefully joyful, developments. I learned subsequently that the rabbi had stayed with the distressed parents all that night, alongside the attendant duty constables; and that he didn't leave until it was time for him to prepare to lead weekday morning prayers at the synagogue. When I got back to the family, the children were thankfully well and fast asleep. But, before

Naomi and I retired to bed, I reported fully to her about what I'd picked up that late evening. Before doing so, I heard from her that Mike, editor of the *Jewish Centaurian*, wanted me to contact him... though I wasn't quite sure why he hadn't communicated with me directly.

Thirty Three

I DECIDED that it was too late for me to return Mike's call; I would get back to him first thing the following morning. When I did make contact, the *Jewish Centaurian* editor immediately said he wanted me to write a front page news story about the missing young girl for the paper's forthcoming debut issue. I enquired, somewhat mystified initially, about how *he* had come to learn about Martha going missing from home the previous day. He informed me that one of his staff members resided in our apartment development; and he'd heard from her that the police were calling at all flats in the building, and about their reason for doing so. And Mike appeared aware also that Naomi and I were good friends of the girl's family. But well before I got in touch with Mike early in the day, indeed when I was lying in bed some hours before and unable – unlike my wife – to get to sleep, I couldn't stop thinking about the time I'd spent in my friends' apartment the preceding night. I just seemed stymied from casting off Brian's conversations, first with Detective Inspector Solomon and then with Rabbi Stellman from our synagogue.

There was one aspect of the exchanges with the senior police officer that I began to wonder about. I couldn't recall him asking the parents to supply some personal information about their daughter; but only that he seemed generally engaged in describing and explaining what had been, and would be, arranged to hunt for her. I didn't think he'd even actually enquired about what night-wear Martha had been wearing when she went to bed. But that fairly expected question aside, it seemed to me important for him to know precisely whether the young girl had gone missing from home, or elsewhere, at any time during her time on Earth; and the cause and outcome of such an incident. Also, I speculated on why Solomon hadn't asked any questions concerning her current, mental wellbeing. That is, about whether she'd been settled in her mind regarding the newly existing, Proxima b situation; or whether the prevailing situation, including attendance at her new school, were having any kind of observably deleterious affect on her.

Surely, I thought, her state of mind that last evening would've been very relevant – and may've been positively significant – for consideration. After all, Martha was still merely a child, albeit a really intelligent one for her age. And, as the material professionals would well know, it mightn't take too much for a youngster – in such an extraordinary set of circumstances as we were all experiencing, unbelievably – to do a strange and uncharacteristic act. These notions crowded into my head and, consequentially, inhibited slumber. In addition, it seemed that I was intent on sublimating any thoughts concerning a possible evil intervention, by any extraneous party or parties, in connection with her absence from home.

Eventually, I did manage to fall into a troubled few hours of shut-eye; but not before I'd reached the virtually comforting conclusion that Brian must've been quizzed on Martha's perceived state of mind, whether healthy or otherwise, when he'd contacted the police originally. This would've been on discovering, alarmingly, that she'd gone missing and after making as good an – albeit abortive – effort as viable to locate her in the vicinity of her home.

On speaking to Mike – who happened to be very busy when I contacted him – he asked, somewhat apologetically, whether I could perhaps pop along to the newspaper offices later that morning for a quick chat about the projected story relating to Martha's disappearance. I agreed, of course, and we fixed a time convenient for him. I couldn't help but feel rather anxious about not knowing of any developments, especially encouraging ones, in the search for the girl; though, as some do say, no news is good news. But I felt it wouldn't necessarily be right for me to just drop in to her parents' flat right then to make some enquiries. There could be much going on there, in any event; and, naturally, I didn't want to be seen as snooping or interfering. I recalled Brian saying that he would keep us in touch with any important progress.

Just before setting out for Mike's office, I did receive a message from Naomi. It was one of her class assistant days at the school, and she mentioned succinctly the sad ambience prevailing there that morning, after teaching and other staff – as well as the pupils, of course – had learned of Martha's unexplained vanishing from her home. Apparently, the headmistress had made diligent arrangements for some care professionals to attend the school premises, in order to offer counselling to those adults and children appearing to be in need of their services during the day.

"Hi, David!" Mike declared in his usual affable fashion, and from behind his computer-occupied desk, as I entered his office. My on-time arrival had been announced by his svelte and youngish PA, who smilingly opened the door for me.

"Hi, Mike!" I responded, sliding onto the chair opposite him; and to which he'd gestured with an outstretched, open palm.

"This is so sad ..." he added, "Martha suddenly disappearing into thin air from the face of the... from the face of Proxima b."

I didn't think the editor was trying to be funny – as opposed to being on the wrong wavelength for an instant; the current situation was far too grim for that sort of quirky approach.

"Yes, Mike," I kind of confirmed.

"Have you heard anything further, David... in the way of any search developments?" he enquired, with due concern in his voice.

"No, Mike," I replied, shaking my head. "I've learned nothing more since last night when, as you know, I spent some time with the parents... and, as you're also aware now, our dear friends ..."

"Yes, I *am* so aware..." Mike stated, but with a wry grin... my staff-member informant, the one who has a flat in your building, told me she has seen you and your wife with Martha's parents chatting amiably at Shabbat morning kiddush after the service in the synagogue, then leaving with them."

"No problem …" I said, matching the editor's dry beam, "but Brian, her father as you doubtless know, said last night that he would try to keep me posted about what's going on in the search process… Quite understandably, I guess, I don't suppose he's been in a position to do that, so far, today. If I don't hear anything from him or whoever before this evening, I could possibly decide, though reticently, to pop round to his apartment. I don't want to bother my friends at this time, and I'm not close family… but I do have, naturally as a parent, strong empathetic feelings about Martha's sudden and inexplicable departure."

Mike nodded, eyes revealing his understanding; then he spoke again.

"I'm sure our potential readers, maybe a good majority of them also being parents, across the territory would seriously wish to know as many details as we can provide in this significant instance," he said in a business-like fashion. "They may want, or need, to take particular precautions concerning their own offspring… it could amount to a crucial security question, we don't know at present. But, hopefully, this will not be a story with a tragic climax. So I'm relying on you, David, and with your many years of investigative journalism, to find out as much as you can about what's happening. I hope that's how you see it, too, David."

I nodded in turn then stated:

"I'll certainly be doing my best, Mike… and not only as the protective father of young kids."

"Ok, David… and if you need my assistance in any way, please don't hesitate to let me know or, in my absence for any reason, my hardworking personal assistant."

I couldn't somehow prevent an image of the trim and sexy brunette inaptly making a fleeting appearance on my mind-screen.

"Thanks, Mike," I said. "And if I can't get the information I require direct from Brian or even his wife Elise, for any overriding reason, I'll have to go out into the field, so to speak, and gather any available data I can from the search HQ personnel or via other means."

"Excellent!" remarked the editor. "Well, many thanks for coming in to see me, David… and we'll keep in close touch."

Mike stood up, we shook hands and I left his office. On my way out, his eye-catching PA and I exchanged little hand waves as I passed her desk.

Walking back to the flat under the now very familiar, bright yellowy sky, I thought I detected expressions on people's faces quite different, on the whole, to the type of looks I was fairly used to seeing when passing pedestrians on the streets. And the thought occurred to me: *Bad news travels fast.*

When I opened the front door to the flat on my return home, I spotted two separate, white pieces of paper lying on the wood floor. Each of them, seemingly and coincidentally, had been slipped under our front door, exposing the side that had manuscript-writing on it, but each clearly from a different hand. Unusual to have such physical message vehicles these days, I felt at once. But then I recollected that old Francophile axiom: *Plus ça change, plus c'est le meme chose.* Anyway, I picked up the notes and read them. Each was addressed to me. One was from Brian, asking me to call round to the flat as soon as I could. The other – a bit surprising, at least in format – was from Diva, who'd written that she'd come to the apartment hoping to see me and discuss the matter of the vanished child. She requested that I advise her as soon as I was back at home, so that she could come along and do just that.

Brian or Diva first …? I had to choose swiftly.

Thirty Four

THERE REALLY was no contest about whether I should go instantly to see Brian, or contact Diva to tell her to come round as I was at home now. I left the apartment and headed smartly to our friends' flat. Though not before sending a message to our other friend, letting her know that I should be back at the apartment and available – I estimated, but without any certainty – in about an hour. I hadn't received a confirmatory reply from Diva by the time I was ringing the bell at Brian's abode.

The male police constable, whom I recognised from last evening, opened the front door and let me in. Brian met me at the other end of the hallway; he nodded then led me into the sitting room. At once, I observed Elise slumped on the sofa, head propped on her chest as if she was asleep; though I could just make out some whimpering sounds emanating from her, and suggesting she was awake. Sitting beside her was a policewoman, but not the one from the night before; the uniformed officer looked up to acknowledge my entrance. Brian tapped my arm and indicated we should sit in the dining area.

I followed him and we sat down, he on a chair at the head of the elongated table with me to his immediate right and facing away from the lounge space. I suspected from my friend's earnest expression that he had some news to report to me; and I assumed, fairly confidently, that it concerned a development in the search for his daughter. But I felt that his facial features appeared somewhat ambiguous, so I wasn't really definite about whether his news was inclined towards the good or the not so good. I hoped for the former. However, and on the basis of his overall approach, I presumed – and with an inward, though perhaps tentative sigh of relief – that what he was on the verge of telling me wasn't tragic. Probably, all this meant that my own face didn't exactly show unconcern in its directed, and inevitably apprehensive, gaze at Brian's unrevealing countenance.

"The police department's search drones, with their amazing telescopic capacity, were launched very early today, David," Brian informed me. "And they've actually found something belonging to Martha ..."

I could almost feel my jaw dropping and eyebrows rising.

"What did they find, Brian?" I asked promptly.

"I don't really know why Elise and I hadn't realised it was missing ..." he continued. "Martha sometimes took her old teddy bear to bed and especially when, our daughter would tell us, she felt a need to closely embrace the brown, furry plaything with its cutely smiling and cheering expression. You might think she would've outgrown the cuddly plaything, but she adored it. Maybe it hadn't occurred to us, when she'd gone to bed that

MARK HARRIS

night, that it was one of those occasions… if, indeed, it was. She'd simply informed us of her weariness after school sports that day, and was sorry she didn't feel awake enough to accompany us to your flat… And we hadn't noticed, in our terrible state of mind when discovering her absence from the apartment, that Freddy the Teddy wasn't in his usual position beside the desk-top, reading lamp in Martha's bedroom …"

"So the police, or rather their drones, have found a teddy bear that you've now identified as your daughter's?" I queried for certainty's sake.

"Yes, David… they brought it here a short while ago for identification purposes, of course, then took it away again," he said.

"But where did they find it?" I enquired further and with, I felt, some trepidation in my voice. "And I take it I'm right in thinking that Martha wasn't found with it, or in its environs?"

Her father took a deep breath then rubbed his furrowed brow, which appeared to be glistening with perspiration despite the temperate climate in the flat.

"Sadly, I can answer your second question in the affirmative," my ostensibly sweating friend responded. "Her teddy bear was discovered in a really odd place, it seemed to everyone …"

"And where was that?" I interjected, full of a sort of aching curiosity.

Brian paused for a brief while, possibly to ensure his level-headedness or self-possession.

"Well, the high-flying drones pinpointed it early this morning," he explained, "as a non-natural object lying on the arranged for, prematurely sky-lightened ground... It's relatively flat terrain, but a landscape scattered with rocks and, evidently, just a few metres beyond the hinterland boundary of our now settled territory."

I wasn't at all certain how I should react now; and both of us remained silent for a short time, collecting some rational thoughts so far as I was personally concerned. Finally, I found some potentially material words.

"B-But is it known how Martha managed to get that far from home, Brian, assuming she did by any means?" I asked, posing the question disquietingly to some extent. "Do the police have any ideas... any clues? Clearly, they've attended at the scene where the teddy bear was found."

"That's correct, of course, David," my friend said. "But the police... well nobody, in fact, has any notion as to why or how our daughter's favoured companion happened to be where it was found... I would merely add for completeness, and as you've just inferred, that because Freddy the Teddy was located where it was doesn't mean necessarily that Martha had been present at that spot, too."

As he noted, I'd already seen the disturbing logic of Brian's additional sentence. At that instance, I turned my head to gaze awkwardly towards the settee. So far as I could make out, there had been no change in the sedentary positions of either Elise or the supportive policewoman; and no break in the continuing, sorrowful sound of distressed whimpering emitted by Martha's mother. I expected that the male constable currently on duty in the flat would still be standing in the hallway. And as if to confirm my belief, he just happened to sneeze at that moment. Then I turned back to Brian.

"So what are the police doing now?" I asked of necessity.

My sorrowing friend placed his firmly clenched hands on the table.

"Well, David," he said, though in a fairly composed manner, "one of DI Solomon's colleagues advised me that they're presently examining, and very meticulously, Martha's teddy bear as well as the locale where it was found for any clues that could be helpful in their quest."

I nodded then opined:

"I sincerely hope the police investigators and evidence analysts detect something useful, and that will provide a distinct pointer regarding your darling daughter's current whereabouts… and as soon as possible."

We spoke for a while longer including, and in a hushed fashion, about poor Elise. I learned from her devoted husband that a medical colleague had attended the flat earlier that morning to examine her. And to make sure that her harrowing, emotional state wasn't having a deleterious affect on her physical health. Both Elise and Brian, I learned and wasn't at all surprised to hear, hadn't been able to grab a wink of sleep since their daughter had gone missing. However, both parents refused to take any pills or tablets. These had been prescribed by the visiting doctor for their insomnia; and to ensure their wellbeing in, as the medic – originally from South Africa, Brian told me – could well understand, the horrifyingly unpredictable circumstances.

But Brian and I conversed also about a hope, parallel to the comprehensive police efforts, that someone from our territory might come forward soon with helpful information. Maybe it would be a person who'd happened to spot Martha the evening before; or possibly at some later time during the night. It could've been an individual who hadn't thought too hard about such a sighting, that's before hearing the now well-circulated news about a young girl's disappearance. And it might've been someone who'd handily taken onboard the description of her physical appearance, and what she may well have been wearing at the time; that is, say, her pink and white pyjamas or otherwise.

Brian mentioned, additionally, the many messages he and Elise had received – from work colleagues, community members, neighbours and others – offering their good wishes, and noting that they were hoping and/or praying that Martha would be found completely well and in the near future.

On saying farewell to Brian, I endeavoured to have a brief word with Elise; but it was sadly impossible for me to get through the sadly emotional barrier. Her husband thanked me for my kind and gentle attempt then shook his head pitiably. Just as he was about to show me out of the apartment, and after I reminded him to keep in touch, the duty constable opened the front door. Coincidentally on the doorstep, and about to ring the bell, was Rabbi Stellman and a woman whom I recognised immediately as his wife. We nodded mutually as I left the flat. And I prayed – yes, actually prayed – inwardly that the community minister, this time with his rebbetzen, could definitely instil some hope and even a trust in *Hashem*, the Almighty, into the mind of each of their pitifully grief-stricken congregants; and, particularly, that of the utterly inconsolable Elise... but not forgetting Brian. When I got back home, I found patiently waiting on my own doorstep the one and only Diva.

Thirty Five

DIVA AND I entered the apartment, and I told her to make herself at home in the living room whilst I popped into the bathroom. Not long afterwards, I emerged and was happy to see her ensconced in an armchair within the lounge area. She accepted my offer of coffee, so I hastened into the kitchen; and feeling myself, too, a dire need for a strong shot of caffeine. A few minutes later, I placed the steaming hot cups on the occasional table then sat down in the armchair opposite my dear friend from way back.

"How are Joshua, Sarah and Naomi?" Diva asked immediately.

Surprisingly or not, it was the first matter she enquired about. I knew, of course, that Diva would have in her head the knowledge of what I was going to say straight away in answer to her kind question. But, as she'd reminded me often, her ability to mind-read – though to that limited extent only... and which capacity seemingly had been inherited by our twins – shouldn't deter or inhibit me from actually expressing myself verbally.

"They're all fine physically, and thankfully," I replied. "And many thanks for asking, Diva."

"That's good," she said, "and doubtless you would've perceived why the question was uppermost in my mind."

After just a moment or two of pondering, I nodded meaningfully.

"Yes, Diva," I added to my head movement, "I'm sadly aware of your likely rationale… and that's why, as you know, I added the word *physically*."

She nodded in turn then kind of changed the implicit subject-matter.

"I thought Naomi might've been at home this morning, David," she remarked. "Isn't today one of those when she doesn't usually work as a part-time, class assistant?"

I nodded then replied vocally.

"You're absolutely correct. Normally, she goes in every other school day. She went in yesterday, so you're right in thinking that today should've been her day off. However, the head teacher requested full, if not extra attendance by all staff, if possible, at this unfortunate and worrying time… As you might expect after Martha's mysterious disappearance, many of the children at her school are, at the very least, in a concerning mood of melancholy and some fear. Naturally, their parents are quite worried, too. Relevant counselling services have been brought in to advise teachers, and to work sympathetically with the pupils. A moment ago, I said that the twins and Naomi are *fine*. Physically, as I've mentioned, that's fortunately the case. But, as we've already hinted, all have been affected variously, in their own individual ways, by their school friend and neighbour strangely going missing suddenly…

Willingly, Naomi answered the head's call and attended school alongside Joshua and Sarah this morning."

I took a deep breath, then a sip of my hot coffee. Diva nodded, empathy and munificence etching her face; and she also took some of her own beverage.

"I take it you know at least as much as we do about developments in the wide-ranging, police search for Martha... including the perhaps odd discovery, by the far-reaching drones, of her teddy bear?" I was kind of asking for confirmation. "And I'm fairly sure that, as an Alpha Centauri team member, you would be kept in the picture as regards any developments by our police investigators... and maybe even approached for any appropriate assistance you might be able to contribute."

"That's absolutely the case, David," Diva reacted. "But what you may not know is that, as you were returning home after speaking with Brian earlier, a report came through, including to me, that some further evidence was found by the police searchers that has confirmed Martha's earlier presence very close to where her teddy was picked up ..."

"Sorry, but what did they find?" I interrupted and perhaps too brusquely, likely disclosing my journalistic obsessions but, principally, an uneasy present status.

"I was coming to that right away, David... and I am aware that Mike has commissioned you to write about all this," she said to a face replete with repentance. "Look, David, let's take it easy... alright?"

I nodded, though I thought she might've been making a small meal of it. I reached across the low table to gently tap one of Diva's hands. Then we both swallowed an intake of coffee from our cups.

"As you may well know," she said, after delicately finger-wiping her moist lips, "your police would've been in possession of samples of the missing girl's DNA, as you term it. Well, apparently, they were able to match something... something somewhat sensitive to mention... something that was found on the fairly level, but rock-strewn ground just a metre or so from her teddy bear ..."

I could barely wait to hear further, but felt a firm need to quash my impatience. So I waited with baited breath, though both ears alert, for Diva to speak again after a short pause.

"It was her urine, David," she said and, maybe unnecessarily, in a rather subdued tone of voice.

I nodded very slowly and deliberately, adding only two words:

"I see."

Perhaps I should've better said something like, *Noted*.

"But I take it, Diva," I went on, "that our police have no idea how she got to that spot or, indeed, why?"

"That's quite so," she responded, "though, and I don't really need to mention this, your police force and relevant associates are striving to locate, and are fully prepared to analyse, any more evidence found in their concerted efforts to solve this shocking conundrum."

I nodded yet again; then, metaphorically of course, I contemplated my navel for a short while as my dear friend further quenched any thirst she might've had.

"There's another aspect to all this, Diva," I advanced after my brief, meditative lull. "And I would be extremely interested to hear your thoughts, as well as any knowledge you might have, in this connection."

"Please go on, David!" she said helpfully, and at once. "I'll do my utmost to respond to your questions."

"Diva... I was wondering what your people, the indigenous population of Proxima b, might be thinking or saying about Martha's disappearance," I began, "and so comparatively soon after arrival on our new planetary home... assuming that, aside from yourself and colleagues, this world's other inhabitants would know about the terribly mystifying matter."

"Yes, David," she said, "your fellow citizens here are very aware of what has happened, and they've been so saddened to hear the fearful news by one media means or another, in your terms. Indeed, our leaders have sent several sympathetic and supportive messages about this serious issue to a number of your relevant organisations... and, naturally, also to Martha's agonised parents."

I hadn't been made aware by Brian of such kind-hearted and empathetic communications received; and I mentioned this to Diva.

"Maybe this would be the last thing on his mind to tell you about," she said, and quite sensibly I believed. "Martha's health and safety would be understandably preoccupying, if not monopolising Brian's head and would doubtless be prioritising his thinking... So far as concerns his wife, I know she's wretchedly and virtually beyond rational thought processes, certainly unsurprising in such a horrible situation."

What else could I do but nod, and fulsomely.

"I've also had some quite morbid notions, Diva," I said, resuming my initial thesis, "… please do forgive me for unleashing them."

"Go ahead, David," she encouraged me.

"You've said, Diva, and more than once in the past, words to the effect that, over an exceedingly lengthy period of time, your people have learned to live perfect lives in a perfect world," I continued. "And that they're now living happily in a kind of *Golden Age* where, although the difference between right and wrong, good and bad, is known and understood, only what's right and good triumphs. Your people, you've said continually, are benevolent and peaceable, caring and considerate, tolerant and loyal, and have learned to cherish one another for the greater good of the planet on which they reside."

"What you say is absolutely true," she responded, "though, as you say, it has taken the people of our world many millennia to attain, achieve and maintain this wonderfully harmonious state of affairs for all of us here on Proxima b."

"And can I say, Diva," I went on, "that since knowing you, over quite a few years now, we've been totally convinced, with you yourself as a glowing illustration, of what you've often been telling us. And not only because you saved the lives of both Naomi and myself in medieval Cambridge or Cantabrigia, nor due to the marvellous children that you've bestowed upon us… for a blessing."

"That's really so good to hear, David, but not at all necessary for you to say," Diva commented, maybe spotting an unstoppable tear pearl or three sliding down my cheeks.

"So do explain expressly the thought you appear to be leading up to, David."

"Of course, I and my brethren and fellow immigrants to Proxima b have not yet had, or been given, the opportunity to meet with your people in their habitable homelands on this planet," I continued. "But I really do believe that day will come soon, and I and my former Earthlings are looking forward to it …"

Diva nodded with a smile.

"But I want also to believe that your own people, or maybe rather an individual member or two of its population," I added, a tad apprehensively, "would've had nothing to do with Martha's disappearance …"

I paused for a moment, and Diva stared at me with more than an intimation of puzzlement in her lovely eyes.

"I can categorically assure you of that, David," she said.

"And I do accept what you say, Diva… without any question or doubt whatsoever," I responded to her justifiable interjection. "And my own brethren will never forget what your people have done in saving, and wholeheartedly welcoming, us as refugees from a likely disastrous, anti-Semitic evil on the other side of our shared galaxy."

My dear friend nodded, this time herself leaning over the low table to lightly touch my forearm.

"Needless to say, but I will say it," I remarked, "my own people from planet Earth, and as you well know, haven't yet enjoyed the kind of *perfect* world that yours have accomplished. But I've got to note that they've been greatly inspired by the other, though as yet unseen, residents of Proxima b to reach that marvellous objective… and sooner rather than later. Nonetheless, coming from an imperfect world, it goes without saying that some of my people are far from perfect, including even those who have a strong religious faith."

Diva peered into my eyes; but in a somewhat disconcerting, if not disturbing manner.

"So, David," she said. "Are you telling me that one of your own brethren could've been responsible for Martha's sudden, inexplicable disappearance?"

"I don't know, I really hope not… though could it be a possibility, leaving no stone unturned?" I answered with another question, which I considered a fair rather than an insulting one, and adding: "It's just something I find so soulfully destroying to contemplate… I think we just have to wait and see what the police investigations reveal. But I do, and ever so truly, hope and believe that my concerning speculations are way off beam …"

"And which I am sure they are, bearing in mind the outcome of our consensus in relation to my own people," Diva responded, with an acceptable resolution. "What can remain for consideration, other than that Martha went off on an exploratory adventure of her own for whatever motivation? Hopefully very shortly, we'll get to know that both the missing young girl and her current escapade or exploit will come to a positively healthy and happy conclusion."

I just couldn't seem to stop my head from nodding over and over, as our conversation seemed to be reaching its conclusion. Diva thanked me for the coffee, adding that she hoped our chat had been helpful... and maybe in more ways than one. This time my strength of will did manage to overrule any further, up-and-down head movements.

"Thank you, my dear friend," I said finally, thinking maybe peculiarly that I'd actually stated the last three words rather than just thought them.

Diva departed the flat, mentioning that she would keep in touch with me. I closed and secured the front door, then just felt like nodding... off.

Thirty Six

FOR MUCH of the remainder of that day, after my sensitively enlightened conversation with Diva, I began composing some copy for the article I would be submitting to Mike for the *Jewish Centaurian* newspaper. When Naomi arrived home with the children, I noted unhappily but understandably that both Joshua and Sarah looked continuingly depressed at the end of what, normally, would be an enjoyable school session. The twins said they wouldn't mind having an earlier supper; and, after their mother had prepared the sensibly light meal a little later and the twins had consumed it in total silence, they slinked off prematurely to their respective bedrooms for the coming night. After exchanging words with my wife about the kids' mood, doubtless related to Martha's 'still missing' status, we had to acknowledge the positive aspect that they were physically, if not at the present time psychologically fit; as well as being safe and secure in their rooms with both parents close at hand to afford them comfort, if required.

During the evening, but after we'd eaten our dinner, Naomi and I cuddled up reassuringly on the settee and listened, almost but not quite relaxingly, to some potentially soothing music of the classical variety that we'd often enjoyed in the *Old Country*. To help us along the road, in efforts to clear our minds of undesirable material, we each indulged in an old-fashioned glass of malt whisky, plus a top-up, from the drinks cabinet. We were rather tempted to down some more wee drams, but nevertheless appreciated the need to be fully sober if the twins happened to need us, and for a hangover-free and upcoming morrow.

Amazingly, and somewhat contrary to my usual bed-time experience after sliding between sheet and duvet, I fell asleep almost immediately. Worryingly, I hadn't heard further from Brian, or anyone else for that matter, about any further developments, major or otherwise, in the search for his daughter. But the night images that assailed my unconscious mind couldn't have been more disconcerting and troubling. I couldn't remember all of the mostly nightmarish scenes on awakening the next morning; but, unfortunately, two of them did return, unheralded, to my waking state.

The first, perhaps predictably, involved a human-sized, floppy, brown-furred teddy bear with moveable arms and legs. When it held onto me, I could feel only a cloying dampness; and, fleetingly in my dream, I did wonder whether that wetness had any connection with certain DNA. Then I realised that the bear was crying, though very softly; and, from the amount of moisture on its body, probably had been for some time. Tears were plummeting down its round face and plump body, making the fur overly sticky to the touch. I recalled seeking to transform the teddy's heart-rending, gloomy and puffed-up face by telling him some – I hoped – funny stories or jokes, if you like. However and maybe as sometimes occurs with my comedic efforts, they didn't bring a belly laugh, or even a modest grin, to my hugging companion's lips.

Then, and all of a sudden, the teddy bear sort of evaporated into thin air; and it was replaced, haphazardly, by a terrifying setting that I couldn't recognise. Somehow, I was gazing down from a nonetheless familiar, yellowy sky at an extraordinarily huge crowd of people crammed into a necessarily expansive square bounded by lofty buildings. There was much shouting, even screaming, rising from the colossal number of assembled individuals – men, women and children – and I could make out numerous placards being held aloft and waved above their heads. Without question, this appeared to me to be some kind of organised, mass protest or demonstration; and certainly about something really troubling the many thousands of apparently enraged participants. From my overseeing heights above the colossal gathering, I strained to read the words I could perceive to be written on the mobile notice boards.

When I did achieve that outcome, I absorbed the phrases with an enormous angst. One placard, with its bold red lettering, sort of shrieked: "*Give us back our Martha!*" Another, emblazoned in thick black letters, kind of cried out: "*Don't trust anyone!*" And yet another, which

I strained to absorb from the distance below me, stated unnervingly: "*To the other citizens of Proxima b – We know you have our Martha. Hand her back to us, and NOW!*" That could've amounted to my final, scarifying enormity that night. But it was accompanied by the grossly terrifying noise of the entire, undulating crowd screaming the same words as appeared on that third placard I'd read. Then, thankfully, I awoke – albeit with a dramatic start – from that frightening and heartbreaking dream-world.

Alas, my sudden and reflexive movement in the bed also stirred my Naomi into wakefulness. I apologised, mentioning that I'd been dreaming; though I didn't feel that I should go into the upsetting details. There was no problem, my wife said at once whilst turning to face me and before hopping from under the covers. In any event, it was nearly time to rise and face the forthcoming day, and whatever it might unforeseeably deliver.

I'd heard from someone, probably Naomi, that the police had visited, and searched thoroughly, Martha's school; and, again, for 'stone-turning' purposes. But also, and as you would expect, they wished to speak with the headmistress, Mrs Goldstein, the girl's teachers and her closer school friends, including our twins. I didn't want to grill them concerning the questions they had been asked by the inquiring officers; and largely because I didn't want to further, and needlessly, upset them. However, and after Naomi had left the flat with Joshua and Sarah for the new school day, I decided to attend the educational centre that morning, if possible. I contacted the head, explained myself and she agreed that I could come along to speak with her about Martha.

So by mid-morning, and having prepared some questions to ask Mrs Goldstein, a former US citizen hailing from New York, I was en route in smart casual gear to her workplace at the nearby school complex. Her PA, hailing from Los Angeles and who met me at the appointed hour just inside the entrance doors, conducted me to the head's study. Friendly-faced Mrs Goldstein – a middle-aged woman, who was wearing a longish, dark-blue dress with a high collar – welcomed me with a warm handshake. Then she indicated the chair on the other side of a large desk to her own, revolving variety of seat. On the way to this spacious room, lined with full bookshelves interspersed with landscape oil paintings demonstrably imported from Earth, I was really impressed by the appealingly modern architecture of the light and airy, school buildings. I glanced along the several lengthy corridors we were walking past, just in case I might spot either my wife or one or other, even perhaps both of the twins. But that wasn't to be the outcome.

"I'm sorry to trouble you, Mrs Goldstein, you must be very busy," I said, being the first to speak. "But thank you very much for seeing me, especially at such short notice and in the present sad and awfully troubling circumstances."

The head – whom Naomi estimated to be in her late forties – exhibited short, curly auburn hair and stood about the same height as me, but with a noticeably fuller curving figure. She presented me with a benign smile.

"Please don't worry about bothering me," she responded graciously and with the expected, though not that broad a transatlantic accent. "My sadly late husband was a journalist for a well-known, Big Apple newspaper. So I quite understand, and can totally appreciate, the basic need for our people to know what's happening in this world... and how it may be affecting their children and our pupils."

After expressing my regret on hearing of the head's widowhood, I asked her the first of my relatively few questions for her. I'd felt the need, in preparing them, not to take up too much of the woman's valuable time, especially then.

"I'm taking it that, as the school's head and with many duties and responsibilities filling your day, you wouldn't have had contact with Martha on any sort of regular basis..."

Mrs Goldstein nodded.

"However," I continued, "did any of her teachers report to you on anything unusual about the girl... anything that might've raised some concerns in your mind about her wellbeing from, say, a psychological viewpoint?"

"No, not at all," the head replied. "I do try my level best, essentially with the help of our excellent and dedicated teaching staff but also directly when I can, to be aware of each individual child at the school. Importantly, I want to know how they're getting along with the education programmes or curricula we have in place for the various year groups, and from a variety of opinions. In that respect,

I've spoken briefly to Martha on a couple of occasions when calling in to her class on my, generally daily, rounds …"

"How was she doing?"

"From reports I'd received, it appeared that Martha was doing very well in her academic studies," Mrs Goldstein replied. "And from my own short exchanges with her, I could readily perceive that she's a youngster with intelligence beyond her years, and revealing much promise. I would expect much from her, by way of positive educational progress as well as personal development, during her coming years here."

"Very good to hear that," I went on, with the hope she might've said the same about my Joshua and Sarah. "And do you happen to know, by any chance, whether she had any particularly favourite subject or subjects?"

"Yes, as it happens I do," was the speedy answer; but it was accompanied by a melancholy expression. "During a fleeting exchange with her one afternoon, I seem to recollect, Martha expressed a particular love of geography. Though the girl added, kind of coyly and knowingly, that she enjoyed all the subjects she was being taught… but she did specifically mention history also."

Her response confirmed what Martha had personally told us; but her favourite subjects of geography and history, now mentioned again, gave me pause for some equivocal thought in the context of her disappearance.

"Thanks for that succinct survey of her scholastic interests, Mrs Goldstein," I said. "I know that, a little while back, Martha had arrived home feeling very tired, at

least that's what she'd told her parents, at the end of one
school session. During that day, as I understand it, she was
involved with various sports activities ..."

The head leaned forward.

"Yes, I know about this," she said earnestly. "I
believe it was the night that, so very sadly, she went to
bed rather earlier than was usually the case... and, later,
was found to be missing. The police told me about that
when they attended here the other day. We try to do
our utmost in ensuring that the children, and especially
during a period of some physical exertion for them,
don't over-tire themselves. But, of course, any individual
pupil may well overdo it, and without any sense of the
possible consequences... The supervising teachers are
trained to keep a vigilant eye out for any tell-tale signs
of fatigue, or any other difficulty. And, for sure, they will
enquire of the more active participants about how they're
feeling... though they won't always receive an honest
reply, particularly if the questioned child is really enjoying
himself or herself."

"I can fully comprehend what you're saying, Mrs
Goldstein," I said. "And thank you so much for your time
today... I'm very grateful."

"No problem," she remarked. "But that's aside, of
course, from the dreadful *problem* of Martha's disappearance.
All of us... myself, teachers, classroom assistants like your
very dedicated and helpful wife Naomi and other staff,
will hope and, at morning assemblies in the great hall, pray
for her safe return to home and school very soon."

We rose from our seats, and the head said she would call her PA to guide me out of the building complex. I responded that it wasn't necessary for me to have an escort; and that I would re-trace my earlier steps to her office. She nodded with a smile, circuited the desk and moved to open her study door. I departed with a crisp but soft "Bye", which Mrs Goldstein reciprocated along with another warm handshake. As I tracked back to the school's main entrance/exit door, and as earlier, I peered down a number of the corridors in the hope that I might see a close family member. But once more, that wasn't to be the case.

Thirty Seven

AS I LEFT the education campus and stepped onto its surrounding stretch of parkland, I was hit by an unwelcome thought. Never could I have imagined that – after our eight-week journey across the cosmos to escape an increasingly militant and horrendous anti-Semitism on Earth, and a relatively short period on our new planetary home – my first assignment as a semi-retired, investigative journalist would be to write about the sudden, perplexing and, as yet, sadly unsolved disappearance of a young Jewish girl from her family abode.

It seemed to me, as I walked pensively across the relatively narrow width of lawn-like greenery, that the overwhelming majority of my immigrant brethren would likely be pondering on a not too dissimilar train of thought. And in that connection, I believed, whatever their age, background or position in our rapidly developing, Proxima b society. Then it struck me that I could give a human touch to my projected, *Jewish Centaurian* news-feature by carrying out a kind of random survey to elicit pithy comments on missing Martha from, so to speak, people on the street. And that's what I resolved to do that very afternoon.

Luckily, my recently issued Press Card was tucked away in an inside pocket of the casual jacket I was sporting. After stepping off the grass but prior to transiting a road, I double-checked that the identification evidence was in place, just in case I needed to show it to potential respondents. As I was about to leave the kerb, I noted a youngish woman crossing the thoroughfare in my direction; and she was holding the hand of a little boy of about six years old. We recognised each other from our synagogue attendance. So I waited for her, a former New Zealander from Christchurch, to reach me with her young son. After a concise exchange of pleasantries, she told me they were hastening back to his school – the one I'd just left – after a visit to their local GP that morning. Apparently, the small lad had hurt his arm in a fall at home, but was fine now… no bones broken, thankfully, just some slight bruising. He smiled at me.

I moved back onto the open green space with the two of them, craved a moment or two of the mother's time, and put the same question to her as I proposed to ask each subsequent, fleeting interviewee in my informal and virtually unsystematic, street survey; using, of course, my trusty gadget to record.

"What has been in your mind when thinking, as I believe you probably have been doing, about Martha suddenly going missing from her home?"

I didn't think I would need to explain that situation to anyone I felt like approaching for a comment.

"As a mum," the woman replied with a grim frown, "I can't tell you how both saddened and nervous I've been since hearing about her disappearance. And I find myself praying constantly for Martha's safe return to her undoubtedly incredulous and tormented parents."

"Thanks," I said, as mother and child began hurrying towards the school entrance.

In the pleasant warmth of the air, and under the bright yellowish sky, I moved on too. I passed a not inconsiderable number, and diversity, of pedestrians going about their day's business. But I decided to stop next at a café that Naomi and I had visited once or twice, and where we'd found our black Americano coffees to be reasonably good. It was owned and run by a middle-aged couple, formerly of Edgware in north-west London. Only a few tables were occupied when I entered, but nobody appeared to be waiting for their hot drinks at the serving counter. So I stepped towards the diminutive, balding and bespectacled husband who, like his dark-haired and even shorter wife, was donned in a full-body, light brown apron. The guy, who also wore what gave the appearance of a chef's traditional white headgear, seemed to recognise me as I asked him *the* question.

"Martha's parents should be thoroughly ashamed of themselves!" he spurted with ill-disguised indignation. "Leaving a small child home all alone at night while they went off drinking somewhere... And I've got no more to say on this awful subject!"

Not even, evidently, to express a hope for the young girl's safe return.

I departed the coffee shop straight away and without more, harbouring the thought that my wife – after I would

311

tell her of the man's observation – and I might not feel like returning there. In any case, the Americano brewed for us hadn't been that brilliant. Though on leaving, and admittedly, I *was* inwardly and perhaps inexorably debating the café owner's – and, possibly, both of its owners' – stance, and its potential justifiability. Not that I wasn't fully aware and, in consequence, unsurprised by the view expressed to me; actually, it proved to be an opinion held by more respondents than the orthodox *barrista*. This attitude did bring back to my mind the sort of guilt complex prevailing in their flat when I'd been with Brian and Elise, not long subsequent to their daughter going missing. And with which, shortly afterwards, community minister Rabbi Stellman had tried his level best to deal.

On my unplanned route, I stopped many more people on the street, some of whom didn't want to make any comment; or didn't have the time to stop and answer my question. One tallish fellow that I approached – he was clean-shaven, black wavy-haired, wearing a dark suit with white shirt and a striped blue, white and red tie – placed his briefcase on the pavement momentarily, then replied to my interrogatory.

"Being Jewish, I would just answer you with another question," he started with a quite stern gaze, rather than an anticipated and whimsical little grin. "Who will be the indigenous population's next bloody victim?"

Somehow, I wasn't entirely amazed to hear this view, either. But it was in a sort of ambivalent way that I'd almost expected someone to bowl this one at me.

Following close on the heels of that quick question-cum-answer-cum-querying comment, I excused myself to stop an elderly, grey-haired couple who were moving slowly arm-in-arm towards me. The man, donning a kind of homburg, was somewhat stooped, wore horn-rimmed glasses and employed a walking stick to aid him along. His younger-looking wife appeared to be rather more bodily vertical and agile. Initially, they seemed to be quite intimidated by my, to them possibly, abrupt intrusion. I did reveal to the pair my Press identification; but I think the lettering on it was perhaps too small for either of them to decipher. The lady explained their initial attitude towards me by asserting that they thought I was a beggar demanding money. I well understood – from my own Earth experiences of being approached by someone saying, "Excuse me" – what they meant. But I really hadn't considered the apparel I'd put on earlier that day would give rise to this kind of impression. The aged gentleman seemed hard of hearing, poor chap, so it was his other half who responded to my question.

"W-We've got a number of children, several grandchildren and a few great-grandchildren," she began and evenly, too; though I did sense a hint of emotion creeping gradually and furtively into her quite lucid voice. "S-some of them are here on this planet... b-but others r-remained b-behind, for w-whatever r-reason, with their f-families... on E-Earth ..."

I could perceive some tear globules forming in her poignant eyes as she strived to reply to me. I was beginning to regret, and somewhat heavy-heartedly, halting them in their gradually advancing tracks. Then my respondent looked like she was taking an abnormally deep but shivery breath; so I readied myself to support her in case, regrettably, she was about to fall down onto the hard sidewalk. To my utter relief, she didn't. Had she done so, it would've plainly been my fault entirely.

"I can't tell you how much we miss seeing those who remained on Earth," she continued, but this time without the hint of a moving stutter. I could feel that, basically, she was a strong woman; but I had rapidly to alter that likely superficial belief when the lady burst into sobs after expressing, with some breath-taking pauses, her next following and unfinished words.

"It's a bit like Martha's parents must feel right now …" she said. "We'll never see again those and other present, and future, members of our family… who decided to stay put on that horribly evil world… It's as if they're all dead to us, just as we must seem dead to them… but we need to pray that …"

I kind of nodded, but felt really uncomfortable to have caused her upset. Then I shuffled away from the couple – the husband having been quite out of the equation – after muttering, guiltily, as soft and tender a *Sorry* and *Thanks* that I could muster. I did wonder whether I should, or could now persist with my vulnerable survey. If truth be told, I didn't want to be the cause of any further anguish or grief by putting my question and hearing any dire reflections and haunting memories to which it might give rise. But having thought the thought, I resolved to go on with the project in order to elicit an authentic spectrum of thinking regarding Martha's virtual vanishing into thin air; and, just possibly, my respondents' comments could prove to be of some utility.

While ambling along, and despite my own preoccupations, I certainly noticed that there were definitely more police on the streets than previously had been the case. The raison d'être was obvious, of course. From time to time, here and there, I did see groups of uniformed officers entering various buildings, both office and residential, on the course I was following. As I walked the very active thoroughfares, it did occur to me that I'd received no further information – by communication from Brian, Diva or anyone else – about any further progress, or whatever, in the search for Martha.

Then I found myself – and that almost allegorically – strolling past a pharmacy. I knew, from passing this remedial services provider on a few previous occasions, that it would be fairly hectic with prospective clients across the year groupings, from teenagers through mid-lifers to third-age members. Whatever their decade, they would be seeking some restorative for their pain, whether physical or mental; and whether or not they had attended previously a clinic or other, now established medical facility to be examined and diagnosed for a prescriptive therapy or remedy.

Probably, it should've been a no-go zone within which to put my clearly sensitive question to a customer or two. And this – practically inescapably, I supposed – would prove to be the case. On entering these extensive premises through the automatic glass doors, I was struck instantaneously by a sense of *déjà vu*! I must've been perambulating in circles… my thought-crammed head partly, if not wholly, to blame for that distinct possibility. For about to exit the chemists' emporium at that moment were two people I recognised right away. Maybe it should've occurred to me, and equally swiftly, why they might be there. The physically arched, bespectacled and elderly man with the stick didn't acknowledge me in any way, even assuming that he'd identified me. But his spouse assuredly did, and had.

It wasn't easy to find the most appropriate words to describe the expression on her only slightly lined face. On being at the fairly disconcerting, receiving end of that look, I determined then and there to draw a close to my survey project; and to go straight home in order to engage in a more upbeat activity, and one that might be less stressful all round. But who knew for sure about anything at that moment in time? Anyway, I backed out between the automatically opening doors and returned hurriedly to our apartment.

Thirty Eight

BEFORE ARRIVING back at the flat, I received a call from Brian. He asked whether I could come round to his apartment. There was much nervous tension in his voice. I didn't really want to squander his time by asking whether he or, indeed, anything was alright because, in any event, nothing *was* for him and, of course, Elise. And he didn't mention anything that would compel me to think differently. He told me that Detective Inspector Solomon had just contacted him to say that he would be attending on Brian shortly. Apparently, the officer had informed Brian that Diva would be accompanying him. Naturally, my neighbour and good friend had asked whether their imminent visit was related to any new developments in the search for his daughter. Solomon, I was advised, responded that they would talk after he and Diva arrived at the flat.

I told Brian that, of course, I would be with him very shortly. Before we finished speaking, however, I did actually feel a gripping need to enquire about his poor wife. Her now edgy-voiced husband explained that, on an independent doctor's advice, he'd engaged a recommended, temporary but full-time carer for his beloved but devastated Elise. It was mentioned that the single woman – who'd been formerly a German citizen residing in Berlin, but with very good English – was with her charge as we spoke; and that Golda was, for the time being, occupying Martha's room. Brian went on to tell me that his spouse currently slept for most of the time, though largely due to the prescription pills she was now having to take; and that he was glad her mind wasn't being tortured continuously. For sure, the hubby said, he wouldn't dream of awakening her to mention the impending arrival of DI Solomon and Diva. Our exchange ended with my telling him to hold on; and that I would be with him in minutes.

As I quickened my pace, my head was almost spinning with concern about what news, if any, the incongruous pair would be bringing with them for Brian and Elise. I felt so deeply, as did Naomi, for the couple. But, at least for the moment, I possessed sufficient equilibrium to send a message to my dear wife, noting where I was headed and why. When I reached our friends' home, Brian – clothed in dark trousers and a short-sleeved, blue-checked shirt – let me in. In the hallway, he told me falteringly that his other expected visitors hadn't turned up as yet.

After I tried to comfort the really distraught-looking man with an arm around his shoulders, we went to sit down in the living room. I could readily perceive that his hands were trembling as they lay on his knees; and that his eyes appeared full of angst and pain. I'd not seen him quite like this before; but I understood, beyond doubt, the terrible motivation for his present bearing or, rather, lack of such. He was obviously, and naturally, fearful of what information might soon be forthcoming. It crossed my mind that the Detective Inspector, when he'd called earlier, probably would've told Brian immediately had he possessed some good news about Martha; though it's also said that hearing no news can amount to good news. In any case, my transient thought prompted even greater concern in me; and I reckoned that my friend, as I gazed sadly at his silent quivering self, could now be psychologically enmeshed in the possibly shocking implications of what Solomon hadn't told him, and for whatever reason.

In my own then brittle state of mind, I jumped a tad on hearing suddenly a door opening off the hall. And whom I took to be Elise's carer – a youngish brunette of medium height and build, with an oval face boasting bright blue eyes and wearing a kind of white smock – entered the lounge. She gave me a wan little smile. Brian looked up and acknowledged the woman who, after a few words with him, then made her way to the kitchen. I'd visited Germany, including its Federal capital, many times for creative writing purposes and other reasons. I'd even attended Shabbat services at synagogues in a number of cities on the, literally, odd occasion for me. So I was able to identify the carer's distinguishable Brandenburg accent accompanying her near-perfect English. On her way back to Elise, she was holding something small in her hand, but which I couldn't quite make out.

I noticed also that Brian appeared to be becoming a trifle more aware. He glanced tensely at his wristwatch then shook his head vaguely. This seemed to turn his mind-tide back again. Maybe he was feeling – and justifiably, I reckoned – that the ominously anticipated duo should've been with him by now, and as promised. I didn't really know what to say to help readjust my friend's frame of mind. But, as it turned out, I didn't need to say anything because there came, what felt like, piercing rings of the doorbell. I do believe that both Brian's and my heart skipped a beat or two at the sudden, reverberating sounds. Although nowhere near as loud, the echoing noise just seemed like a warning alarm going off. With whatever physical energy reserves he could draw together now, Brian launched himself off his armchair and into the hall; and with a sort of tenterhooks expression masking his face.

From where my seat was situated in the room, I couldn't see directly the other end of the hallway. But on rising from my armchair, I heard the front door being opened; though not clearly enough the words then being exchanged. So I waited, impatiently and with baited breath, for Brian to bring Solomon and Diva – both of whose voices I recognised at once – into the sitting room. I was given an acknowledgement nod from each of the visitors as they sat down, each against one arm of the three-seat sofa. Quickly, Brian and I resumed our armchair accommodation.

DI Solomon spoke first, addressing Brian.

"I'm sorry for not telling you about the current position when I contacted you earlier," he said candidly. "I appreciate how you're feeling right now. But we prefer, generally, not to talk about such matters other than on an actually personal and one-to-one basis… I hope you'll understand, and forgive me …"

"But what about Martha?" her father interrupted with a terrified urgency in his voice.

"Unfortunately," Solomon went on, "we haven't yet located her, and despite our currently widespread search procedures… though there's much that we do need to cover."

I couldn't tell whether the look then creasing Brian's face was one of frustration, neo-horror or relief; or perhaps all three feelings combined. Though I could divine from his again altered features, and also by his fleeting glances towards the hall, that he perceived no reason to awaken or otherwise disturb his wife.

"But something else, aside from Martha's teddy bear and the evidence of her urine," the DI continued, "has been found, and which could possibly have a connection to her …"

My ears pricked up, hopefully; and not necessarily from a selfish, journalistic point of view.

"And what is that *something*?" Brian enquired with emphasis; but also some discernible optimism, hope or faith.

"I should explain," Solomon added, "that our police force has been closely in touch with the leaders of Proxima b via Diva's team. Because Martha's teddy was found externally to, although only just outside, our settlement territory, we considered there should be, and there is, very helpful cooperation in the search for your daughter... and as necessary, we believe. Bearing in mind also the valuable potential contribution of the relevant experts, who can be made available with their extraordinarily advanced, technological means for search purposes... So let me hand you over to Diva, who'll explain the most recent discovery."

He gestured with a hand in her direction. Diva nodded reactively and, largely facing Brian, began her narrative.

"What we've found," she said, "and about halfway between your territory and an extensive, inhabited zone where millions of our people reside, is evidence of a small amount of dampness on the ground... Perhaps I should say, and at once, that it wasn't another sample of Martha's pee. It was discovered, in an area where the presence of moisture would be most unusual, by means well beyond the capabilities of the camera-bearing drones ..."

I noticed DI Solomon nodding; and with no facial hint of finding any fault with Diva's factual statement which, doubtless, was intended as no more than such.

"The presence of a patch of wetness," she went on, "in the arid and rocky terrain where it was located is, as I mentioned, virtually unprecedented. Analytical tests indicated that it was water-based... and that the water would've been produced to be drinkable. This was somewhat amazing and, because there was no other material evidence, we came to the, albeit provisional conclusion that it could've been spilled by someone drinking, say, from a bottle of water. There's absolutely no support, we know, for asserting that any of our own indigenous citizens were out there drinking water. But in light of Martha's evidential presence just inside the perimeter of this inter-habitable region, we've considered whether she might've been carrying potable water into it, drunk it and also spilled it. We don't have the precise answer to that complicated conundrum at present... nor do we know how the nine-year-old might've journeyed so far from the borders of your territory, and in a relatively compact period of time. Assuming always that Martha was, indeed, at that geographical location. For now, we have no certain evidence that the water was connected to *her* presence there."

I could tell that Brian was rendered speechless by Diva's account; though, possibly, only in the sense that my friend hadn't a clue as to how he should respond. Needless to say, but I wouldn't have been any clearer in my own mind, either. The information put forward by my longer-time friend, however, did stir me to think of the pointedly dismal reaction – with its assured presumption of Martha's abduction – from the man in the formal outfit with a business-like briefcase, and to whom I'd put my survey question earlier that afternoon. Diva now looked askance at the senior police officer, and indicated that he should take the floor again.

"So that's the present and rather puzzling position regarding the search for your daughter," he said, again speaking to Brian directly. "I regret we haven't anything more positive for you and your wife... so we'll take leave of you for the time being. Of course, we'll keep you in touch with any further developments we learn about from our searches. And I would also say this… please don't give up hope… the recent find may well suggest that your daughter is ok."

With those closing and faintly optimistic words, Solomon and Diva rose – as did Brian and I – then made for the hallway. They left through the front door, which was opened by Martha's rather pensive father. After closing it, he returned to the lounge area and sat down again, this time on the settee. I resumed my armchair seat; and my host then stared meaningfully at me.

"I've been harbouring an idea, David," he said, and really determinedly.

"And what's that about, Brian?" I queried with some aroused interest.

"I'm going to look for Martha myself… and I hope you'll feel able to accompany me, David."

Thirty Nine

I COULDN'T believe the words I heard emerging from Brian's mouth. So I asked him to repeat what he'd just said. He did, but I still wasn't able to absorb what my friend had uttered. After a dithering pause, I found my voice at last.

"M-May I ask why, Brian?" I managed to say. "And not... *Why are you asking me to accompany you on your mission*? But... *Why are* you *going to search for Martha?* Even our territory's police force, and with the full assistance of Diva's team and other of her tech colleagues, have been unable to locate her... at least, so far."

Brian sighed miserably profoundly.

"My good friend, it's just that I, as her father, feel a dire but compellingly urgent need to do something myself, constructively and actively, to find our darling daughter," he explained clearly but with a categorically suppressed emotion. "I can't just sit in the flat any longer... merely waiting to hear something... hoping, and praying to the Almighty, for Martha's safe return... only watching my broken-hearted Elise going to pieces. I really cannot remain inactive here any longer... and thus do nothing to seek out our beloved child."

"I understand fully, Brian," I responded. "And I'm fairly certain my Naomi will, too, when I tell her that I'm proposing to accompany you in your own quest for Martha …"

"Please don't tell anyone other than your wife about this plan, David," he said firmly, his eyes pleading the case.

"Ok," I reacted, rather prolonging the two letters, vowel and consonant. "But such a venture, needless to say I'm sure, could be dangerous… and maybe in more ways than one, Brian."

"I really don't care now, David," he reacted, bunching his lips and creasing his brow to create a kind of concerted frown. "And I don't think Martha's mother would find fault with that feeling, if she was capable of doing anything at the moment. But, of course, it's up to you, David… whether you would wish to face any perils alongside me."

"No problem, Brian," I said and added, I believed quite rationally: "But how would *you* or, maybe rather, *we* know where to look for Martha?"

"Bearing in mind the three finds so far," my friend started to explain, "that is, her teddy bear, her urine and possibly her drink spillage, I'm planning to follow on from that trail in the hope of identifying something significant… and even, may the Almighty hear my voice, of finding our darling Martha safe and sound."

Hearing that, I commented questioningly:

"Is anything noticeable likely to have been missed by the extremely advanced hardware and software, airborne and other search equipment now being utilised to locate Martha's presence?"

"Who knows, David?" he answered, equally quizzically. "I certainly don't... but what I do know is that our lovely Martha hasn't been found yet, and despite the superlative, technological assistance being provided apparently."

I nodded empathetically.

"So when would we leave on our mission?" I enquired. "How would we travel? And what would we need to take with us, Brian? It could be a lengthy trip."

"All good questions... and you're right," he replied. "I've been shown by Solomon, who knows nothing of my own search scheme, the sky-taken images of the area in which the items I've mentioned were found. It's mostly level though fairly rough terrain, a largely flattish landscape scattered with stones and boulders... but also revealing some quite substantial, rocky outcrops if not hillocks or ridges of various descriptions. I seem to recall Solomon, or Diva, saying that the distance between the boundary of our territory and the nearest relevant border of the indigenous citizens' populated areas measures about forty of our Earth-kilometres. That's not just around the corner, but I believe it to be a manageable walking trek for the pair of us. And do you know what, I really can't credit that I'm saying all this, I really can't... I just can't help wondering, at times, whether we're personally in a worse situation than we would've been had we continued to reside on Earth."

I nodded sympathetically, knowing precisely what he meant and why he meant it. But *I* couldn't help wondering how Martha might've transited at least half and possibly almost the entire distance alluded to by her father; and if she had done either, in actual fact. It was as much an astonishingly inscrutable puzzle to me as it was, demonstrably, to everyone involved with this sad and baffling matter.

"Are you contingency planning to enter the indigenously populated zone, if need be?" I quizzed Brian tentatively, if not apprehensively. "As I think you know, and as Diva and her team have explained to us and our brethren, it's not proposed by Proxima b's respective immigrant and indigenous leaders that we get together, and potentially integrate, with each other until after we former Earthlings have finally and comfortably settled into our new home territory."

"Yes, I am *au fait* with that arguably informal agreement, David," my friend responded wistfully, "and I wasn't at all proposing that we should do what you've just referred to… I don't want to contravene any applicable convention or consensus in our own search for Martha… unless, of course, I feel desperately that we've got no choice in the matter …"

I nodded again but, in this instance, somewhat reluctantly.

"I think we should move, and very cautiously, only during the so-called night hours, David," he went on. "It's darker, of course, than our artificially enhanced and so-called *daytime*… and we'd sort of hole-up then for some rest. But, as you know, our *night* sky here in Proxima b's habitable zone is gorgeous, no other word for it… it's like a continuous and beautiful sunset, with the most amazing twilight colours to match."

I gave a reiterative nod then delivered another enquiry.

"But what's your thinking about the nature of our supplies etcetera, Brian?"

"Naturally, we'll take food and water with us …" he began. "The *days* and *nights* are relatively mild, so we'll don whatever we want to wear for our comfort. You may be aware that a store has now opened, and not too far from our development. The shop sells stuff like camping, hiking and some intriguing, and possibly appropriate and useful, orienteering kit. It's primarily intended for the time when our brethren, or rather those of us who may wish to do so, go wandering and in whatever direction beyond the territory we live in here and now… that is, when it becomes generally acceptable to do so of course."

"Yes, I do know about that retail outlet, Brian," I remarked with maybe an unintended smidgeon of a grin. "Incidentally, it was our Joshua and Sarah who told us about this supplier. Apparently, their school has already bought and stored away some items for the time when its pupils can be taken on the kind of trips or activities which you've just mentioned."

"I'm proposing to get a few articles from the shop tomorrow morning," my friend and impending trek companion advised me, "and with the intention of leaving here when our bright yellowy daylight has faded tomorrow evening... Will that be alright with you, David?"

"Yes, it will," I replied at once, confident – or, perhaps, reasonably confident – that it would be more or less alright with my wife, too... at least, I hoped so. "I'll be telling Naomi about all this when I get home. She should be back at the flat with the kids now, or very soon anyway. I'll make sure that I inform her outside of the twins' earshot and presence, if you know what I mean. And I'll tell their mum what precisely to inform them about my absence from home, probably a journalistic excuse, because the clever little imps would otherwise quiz her relentlessly about it... and without the shadow of a doubt!"

This time it was Brian's turn to nod, and with the merest of wry smiles. Then he spoke again.

"Don't worry about bringing anything with you here tomorrow night, other than the necessarily appropriate clothes you'll be wearing plus some suitable changes of you-know-what. I'll have everything else we should need, no problem, including backpacks. Hopefully, as we proceed on our route, I'll still be able to receive, as you will also, any messages from whomever about any fresh developments in the, so to speak, parallel search for Martha. Well, I think that's about the lot for now, David... so see you soon."

Just prior to my exiting his apartment, I asked Brian about Elise in connection with *his* – or, rather, *our* – imminent mission; and in the context of our not knowing exactly, or even at all, how long the period of his and my absence from home would likely be.

"I've told Golda that I'll be away from home for a while regarding an aspect of my vital, medical research work," he related to me. "And that, if my wife happens to want to see me, or just enquires about where I am, she should be told I'll be returning home quite soon. To be frank, but desolately so, I doubt very much that, in Elise's currently chaotic state of mind, she would think to enquire about me… and, in the dreadful circumstances, I say that without any hurt on my part."

I nodded finally, and with an unavoidably despondent expression.

"I'll see you tomorrow night, Brian," I added, then went to my apartment.

Forty

I GOT BACK to the apartment just as Naomi was arriving home from school with the kids. All three of them looked quite down in the dumps; and it didn't take much deliberation, on my part, to comprehend the likely cause. No sooner had we entered the hallway than Joshua and Sarah dashed into their respective bedroom and shut its door. But not before they speedily asked their mother to please bring their usual, back-from-school refreshments to their rooms. After Naomi had kind of refreshed herself in our en suite, she joined me in the kitchen. I was beginning to prepare some sandwiches and hot drinks for all of us.

As my wife joined me to do so, total silence reigned in the workplace... and, without a shred of doubt, she was thinking about her hours at school. I was reflecting on my, in a way, newsworthy day, and its incredible outcome at the close of my time with Brian; and on my earlier, memorable afternoon. As we worked, Naomi and I glanced blankly at each other now and again, implicitly acting on an agreement that we would talk after serving the twins and settling down – if we could, in a sense – to munch and sip in the lounge. That time came soon; and, as it happened, Naomi didn't have a great deal to inform me, as opposed to philosophise about. However, she did speak first; but only subsequent to both of us taking some of our black Americano coffee from the cups I'd placed on the nearby, occasional table.

"The atmosphere in school is still terrible," Naomi said with a pronounced sigh, and kind of confirming my recent thoughts as we all returned home simultaneously. "There's so much fear and nervousness in the children, I can't tell you David... the attending counsellors, as well as us assistants, have our work cut out for us. It's quite sad and distressing, really. Of course, we try hard not to disclose our emotions to the pupils, lest they become even more disturbed and scarified. Naturally, we don't know what their parents, or any other close relatives, are telling them. But we've got wind of the fact that there are many, often appalling and harrowing rumours circulating and concerning Martha's sudden and still unexplained disappearance... as well as her possibly tragic fate. It's no wonder our kids just rushed to their rooms after getting home. And when I delivered their tea just before, both were stretched flat on their backs in bed, with Joshua's eyes staring up at the ceiling and Sarah's tight shut as she whimpered quietly..."

We were now sitting in the armchairs, not together on the settee, but close enough for me to grasp Naomi's clenched fingers.

"I do understand, darling," I offered, while gently squeezing her hands.

With my wife's reference to *appalling and harrowing rumours* well in mind, I mentioned my prematurely aborted, random street survey that day; and some of the hardened reactions I'd received from its respondents. Naomi nodded, smoothly uncoupled her digits from my caressing grip and rubbed her forehead forlornly. Then we took a little more of our hot coffees.

"I'm not at all surprised by what you're telling me," she said, after another pause to set down her cup. "But I'm not really sure why some people think, or even believe, the worst... and I include, of course, the worst about other people. It's mere speculation, without any corroborative evidence... or maybe simply prejudice against *the other* ..."

"It's human nature," I responded instantly. "We shouldn't be amazed... human beings have a lot to learn. We must continue to be aware of why we fled our former home planet and of the centuries-long history of discrimination, segregation, tropes, abuse, persecution, violence... and, as we know, six million times worse. We need to seek the perfection in all things that, as we've been told frequently by Diva, has led Proxima b to become an ideal, if not idyllic world for its indigenous citizens..."

Naomi nodded then added a comment.

"It could take time, though I'm fairly optimistic that those of our brethren who may be falling a little way behind at the moment, but at this quite early stage in our presence here, will learn from the vast majority of them who desire strongly, and so very understandably, to achieve and live harmoniously within a perfect society..."

It was my turn to nod, and I sort of changed the subject.

"And now for my *piece de resistance*," I remarked then perhaps regretting the too glib, Francophone phrase; and especially in the presently troubled context.

"Sorry?" Naomi uttered, obviously bewildered by my plain silly intro.

"No, *I* am sorry," I apologised. "Let me start again… and more sensibly this time."

"Ok."

"Brian told me this afternoon that he has decided to himself search for Martha," I reported, "and he would like me to accompany him… but only if I and, of course, you would feel alright about it."

Then I explained in detail, with due gaps in my narrative to allow for mutual refreshment, the earlier proceedings in our friends' flat. I could see that my wife was almost spellbound when hearing about the latest discovery in the current search pattern, and its equivocal implications… though then she looked particularly sad due, I supposed, to Martha not having been located as yet.

"I've got no serious reservations about you going with Brian on what amounts to an independent search mission to find his daughter …" Naomi said at last.

I was gladdened to hear my wife's authentic approval.

"But, as I'm sure has been taken onboard, both of you must proceed with extreme care," she went on, and with an unyielding tone in her voice. "There could be unknown and unexpected perils on the way through your search area… though I, myself, don't believe they would derive from this planet's indigenous population. And I would just add that our more religiously orthodox brethren, safely landed refugees from a dangerous Earth and sympathetic to that way of thinking, would be placing their faith and trust in the Almighty in this connection."

"I'm pleased to hear your view on this, darling," I reacted with maybe the trace of a smile. "I certainly wouldn't feel good about letting Brian venture forth all alone… and, of course, I want Martha to be found safe, well and as soon as possible now."

Naomi nodded sympathetically then mentioned her own feelings in that connect; and she included, especially, her angst-ridden thoughts also for Elise and her terribly grim state of mind.

"S-So, with all my heart, I wish both of you every success in your heroic efforts to locate Martha," my wife declared, and I could detect a few tear pearls starting to roll from her eyes. "I-I hope and pray you are more fortunate in your search than others have been… as yet."

I raised myself from the armchair and went down on my haunches directly in front of Naomi, in the process carefully shifting the coffee table to give myself more space to manoeuvre. I leaned forward and just embraced my wife very closely. After a short while, she relaxed and gradually leaned back against the cushion. My upper body advanced a little and I pressed my lips against hers, tasting some salty tears that somehow had slid onto them from Naomi's wan, moist cheeks.

"There's another reason why I would wholeheartedly support your courageous attempt to help find Martha," she said."

"And what would that be, my love?" I asked, grasping her hands again.

"Y-You know we personally wouldn't be here now, on this mind-blowing planet and talking to each other like this, David," she observed with feeling, "if it hadn't been for Diva crossing the centuries back to medieval Cambridge to save and preserve our lives."

"Y-Yes, I know, darling," I responded, almost becoming tearful myself with the reminiscence. "And, like you m-my love, I'll never f-forget what she did for us."

We kissed firmly on the lips again.

"I'll be leaving for Brian's flat shortly after dinner tomorrow evening," I told Naomi. "In the meantime, I'll prepare myself and what I need to take with me… which won't amount to much, aside from the hopefully appropriate gear I'll be wearing. Our good friend tells me he'll be responsible for collecting together everything else we're likely to require. This would be equipment-wise… and including, necessarily, roughly estimated supplies of food and drink."

"Great!" my wife opined and very succinctly, then rising from her seat as I hoisted myself from my awkwardly crouched position. "So I think I'll be off now for a nap, before getting supper ready. What are you going to do, darling?"

"Think I'll join you shortly, my love," I replied, picking up the empty cups etcetera, "after I've cleared up in the kitchen… but I must mention to you, before I forget, that if the kids or anyone else for that matter, including Diva and Mike, ask where I am, do tell them I'm away doing some journalistic research for a while… And you're not to tell anyone about my true mission, ok?"

My wife nodded her assent.

While Naomi proceeded to our bedroom, I popped into each of the twins' rooms to collect their now used, tea-time crockery. On entering each, I noted immediately that brother and sister were – though somewhat prematurely – deep into their slumbers.

Forty One

FOR MUCH of the following day, while Naomi and the kids were at school, I was getting myself ready – in large measure, mentally – for the mission, alongside Brian, into the wilderness and in search of his daughter Martha. When that word, *wilderness*, fleetingly entered my mind during a much-needed, morning coffee break, I hoped that my next thought of 40 years crossing it was just an inaptly and pessimistically, whimsical one. But for a brief while I did muse on the first *Exodus*, the biblical fleeing of the Israelites from slavery in ancient Egypt to the Promised Land. I also reflected on what many of my brethren alluded to as the *Second Exodus...* our flight, in both senses, across the Milky Way galaxy from the Solar System to planet Proxima b, in the dwarf star Proxima Centauri's habitable zone. And from the appalling catastrophe of anti-Semitism on Earth, as well as the slavery of dread and panic that was prevailing amongst our Jewish people world-wide.

Dinner with my family that evening was an emotional meal for me, being on the brink of entering unknown territory; though I did strive, hopefully with success, not to reveal my apprehensions. The kids ate unusually silently and with fairly serious expressions, whilst Naomi and I exchanged few words. But, of course, I was fully aware, and quite worryingly, that Joshua and Sarah, bless them, seemed generally capable of reading a person's instant thoughts; and even though they weren't expressed orally. So I did trust, no doubt uselessly, that my physical feelings could be separated off from my verbal notions. Maybe it was the failure of such a theoretical division that caused the twins to possibly withhold conversation; though my guess was that it stemmed from the current, cloudy climate of concern at their school. This could've been preoccupying their minds, so that they weren't being too attentive to my imminently unexpressed thoughts, if I could put it in that bizarre way.

After supper, the children retreated after their parents had kissed them goodnight – with my lip pressure on their cheeks maybe more than a bit emphasised that evening – but without either of us enquiring whether they were now going to bed. I spent some time cuddling an understandably tearful Naomi on the sofa; and we spoke the kind of loving words normally exchanged by husband and wife when one of the them is about to depart on a long journey. After that, I donned my dark blue anorak and colour-matched, woollen hat, retrieved the bag of fresh underwear from our bedroom and stood in the hallway. I wasn't taking much with me from home in view of Brian's advice that he would have available everything else we needed for our venturing forth to find Martha. Before opening the front door, I embraced and lip-kissed Naomi lingeringly… then I left the flat.

I was a bit surprised when Golda opened the front door of Brian's apartment.

She smiled and told me he was waiting in the living room. She then disappeared into what was Martha's room, so I assumed that Elise was sleeping. My friend, somewhat remarkably clothed in what appeared to be a sort of brownish camouflage outfit and headgear oddly not too dissimilar from mine, greeted me with a firm handshake. Quickly, and a bit like an inspecting sergeant major, he looked me up and down; then he instructed me kindly to don, additionally, the apparel matching his and that, as he indicated, lay folded up on the settee.

"I hope it fits you snugly," he said. "Thought this attire could be helpful... you know what I'm saying, David. I got the tunics, and several other articles, at that camping store this morning... just as I said that I would."

I nodded, noticing a couple of open backpacks on the floor; and into which Brian had been stuffing certain requisite items.

"Which one's mine?" I enquired, pointing at the not overly sizeable or totally unmanageable, canvas-type bags; though they looked to possess a certain weight.

Brian gestured, and I placed my underwear in the one allotted to me.

"Can I fasten them up now?" he asked.

I nodded again then, whilst my friend and fellow searcher-to-be did just that, I put on the alleged camouflage kit then turned to face him.

"Looks fine," he said. "Take it that I estimated your size near enough."

"Yes, it fits me well, thanks," I responded, but definitely not asking whether I could look at myself in the full-length mirror in their bathroom; and which, of course, I knew about from previous visits to the flat.

"Now take off your trainers, and put on those trek boots over there," he said, pointing to a spot beyond the sofa.

Accepting the undoubted daftness of my trainers, I changed over at once to the rather more appropriate, cross-country footwear.

"Ok then, let's go, David," he said with a certain confidence in his voice, and which I hoped would be satisfied.

He picked up his pack, and I picked up mine; then we dragged them into the hallway.

"We'll swing them up onto our backs when we get outside," he said, possibly thinking also that *swing* may've been a bit too much like wishful thinking.

"Agreed," I said.

Before we exited the apartment, Brian opened quietly the door to his bedroom. With the not too bright light from the hallway, we could see that Elise appeared to be slumbering calmly. Brian blew his wife an air-kiss then, ever so carefully, he shut the door. Next, he tapped gently on the closed door of what was Martha's room. Golda's hearing was clearly very good… she opened up almost instantly. Brian told her, though it would've been quite obvious, that we were off now. She nodded and, after a timid little wave, she closed and soundly locked the front door behind us.

Naturally, it didn't take us too long to reach the relevant boundary of our settlement territory; on beginning our trek, we were much closer to this perimeter than many other sections would be. Fortunately, the backpacks rested fairly comfortably, and not too burdensomely, strapped over our shoulders. These significant effects, I reflected as we silently lengthened our stride after leaving the building complex, were doubtless due to the equipment being of excellent quality and manufacture. The yellowy day period was now substituted by Proxima b's gorgeous twilight firmament, with its beautifully hued bands of red, crimson, orange, dark blue and even emerald green. The heavens here were so staggeringly breathtaking to behold. Brian and I couldn't help glancing upwards from time to time, admiring the astonishing strata of colour arrayed above us then nodding evocatively at each other.

The ubiquitous streetlamps cast a soft glow across our route; but, for some time, we saw nobody moving under their subtle illumination. We knew that would likely be the case; normally, not that many people would be out and about after the relatively bright *day* sky had transmuted into the somewhat more natural night one. Once home from work or whatever, our brethren would generally stay put. Although they weren't necessarily frightened to go out in their new and astounding world – theatres and other places of entertainment were usually well-attended

– the still unexplained disappearance of a young Jewish girl could've been an inhibiting factor; and in their sort of night-time, *al fresco* thinking at that time. So far as we could, Brian and I kept to the deeper shadows, hugging the sides of the buildings we passed, some with the windows of their diverse retail outlets still well lit. Slinking along with our backpacks, we did realise, could've aroused dour suspicions and with abortive consequences. So we really needed to retain a low profile with our rucksacks.

All of a sudden, Brian – who was striding directly ahead of me – indicated with some rapid hand movements that I should back into a dark and nearby doorway, and get low swiftly… as then he did similarly. We crouched tightly together, and as best we could with our attached packs, in the rather confined space. I think we were lucky there wasn't a streetlamp in the immediate vicinity. My friend turned his face towards me, and placed an index finger upright against his lips. After that, he looked and pointed across the wide roadway. Filled with concern, I could make out three uniformed police officers, with another guy in *mufti* and possibly a plain-clothes detective, standing outside the impressive, glass entrance doors to what appeared to be a quite lofty office building. They seemed to be waiting, whilst looking expectantly through the apparently closed, and probably locked and secured, entranceway. One or two of the policemen turned round occasionally – rather worryingly for us cowering pair – and gazed up and down the otherwise deserted thoroughfare. Fortunately, they didn't look specifically across the highway and in our direction. Next we observed the lights going on in the likely reception area beyond the glass doors, and a man approaching them from within. The doors were opened, and the police entered quickly. They appeared to follow the man – perhaps a caretaker or security guard – further into the building; and a very short time later, the lighting in the foyer area dimmed then went out.

Brian glanced awkwardly over his shoulder and beckoned me to follow him out of our refuge, whispering that we must proceed very cautiously. As I lifted myself, a trifle achingly, it did occur to me to wonder whether the police we'd just witnessed were engaged diligently in an investigative aspect of the search for Martha. And that made me, albeit internally, question again the practicality of our current mission to locate her. Rapidly casting that rumination aside, however, I now followed Brian hurriedly along the street. After a time, we began to enter the not so built-up, residential sector approaching the border area of our territory. Rows of houses of varying design – and akin to, say, a big Earth-city's suburbia – were more evident here than blocks of flats and similar developments. And there was rather more abundant greenery around in this district than further into the metropolitan zone through which we'd trekked. Now we were hiking, along the edge of a more isolated neighbourhood, towards the start of the *wilderness* separating our people's territory from another habitable region where, we'd been informed, a very substantial number of Proxima b's indigenous population resided.

Then I noticed Brian reaching a hand behind him to his backpack, and taking an item from one of its side-pockets.

"What's that?" I asked whisperingly, coming up beside him.

"It's an advanced piece of orienteering equipment, David," he answered, while pressing some buttons on the hand-held article.

I could see that the gadget possessed a smallish screen but, maybe fortuitously, it was partially hooded. Not being as scientifically or technologically minded as I believed Brian was, as a doctor and medical researcher of some renown, I refrained from delving into the no doubt meticulous details of the device's capabilities. I merely accepted that my professional friend considered it would be very useful to us in transiting the terrain we were now about to enter. I could've been forgiven for thinking that he was becoming something of a mind-reader, too, when he next addressed me.

"This piece of equipment will be very helpful in steering us over the landscape we're now fast approaching, David," Brian said.

I had to stifle what would've been an unbecoming little chuckle. After all, this was the most serious of matters with which we were occupied.

"We know, from the expert analysts' scrupulous examination of her urine," he continued, "that it was actually and definitely deposited, so to speak, by Martha herself at the spot that we'll very soon reach. Before this positive conclusion of that analysis, it could've been argued that her urine might've been taken and deposited there along with her teddy bear. But now we know for certain that my daughter was present at that spot."

I nodded with the thought that, moving onwards purposefully into uninhabited terrain, at least we could talk to each other now without the disquiet felt earlier about conversing openly and in a reasonably normal voice.

"Of course, we don't know how or why Martha, and almost miraculously, came to be at that point... and possibly well beyond it," I observed, "bearing in mind the later, drinking water discovery. But if, say and for whatever reason, she was heading towards the zone of indigenous population, why do you think she didn't travel by way of, and assuming she knew about it, a possible and maybe easier route along the seaside?"

"She knew the sea existed, of course," Brian replied, "and of the importance of water in making Proxima b habitable. She'd learned about some of the geography of the area, etcetera at school... though, naturally, only to the extent that Martha's teachers were knowledgeable enough to pass on any material data they had gathered and absorbed ..."

As her father paused momentarily, I nodded again.

"But I do believe," he went on, "that she wouldn't have taken the water-side route, in any event, David?"

"Why's that?" I enquired with an edge of curiosity.

"Well, David, our daughter doesn't really like water... in fact, she is fearful of it. And that's why we've needed to explain to her PE teacher that, although Martha is enthusiastic about other sports and gymnastics, she's unable to attend the swimming class or go anywhere near the school's own large pool …"

"Tell me, Brian."

"Her continuing phobia began a couple of years ago," he went on. "The three of us were holidaying in the lovely seaside resort of Netanya. This was Martha's first time in Israel, and she was really enjoying herself. We were staying at a fine hotel, which had an extensive swimming pool in its beautiful gardens. On our third day there, we were all stretched out sunbathing on lounging-beds beside the pool... though more healthily from under all-embracing parasols, you understand. We'd been for a swim earlier, with Elise kind of trying to improve our daughter's L-plate technique, so to speak. When we returned to relax in the shade of our sun umbrellas, she curled up with her mum and, shortly afterwards, we were all asleep. However, as we learned subsequently from neighbouring sunbathers, Martha had apparently awakened, slipped a bit dozily out of her slumbering mother's grasp and, after a few dodgy steps, fell headlong and shrieking into the deep end of the pool …"

"Oh my goodness, Brian …!" I exclaimed, then apologised for interrupting.

"That's ok, David," he said, then going on with the story. "It was lucky that two men, strong swimmers and fathers of young children, happened to be chatting proximate to the spot where Martha had fallen into the water. Alerted by her screams as she plunged into the pool, they jumped in and, together, brought her up from the depths. Of course, we were now aware of what had transpired. We dashed to the side of the pool where the two caring guys had initially laid supine our terrified daughter, but who was now spluttering loudly and coughing up water. The hotel called a doctor forthwith, and despite the fact that yours truly was present and correct in tending his daughter. Fortunately, Martha was physically ok. But she suffered a lot of post-traumatic stress, and even after we'd returned home. Happily, however, that psychological disorder passed on eventually... though our daughter did tell us, and quite firmly, that she didn't want to be close to stretches of water ever again."

"Say no more, Brian," I reacted. "I'm so glad that things turned out well for her. But I do realise now why she wouldn't have taken any route along the seashore here."

"Thanks for that, David," her dad said, and now studying earnestly the gadget in his hand.

"We're shortly about to cross over the territorial perimeter," he informed me, "and in not too many steps beyond that, according to the programmed contrivance I'm clutching, we'll be standing at the exact locations where Martha's teddy bear and, subsequently, her urine were found."

I took Brian's word for it; and when we reached the exact positions where his daughter had stood or squatted, he said we should rest up for a while. I removed my backpack, placed the sort of camper's holdall on its side then lay down, with my head resting back against it. After my companion performed likewise with his own bulging bag, he went down on his haunches beside the precise spot where Freddy the Teddy had been found. Brian was facing me from a few metres away, but with his eyelids closed. He placed a hand on the pertinent ground, and I could perceive that his lips were now moving perceptibly. I just knew that my friend and search companion was praying to the Almighty, and I understood for sure also for what he was praying …

Forty Two

AFTER BRIAN and I had reposed, but for a relatively short period – stretched out on the rough ground in our endearing camouflage gear, heads resting on the backpacks – we re-launched ourselves and re-strapped the bags to our upper rears. But as we'd rested, quite near to each other, from our slog across the settlement territory and from time to time, I glanced wakefully at my flat-on-his-back, trek buddy. Whenever I glimpsed the guy's face, his eyelids were closed; though his lips moved continuously. I felt pretty certain that he was repeatedly reciting the prayers he'd begun to say earlier, at the spot where Martha's teddy playmate had been discovered. For my part, and otherwise, I just stared up at the sky – into its magnificent twilight – to the dazzling strands of heavenly colour.

As I trudged onwards in silence, though observationally alert and wary – with Brian beside me, and constantly consulting his hand-held thingamabob – a possibly relevant thought occurred to me... so I expressed it.

"Brian," I began, "I understood that the terrain we would be crossing was said to be almost entirely level, but that doesn't appear to be quite the case... Aside from the ancient rocks and boulders scattered over this often horizontal ground we're now transiting, I can make out more than one stretch of pinnacle-topped ridges up ahead. Will we need to get over them whenever they cross our path… and in order for us to advance conveniently and without difficulty?"

"W–We may well have to do that, David," my friend answered promptly, apparently but only slightly unnerved by the sudden sound of my voice in the quiet air; that is, apart from the crunching noise of our sturdy boots on the coarse topography. "But the rocky upland areas aren't that high, and their inclines would be quite manageable… even with our backpacks, I do believe. Once we've reached the crests, and then proceed over them and downwards, we'll be able to survey a lot more of the land around and ahead of us."

I wasn't sure that Brian noticed me nodding. But with the requisite surveying aspect in mind, I posed another query for his attention.

"Is it known for sure what Martha was wearing when she disappeared?"

"Well, David… we do know that, when Martha went to bed that evening, she had on her pink and white striped pyjamas," he replied. "But that's as much as we know for certain. Apart from the fact that, after a seriously distraught and panicky Elise had searched frantically through our daughter's wardrobe and cabinet drawers, on police advice after I'd called them originally to report her missing, my wife had said, but almost hysterically, that Martha's clothes and footwear etcetera were all in place."

"Do you think that, in Elise's terrible state of mind at the time," I put it, "she could've been easily mistaken about that?"

"No, I don't think so, David," Brian replied, as our reasonably celeritous, marching gait carried us quickly towards the first ridge in our projected line of advance. "You see, David, I'd held the selfsame question in my mind that you've just asked me... So I doubly checked, with Elise alongside, to make sure of her findings."

Again, I didn't know whether he was aware of my nodding head. Quite correctly, his visual focus – as mine should've been – was on the surrounding geography and environment. Shortly afterwards, we started to climb, as my friend had foretold accurately, the first ridge's not too steep an incline-gradient. On our nonetheless gradual ascent to the craggy peaks, some 50 metres or so above ground level, we passed the occasional hole – for want of a better word – in the surface rock. Inevitably, and with a mindful inquisitiveness, we went down on our knees and poked our heads into the about metre-sized openings in the rock. Some of the interior and cocoon-like spaces or – as I imagined them – mini-caves could've easily held a child of Martha's compact dimensions.

When Brian gazed at me after a few of our peeps inside the hollows, I read his eyes to mean that we were speculating on similar notions.

"But we can't possibly peer into every one of the countless holes or gaps that undoubtedly exist across this entire wilderness, can we Brian?" I posed.

"I know that, David," he confirmed readily, "but I don't want to be persistently just calling out my daughter's name… I hope you get my motivation."

I did, of course; and, on this occasion, he definitely noted my emphatic nod.

"If she *is* hiding, or otherwise concealed, down one of these holes in the rock," Brian continued, "I can't comprehend why Diva's super-tech colleagues, with their ultra-powerful contraptions criss-crossing this terrain from on high, haven't located her already… assuming, of course, she *is* somewhere in this region."

"Maybe they can't accomplish everything under the sun …" I remarked somewhat mordantly, "meaning their dwarf star Proxima Centauri, of course."

"Or possibly," my friend commented further, "they haven't yet had sufficient time to cover every single square metre of this quite expansive zone."

I nodded slowly in agreement, and he returned the gesture.

So we moved to the crinkly, spirally-rock crest, peered about and below us for a while then descended warily. Brian and I needed to ensure, in as optimum a way as possible and practicable, that we didn't trip over a loose rock, fall into one of those ubiquitous, vertical mini-caves or lose balance completely and tumble headlong down the hill. As we moved on – thankfully with steadiness, and accident-free – across the landscape, we encountered and overcame comparable geological formations. We kept a sharp eye on the terrain, but saw neither give-away signs nor noticed any suspicious movements. After quite a lengthy period of breath-saving, silent and continuous trekking, Brian announced suddenly that, maybe unbelievably, we were coming up to the halfway point between our territory and its nearest habitable zone in which resided a very large number of citizens from the indigenous population. My friend studied closely the gadget virtually glued to his left palm, then pointed to a particular spot on the comparatively flat ground not too far in front of us.

"That's where the ambiguous spillage of drinkable water was found," he said as, rapidly, we approached the site. When we reached the strangely still apparent stain, which appeared imprinted on ground adjoining a rocky outcrop, I noted Brian closing his eyelids and moving his lips, just like on recent occasions. I was convinced, once again, that my dear pal was engaged in praying to the Almighty.

"I think we should have another rest-break at this juncture," he said, looking meaningfully at me, "and right here... if that's ok with you, David?"

I nodded my concurrence and, after consuming some tasty sandwiches and drinking from our water supply – all of which my friend took from his backpack – we propped our bags against a huge boulder and lay down, with some inevitable fatigue creeping into our bones. Before we sunk into our respective and likely sea of unhappy, even morbid thoughts, I presented to the nearby and reclining Brian a few versions of what amounted to the same question. I felt somewhat uncomfortable about putting it to him, but I really couldn't prevent myself from doing so.

"Do you think we've bitten off more than we can chew, Brian? Are we out of our league and depths here? Doesn't it seem very unlikely that we'll be finding Martha by ourselves and with our limited means of doing so?"

I heard my companion shifting his position.

"I hear what you're variously saying, David," he responded, "but I do feel that I've just got to do what I need to do... it's as simple, or as complex, as that."

I remained still and silent for a brief while, then spoke again.

"I'm so sorry, my dear friend... I really don't know why I troubled you just now... I fully comprehend your motivation, and that's the reason for my being at your side here and now. Please forgive me for raising this, Brian."

"There's absolutely no necessity for that," he said empathetically. "I do understand also... so rest now, *my* dear friend."

After that short and difficult exchange, I did lower my head onto my sideways-on backpack to take it easy... and as best I could in all the stressful and multi-faceted circumstances. Actually, and maybe unsurprisingly, both of us slipped into the Land of Nod. When Brian stirred me, and I did jump at his wake-up call then prod, we had another bite and a drink, subsequently carried out our ablutions as hygienically as viable then resumed our primary undertaking. After marching for a further, not insignificant length of time across both rock-scattered, level topography and more ridges with their distinctive 'cocoons' – or 'Swiss cheese' holes, as I oddly thought of them – and pinnacle-topped peaks, Brian announced suddenly that we were a mere kilometre or so from the boundary of that closest of the indigenous people's habitable zones.

Naturally, he'd been solicitously consulting his rather special, clearly fascinating and very practical item of pocket-sized, orienteering kit. We couldn't yet observe the border area because another, apparently final stretch of ridge intervened a short distance ahead of us. Although we'd kept a crucial and continuous lookout for any likely indications of Martha's presence, we'd still seen nothing. I wasn't at all astonished by this vacant and unhappy result. When now I looked at Brian's face, I couldn't help but feel so abysmally sad. The image of deep emotional hurt confronting me appeared, in a way, akin to that doubtless evidencing the frightful feelings I was experiencing inwardly. But his pain, and naturally, went so many more fathoms deeper than mine. After all was said and done, *he* was the missing child's father.

"We'll go no further than the crest of that last ridge looming up ahead," he said with a melancholy resignation, whilst waving a hand forward.

"Ok," I reacted, preparing myself again for an imminent ridge-ascent.

Very soon, we were clumping over the pebble-cluttered kind of entry-way to our fairly easy, 50-metre or thereabouts climb to the summit. I was anticipating some truly stunning vistas of the region ahead of us when we would finally attain the peak; and, especially, of an anticipated 'sci-fi' metropolitan zone. Close by, on our route to the top, we passed a few more of the now familiar holes we'd come across on earlier ridge ascents and descents. Needless to state, there were others that we could perceive scattered further away on our left and right flanks. When Brian and I, ascending side by side, came within striking distance of the ridge's peak, only a few more metres away, I heard something behind us that almost gave me a heart attack. A swift, panicky glance at my friend's face revealed an identical, incipient assault on his own vital body organ. We steadied ourselves on the sloping rock surface, staring at each other now in a completely uncomprehending manner. Then the sound came again… it was actually a high-pitched but vaguely recognisable voice.

"Daddy …! Daddy …!"

In that breathtaking instant, or maybe 'Eureka' moment, we swivelled round briskly on our bulky heels with flaring eyes urgently scrutinising the slope below us.

"Over there, Brian!" I screamed, pointing shakily to a spot several metres to the right of our chosen route upwards. His eyes followed my indication and riveted themselves on the specific location. Yes, oh yes… it *was* Martha! Her small eyes were peeping at us over the rim of one of those, ubiquitous surface holes in the rock-face. Just in case we were dreaming, fantasising or even seeing a mirage – and almost simultaneously, though clumsily – Brian and I sought to grip each other's hands. Then her father shouted:

"Martha!... Martha! It *is* you, isn't it?"

"Yes, Daddy!" she cried out in reply, and with what I was glad to see amounted to a kind of smile on her cute little face. Fortunately, that hint of a grin appeared to be saying, and unreservedly: *Please don't worry, Daddy and Uncle David... I'm quite alright... Really!*

"Stay where you are, my baby... I'm coming to get you, Martha... and right now!" Brian bellowed with full volume.

He leapt downwards in her direction, his monopolised mind concentrated 100 percent, and without question, on a matter other than his possibly slipping or tripping. At this joyous and no less than miraculous and wonderful moment, I thought that I should let him go to his daughter by himself. I watched this incredibly marvellous scene playing out, as my friend reached his daughter, so tenderly and cautiously lifted her out of the 'cocoon' then kissed her cheeks and embraced the child like, probably, never previously. After holding his beloved Martha close to his doubtless rapidly beating heart, and for what seemed like ages, the now even more emotionally overcome if not blissfully ecstatic parent rested her gently on the ground. I could just make out that she was wearing a kind of hooded, dark anorak together with trousers of some slightly lighter hue. I wasn't at all amazed to then witness Brian obviously transmitting an exceedingly important message – and without a doubt to Elise – informing her of his extraordinary, if not unbelievably momentous breakthrough. After that, he turned to me and, with a so happily tearful face, presented an emphatic thumbs-up sign. I reciprocated the gesture, and with what could've counted amongst my gladdest expressions ever.

I was about to move off to join him and Martha – to say a fond *Hello* to the girl, and maybe to hear her dad's inevitable *Why?* and *How?* and, possibly, also *Who?* questions to the child – when there was another unexpected happening. Like the one I'd now witnessed, it nearly caused me a serious heart problem. Out of the blue, with utter incredulity and bewilderment, I spotted another person coming towards me up the ridge, someone I recognised immediately… it was Diva! Perhaps I shouldn't have been so totally gob-smacked. I knew well enough that this remarkable woman was capable of suddenly turning up wherever, and at any time. Even so, I couldn't refrain from being nonplussed at her imminent presence within a metre of my quivering body, poor weak thing that it was becoming. However and prior to her reaching me, my longstanding and one-time more than just good friend veered smilingly towards Martha and her father. I heard only the last words Diva addressed directly to Brian, which she voiced rather louder than her earlier ones to him; and also, of course, to his now certainly secure daughter.

"My team colleagues, including a medic, will be with you in just a moment or two," I heard her say to Brian. "They will get you and Martha back home, safe and sound, really quickly."

I espied Brian nodding with gratitude. And time-wise, naturally, Diva was being orally literal. In the instant, and as she stepped up across the space separating us, I noted three of her workmates coming fast up the incline, angling their course towards father and daughter. When she got to me, Diva said and fairly earnestly:

"Hi, David, *I* will be taking you back to your apartment... to Naomi and the twins, so let's climb first to the summit area. I have informed your wife of the current, happy conclusion to your exploit. She was really delighted. So you can take a well-deserved breather atop this ridge for a brief while... you must be utterly exhausted by now, and I mean mentally as well as physically... Ok?"

"Hi Diva, and thanks," I replied. "And you're quite right... so I'm definitely ok with your thoughtful suggestion."

Just prior to attaining the peak, I stopped and Diva halted too. Then I asked her a quite foolish question which, of course, she knew I was about to pose.

"How did you know where Brian and I were precisely situated?"

The woman grinned then sort of frivolously prodded my chest with a bunched fist.

"We have been tracking both of you since the moment you entered the *wilderness*, your word David ..."

There was nothing more I could say.

"That was just in case you had gathered some information about Martha's disappearance, and her possible whereabouts, that we hadn't been alerted to for some reason... But, for the most part, we wanted to ensure your safety and to help you, if need be... The terrain looks fairly easy to manage, but sometimes that is really not so if it isn't familiar territory."

Then I did think of something I should say. And it was far from an expression of annoyance that Brian and I had been spied upon.

"Thanks for that, Diva," I said warmly. "I wouldn't have expected otherwise."

We moved aloft the mere few remaining metres, and pulled ourselves up to a standing position facing towards one of the other populated regions of Proxima b's habitable zone. And I almost collapsed with a yet further assault on my now over-palpitating heart, plus a kind of almost stunning blow to my cerebral processes. I felt Diva's lovely blue eyes fixated on my facial features as, on gazing in the direction of the inhabited zone, my innermost sensibilities and sensitivities became virtually paralysed; though, fortunately, not realistically so.

The view spreading out before us was doubtless well known to Diva, but absolutely and astonishingly implausible to me. However, that personal disbelief – and perhaps astoundingly – wasn't at all related to the mind-boggling, 'future world' structures that confronted me from less than a kilometre away and into the visible distance. It was something else entirely. Just beyond the zone boundary, and not that far ahead of us, was a level and extended green space. At the innermost end of that open ground was a most beautiful building, one of an architectural genre, style and design of a time much earlier than, and which stood in stark contrast to, the startlingly futuristic 'skyscrapers' of sorts that flanked and backed it.

The edifice in my sights was extremely imposing, boasting a gorgeous dome and flanking towers, with lofty arched and stained-glass windows and decorative motifs on its frontage. I was convinced that I'd seen photographs – black and white or sepia-tone – on Earth of similar buildings. After a moment or two of further reflection, I pinned them down to Germany. Then I spotted a couple of pieces of stonework affixed and displayed on the magnificent structure's masonry that might've resulted in my experiencing a third, and this time potentially fatal heart attack. At last I realised, though with at least a shocking belief problem, what kind of structure I was now fixated on and by which I was comprehensively magnetised. The two items, one a few metres above the other and in central positions on the really eye-catching façade, constituted a Star of David and a representation of the stone Tablets on which the Ten Commandments, received by Moses from the Almighty on Mount Sinai, had been inscribed. So finally, the grand yet elegant building struck me, but unbelievably, as being akin to the many handsome synagogues that had existed in German cities from the 19th century until evilly set ablaze and destroyed by the fanatically anti-Semitic Nazis on and around Kristallnacht – the so-called 'Night of Broken Glass' – during the dark hours of 9th to 10th November 1938.

I turned to face Diva and with a definitely deeply puzzled, if not out of this or any world expression. Her visage took on the semblance of a strangely wry smile, which activated her features in a whimsical manner. Needless for me to think, but she knew precisely what I was almost dying to know, absorb and comprehend.

"Thought you might be interested in that building …" she said with, in my opinion, a massive degree of understatement. Almost wholly disorientated, I merely nodded silently several times. Perhaps this was due to my being rendered utterly speechless.

"It *is* a synagogue," she confirmed, "and similar to ones built in the style, time and place you've just been envisaging."

"Is it active?" I enquired, hardly crediting that I was back on track and what I was asking in my new-found voice.

"It is, indeed," Diva replied instantly, but rather too succinctly for my present contextual liking.

"H-How come …?" I persisted, with an all-encapsulating confusion. "I thought my brethren from contemporary Earth, fairly recently arrived on Proxima b as you well know, are the only Jewish inhabitants on this planet …"

"Well I never actually said that was the case, David," she interjected.

"I'm more than perplexed, Diva," I remarked, doubtless with an overwhelmingly mystified look and tone to match my choice of words.

"Ok," she said.

"*P-Please* explain all this to me," I implored her. "Because I'm getting the rather unexpected feeling, Diva, that ours wasn't what has been alluded to by some of my brethren as the *Second Exodus*, and after the first, Moses-led *Exodus* from the ancient Egypt of the Pharaohs... but rather, and in reality, maybe the *Third or whatever Exodus!*"

"Well deduced, David," my long-time friend continued, with a seemingly uncharacteristic element of condescension; though, admittedly, I might've been quite wrong about that estimation and many other matters. "Between the time that Hitler came to power in Germany with his Third Reich in 1933 and the outbreak of the Second World War in 1939, nearly 100,000 Jewish people managed to escape the country... But not all of them by virtue of having obtained visas or other valid permits for emigration to another nation. A substantial number of the German-Jewish population could not, or did not even try, to obtain the vital and potentially life-saving documentation ..."

"Sorry for interrupting, Diva," I apologised, "but, on this occasion, I do believe that *I* can read *your* mind... Your people rescued those Jewish people, didn't they, and brought them here to Proxima b?"

"That is right, David... you have hit the proverbial nail on the head, in a manner of speaking."

"But tell me, Diva, why do you focus on giving to Jewish people sanctuary from anti-Semitic evil, and almost certain catastrophe?" was a question I considered germane to put to my good and kind friend.

"If that is in fact the case," she answered mysteriously, but added quickly:

"We have got to leave now, David... I need to get you back home to your family, to Naomi and the twins."

"B–But ..." I began to utter, and with an even greater sense of confusion.

Diva cut me off politely with a gently raised hand.

"We will maybe talk another time about what is now playing on your mind," she offered. "Though my reference to the twins just now has reminded me that if, sadly, Martha hadn't been found... or had been discovered but not to have made it, we had been considering whether to offer Brian and Elise the offspring of Ziva's pregnancy... Naturally, it could have been a very difficult decision to make in all such circumstances."

There wasn't time for me to say anything more before we began our descent of the ridge. Nevertheless, there was a moment for me to seize another quick glimpse of the superb synagogue building. As I turned away from viewing it, there seemed so much more for me to learn about Proxima b in the Alpha Centauri star system. In the meantime, I was sure Mike would be delighted that I could give him a superlative news-feature with a happy, as well as an intriguing ending; though I could hardly wait to hear about Martha's story ...

THE END
(For Now)

Praise for
"The Shtetl
and other Jewish stories"

"Humorous, sad, thought-provoking and relevant to each of us and our life-style today… I enjoyed this book more than I could ever have thought possible."

Reggie Ross, *Belfast Jewish Recorder*

"Mark Harris follows brilliantly in the tradition of a writer with a gift for descriptive narrative and the ability to paint his characters so accurately that you can see them in your mind's eye… The author senses he is building a pipeline for the thoughts and emotions of the characters that walk through the pages. And he does it with style and feeling."

Manny Robinson, *Essex Jewish News*

367

Praise for

"The Chorister and other Jewish stories"

"Mark Harris' style makes for easy reading and comprehension. He paints the background to each story with a delicate, gentle and at times humorous touch. The subjects of his stories are seldom light-hearted, dealing with sensitive issues… but they are all worth reading."

D J Coppel, BJR

"The author meticulously outlines the theme of love, an emotion that weaves like a piece of tapestry through the pages… In many of the stories there is a twist in the tale. And that perhaps is Mark Harris' greatest strength… having the ability to describe a seemingly everyday scenario and make the reader sit up at the surprise ending."

M Robinson, EJN

Praise for

"The Music Makers and other Jewish stories"

"The third of Mark Harris' trilogy of his Jewish short story anthologies carries, in the main, a theme of Jewish suffering that extends across the Holocaust of the Second World War, the persecutions before that period and, indeed, anti-Semitic attacks subsequent to it. The author invites the reader to use his or her imagination to visualise the dialogue-based stories... Mark Harris writes with clarity, and his knowledge of Jewish custom and practice is lovingly transmitted through the pages... There are stories that are sombre and stories that are horrific, but also some lighter tales. Many of them carry in their words both faith in the Almighty and a belief in a better future for the Jewish people."

Manny Robinson, *Essex Jewish News*

Praise for

"Last Days in Berlin"

"Mark Harris' debut novel is a serious story about a married, retired professional man and fiction author in his early 60s, who is on a creative journey in Berlin. Being Jewish, he harbours some ambivalence for a city he has visited many times; and he has sought to understand its complex and enigmatic character. But he embarks also on another kind of voyage of discovery with two fellow passengers - both of them women, other than his spouse - that could end in tragedy. The capital of the Federal German Republic has a fascination for many people. And in this well-written, meticulously observed book, Mark Harris presents a unique perspective of Berlin as seen through the eyes of a man whose personal dilemmas seem to mirror the city's own uncertainties."

Manny Robinson, *EJN*

Praise for
"A Virtual Reality"

"Mark Harris has boldly gone where no... writer has gone before. His leading character, David... a divorcee and early retired, investigative journalist... ventures back in time to the Jewish community living in and around Cambridge... or Cantabrigia... in 1275. The remarkable opportunity is accorded to him by Diva, a beautiful woman – you could say she was out of this world – from another star system, Alpha Centauri, in our Milky Way galaxy ...

Mark Harris is a meticulous researcher; and... rather than go on a Cook's tour across the 13th century Cambridge, he tells the story of the suffering of the Jews at the hands of anti-Semites in the first person, making his principal character part and parcel of the narrative... Entwined with the terrors of anti-Semitic abuse and assault, there is also a tender love story that lifts the plot from the usual time travel tales ..."

Manny Robinson, *EJN*

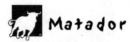